Praise for

Judith Arnold

"This novel's strength lies in its realistic characters. Readers...will be charmed by this down-to-earth romance."
—*Booklist* on *The Fixer Upper*

"Simple and scrumptious...this novel has all the makings of a memorable summer read."
—*Publishers Weekly* on *Blooming All Over*

"Judith Arnold has one of the most original voices in romance fiction today. Her books are filled with warmth and emotion, believable characters and real problems, and she handles them all with a tenderness and dexterity that is both touching and mesmerizing."
—*New York Times* bestselling author Anne Stuart

"*Looking for Laura* will leave readers looking for more of Judith Arnold's books."
—*New York Times* bestselling author Debbie Macomber

"Arnold excels at telling stories about ordinary people.... Enchantingly charming, and perfect for any occasion."
—*The Romance Reader* on *Heart on the Line*

"Arnold's characterization is superb and her writing is quietly lyrical. Highly recommended!"
—*Romance Readers Anonymous* on *The Marriage Bed*

"Reading a Judith Arnold book is like eating chocolate— I can never get enough."
—*RomEx Reviews*

Dear Reader,

When I moved to Providence, Rhode Island, to attend graduate school at Brown University, I was enchanted by the names of many of the streets in the East Side neighborhood surrounding the campus: Benefit Street, Benevolent Street, Power Street, Prospect Street and of course Hope Street. (I also loved Arnold Street, for obvious reasons!) Hope Street was lined with old brick and brownstone apartment buildings, triple-deckers, a few shops and an unsavory bar reputed to have on display a fish tank full of piranhas. (I was afraid to enter the place and see for myself.) It wasn't a particularly pretty street in those days; the apartments were occupied mostly by students and young people who couldn't afford high rents. Yet I adored the street's name and regretted that I never had a chance to live there.

Curt Frost, the hero of *Hope Street,* did get to live there, and to share his apartment with Ellie Brennan, the fellow student who would become his wife. Exuberantly in love, Curt promised Ellie that no matter where life took them, as long as they were together they'd be on Hope Street. Just as deeply in love, Ellie believed him.

But life doesn't always take us down the road we've mapped for ourselves. *Hope Street* explores what happens when our journey takes a tragic detour and we become lost. How do we survive? Can love be enough to save us?

I wept while writing the story of Curt and Ellie Frost's difficult trip back to Hope Street. I think you'll weep while reading it. But I promise that you'll close the book convinced of the power of love to heal us and guide us home.

Feel free to visit my Web site, www.juditharnold.com. Happy reading!

Judith

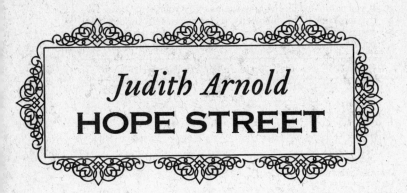

Judith Arnold

HOPE STREET

HARLEQUIN®

TORONTO • NEW YORK • LONDON
AMSTERDAM • PARIS • SYDNEY • HAMBURG
STOCKHOLM • ATHENS • TOKYO • MILAN • MADRID
PRAGUE • WARSAW • BUDAPEST • AUCKLAND

Recycling programs
for this product may
not exist in your area.

ISBN-13: 978-0-373-23072-3
ISBN-10:   0-373-23072-9

HOPE STREET

The publisher acknowledges the copyright holder of the individual works as follows:

HOPE STREET

THE MARRIAGE BED

This is a work of fiction. Names, characters, places and incidents are either the product of the author's imagination or are used fictitiously, and any resemblance to actual persons, living or dead, business establishments, events or locales is entirely coincidental.

This edition published by arrangement with Harlequin Books S.A.

® and TM are trademarks of the publisher. Trademarks indicated with ® are registered in the United States Patent and Trademark Office, the Canadian Trade Marks Office and in other countries.

www.eHarlequin.com

Printed in U.S.A.

CONTENTS

HOPE STREET 9

THE MARRIAGE BED 251

HOPE STREET

To my sons

ONE

"SO, WE'RE NOT GOING to tell them," Curt said. His gaze remained fixed on the road ahead. Dusk spread a warm pink glaze over the asphalt, the forest of pine trees lining the road and the windshield of his BMW Z4. His "midlife crisis," Ellie had dubbed the coupe when he'd bought it last year. Not that either of them believed an expensive sports car was the solution to a crisis. But his daughters were grown and gone, and a man turned fifty only once in his life—if he was lucky enough to live that long.

He loved the car's snug cockpit, the burled-wood dashboard and the upholstery's leather smell. Right now, however, the coupe seemed too small, too intimate. They should have taken Ellie's old Toyota. Maybe he would have been able to breathe in that car.

"We're not going to tell them," she confirmed. "We've already decided the girls are the first people we'll tell, and we aren't going to dump this on them over the phone. They'll be home for Thanksgiving. We'll discuss it with them then, face-to-face."

"And in the meantime, we're just supposed to pretend everything is fine."

"I think we can fake it for an evening, don't you?"

He sighed. They'd been faking it for a long time already, he supposed. He wasn't sure exactly when in the past few months he and Ellie had decided to get a divorce, at what point they'd crossed that line, at what moment they'd acknowledged that certain wounds just weren't going to heal. But the word *divorce* had finally invaded their conversations, and neither had flinched or backed off from it. They'd been moving in this direction for a long time, and now the destination was in sight.

So how the hell were they supposed to get through dinner with Ellie's parents tonight? "It's Ellie's fiftieth birthday," his mother-in-law had pointed out. "Curt got himself that expensive hot rod when he turned fifty. The least you can do is let us take the two of you out for dinner to celebrate Ellie's milestone." She'd made a reservation at a historical inn twenty miles away, one of those quaint, pretty places that Curt and Ellie had always intended to check out but never had.

Curt got along with his in-laws—sometimes better than Ellie did. He was the Harvard Law School graduate who'd married their headstrong daughter. How could they not adore him?

But he sure as hell didn't want to spend the evening with them, listening to them sing "Happy Birthday" to Ellie when he and she were already mulling over who should get custody of the snowblower and the china.

He could feel the tension wrapped around her like a silent hum as she sat in the scoop-shaped seat beside him. He didn't have to look at her to picture the tight line of her mouth, the clench of her jaw, but he glanced in her direction anyway. Her hands lay rigid in her lap, as if she was struggling not to curl them into fists. He could practically see her nostrils quiver with each breath she took.

Ever since she'd come home from Ghana, she'd looked...fantastic, damn it. She'd lost weight while she was gone—not that she'd been fat, but she'd accumulated a little extra padding during the past few, awful years, and it had melted away beneath the African sun. Her profile was sleek now, her cheeks almost gaunt, making her eyes appear twice as big as before. She'd cut her hair short, but it had grown back a bit and now fell in a chin-length pageboy, the brown laced with strands of silver. No more of those reddish-blond highlights she used to have bleached into her tresses at the salon. He'd never been a big fan of that streaky hair coloring. Silver was more honest, more stripped down—like everything that remained of their life together.

She also dressed differently since returning from Africa, favoring shapeless, swirling outfits in bold patterns and neutral colors, fabrics that draped over her taut body and emphasized her slenderness. She'd abandoned the fancy jewelry she used to love—the diamond stud earrings, the tennis bracelet, all the glittery, expensive trinkets Curt had given her over the years. Tonight she had on simple gold hoop earrings and a necklace made of rough-hewn chunks of amber.

And her wedding band, along with the diamond eternity ring he'd given her as a tenth-anniversary present. If they were faking it, she needed to wear her rings.

He wore his wedding band, too. He'd removed it a month ago in a final concession to the inevitable. She hadn't been wearing hers when she'd arrived home from Ghana. He wondered exactly when she'd removed it, if she'd taken it off for a specific reason. He'd asked her more than once, and her refusal to offer him a straight answer was still eating at him.

Fake it, he reminded himself, pushing his anger away. *Just for tonight. Get through this evening.*

Pretending to be her devoted, loving husband for the time it took to eat dinner might just be the most costly birthday present he'd ever given her.

SHE KNEW CURT DIDN'T WANT to drive to this stupid inn for dinner. She didn't want to, either. But how did you deny your parents the pleasure of celebrating your fiftieth birthday? She couldn't have said, *Curt and I don't feel like partying, Mom. We're getting a divorce.*

They'd already agreed that their daughters would be the first people they informed of their decision. And with Jessie away at college and Katie working as an intern for one of the television networks in New York City—glamorous work, lousy pay, but it was a start—Ellie just couldn't break the news to the girls long-distance. It was the kind of thing parents ought to tell their children in person, so they could comfort and reassure them, hug them and wipe their tears.

"Should we have some small talk ready?" Curt asked. "Something we can tell your folks when they ask how everything is? Maybe we should rehearse. Come up with a script."

"If we're putting on a show, you can sing that song from *Evita,*" she suggested, allowing herself a slight smile. Curt often broke into a chorus of "Don't Cry for Me, Argentina," except that he always substituted a more relevant phrase in place of *Argentina.* "Don't cry for me, Martha Stewart," he'd sung to the TV set when the domestic diva had faced her legal struggles. "Don't cry for me, burger patties," he would croon as he fired up the grill. "Don't cry for me, Kate and Jessie," he used to serenade his daughters when they were in high school and pestering him for bigger allowances and later curfews.

"If I sing, they'll kick us out of the restaurant."

"No, they won't. You have a lovely voice."

Curt shot her a quick glance, as if not quite believing she could have said something nice about him. She could think of plenty of valid compliments, though. He did have a beautiful voice, and he was a superb lawyer, and he was as handsome today as the evening he'd run into her on the campus green some thirty years ago, and invited her back to the apartment on Hope Street that he'd been sharing with his friend Steve, and poured her a glass of bourbon and assured her that she wasn't a disaster, even though everyone else who mattered had done their best to convince her that she was.

Along with the compliments, she could also say about Curt that he had made a major mistake—just as she had—and that some mistakes could not be overcome. No matter how hard you tried, no matter how willing you were to forgive, no matter how many sutures you used to close a wound, sometimes the scar was simply too ugly to bear.

"We don't have to rehearse," she assured him, staring forward. He directed his attention back to the road, but when they stopped for a red light he looked at her again. She pretended his gaze didn't unsettle her. "My parents will ask you about work. You always have plenty to say about that. They'll ask me about work. I'll tell them it's fine. Then they'll ask about the girls. That ought to carry us through to dessert."

He nodded, then shifted gears when the light turned green. "The driveway should be coming up soon," he said.

She scrutinized the road, searching for the sign that would direct them to the inn. At another time—a few years ago, in a happier past—she would have been eager to dine at the landmark restaurant. It had been written up in tourist brochures and history books, a must-see for people in the area. She wondered what magic her parents had performed to get a dinner reservation on a Saturday evening during the peak leaf season, when visitors from all over the country spilled into New England to admire the region's autumn foliage.

Even as a native New Englander, Ellie used to get excited about the leaves blazing with color each fall. This year, however, she couldn't get excited about anything. Not the autumn foliage. Not dinner at a famous inn. Not her fiftieth birthday.

The sky had faded to a deep blue by the time they found the driveway. Sunset leeched all the color from the scenery, turning the trees into silhouettes and shrubs into clouds of black resting along the ground. Up ahead, at the end of a winding drive, the inn sprawled grandly, two white-clapboard stories below a steeply peaked roof, with wings extending on either side. Lights designed to resemble gas lamps illuminated the slate walk from the parking lot to the pillared front porch, which was bathed in a welcoming glow from wrought-iron lamps flanking the paneled front door.

"Charming," Curt said dryly. He'd always been immune to old New England charm—"Old-ee," he called it, spoofing the many establishments in the Boston suburbs that featured the word *Olde* in their names. Ellie's parents loved "old-ee" things. The decor of their modest house was colonial, and every horizontal surface held "old-ee" knickknacks and collectibles. Her parents couldn't afford *old* things—genuine antiques—so they compensated with an abundance of "old-ee" dust collectors.

Curt parked the car, and Ellie climbed out before he could circle around to assist her. A serenade of late-season crickets greeted her as she straightened, and her lungs filled with the scent of pine needles and damp earth and wood-burning fire-places. She adjusted the gauzy black jacket of her outfit, felt to make sure the clasp of her necklace was positioned at her nape, finger-combed her hair smooth—and ordered herself to stop fidgeting. The time for faking had arrived.

Curt locked the car, then reached for her hand and tucked it into the bend of his elbow—his own attempt to fake it. The wool of his suit jacket was smooth and soft against her palm, and his conservative silk tie was knotted tight against his throat. He hated having to dress up on the weekends—five days a week was more than enough, he insisted—but he'd been willing to costume himself appropriately for the role he had to play tonight: the doting husband of the birthday girl.

Ellie would play her role, too: the loving wife. In her bid for an Oscar, she let her hand rest on his sleeve in the crook of his arm and matched her steps to his as he escorted her up the walk to the inn's entrance.

She and Curt touched each other so rarely lately. Sometimes they seemed to go out of their way to avoid accidentally bumping into each other at the kitchen sink or in the garage, or in bed. Either of them could have moved into one of the house's three other bedrooms, but they hadn't. Stubbornness, maybe. Habit. Whatever it was that kept them in the same bed, they'd learned how to leave a safe buffer of space between their bodies on the king-size mattress.

A hostess in a colonial dress of pale blue topped with a frilly white pinafore greeted them as they entered the inn. The aromas of hearty food and pine logs burning in hearths surrounded them. Ellie's hand instinctively tightened around Curt's elbow. She wanted to comment on the delicious fragrances, the ancient patterned rug running the length of the entry hall, the elegant brass wall sconces and the dimly lit taproom to their right. Years ago she and Curt would have swapped their opinions about the inn, compared impressions, debated which artifacts were old and which were "old-ee." Now she simply stood beside him, clinging but trying not to, while he gave the hostess their name.

"Yes, of course," the hostess said, skimming the reservations book spread open on her desk and then smiling at them. Her blond curls were tucked under a quaint bonnet, but her makeup was decidedly twenty-first century. "Please follow me."

She led them past the taproom, past a large, bustling dining room and down another hall. "Jeez," Curt muttered, softly enough that only Ellie would hear him. "Where are they seating us? In the kitchen?"

"Maybe you have to bribe someone to get a good table," Ellie muttered back. "My parents would never have thought of that."

Around a corner and down another short hall, the hostess halted in front of a closed door. "Your party is waiting for you here," she said, rapping the door with her knuckles and then swinging it open.

Ellie realized how literally she'd meant *party* when a raucous chorus of "Surprise!" and "Happy birthday, Ellie!" exploded through the doorway, a barrage of cheers and hollers aimed at her. She staggered backward, but Curt stood behind her, blocking her escape and also preventing her from falling.

She twisted to glare at him; if he'd conspired with her parents behind her back, especially with their marriage in its death throes, she would never forgive him. But he looked as shocked as she felt, and he shook his head. "I swear, Ellie..." he whispered. He didn't have to say more. She knew he hadn't been in on this.

Sucking in a breath, she cautiously entered the room. In the crowd she spotted her parents, a few neighbors and coworkers, her brothers and sisters-in-law, college friends and—God help her—her daughters. Katie and Jessie, in dresses and high heels and nylons, grinned gleefully and lifted goblets of wine in Ellie's direction. Jessie was only twenty. Who had served her a glass of wine?

As if that mattered. As if anything mattered besides the fact that this room was filled with her loved ones and her husband stood at her back, and faking it would now force them to perform in front of a much larger audience than she'd ever expected.

CURT HATED SURPRISES. He wasn't a big fan of birthday parties, either. When his fiftieth birthday had approached last year, Ellie had asked if he wanted any sort of celebration, and he'd told her he'd be satisfied with his dream car. Despite its steep sticker price, she'd told him to go ahead and buy it. Big parties weren't exactly her thing, either, especially not in the past few years.

But there she was, clutching a champagne flute full of bubbly while her mother, some of Ellie's friends from work and Anna, her college roommate, clustered around her, all yammering at once. Anna had dated Curt's roommate Steve for a few years, long enough for Ellie and Curt to have found each other. By the time Curt and Steve had graduated, Steve and Anna were history. She'd gone on to marry a professor of film studies at some tiny college in New Hampshire—a pedantic bore, as far as Curt was concerned, but when the two couples got together he was a dutiful host and sat politely, nodding to indicate his fascination with the guy's lectures on Hitchcock and Godard. He'd always been so grateful to Anna for having enabled him to meet Ellie, he'd never really minded the old windbag's pontificating.

For some reason, he was still grateful. Even though their marriage was over, it had been wonderful for a whole lot of years. He had Anna to thank for those years.

He accepted a glass of Chivas neat from the bartender who'd set up shop in one corner of the room, and watched as Ellie was ushered over to a table draped in white linen and stacked high with gifts. Next to the table was a fireplace—not burning, thank God; with all the people in the room, a fire would have turned the space into a sauna. Above the ornately carved mantel hung a curving satin banner with Happy 50th Birthday, Ellie! printed on it. Her mother's dress was a glittery gold number, and Anna's cocktail dress was emerald green. In her gauzy black outfit, with her austere haircut and her large, soulful eyes, Ellie seemed out of place, even though she was the guest of honor.

Jessie sidled up to Curt, beaming like the sun in August. "So, what do you think, Dad? We pulled one over on you guys, huh?"

He managed a smile. In the past year, his younger daughter had turned into a woman, all curves and sophisticated airs. She looked even older with that wineglass in her hand, but he wasn't going to get on her case about a few sips of Chardonnay. "You and Katie hatched this thing with Nana and Poppa?"

Her grin widening, she nodded. "Grandma and Grandpa were hoping to come, too, but with Grandpa's knee surgery, the doctors said they couldn't fly." Curt's parents had retired to Phoenix a few years ago, and joint by joint, his arthritic father was being transformed into the Six Million Dollar Man. "But they sent the coolest present."

"What?"

"You'll see," she said cryptically. "Actually, I think maybe Katie's and my present is even cooler."

"Your mother isn't going to open all those presents in front of everybody," Curt warned, eyeing Ellie from across the room. She was smiling bashfully, shaking her head as her mother gesticulated at the gift-wrapped packages heaped on the table. "This isn't like the birthday parties you used to have when you were kids, where everyone tears the paper and shrieks over each little Barbie outfit."

"What? No tearing paper and shrieking?" Jessie feigned horror. "Katie and I figured we'd truck all the presents back to the house, and Mom can open them tomorrow."

"Tomorrow? Why not later tonight?"

Jessie pressed her hand to her mouth, then giggled. "Oops. Well, act surprised when Mom opens her gift from Grandma and Grandpa. They reserved a room here at the inn for you two for tonight. Katie and I put together a bag full of toiletries for you, too, so you don't have to go home to get stuff. You can just go upstairs after dinner and spend the night. The rooms here are supposed to be *très* romantic."

Oh, Christ. Just what Curt and Ellie needed—a *très* romantic room at the old-ee inn for the night. How much had his parents splurged on that little goodie? Rooms at inns like this didn't come cheap, especially during leaf season.

He eyed Ellie again, admiring her graceful posture, the way she held her head, her shoulders. She could have been a dancer, he thought. Her long legs and arms, her slim hips—especially now, the new, streamlined version of Ellie, as slender as she'd been in college—and her posture all gave her the lissome stance of a prima ballerina.

If the room at the inn was already paid for…what the heck. They weren't divorced yet. They could make the best of it. Why let his parents' generosity go to waste?

It had been so long since he'd made love with Ellie. So long. So much anger, so much penance, the months she'd been away… He'd made his peace with the idea of divorcing her. But he wasn't sure he'd quite accepted the prospect of never having sex with her again.

Tonight, for old time's sake, because at this time of year his parents must have gone through an enormous effort to reserve a *très* romantic room for them…he could give Ellie a birthday night to remember. A night to remember him by. A farewell… whatever.

"Since you've spilled the beans about Grandma and Grandpa's present, how about yours and Katie's?"

"You want to know?" Jessie's eyes sparkled. They were hazel, like his, and her hair was a few shades lighter than his pale brown, but as straight as her mother's. She was going to break hearts someday, he thought. She'd probably already broken a few.

"I want to know," he confirmed.

"It's a DVD. We videotaped people talking about Mom, grabbed a bunch of photos and home movies and made a little documentary about Mom's life. Katie edited it at work. They let her use the editing room there."

"God, you two are creative."

"Yes, Dad," Jessie deadpanned. "We're beyond brilliant. I wonder whose genes we have to thank for that."

"Your mother's," Curt said, not having to think about it. Ellie was the imaginative one, the parent with instant access to her emotions. She was the one who'd taught the girls to view the world in a variety of ways, to see it in all its squalor and splendor. He knew his business, knew how to make a lot of money, knew how to argue and negotiate and recite case law. But Ellie knew how to paint the world with color.

One long, special night with Ellie, he thought, watching as she circled the room, pausing to chat with her sister-in-law, with Bill and Marlene from across the street, with her aunt Louisa. One night in a *très* romantic room with her. Where was the harm in it?

They could get back to planning their divorce tomorrow.

SHE HADN'T REALIZED HOW hard faking it would be.

All these people, so happy for her, happy that she'd enjoyed fifty years of living, happy that she'd returned home after six months in Africa with a new sense of purpose, a new way of approaching the world. Happy that she was no longer flailing, no longer brooding and moping and staggering around, wallowing in so much grief people were afraid to approach her.

Everyone was so happy that she and Curt had emerged from the far side of hell and were still together.

"...And I was saying, my God, how can she be fifty? She looks younger than me!"

"...Now, tell me, Katie, is Manhattan full of eligible bachelors?"

"...I always say, we shouldn't just get together for sad occasions. When was the last time I saw you? Whose funeral? We need more parties...."

Voices churned around her in an atonal chorus. She sipped her champagne, remembering much too vividly that the funeral where she'd last seen her aunt Louisa had been Peter's. One more sip and she realized she hated champagne. She realized, as well, that there was no tactful way for her to extricate herself from the group of well-wishers gathered around her. Finally, her smile causing her cheeks to cramp, she said, "I'll be right back," and made a break for the bar.

The bartender had three bottles of beer lined up on display, one premium, one regular and one light. She still missed the thick, sour beer she'd grown accustomed to in Kumasi. American beers tasted bland in comparison. She asked for a glass of red wine.

"For the lady of the hour," the bartender said, then winked. He was a young fellow with a thick mustache and broad shoulders, and for a moment she wondered whether that wink meant he was flirting with her. She had her wedding ring on, and if he knew she was the birthday girl, he also undoubtedly knew she was here with her husband, her parents and her daughters. Besides which, she was fifty years old. Why would a buff stud like him be flirting with her?

She felt a hand on her shoulder, warm and familiar, almost possessive. "How are you doing?" she asked Curt, not meeting his eyes. "Holding up okay?"

"Yeah." He squeezed her shoulder gently, then released her and gave the bartender a brisk nod, as if to say, *Save your moves for someone else. She's mine.*

For tonight, for as long as this party lasted and they had to keep faking it, she was indeed his. If he felt the need to signal the bartender by putting his arm around Ellie, maybe she hadn't been crazy to think the young man had been coming on to her.

"Have you checked out your presents?" Curt asked as he led her away from the bar. His glass held a golden liquid—Scotch, she assumed. She clasped the stem of her wine goblet and shook her head to dismiss a waiter approaching with a tray of canapés.

"My mother gave me a quick tour of the packages. What am I going to do with all that stuff?"

"Write a lot of thank-you notes," he suggested. "I've got to give you a heads-up, Ellie. If you're annoyed at your parents for organizing this bash with the girls, you'll be even more annoyed at my parents for their gift."

Curiosity twitched awake inside her. "What did they give me?"

Curt looked pained. "A night here at the inn, with me. In a room that, according to Jessie, is *très* romantic."

She grimaced. She and Curt had learned to share their house without arguing, without sniping—basically without engaging each other any more than they had to. But there was nothing romantic about the Dutch Colonial they'd lived in for more than twenty years. Nostalgia dwelled within the walls, memories marked each room, but all the romance that had once electrified the place must have escaped through the cracks and screen windows, because not a hint of it remained inside the house.

"We can stay in the room a couple of hours and then sneak home," she suggested.

"The girls are spending the night at the house. They'd know if we came home."

"Then we could tell them we came home because we wanted to spend a little more time with them before they went back to college and New York."

He scowled and shook his head. "The girls would be really pissed if we did that. They think my parents are the coolest people in the world for booking this room for us."

"All right." She sighed. "We'll get through it." After all, it was her birthday. Why shouldn't she spend the night in a lovely room at a lovely inn with the man she was planning to divorce?

She'd survived worse. She could survive a night at a romantic inn with Curt.

TWO

THE ROOM WAS DEFINITELY romantic. Large and square, it featured peach-hued walls with white wainscoting, two enormous windows overlooking the field behind the inn, a rustic armoire with a pair of plush white bathrobes hanging inside it, a fireplace with split wood piled on the grate, requiring only the strike of a match to set it burning, an apparently antique cabinet that deftly concealed all the room's twenty-first century items— television, DVD player, minibar—and a queen-size brass bed covered with a quilt and embroidered pillows that matched the drapes. The room smelled faintly of vanilla, and a decanter of port and two glasses stood on a slightly tarnished silver tray on the dresser.

Curt followed Ellie into the room. He shut the door, tossed the old-fashioned brass key on the dresser and tugged at the knot of his tie. He looked exhausted.

Ellie stepped out of her shoes, then removed her earrings and necklace and dropped them onto the dresser. She carried the tote full of toiletries the girls had given her into the bathroom. Returning to the bedroom, she crossed to one of the windows and peered out into the darkness. She saw nothing but her ghostly reflection in the glass. With a sigh, she released the swags on the drapes and let them fall shut.

"It's a very nice room," she said without facing Curt. She knew he must be feeling as uncomfortable as she was, and it broke her heart to think that after all these years they could feel so ill at ease with each other. It was one thing to be together in the house they'd shared for so long, but quite another to find themselves trapped in this unbearably romantic room when *romantic* was the last word to describe how they felt about each other.

"If you want," he addressed her back, "we can stay here for a little while and then go home. Just because my parents got this crazy idea about what to give you for your birthday doesn't mean you have to keep it. Presents can be returned."

"We already discussed this," she reminded him. "If we go home, the girls will be there."

"And we'll tell them what we're doing. No law says we have to wait until Thanksgiving."

But Thanksgiving was what she and Curt had planned on. It had been an arbitrary deadline for Ellie, a date that gave her time to figure out just how to break the news to Katie and Jessie. Tonight—the second weekend in October—she wasn't ready yet.

Maybe Curt wanted to go home. Maybe the prospect of spending the night at the inn with her was so appalling he would rather face his daughters than share that beautiful brass bed with her for a night.

Fine, then. He could go home without her and she could have the room to herself. While he was home, he could break the news to the girls and spare Ellie the trauma. Now, *that* would be a birthday present she'd appreciate.

Turning, she scrutinized his face. She'd known him long

enough to be able to read his thoughts in his eyes, in the curve of his mouth. No, he didn't want to go home. He didn't want to face the girls any more than she did.

He confirmed her guess by moving to the armoire and arranging his jacket on an empty hanger. Then he rolled up his sleeves and twisted his head left and right to loosen the muscles in his neck. "Okay," he said. "Let's have some port." His tone was so brusque he might as well have said, *Let's get this over with.*

She used to love coming home from parties with Curt. Sometimes they'd have port, sometimes water, sometimes sloppy bowls of ice cream drizzled with chocolate syrup, and they'd share all the gossip they'd picked up that evening. She'd tell him that Lois had decided to go ahead with the cochlear implant surgery for her son, and he'd inform her that Tom had bragged about buying a boat, but Lorraine had said Tom was nuts and they could barely afford the Audi he'd just bought. Ellie and Curt would laugh and compare notes, click their tongues over the challenges confronting their friends and feel just a bit smug about their own contentment.

Curt filled the two crystal glasses with port and handed one to her. Then he settled into the wingback chair near the fireplace. Ellie's choices for sitting were a wooden rocking chair and the bed. She opted for the bed, propping a few pillows up behind her shoulders and stretching out her legs.

To her surprise, Curt held his glass up in a toast. "To you, Ellie. Happy birthday."

"Thank you." As weary as he looked, his hazel eyes still radiated sparks of silver-and-gold light. He was a handsome man, she thought, as lean and fit as the day she'd met him. His tawny hair might be fading to gray, but it was thick and wavy. The lines framing his eyes had deepened, but his smile still dazzled.

If only they could turn back the clock, flip backward through the pages of the calendar, return to a time when everything was good between them. If only he hadn't done what he'd done, if only she hadn't done what she'd done. If only their family was still whole. If only…

"The girls sure clean up nicely," he commented.

Ellie was grateful to him for dragging her mind away from painful if-onlys. "Where did Katie get that dress?" she wondered aloud. "I hope she doesn't wear it on the streets of New York. She'll get attacked."

"It was a little skimpy," Curt concurred. "Thank God we made her enroll in that self-defense course in high school. She'll be able to fight off the creeps."

"I hope so. A gorgeous young woman, all by herself in Manhattan…"

"She's got two roommates," Curt reminded her. "And she's smart. I trust her to take care of herself."

Ellie sipped her port to keep from retorting that trust came more easily to Curt than to her because no one had broken his trust the way he'd broken hers. She had her own sins to answer for, but she'd never betrayed him.

Discussing all that would make sharing this room for the night impossible, so she steered her thoughts back to their daughters. "Jessie looked amazing, too. I didn't know she could walk in high heels. All she ever wears are those rubber flip-flops."

"In honor of her mother's birthday, she put on the stilettos."

"They weren't quite stilettos," Ellie corrected him. "They were high enough, though."

"Do you have the DVD they made, or did you send it home with the other gifts?"

She hadn't opened most of her gifts. God knew what her

friends and relatives had given her. Would those presents qualify as community property and have to be divvied up in the settlement because she'd received them before divorcing Curt? Would she even want to keep the presents, which would always remind her of the misery she'd been experiencing on her fiftieth birthday?

"I held on to the DVD," she remembered to answer Curt. "It's in my purse. Katie insisted that I take it. She thought we might want to watch it tonight." Actually, she'd said that if Ellie and Curt ran out of other things to do in their *très* romantic room, they could always catch their breath and watch the DVD. Ellie had pretended to be amused and mildly scandalized by Katie's bawdy remark. The only activity that left Curt and Ellie breathless anymore was arguing, and they'd pretty much lost their passion even for that. Two civilized people who'd once loved each other could talk about divorce without becoming hysterical.

"Why don't we check it out." Curt rose from the chair and crossed to the dresser, where Ellie had left her purse. "Mind if I get it?"

"Go ahead." Her purse contained no secrets. He could rummage through it if he wished.

He pulled out the DVD case, which featured the title *Eleanor Brennan Frost: The First Fifty Years* and a pen-and-ink drawing of Ellie—a pretty decent likeness, she'd had to admit. Jessie had designed it, according to the notes inside, which solemnly listed the credits: "Written by Katherine and Jessica Frost. Produced by Katherine Frost. Package Design by Jessica Frost."

Curt moved to the cabinet that contained the TV, opened the doors wide and fussed with the remote control until he had both the television and the DVD player on. Ellie suffered a twinge of apprehension—what if the video was schmaltzy and sentimental? What if it made her cry?

If it did, it did. She'd noticed a box of tissues in the bathroom.

Remote in one hand and glass in the other, Curt settled back into his chair and clicked a button. The screen went dark, and then they heard the familiar strains of the song from *Evita,* and a strange man's voice singing, "Don't cry for me, birthday woman…"

Curt laughed. So did Ellie. If the movie continued in that vein, she wouldn't have to worry about running through the bathroom's supply of tissues.

Eleanor Brennan Frost: The First Fifty Years spread in block letters across the screen, white on black, followed by a snapshot of Ellie as an infant, bundled in a blanket and cradled in her mother's arms. She knew that picture from her mother's photo album. Katie's voice took over the narration: "Ellie's life started when she was born. She was quite young at the time. Gradually, she grew." The screen filled with a series of photos—Ellie as a toddler, sucking her thumb. Ellie as a four-year-old, seated proudly on her tricycle, with plastic streamers dangling from the ends of the handlebars. Ellie in a crisp plaid dress, white anklets and Mary Jane shoes, boarding a big yellow bus on her first day of kindergarten, her stick-straight brown hair cut with ruler-edge precision. Her mother had cut her hair, she recalled. And she'd sewn that dress. Ellie's family hadn't been poor, just proudly blue-collar. They'd lived frugally.

A class photo appeared—Ellie seated at her desk with her hands folded primly in front of her and an artificial smile stretching her cheeks—followed by a picture of Ellie's third-grade report card. Jessie's voice entered the narration: "'Ellie is a bright little girl who will accomplish great things if she keeps her focus. This year she excelled in social studies and science. Her book reports improved throughout the year. She participated in all class activities and played well with others.' Mrs. Birnbaum, Grissom Elementary School."

Curt laughed again. "Those daughters of yours are wicked," he said.

"Oh, they're *my* daughters?" Ellie shot back. She was laughing, too. The video spoofed all those somber documentaries the Public Broadcasting Service was forever airing. Photos, narrators speaking in grave, measured tones and reading from documents, accompanied by an occasional snippet of haunting music.

The TV screen filled with a shot of Mrs. Carmody, who'd lived next door to Ellie's family when she was growing up and, like Ellie's parents, still occupied the house in which she'd raised her children. Her hair was silver now, and her face had pruned with wrinkles, but she sat in her spotless parlor and smiled at the camera. A caption identifying her as "Frances Carmody, neighbor" appeared at the bottom of the frame. "When Ellie was about nine or ten, she made herself a skateboard. Not one of those slick skateboards with the plastic wheels like the kids have today and do all those tricks on. This was a plain pine board with metal roller skates screwed on to the underside. She'd roll up and down the sidewalk all day on that thing. The wheels were very noisy."

"I remember that!" Ellie exclaimed. She'd sacrificed her roller skates to make the skateboard, and she'd spent countless hours rattling along the uneven sidewalk. When she was twelve, she'd passed the board along to her brothers. By then, she'd been too mature for such toys.

"You made it yourself?" Curt eyed her with curiosity.

"Of course I did. I'm handy. I fix things all the time."

"But you were only ten."

"A hammer, a screwdriver—it wasn't rocket science, Curt."

She pressed her lips together, unsure why his respect for her accomplishment should rankle. She often did household repairs, hung paintings, scrubbed the innards of spitting faucets and freshened the grouting around the bathtubs. He'd always appreciated her efforts, but he'd never made a big deal about it, and she'd been glad.

She gave herself a mental shake. No reason to be so touchy. All he'd done was ask a question.

Sipping her port, she directed her attention back to the television screen. Katie was narrating again: "In high school, Ellie continued to play well with others," she recited as a montage of photographs of Ellie appeared—with a couple of her girlfriends at Revere Beach, with a dozen friends in the rec room in Lynne Schwartz's basement at Lynne's sweet-sixteen party. The yearbook photo of the Future Doctors of America Club, with Ellie prominently positioned at the front, one of only two girls in the club. A portrait of her and Jimmy Kilpatrick taken in an anteroom at the hotel where her senior prom had been held. Her gown had been banana-yellow—a ghastly color for her, she realized in retrospect—and Jimmy had worn a frilly tux, his hair frizzing out from his face in a bright red afro. They'd been good friends, neither going steady with anyone, and they'd probably had a better time at the prom than all those hot-and-heavy couples who'd had impossibly high expectations about the big night.

The high-school collage ended with a photo of Ellie in a cap and gown, holding her diploma high in the air as she marched from the platform that had been set up in the football stadium at her high school. Jessie's voice said, "Ellie Brennan, Pinebrook High School class of '74, member of the Honor Society and National Merit Scholar, got into Brown University on a scholarship." The word *scholarship* was accompanied by a photo of

Ellie's parents gleefully smiling. Curt laughed, and Ellie relaxed and laughed, too.

"At Brown," the narration continued as the screen filled with a photo of the university's famous Van Wickle Gates, "Ellie found true love." There followed a series of photos of Ellie with that mildly pimply boy she'd gone out with a couple of times freshman year—what the hell was his name? And then a photo of Martin, with his long black hair and narrow face—Ellie grimaced. And finally a picture of Ellie with Curt.

Her breath caught in her throat. God, he'd been cute then. Lanky, but with the kind of firm shoulders a woman could lean on—or so Ellie had thought back then. Hair the color of honey, long but not too shaggy. Clean, straight features and hypnotic hazel eyes, and a smile that could melt a polar ice cap. How could Ellie have not fallen in love with him?

There was photo after photo—Ellie and Curt outside Sayles Hall, Ellie and Curt in the Hope Street apartment he'd shared with Steve Rogers, Ellie and Curt and a bunch of other people at Narragansett Beach. Ellie sitting on Curt's lap at some rowdy party, with other faces crowding the frame and plastic beer cups scattered about. Ellie and Curt at the big campus dance before his graduation, her hair long and silky, his barely tamed, and both of them dressed in the nicest clothes they owned, she in a flowing Indian-print dress with little mirrors stitched into the fabric and he in a pair of slightly wrinkled khaki trousers and a Harris-tweed blazer. Ellie and Curt at his graduation, a year before hers, Curt in his brown academic robe and Ellie in a cotton sundress, holding a bouquet of roses. He'd been the graduate, but he'd given her those flowers that day. He'd also asked her to marry him.

"Jesus. Were we ever that young?" Curt murmured.

The tears she'd anticipated arrived in a rush. Yes, they'd been that young. They'd been that naive. They'd believed that nothing bad could ever happen to them, nothing so terrible it could break them apart. Nothing so dreadful their love wouldn't be enough to overcome it. They'd honestly believed that.

The screen blurred and she closed her eyes. The bathroom—she had to get to that box of tissues if she didn't want to flood the bed with her tears.

Before she could swing her legs over the side of the mattress, it shifted under her. Curt climbed on beside her, stuffed his linen handkerchief into her hand and looped his arm around her.

She sagged against him, resting her cheek against the soft, warm cotton of his shirt, and sobbed for everything they'd lost—their love, their marriage, their dreams of growing old together. Their trust. Their friendship. Their son.

It was all gone. But at least for this one moment, in this room so far from the reality they lived every day, so far from a world full of awful things, Ellie discovered that Curt's shoulders were still sturdy enough to lean on.

THREE

Thirty years earlier

HE FOUND HER SITTING all alone on the slate steps outside Faunce House. Night had fallen on the campus, a crisp, clear October evening lit by an amber harvest moon. Heading back from the Rock, as Brown University's Rockefeller Library was affectionately known, he was strolling across the green toward Faunce— a dowdy block-long building that housed lounges, snack bars and vending machines, along with a theater and the campus post office—and debating with himself about whether to buy something to eat. He and Steve had food in their apartment, but for some reason their fridge never seemed to contain exactly the thing he had a hankering for.

Tonight he was in the mood for a salty snack. Potato chips, corn chips, pretzels, something he could crunch with his teeth. Whatever edibles he might exhume from the dark recesses of their kitchen would likely be soggy or stale. And he didn't feel like trekking to the supermarket. Faunce was so much closer.

His hunger for chips went forgotten when he spotted Ellie

Brennan seated outside the building. He knew her because Steve was going with her roommate Anna, which meant their social circles frequently intersected. Ellie was dating a long-haired, artsy-fartsy type. What was his name? Curt had met him at a couple of parties. The guy was thin and intense, with hair longer than Ellie's.

She was alone now, though. More than alone, she was *alone*. She looked abandoned, forlorn, her straight brown hair drooping into her face, her elbows propped on her knees and her chin resting in her cupped hands. Her blue jeans were worn white along her thighs, and she had a thick brown-and-white scarf wrapped around her neck. Next to her on the steps sat a bulky sack of a purse made of a bright red fabric.

Sad as she seemed, she was strikingly pretty. Curt had noticed her beauty the first time she'd accompanied Anna to the apartment, and every time he'd seen her since then. But Steve had alerted him to the fact that she wasn't available, and Curt respected that kind of thing. He didn't like guys trying to poach on his territory, and he sure wasn't going to poach on anyone else's. Even if the guy had stringy black hair and a snooty way of talking.

Asking her if everything was all right wouldn't qualify as poaching, though. It was simply being considerate. She seemed distraught, and ignoring her under the circumstances would be rude.

"Ellie?" he called out as he strode over the grass to the steps.

She glanced up and her eyes focused on him. A feeble smile curved her lips. "Hi, Curt."

He drew to a halt in front of her, then hunkered down. "You okay?"

"Oh, I'm just great," she said in a wobbly voice.

"You don't look so great," he argued. "I mean, if it's none of my business, say so, but you look…" He didn't know how to finish the sentence. If he told her she looked terrible, she'd be insulted. Could he say she looked beautiful and terrible at the same time?

She dropped the phony smile and sighed. "Apparently, according to people who supposedly love me, I'm the world's biggest loser."

Curt swore softly. "Whoever told you that doesn't love you."

"Whoever told me that may or may not love me, but they've got their own ideas about who I am and what I should do. And go ahead, sue me, but I think I know myself better than they know me."

She was being cryptic, but she wasn't telling him to go away. He sensed that she wanted to talk, maybe even needed to, and he was all done studying for the night. "You want to go get something to drink?" he asked.

"I'm only twenty," she said. "Unless you've got a stash of liquor somewhere, I can't drink."

"I've got a stash," he informed her. "Come on." He straightened, then extended his hand. She took it and let him hoist her to her feet. As soon as he let go, she slung her purse strap over her shoulder and fell into step next to him.

They walked in and out of the round blotches of light shed by the lamps that stood along the walkways crisscrossing the campus green. Ellie didn't speak as they strolled off the campus onto Thayer Street and past it to Hope Street, where Curt lived. Although he would never publicly admit to such a corny notion, he loved living on a street called Hope. Brown University's neighborhood, the east side of Providence, was full of streets with inspiring names: Hope Street, Benefit Street, Benevolent Street, Power Street, Prospect Street, even Angell Street, which was probably named after a person, with that extra *L* stuck on, but Curt liked to believe it was named after a heavenly creature. He'd grown up in Manhattan, where roads had names like Third Avenue and East 65th Street. Hope Street sounded…hopeful.

The apartment he shared with Steve wasn't quite as auspicious as its address implied. It occupied the top floor of a ramshackle three-story walk-up with paint chipping from the clapboards and ratty old furniture sitting on the porches that abutted each level in front. The place was overpriced because its tenants were all Brown students and the landlord clearly felt justified in gouging them. But Curt and Steve had the best of the three apartments on the third floor—the front apartment, with access to a porch. The living room and kitchen might be dreary, the two bedrooms not much bigger than coffins, heat sporadic and air-conditioning nonexistent, but they did have that porch.

The porch was where he led Ellie, after a quick detour into the kitchen to grab a bottle of bourbon and a couple of mismatched, but clean, glasses. The bourbon was one of his first liquor purchases since he'd turned twenty-one a few weeks after arriving on campus at the start of this, his senior, year. In fact, the party he and Steve had thrown to celebrate Curt's arrival into adulthood might have been the last time he'd seen Ellie. They'd had maybe forty people crammed into the apartment, but he'd remembered she was there—with Stringy-Hair.

Curt hadn't paid them much attention. The Lennox sisters had been all over him that evening, arguing over who was going to win the privilege of taking the birthday boy to bed. Yes, that had been a fine night…and as he recalled, Ellie Brennan hadn't been an essential part of it.

But Stringy-Hair wasn't present now, nor were the Lennox sisters. For some reason, he believed that cheering Ellie Brennan

up was imperative. A little bourbon, a little company, a sympathetic ear and the cool autumn air on the porch overlooking
Hope Street… Maybe he could pull it off.

They settled on an overstuffed sofa on the porch. It smelled
only slightly mildewy; the porch's overhang protected it from
rain and snow, and it was much more comfortable than plastic
furniture would have been. Curt filled the two glasses with a
couple of inches of Wild Turkey and handed one glass to Ellie.
She took a tiny sip, winced and then snuggled into the sofa's
puffy upholstery.

"So," Curt said, "what jackass called you a loser?"

"My parents," she said. "Not in so many words, of course. But
they did, and my advisor did, and Martin did."

Martin. Right, that was Stringy-Hair's name. "And what led
them to this ridiculous assessment?"

His academic phrasing sparked a laugh from her. "I told them
I wanted to be a nurse."

"A nurse." Curt pretended to mull this over. "Oh, yeah.
There's a real loser career. I hate nurses. They contribute absolutely nothing to society. My greatest fear is that I might someday
have kids who want to grow up to be nurses."

She laughed again. He liked the sound of her laughter, especially since she'd been so glum when he'd found her. But he
wasn't just trying to make her laugh, even if that had been his
primary goal when he'd brought her here. He really was
stumped about how anyone could possibly find Ellie's choice of
career objectionable.

She solved that mystery for him. "Everyone assumed I was
going to medical school. I'm the first person in my family to go
to college, Curt. My parents pinned a lot of dreams on me. My
dad works for the postal service. My mom does part-time sec-

retarial work. And here I am, their firstborn child, going to an Ivy League university. How could I possibly become a *nurse? I* was supposed to be a doctor."

"And you don't want to be a doctor?"

"I've thought about it," she said, then took another sip of bourbon. She didn't wince this time. "My advisor wanted to get me into a special program that would lead directly into Brown Medical School. He said I had the grades for it. I just don't have..." She considered her words, then shook her head. "I was going to say I don't have the ambition. But I *am* ambitious. I want to be a nurse. I want to be a terrific nurse. I just don't want to be a doctor."

"Any particular reason?" Curt asked. "They're both healing professions. Either way, you'd work in a hospital and have one of those stethoscope things looped around your neck. So what's the difference—besides a lot more years of schooling?"

"Doctors treat diseases. I want to treat people." She drank a little more, sank deeper into the sofa and propped her legs up on the porch railing. Her hair spilled around her shoulders. Light from a street lamp below them painted intriguing shadows over her face. "I've been doing volunteer work at Women & Infants' Hospital downtown, and I just...I don't know. I feel such an affinity for the nurses. The doctors sweep in, examine a patient, make a few pronouncements and sweep out. The nurses stick around and make the patients feel better, and bolster their spirits. That's what I want to do. I want to make patients feel better."

Curt twisted to look at her. Her expression was earnest, intense. "That sounds great. I don't see how anyone could call you a loser for wanting that."

"I'm not going to be Dr. Brennan. That's breaking my parents' hearts. I'm going to wind up being a lowly nurse. As far as they're concerned, it's a disaster. *I'm* a disaster."

"There's nothing lowly about becoming a nurse. And for God's sake, Ellie, you aren't a disaster. Anyone who says you're a disaster is an idiot."

"Even my advisor?"

"No. He's an asshole." Curt tucked his thumb under her chin and tilted her face so they were looking directly at each other. He'd never before realized how large her eyes were. They seemed as big as Oreo cookies, and every bit as dark and deliciously sweet. "Listen to me, Ellie. If becoming a nurse is your calling, you should become a nurse."

She took a moment to absorb his words. "You're right, Curt. It's my calling." She drank a little more. "Anna says you're going to law school."

"Assuming I get accepted into one, yeah."

"Is that your calling? Or do you just want to be a lawyer to get rich?"

He grinned. He was already rich, at least by birth. Unlike Ellie, he was not the first person from his family to go to college. At least six other Frosts had graduated from Brown over the past century, and several—including his father—had become lawyers. But Curt didn't want to attend law school to follow in his father's footsteps. It was more in spite of his father that he wanted to go. His father worked in corporate law. Curt was more interested in the drama, the arguments, the challenges of litigation. Figuring out how the law worked was like solving riddles and brainteasers and intense puzzles. Whenever he read law cases or followed a local trial, his mind sang.

"Rich is nice," he conceded, "but yeah, I think it's my calling."

"Have you sent your applications out yet?"

"Back in September."

"You seem so calm. Aren't you nervous about it?"

"I'll get in somewhere," he said, hoping he didn't sound too cocky. He wouldn't even need his alumni connections to get into a good law school. His grades were solid and he'd gotten a stratospherically high score on the LSAT exam. He'd also done volunteer work at a legal-aid clinic. Surely at least one law school out of the six he'd applied to would consider him worthy.

"You're so confident," she said, a simple observation. "If I were you, I'd be a basket case by now."

"If you were me, you'd have my personality," Curt pointed out. "I'm never a basket case. Look at me—nerves of steel." He held one hand out in front of him so she could see how steady his fingers were.

She laughed again. "I'm glad you found me over at Faunce House," she said. "I'm feeling a lot better already."

"Must be the bourbon," he said, adding a little more to their glasses. He wasn't sure what her tolerance for liquor was, but his purpose wasn't to get her drunk. Just to improve her spirits. Tonight, improving her spirits was his calling.

Not that he was responsible for her or anything. They were two people tossing back a few. Two friends, nothing more. She wasn't available.

Except that Stringy-Hair—Martin—thought she was a loser. "So...what's the deal with your boyfriend? He thinks you should be a doctor?"

"He's not my boyfriend," Ellie muttered, her smile vanishing and her face receding into the shadows again. "But, yes, he thinks I should be a doctor."

"Not to judge a book by its cover, but he doesn't really seem the type who would care." Curt wasn't the most clean-cut guy around—like Ellie, he was wearing jeans that featured fraying hems and a few patches, and his hair was long enough to cause his parents to sentence him to hard time in a barber's chair whenever he went home—but compared with Martin, Curt could pass for a Republican. "I don't know the guy, but he looks like the sort of person who'd think becoming a doctor was selling out."

"Martin is an artist," Ellie said dryly. "He makes video installments. Vidiot installments, I call them. But anyway, okay, they're artistic. He was figuring I'd become a doctor and make lots of money so he could afford to make his vidiot installments and still enjoy the finer things in life."

"He was expecting you to support him?"

"Hey, I'm a proud feminist. I have no problem with supporting a man."

"I like the sound of that," Curt joked.

She plowed ahead, undeterred. "What I *do* have a problem with is some artist who expects me to pursue a career I don't want just so he can do what *he* wants. I keep telling him to take some education courses so he can be an art teacher while he does vidiot stuff. Or at the very least learn how to type so he can work in an office. It's one thing to support an artist, and another to support a freeloader. And you know, nurses make decent money. I could support him as a nurse, but that's not good enough for him. He wants me to be a doctor and rake in tons of money."

"He sounds like a schmuck," Curt said. "Nothing personal, of course."

"You're right. He *is* a schmuck. And he's not my boyfriend. Not anymore."

She's available. Curt wasn't sure where Steve was—probably balling his brains out with Anna somewhere—but the next time he saw his roommate, he'd break the news that Ellie

Brennan was now fair game. That Stringy-Hair was out of the picture gave Curt an entirely new perspective on things. Not just on Ellie but on everything: the mellow burn of the bourbon sliding down his throat, the crisp October air embracing the third-floor porch, the whisper and occasional rattle of cars cruising down Hope Street below them, the prospect of law school and pursuing his calling and the entire future spreading before him.

That future could include someone like Ellie. A proud feminist, the first in her family to get a college education, a woman who wanted to make people feel better. He'd never met a girl who had that dream. It was a damn terrific dream.

She was slouching lower in the sofa, consuming her drink one dainty sip at a time but definitely working her way through it. Suddenly he wished he hadn't given her any bourbon. With her long, slim legs and her long, long hair and those big, expressive eyes… A guy couldn't help but get ideas. And the ideas he was getting weren't what he ought to be thinking about a woman who was slowly but surely getting drunk.

Too late. She held her glass out for another refill, and he obliged. "This stuff'll smack you in the skull later," he cautioned her. "You may not be feeling it now, but you might have trouble standing up."

"I'm Boston Irish," she argued. "I'm genetically programmed to handle booze."

"Boston Irish, huh," he repeated, and for the next hour, as they polished off a significant amount of Wild Turkey, they talked about themselves. She told him about growing up in the Boston suburb of Pinebrook, about playing stickball and hopscotch in the street outside her house and riding the T into the city to visit the Museum of Science or cheer herself hoarse at a Red

Sox game or, every Independence Day, hear the Boston Pops perform free at the Esplanade, a park adjacent to the Charles River. She told him about her pesky younger brothers, one of them a senior in high school and the other a freshman, each of them convinced that he would be the next Carl Yastrzemski, leading the Red Sox to glory and triumph. She told him that even though her brothers were obnoxious, she loved kids. She wanted to be a pediatrics nurse so she could work with kids forever. She wanted kids of her own. At least two, maybe three. Probably not more than three, because growing up as one of three children had taught her that the more kids a family had, the more they had to compete for their parents' attention, and she didn't want her kids to be competing all the time for her attention.

Curt told her he was an only child, but he thought he'd like to have kids, plural, someday. He told her about growing up in a spacious apartment on Manhattan's Upper East Side, and attending an exclusive private school, and viewing the city as his own backyard. He told her about his father's esteemed career as a corporate lawyer—an area of law that he found painfully boring—and his mother's numerous charitable activities. He hadn't had to compete with siblings for his parents' attention, but they were too busy—his father with his career and his mother with her fundraising drives for the Metropolitan Museum of Art and the Arthritis Foundation—to smother him, for which he was grateful.

Eventually, Ellie emptied her glass, and shook her head when he lifted the bottle to refill it. "So you think I'm going to have trouble standing up?" she asked.

"You're Boston Irish. You tell me," he goaded her.

She pushed herself to her feet, swayed slightly but remained upright. "Well, I mastered that. Walking back to campus should be a piece of cake."

Curt glanced at his watch. After midnight. And she lived all the way north on the Pembroke campus. He couldn't let her walk back alone, not this late at night. But he wasn't too keen on making that long walk round-trip himself. "You could spend the night here," he said, trying to keep his voice light.

"Where? On the living-room couch?"

He scowled. She wouldn't want to know how much crap had been spilled on that couch, how much trash had gotten lodged between its cushions. "I'll take the couch," he said chivalrously. "You can have my bed."

"Look, Curt—" she swayed again, and he clasped her elbow to steady her "—I trust you. I mean, I'm not getting undressed, anyway. So why don't we just share the bed."

He gazed at her in the diffuse light from the street lamps and the harvest moon. She was no longer swaying, but...hell, she was beautiful. Lying next to her all night and not touching her was going to be some kind of torture, even if they were both fully clothed.

Yet if he rejected her suggestion, he'd be admitting that he wasn't trustworthy. She'd told him she trusted him. He had no choice but to live up to her faith in him.

"Sure," he said, opening the door back into the apartment.

He directed her to the bathroom, which he wished was cleaner than its usual dingy, moldy state. He didn't have a spare toothbrush, but she told him she didn't mind; she'd use some toothpaste on her finger to clean her teeth. While she washed, he raced around his bedroom, tidying it as best he could, tossing his sneakers into the closet, hanging up the flannel shirt he'd dumped on his chair two days ago, arranging the textbooks on his desk into a neat pile. He fluffed the pillows and thanked God that he'd laundered his sheets that past weekend. The bed, pushed up against the wall, was a twin—large enough to fit two people, but nowhere near large enough for him to sleep next to Ellie without going half-crazy.

Big deal. He'd go half-crazy. Given how much bourbon he'd put away, he wouldn't be at his best even if she was receptive to an overture. And somehow he knew that if he ever had sex with Ellie Brennan, he'd have to be at his best.

She returned from the bathroom, and he took his turn washing up. The tiny, windowless room smelled of toothpaste and Ivory soap and something unfamiliar, something feminine. Anna had slept at their apartment lots of times, but this wasn't her scent. It was Ellie's, and despite the hour, his exhaustion and the Wild Turkey pumping through his veins, Curt got a world-class boner just from the smell and from the thought of her in his bed. Christ. Why the hell did she have to say she trusted him?

When he got back to his room, he found her seated on the bed, her shoes—a pair of ankle-high work boots—standing side by side against the wall. Her socks were garishly striped in rainbow colors. They made him laugh, and that helped to relax him.

He could see her clearly in the glaring light from the goose-neck lamp beside his bed. Her eyes were still uncannily big and dark, her complexion smooth and pale. He'd never really noticed her cheekbones before, not in any conscious way. Now… Now he *wished* he'd never noticed them.

"I don't know what side of the bed you prefer," she said. Her voice was soft but certain. She had no doubts about his integrity. He wondered if he should be insulted.

"This side," he said, pointing to the night table with the lamp on it. "You get the wall. I hope you don't mind."

She eyed the wall and smiled. "I won't have to worry about falling out," she said.

I won't let you fall, he almost blurted, but he clamped his mouth shut, holding the words inside. Why should he feel protective of her? Her parents and her ex-boyfriend and even her advisor might be asses, but she didn't need Curt's protection. A little ranting, a little bourbon and she could handle anything.

She climbed into bed, snuggled down under the covers and looked up at him. He swallowed and turned away so she wouldn't notice the erection bulging beneath the fly of his jeans. He yanked off his shoes and flung them toward the closet, where they landed in two thumps, and then pulled off his sweater and draped it over the back of his chair. Ellie's scarf lay coiled like a cobra on the seat. He smoothed his gray T-shirt into the waistband of his jeans, removed his belt for comfort's sake and, inhaling for courage and praying for willpower, slid under the covers beside her and snapped off the lamp.

To his surprise, sleeping next to Ellie Brennan was easy. After a murmured good-night, she drifted into a deep slumber. He could tell by the steady rhythm of her respiration, the gentle stillness of her body, that she was out cold. With a yawn, he closed his eyes and quickly joined her in oblivion.

When he woke up, a milky predawn light was seeping through the flimsy curtains covering his window. He glanced at the clock on his night table: six-seventeen. Much too early to get out of bed.

Ellie was cuddled up next to him, her head on his shoulder and her hair spilled over his arm, cool and slippery. The blanket had skidded down to their waists and her body exuded warmth.

His groin stirred—that particular part of him couldn't help but be excited to have this beautiful, sweet-smelling woman so close—but he felt more than standard college-boy lust. He felt peaceful. He felt relaxed. Having Ellie in his bed seemed right.

Then she opened her eyes.

They stared at each other in the pale light for several silent, potent seconds. He ought to say something. *Good morning* would do, or *How did you sleep?* or *Any aftereffects from the bourbon?* But she just kept gazing at him, searching his face with those profoundly dark eyes of hers…and instead of speaking, he kissed her.

She could have recoiled. Could have said no. Could have slapped him, slammed her pillow into his face, sprung from the bed and fled to the safety of the living room. What she did was kiss him back.

Man, how she kissed. Lips, tongue, taste, breath——she poured herself into the kiss, hurled herself into it, kissed him as if she'd spent the entire night dreaming about this kiss and was determined to make her dream come true.

Maybe he was the one dreaming. Maybe this wasn't actually happening. Maybe she wasn't skimming her hand along his bristly cheek and threading her fingers into his hair, and her breasts weren't pressing against his chest through her sweater and his T-shirt, and her legs weren't shifting restlessly under the blanket, tangling with his. He recalled her multicolored socks and almost laughed, but how could he laugh with Ellie's mouth open on his and her body half on top of his?

Maybe he'd dreamed her socks, too. Maybe last night he'd said hi to her on his way across the green, and then he'd come home alone to his empty apartment and drunk Wild Turkey on the porch by himself, and now, in some bourbon-induced stupor, he was imagining this entire episode.

No. His imagination wasn't that creative. This was real.

He pulled back and stared at her again, another prolonged moment of weighty silence. Finally he cleared his throat and asked, "Are you drunk?"

She laughed.

He saw nothing funny in his question. "Because I don't want to—I mean, if you're drunk and I'm taking advantage here—"

"I'm not drunk," she said. "Not the least bit."

"Hungover?"

Smiling, she shook her head, causing her hair to ripple.

"Because if we're both sober, both cognizant—"

"I'm very cognizant, Curt."

Now what? Should he resume kissing her, or should he keep talking? Should he discuss what he wanted to do or just do it? If he just did it, would she think he was presumptuous? Last night she'd boasted she was a proud feminist, after all. She might think he was some pushy, macho pig or something.

"I want you," he said. Honest, blunt—possibly presumptuous, but he didn't care. "I know this is crazy, but—"

"No, Curt," she whispered, her smile gone. "It's not crazy." And then she leaned toward him and offered her lips for another kiss.

Time melted away. The edges of reality blurred. He kissed her, kissed her forcefully, kissed her in a way that let her know just how much he wanted her. He rose and guided her onto her back and then came down to meet her mouth, hard and hungry. If she didn't think this was crazy, it wasn't. It was simply what had to be.

He eased his hands under her sweater. She lifted her shoulders high enough for him to pull it over her head and off. He made quick work of her bra and sent it to the floor with her sweater. Then he bowed to kiss her breasts. They were small and sweet, and he kissed and sucked until she clenched her hands in his hair and shuddered beneath him. Did she want him to stop? Go slower? She'd have to tell him, because her movements, her sighs and gasps and tiny moans all seemed to be saying she wanted more and she wanted it now.

He reared up and caught his breath. Naked to the waist, she reminded him of a mermaid, her hair swirling around her head, her nipples hard and wet from his kisses, her lower body hidden beneath the blanket. To make sure her legs hadn't transformed into fins and scales, he swept the blanket down to the end of the bed. Two legs, he noted. Two legs clothed in denim and loudly striped socks.

He attacked the fly of her jeans. She attacked the fly of his. He paused long enough to shuck his T-shirt, then went back to work on her jeans. By the time she'd gotten his button undone, he had her zipper open and was gliding the jeans and her panties over the soft swell of her bottom. She wiggled her legs and freed one from the worn blue denim. He tugged the jeans free of her other leg—the sock came along with it—and tossed everything over the side of the bed. She still had one sock on.

He left it alone. Perhaps she'd be offended to know that at that moment her feet were pretty much the least interesting part of her body, as far as he was concerned. Her legs were long and slim, her thighs sleek and pale, the skin of her abdomen tight and smooth between her hip bones. A tuft of brown curls adorned her crotch. Poets might believe a woman's eyes were the windows to her soul. Right now, Curt preferred to reach her soul another way.

He shimmied down to the foot of the bed, knelt between her legs and pressed his mouth to her. Some guys did this because they felt they had to; some did it because afterward a girl would be obliged to give them a blow job. Curt did it because he loved it. He loved the smell of a woman's arousal, a flowery, musky perfume, and the way her skin spread and quivered and grew moist. He loved knowing something so simple could make a woman feel so good. He loved—all right, he'd admit it—the power, the ego trip of believing he could reduce a woman to mindlessness with a flick of his tongue, a nip of his lips, a well-directed breath.

Ellie writhed, her hips arching against him, her knees flexing, the heel of her socked foot digging into his thigh. He slid his tongue deep and she moaned, her body heaving, pulsing against his mouth.

Suddenly, he didn't feel so powerful. It was as if by reducing Ellie to mindlessness he'd lost his mind, too. He couldn't think. He could scarcely breathe. All he could do was want. More. All of her.

The pressure of her hands on his shoulders helped to bring him back to—what was his word? Cognizance? God, he was a jerk to use that word. A pompous ass. It was amazing she hadn't laughed him right out of the bed.

When he lifted his head, he could see she wasn't laughing. She was staring at him again, her eyes reaching to him as her hands did, pulling him up onto her. His jeans were in the way, and given his hard-on he had trouble getting them off. But he did, somehow. Somehow he managed to pull a condom from his night-table drawer, somehow he managed to get the damn thing out of its package and where he needed it.

She reached for him, squeezed him, stroked him and then opened that womanly, wonderful window to her soul, spreading for him, taking him in. She wrapped her arms around his shoulders, her legs around his waist and held him so tight he felt as if his entire body was inside her, his shoulders, his back, his hips. His soul. This was what he wanted, what he needed. Everything inside her, a part of her.

He didn't last long, but that was all right. She didn't last long, either. Just a few strong thrusts and she was coming again, sighing and clenching her thighs and throbbing around him, her body practically levitating off the mattress as she pressed her mouth to the ridge of his shoulder and released a muffled sob of pleasure. And then he was there, groaning right along with her, pushing her back down with a final surge.

Reality went blurry again. Time vanished. The fire burning through his body slowly, slowly cooled. His lungs remembered how to function. The drumming of his pulse inside his skull faded. Ellie's arms and legs relaxed, went slack, released him from their glorious bondage.

He propped himself up, and there were those dark, haunting eyes, watching him. She smiled, the most beautiful smile he'd ever seen.

He knew right then that Ellie Brennan was all he'd ever wanted and all he would ever want....

FOUR

EVENTUALLY SHE WOUND DOWN, her tears spent. Cuddling up to Curt, resting her cheek against his shoulder and drinking in his familiar scent felt too good. She used to feel so safe when he held her this way. But now she knew any safety he offered was illusory. He couldn't keep bad things away.

Sheepish about her display of waterworks, she eased out of his arms, dabbed her damp cheeks with his handkerchief and then returned it to him. The TV screen held the frozen image of her and Curt on the day he'd graduated from college, both of them smiling, wildly in love. He must have paused the DVD while she'd suffered her little meltdown.

"I can't watch this," she said, swinging her legs over the side of the bed and standing. "I need some fresh air."

"Sure." He pushed away from the bed as well.

God, no. She didn't want him to accompany her. She had to get away from him before she sank into his arms again. "I'm just taking a walk," she said brusquely. "You don't have to escort me."

"It's late." He glanced toward the windows, their closed drapes blocking out the night. When he turned back, she noticed the shadow of moisture her tears had left on his shirt and suffered a pang of remorse. She shouldn't have fallen apart like that. Not on his shoulder.

"I'm just going to step outside the building for a few minutes. I'll be fine." Like hell she would, but she had to find her own strength. She couldn't rely on him to wipe her tears and make everything better.

She slid her feet into her shoes, grabbed the room key from the dresser and swung through the door. Only after it had shut behind her and she was halfway down the hall to the stairs did she draw in a breath. Her tongue tasted salty from her tears. She needed air. She needed the night.

She needed to get away from Curt, from his arms and his warmth and all the memories of the love they'd once shared.

The key weighed cold and heavy in her palm. Its quaintness—not one of those computer-programmed card keys—appealed to her. And the fact that she had it and Curt didn't meant he probably wouldn't come after her. If he did, he'd be locked out of the room. They had only one key between them.

Still, she hesitated on the stairway landing for a minute, waiting. Curt didn't emerge.

She continued the rest of the way down the stairs, which ended in the front hall near the taproom. Cheerful conversation bubbled out of the room, and she hurried past it. She'd endured enough cheerful conversation at her birthday party to last the next fifty years. Faking happiness, she'd learned, could drain a person of energy.

Stepping outside the inn's front door, she let the cool night wrap around her. A couple of paunchy older men stood on the path near the porch, smoking cigarettes. A young man and a woman strolled toward the parking lot, their arms wrapped around each other. After a candlelit meal at the inn's restaurant, they were probably heading home for a *très* romantic night. Ellie felt a twinge beneath her breastbone as she watched them recede into the shadows. Not jealousy. Just...regret. Loss. Emptiness.

She spotted a bench on a side path that led to a small garden near the inn. The carved wooden slats were stiff and chilly against her back and thighs, but at least she had the night, a sky full of stars above her and the scent of pine around her. The air was nippy, and she hugged herself warm.

You're allowed to be a basket case, she assured herself. *You've just turned fifty. You're on the verge of a divorce. Mere minutes ago, you dissolved into a blubbering fool and let Curt—the man you're planning to divorce—comfort you. Anxiety is acceptable under the circumstances.*

She wasn't sure what she felt was anxiety, though. It was more those other things—regret, loss, emptiness.

Being held by Curt had felt so good. But why the hell shouldn't it feel good? He was a man, and for many years, Ellie had associated being held by him with joy and love and fabulous sex. Just because she was prepared to walk away from what used to be didn't mean she couldn't feel wistful about her decision. Any woman would feel the way she did, especially after going so long without a man's arms around her.

She sat straighter and gave her head a shake. It hadn't been so long, she reminded herself. She'd had a man's arms around her just a few months back, when she'd been in Ghana.

Ten months ago

"DON'T GET IDEAS ABOUT ADRIAN," Rose warned Ellie. In her sixties, stout and bristling with energy, boasting a crisp British accent to match her crisp blue dress, Rose Hampton was the ad-

ministrator of the clinic where Ellie would be working. During
the drive from the airport, Rose had provided Ellie with a brief
biography of herself. She was a widow whose late husband had
been in the foreign service. His last posting had been in Ghana,
and after his death she'd stayed on, putting her management skills
to work at the clinic so Dr. Adrian Wesker could be brilliant and
perform his healing magic free of bureaucratic demands.

She continued to talk about Dr. Wesker's extraordinary abil-
ities as Ellie unpacked her things in the cramped cubicle of a
bedroom she'd been assigned to in the residence compound
next door to the clinic. Fortunately, she'd packed light. Had she
brought more clothing, she'd have had no place to store it. The
room featured a three-drawer chest, a closet the size of a high-
school locker, a narrow bed with a foam mattress and a nightstand. Thin cotton drapes hung across the tiny window, which
overlooked the cinderblock side wall of the clinic.

If Ellie had wanted a four-star resort, she wouldn't have
come here. The stark, cell-like room would serve as a perfectly
adequate home for the next six months.

"Every woman who passes through the clinic gets a crush on
him," Rose warned, looming in the doorway and watching
Ellie sort her clothes into the snug drawers. "Some men, too,
I'd imagine. I must warn you that his first, last and only love
is the clinic."

"I'm here because I want to fall in love with the clinic, too,"
Ellie assured her with a smile. The notion of getting a crush on
some single-minded, charismatic doctor with supernatural talents
amused her. She was too old and weary for that kind of thing.

"He's been here seven years now," Rose continued. She
entered the room, crowding it with her bulk, and settled herself
on the wooden stool at the foot of Ellie's bed, which was made

with fresh white sheets and a cotton spread. "I daresay he'll wind up dying here. He hardly ever goes back to London anymore, except on fund-raising missions. His passion is here, with his patients. The women and children. You've familiarized yourself with the literature we sent, I presume?"

"Yes." Ellie had read about the economic upheaval in the villages surrounding Kumasi, Ghana's second-largest city. Developers were sometimes buying and sometimes simply stealing the small farms that surrounded the city, often with the complicity of village chiefs. Men tended to own and work on farms farther out from the city, cultivating land too distant from Kumasi's urban center to interest the developers. But the smaller, closer farms were generally owned and worked by women. Once these women lost their plots, they could no longer feed their families and earn money with their home-grown crops.

Funded by several international charities, Dr. Wesker's clinic served the medical needs of those economically displaced women and their children, as well as the farm women and children living in the territory surrounding the city. The clinic was always looking for pediatric nurses willing to serve a few months in exchange for free room and board, an exotic experience and a chance to feel they'd made some small contribution to the world.

When Ellie had learned about the program, she'd lunged at the opportunity. Both her daughters had flown from the nest and the house was painfully silent. A boy should have been thumping up and down the stairs, leaving trails of mud with his soccer cleats, devouring groceries faster than she could buy them, blasting god-awful hip-hop music through the speaker of his laptop and pretending he wasn't excited about the female classmates who called to talk to him and giggled as they passed along the news that some other girl—never the callers themselves, of course—had a thing for him.

But no boy clamored through Ellie's house anymore, complaining about too much math homework and asking what was for dinner. Peter was dead, and so was a huge chunk of Ellie's soul. And now her marriage was dying, too. She'd had to get away.

"I assure you," she told Rose, "I have no intention of getting a crush on Dr. Wesker."

Rose shook her head, unconvinced. "They all say that."

Ellie laughed. "I'm here to give vaccinations and take throat cultures for strep. The last thing I need in my life is romance."

Rose's eyes narrowed slightly. "You're not a lesbian, are you? Not that I mind, one way or the other, but you do have to share this floor with three other ladies. They're rather young, I'm afraid. College girls on an academic semester abroad." She gestured through the doorway toward the hall, onto which several other rooms opened. "No medical skills to speak of. They're very good with the children, handing out suckers and jelly beans after the little ones have received shots. One of them has been a godsend when it comes to processing the paperwork. The other two may someday make suitable nannies, but I don't see much more in their futures. Certainly nothing in the healing arts."

"I'm sure we'll get along fine," Ellie said.

"They all have crushes on Adrian," Rose added.

Ellie laughed again. Not strained, hysterical laughter but relaxed, comfortable laughter. Coming here—flying across an ocean and landing somewhere near the equator, in a country that smelled of ferns and spice and cocoa, where people dressed in cool, colorful linens and spoke a language called Twi as well as a pungently accented English, and where impoverished women and their children needed access to free medical care—had been a wise move. When Ellie had exited the airport with Rose and stepped into the warm African morning, she'd felt her spine straighten, her eyes widen. The darkness that had been her companion for nearly two long, horrible years melted away beneath that fine tropical sun.

Once Ellie had finished unpacking, Rose took her on a tour of the clinic. The boxy, functional building wasn't much to look at, but it included the basics: a waiting room with a spacious play area full of toys for the children, two examining rooms, a modest surgery—"Anything major we refer to one of the hospitals in the city," Rose explained—and a six-bed ward. Currently two beds were occupied by thin, sad-eyed children battling the flu. "Dehydration, both of them," Rose noted, pointing to their IV drips. "They'll recover shortly. Be prepared to encounter lots of childhood diseases you thought had vanished from the face of the earth. Measles, rubella, chicken pox. These children don't get inoculated the way your children back home do."

Ellie nodded, taking it all in. She gave each of the young patients a warm smile before leaving the ward.

Rose walked her through the nurses' station, which contained a small pharmacy, two desks and a computer that would have been obsolete ten years ago. Ellie recalled the nurses' station at Children's Hospital in Boston, where she'd taken her first job after receiving her RN degree. It had boasted clean, sleek counters, bright lighting and all the high-tech equipment a nurse could dream of. Even her office at the Felton Primary School made this clinic on the outskirts of Kumasi seem about twelve rungs lower than primitive.

But a nurse didn't need a fancy computer to make a child with chicken pox feel better. Just lots of liquids, cool baths, calamine lotion and ice cream to slide down a tender throat.

Dr. Wesker's office door was closed, and Rose warned Ellie not to disturb him when he was shut up inside, unless it was an emergency. So Ellie didn't meet the doctor until that evening at dinner, in the dining room on the first floor of the residential compound. A long, family-style table took up most of the room, which had windows along one wall and a colorful abstract mural painted on another. She'd taken a seat at the table with the three college interns, who were bouncy and bubbly and eager to fill Ellie in on everything they felt she needed to know: "The market's a great place to connect with the women— they're always shopping and bartering. Whenever we see one with a kid, we go over and tell her about the clinic," one of the girls informed Ellie.

"And we go into the school and give talks on hygiene and the importance of vaccinations."

"A little sex ed, too," the third girl said with a grin. "I'm planning to teach middle school, so I like doing the sex-ed stuff." All three girls were from Georgetown University, they told Ellie, although their manner of speech indicated they heralded from different regions of the United States. One girl had a thick Southern drawl, another the flat intonations of the Midwest and the third, from central New Jersey, could have been a speech coach for the cast of *The Sopranos*.

Abruptly they nudged one another and fell silent. They were gazing past Ellie, and she twisted in her seat to find out what had caught their attention.

The brilliant doctor who performed magic had entered the room.

At least, she assumed that was the identity of the man walking toward their table, a plate heaped with steaming pork stew and rice balanced in one hand and a dark beer bottle in the other. He wore blue surgical scrubs and scuffed leather sneakers, and his lean body moved with a boneless grace. His wavy chestnut-brown hair was too long, tucked behind his ears to keep from spilling into his face, and his eyes had the permanent squint of someone who'd spent too much time staring at something bright and painful.

He was undeniably handsome. His weathered face, his economical physique, the sinuous muscles in his forearms and his smooth, elegant gait... Not that Ellie cared, but yes, she could understand how some women might find him appealing.

He circled the table and set his plate down in front of the empty chair facing Ellie. "Our new nurse, then?" he asked, his accent every bit as British as Rose's.

She extended her right hand. "Eleanor Frost," she introduced herself. "You must be Dr. Wesker."

The college girls remained silent, gazing at him with adoration. He ignored them. "Eleanor Frost," he echoed, unrolling the napkin that held his silverware and spreading the square of cloth across his lap. "Pleasure to meet you. Rose tells me you're a school nurse. Good at mopping up bloody noses, I presume."

"We get our share at my school," she confirmed.

"We get our share here, too—although here, bloody noses can be a symptom of a multitude of other problems. Medicine is slightly different in this clinic than what you're likely used to." He eyed her speculatively. "You're a bit more mature than most of our volunteers," he added, shooting a meaningful glance at the college girls, who dissolved in laughter. "A little maturity should do us all some good."

"Dr. Wesker," one of the girls protested. "We're very mature."

"Terribly mature, yes." He shot Ellie a smile. "Do you prefer to be called Nurse Frost or Sister Frost?"

"Ellie would be fine," she said. His eyes, she noticed, were the same glinting color as his fork, a cool, metallic silver. She imagined they would be blinding if he ever opened them fully.

"Ellie it is, then. And you may call me Adrian. We don't stand on ceremony here, as long as everyone recognizes that I am the boss and treats me with the proper deference." He smiled again. Ellie smiled back.

The college girls dominated most of the dinner conversation, describing their most recent shopping expedition in downtown Kumasi. Once they'd all finished eating, Adrian filled two mugs with rich, dark coffee and ushered Ellie outside. The heat of the day had evaporated, and the evening air smelled like foliage and moist soil. He gestured for her to sit on the concrete steps leading down from the back door of the residence compound, then lowered himself beside her. His knees were only an inch from hers, the smooth blue cotton of his scrubs contrasting with her khaki slacks. She considered putting more space between them, but the stairway railing was at her back. And he might be insulted if she shifted away. He'd chosen this place to sit with her, so she decided to accept his nearness without making a fuss.

Perhaps his subtle body language was his way of conveying the way things worked at the clinic. Volunteers worked together. They ate together. They shared a residence—except for Dr. Wesker, who, Rose had informed Ellie, lived in a small cottage just up the street, and Rose herself, who remained in the house she'd shared with her late husband.

Personal space might be a luxury unavailable in this village on the outskirts of Kumasi, at least for the volunteers.

"They're lovely birds," he said, "but rather too giddy."

It took Ellie a minute to realize he was referring to the college interns. "They're women, not birds," she said, a stern display of feminism.

"I imagine they'd prefer to be thought of as birds. At least they'd prefer that I refer to them that way. They twitter and flutter a lot. They mean well, but our older staff tend to be more productive. You've met the other nurses?"

She had. One was a thin, towering Kumasi native named Atu. He'd said little when Rose had introduced Ellie to him, but he'd had a marvelous smile. The other nurse, Gerda, was from Scotland and was, according to Rose, a fanatic about sterility. Ellie had contended that in a medical setting, being fanatical about sterility was not such a terrible thing.

Atu appeared younger than thirty. Gerda looked closer to sixty. Both, Ellie assumed, met Adrian's definition of mature.

"You're here for six months, then?" he asked.

She nodded. "That's the plan."

"You will work far harder during these six months than you have ever worked in your American practice, Ellie. You will see health problems you haven't heard of before. Your heart will break ten times over, and it will soar at least twice as often."

"I'm looking forward to the soaring part," she said with a smile.

He smiled back, his eyes nearly disappearing. "Tell me, then," he asked, "why are you here?"

"A friend mentioned your program to me, and I researched it on the Internet," she said. "It sounded interesting. I thought I'd enjoy it, and I knew I'd have something to contribute—"

He cut her off with a snort. "Spare me the do-gooder speech. Everyone who passes through here is oh, so altruistic, so eager to save the world." He tempered his cynical tone with a chuckle.

Deep lines framed his mouth and dented his cheeks. At one time, they might have been dimples. Ellie wondered how old he was. His hair was more brown than gray and his forehead was relatively smooth. But the creases framing his eyes and mouth indicated that he'd spent many years in the sun.

He shifted on the steps so he was facing her, his back against the wrought-iron rail and his knees bent toward his chest, and took a sip of his coffee. "People come here for one of two reasons. They come here to lose themselves, or they come here to find themselves. Which reason fits your purposes?"

She leaned back against the cast-iron posts of the railing and drank some coffee, using the time to contemplate his question. Had she come here to lose herself? Hell, she was already lost— but she'd come to get even further away from everything that was wrong with her life back home. Her empty, echoing house. Her bone-aching grief. Her husband's betrayal. Her dread of the darkness that kept threatening to swallow her.

Yes, she'd wanted to lose herself.

But she'd also wanted to stand tall again, and feel as if her life had purpose. She'd wanted to save sick children. Her own son had died, and she would never get over that. But if she could save enough other children, if she could bring them health and the promise of long, happy futures... Would that qualify as finding herself?

"Both," she told Adrian. "I think I've come here for both...."

FIVE

AT WHAT POINT should Curt start worrying? At what point should he surrender to his Neanderthal instincts and go after Ellie? Not that worrying about her safety was Neanderthal, but she would probably think it was.

Ellie had always been a stubborn feminist, and now, more than before, she was determined to prove she didn't need him. Yet sometimes she did. When her heart was breaking, when the memories were like razors cutting her to shreds, when she needed a shoulder to cry on, the way she'd needed his shoulder after she'd been overcome by the movie the girls had made...

Once he and Ellie were divorced, he supposed, she would find another shoulder. A shoulder that belonged to a man who hadn't wounded her the way Curt had.

As far as he knew, she hadn't found that other shoulder yet. His remained the only available shoulder, and rather than let it absorb any more of her tears, she'd bolted from the room. Now she was off somewhere, wandering around late at night at an inn on a dark country road. Damn it, he wished she'd left him the key. The night clerk probably had a spare; he could go downstairs, get the extra key and then head outside in search of Ellie.

Not to control her, not to force her back to the room. Just to make sure she was all right.

His gaze snagged on the frozen image on the TV screen: him in his graduation robe and Ellie tucked into the curve of his arm, holding the roses he'd bought her. He wasn't sure why he'd thought he should present her with roses as well as a diamond ring when he asked her to marry him. She'd already told him a million times she loved him, in a million different ways. They'd constantly discussed the distance between Brown's campus and Harvard Law School, how they'd still be able to see each other regularly, how she would only apply to nursing programs in Boston so she could join him there once she graduated. They'd talked about the children they hoped to have. She desperately wanted to be a mother, and he couldn't think of anything better than to make a few babies with her.

Over winter break his senior year, he'd traveled to Pinebrook to meet her parents, and they'd fawned all over him, probably because he'd brought her family impressive Christmas presents: a staggeringly expensive bottle of Scotch for Ellie's father, a crystal bud vase for her mother and Carl Yastrzemski baseball jerseys for her brothers. Ellie had traveled to New York City to meet his family over spring break, and they'd adored her. They would have loved her even if she hadn't brought his mother a potted Easter lily. Gifts didn't dazzle them. Ellie's intelligence, her humor and her commitment to her calling did.

Despite all that, despite the family introductions and the planning and the fact that they spent nearly every night together in his bed in his scruffy third-floor walk-up on Hope Street, she could have said no when he'd proposed. She could have come up with some logical argument about how they should wait to figure out how they felt about each other when they were done with their schooling. She could have pointed out that he wasn't Catholic and she was. She could have told him she loved him as a college boyfriend but not *really,* not till-death-do-us-part.

So he'd softened her up with a dozen red roses to hold during the graduation ceremony. And he'd sent his parents to their hotel room for an hour and walked Ellie back to his apartment and out onto the porch where he'd first started falling in love with her, and he'd reached through the flaps of his graduation gown to the little velvet-lined box he'd stashed in a pocket of his trousers. He'd handed the box to her and told her he wanted to spend the rest of his life with her. He'd said, "If you say yes, Ellie, I promise you, it will always be Hope Street. Wherever we live, wherever life takes us, we'll live on the street of hope."

And she'd wept, her tears sprinkling all over the velvety petals of the roses, and said yes.

So much for that promise. So much for hope.

People got divorced. He and Ellie weren't the first couple to have their hope shattered, to prove unable to survive the worst kind of tragedy. They'd get through this unpleasant step and move on with their lives as best they could. She'd find someone else to hold her together—if she ever allowed herself to fall apart again the way she had with him. And maybe he'd find some other woman who didn't mind crying on his shoulder every now and then. Ellie would no longer be his responsibility. He'd remind himself, every day if he had to, that he wasn't supposed to worry about her anymore.

But damn it, she could get hurt out there in the dark. She'd been gone too long. They weren't divorced yet, and he worried.

Turning his back to the television, he closed his hand around the doorknob. It twisted in his palm and the door swung inward. Ellie had come back.

She stood in the doorway, apparently startled to see him. The perfume of an October night clung to her. Her hair hung loose around her face and her cheeks were flushed.

"I was just going to look for you," he said, backing into the room and wondering whether she'd cross the threshold.

She did. "That wasn't necessary," she said tersely as she set the key down on the dresser.

"So shoot me. I was worried. You were all alone out there." At least he assumed she was.

"I sat on a bench for a while and then I got cold and came inside. You don't have to take care of me, Curt. I'm fine."

His gaze collided with hers. Like hell she was fine. Just before she'd fled the room she'd been a wreck. The only reason she'd fled was that she couldn't bear the idea of letting Curt clean up her wreckage.

Skeptical about just how fine she was, he decided to test her. "How about watching a little more of the girls' video?"

Her lips tensed. She knew he was challenging her, and she was too proud to hand him a victory. "Sure," she said, a bit too readily. She returned to the bed, settled onto it, kicked off her shoes and swung her feet up onto the mattress. Then she reached for her glass of port, which she'd left on the nightstand when she'd bolted. She took a sip and nodded at him. "Let's watch some more."

She'd passed that test. Why not give her another? He carried the decanter over to the other nightstand, then climbed onto the bed next to her, propping a few pillows behind his head and shoulders. He shot her a smile that he hoped looked more confident than it felt, aimed the remote at the TV set and clicked the button.

Accompanied by music from the *Evita* soundtrack, a series of photos depicted Ellie's final year at Brown. Ellie grinned at the photographs of her at assorted social gatherings and sports events. Jessie's voice broke through the background music to intone, "'In a way, our last year at Brown was great because Ellie had more time to spend with her friends. Sure, she missed Curt and spent most weekends with him in Boston, but when he wasn't around, we hung out together, danced all night at Lupo's Heartbreak Hotel and volunteered to be stagehands for this bizarre campus production of a play called *Ovum*. It was about an egg.' Anna Krozik."

"Ovum?" Curt scowled. "I don't remember that."

"I didn't tell you everything I was doing while you were in law school," Ellie said, sounding a bit smug.

"Dancing at Lupo's? I used to take you to Lupo's."

"When you were in Providence. Once you moved to Boston, I went to Lupo's with Anna, instead. And other friends."

"Hmm." Of course he'd known that she'd had a life in Providence while he'd been busting his ass at Harvard. He'd had a life, too. He'd hit the bars with his classmates, scored occasional tickets to Red Sox games, caught Bonnie Raitt performing one night at a coffeehouse near Harvard Square. But he couldn't recall dancing at a rock club with anyone other than Ellie. And he certainly hadn't worked backstage at a show called *Ovum.* "What was that play about?"

"You heard what Anna said. It was about an egg." Her cryptic smile let him know she was enjoying herself at his expense.

He played along. "So, what did the stagehands do? Build a nest on the stage?"

"It wasn't a chicken egg. It was a human egg. The play explored reproductive issues. Two guys played sperm."

"Lucky guys."

"They were the comic relief."

He feigned indignation, but inside he was laughing. All right, so maybe Ellie *was* fine. He detected no lingering symptoms of her earlier despair.

The movie moved on to Ellie's graduation from Brown. This time she was the one in the flowing brown graduation robe, while Curt was dressed in civilian attire. One photo showed her flanked by her parents; one featured just Ellie and Curt. In that one, she was holding another bouquet of roses that he'd given her.

When was the last time Curt had given her flowers? Maybe if he'd showered her with bouquets, she wouldn't be divorcing him now.

Yeah, right. A gift of flowers would have infuriated her. In the days after Peter's death, their house had filled with flowers. Flowers from friends, from neighbors, from relatives, from Peter's classmates and teachers. So many flowers that the perfume had cloyed, and then the flowers had died. Day by day, petals had faded to brown and dropped from their stems. Day by day, stalks had drooped and pollen had spread in a fine, pale dust under each vase. Watching the bouquets die was like reliving Peter's death over and over.

Two weeks after the funeral, Curt had arrived home to find Ellie cramming all the dying bouquets into a huge black trash bag. He couldn't imagine bringing her flowers after that.

Shoving away the memory, he focused on the video. A few shots of the nursing-school building at Boston University, where Ellie had received her RN degree. A few shots of Children's Hospital, where she'd worked while he'd finished law school.

A few shots of the building that had housed their first apartment, in Allston. He'd had to commute on the T across the Charles River and into Cambridge to reach the law school every day, but the place had been cheaper than the rentals on the Cambridge side of the river, and with Ellie often working a night shift, he'd wanted her to have a quick commute.

They'd been happy then, he recalled. Shabby apartment, budgeting their pennies, both of them working like dogs, sometimes too tired to eat, let alone make love—but they'd been so exuberantly happy. Their flat had been furnished with Salvation Army castoffs and they'd dined on macaroni and cheese several nights a week. Ellie's parents had been appalled that she was living with Curt without the benefit of marriage. "He's never going to marry you if you live with him, Ellie. You know the saying. Why buy the cow when you can get the milk free?" Ellie's mother had often nagged. But her parents *did* like him, and once he'd finished law school, he'd bought the cow.

A title appeared on the screen: *The Wedding.* "Oh, God," Ellie muttered.

"We survived it," he reminded her.

"Barely. I wonder how the girls are going to spin this part of the story." She nestled back against the pillows and sipped some port.

The screen filled with a photo of an engraved wedding invitation and then a faded clipping of the engagement announcement that had appeared in the *New York Times.* "I'd forgotten that," Ellie murmured. "Your mother got our engagement into the *Times.*"

"My mother could have gotten it onto a billboard in Times Square," Curt noted. "She was very well connected in the city. She probably still is, even though they don't live there anymore."

"My parents were blown away by that. They'd thought it was the pinnacle of something that they'd gotten an announcement into the *Pinebrook Weekly News.* Then, when they found out your mother got us mentioned in the *Times,* they freaked out."

Curt shrugged. He remembered how intimidated Ellie's parents had been by his parents. They'd always thought his privileged background was something to be awed, and because Curtis Frost, this blue-blood scion of the American aristocracy, had deigned to marry their daughter, the product of their humble family, they'd ultimately forgiven Ellie for skipping medical school and living with Curt before they were legally wed. That his family, while affluent, was far from the ranks of the megamillionaires hadn't mattered to them. As far as they'd been concerned, a Harvard Law School graduate who belonged to a clan with dozens of Ivy Leaguers dangling like ripe fruit from the family tree, and a mother who could get her son's engagement announcement into the *Times,* was an aristocrat.

"The wedding of the decade took place at St. Bridget's in Pinebrook," Jessie narrated as the screen displayed a photo of the modest neighborhood church where Curt and Ellie had exchanged vows. "A reception at the Field House of the Pinebrook Country Day School followed."

"To my mother's everlasting fury," Ellie added.

"That was a beautiful place," Curt recalled, his memory confirmed by the pictures of the stone field house overlooking a pond on the campus of a ritzy private school in Ellie's hometown. "I never understood why your mother was opposed to our having the reception there."

"She hated everything I wanted," Ellie reminded him. "First she wanted the reception to be at a wedding factory in Waltham, one of those places that had six weddings going on at once. Then, when your mother got our announcement into the *Times,* she decided the Frosts were too classy for that wedding mill. She announced that she and my father would take a home-equity loan and host the wedding at one of the downtown hotels. The Ritz-Carlton was her first choice because it sounded ritzy."

Curt grimaced. "No one should have to go into that much debt just for a wedding."

"Tell that to your daughters when they decide to get married," Ellie joked. "I'm figuring they'll cost us fifty thousand apiece, minimum."

"I'll buy them each a ladder. They can elope."

Ellie chuckled. "More than a few times during the planning of our wedding, I was ready to buy us a ladder and elope. My mother insisted the field house was going to smell like gym socks. I told her it was a beautiful facility, and it had a full kitchen for the caterers to work out of. I told her lots of parties were held there. She was sure the place would be full of hockey sticks and football helmets."

A photo appeared on the screen of Ellie in a bridal gown surrounded by her bridesmaids—Anna as her maid of honor and two cousins as additional attendants. Ellie hooted with scornful laughter. "Oh, Lord, the bridesmaids' dresses. The battle my mother and I had over those dresses nearly started World War III."

"Why?" Curt paused the DVD to study the dresses. "What's wrong with those dresses?"

"I decided my attendants should wear tea-length dresses instead of full-length, so they could get more than one wearing out of them."

The bridesmaids' dresses seemed nice enough to Curt, not that he was any expert. He wasn't even sure what *tea-length* meant. "Your mother didn't approve of tea-length?"

"She wanted them to wear full-length dresses in this hideous green color that made everyone look jaundiced. She thought navy blue was too wintry."

"Those dresses are sleeveless. That's not wintry. Who wears sleeveless dresses in the winter?"

"It didn't matter to her. She told me I was a thankless girl with no taste."

"Yeah, that's you," Curt teased her gently.

"And then there was..." She dissolved into laughter.

"What?"

"The silk purse."

"What silk purse?"

"I never told you about the silk purse?" More laughter, deep and throaty and sexy. Curt might have fallen in love with her after their first, fantastic sexual encounter, but her laughter had clinched the deal. When Ellie really laughed—something she did far too rarely these days—her entire body seemed to glow.

It took her a moment to collect herself. This time, at least, the tears glistening in her eyes weren't from sorrow. While she sniffled and chuckled and dabbed her eyes, he refilled his glass with port. Swallowing the last shimmers of her laughter, she extended her glass and he topped it off, as well.

"My mother wanted me to wear a silk purse around my wrist," she said. "It was a long, narrow thing—they actually sell them in bridal shops, although she was willing to sew one for me."

"What would you need a purse for? It's not like you'd be driving off in your wedding gown. I had our keys and a wallet."

"The purse is for collecting money gifts. Instead of having you stuff all those checks and envelopes into your pockets, I would have them hanging off my wrist."

"For the whole wedding?" Curt didn't get it. Why would someone want to spend an entire evening wearing a sack stuffed with money dangling from her arm?

"My mother insisted this was the correct thing to do. I told her I'd rather cut off my hand than wear one of those things."

Curt nodded. "That sounds like something you'd say."

"We had one of the biggest fights of our life over that stupid purse. Bad enough my bridesmaids weren't wearing full-length gowns. Bad enough I wasn't going to have a flower girl or a ring bearer. Bad enough we were having the party at the field house instead of the Ritz-Carlton. Bad enough I wanted to wear my hair straight, the way I always wore it, instead of spending the morning of the wedding at a salon getting it sprayed and gelled into some weird configuration—and that I polished my own nails the night before the wedding instead of getting a professional manicure. But my passing on the silk purse? My mother sewed one against my wishes and brought it with her to the field house, insisting that I wear it. There we were, in the powder room, having this violent argument through clenched teeth while all the guests were wandering in and out to pee and touch up their lipstick."

"You should have worn the purse," he said.

Ellie eyed him incredulously. "Are you kidding?"

"In fact, I think both girls should wear silk purses when they get married, too. I think we should insist on it." He tried to keep his expression deadpan, but evidently, he couldn't suppress a small grin.

Ellie poked him in the arm and snorted. "I'll make you wear a silk bag over your head," she grumbled, and they both laughed.

In the midst of his laughter, a wave of sorrow knocked him sideways. When was the last time he and Ellie had laughed together? When had they last teased each other, joked with each other, pulled each other's legs? God, he missed this. He wanted it back.

Well, he couldn't have it back. During the worst period of their lives, Ellie had shut herself off from him, and he'd dealt with her rejection in a bad way, and too much damage had been done. All the king's horses and all the king's men couldn't put their shattered marriage back together again.

Next to him, Ellie grew quiet, as well. He wondered if she was feeling what he was feeling—that profound loss, that dizzying sorrow. Probably not. He still loved her, despite his anger and resentment, but she no longer loved him. Not after what he'd done. She couldn't forgive him, wouldn't forgive him. He knew that.

He pressed the remote button and the DVD started up again.

OH, GOD, THE WEDDING. Before now, whenever Ellie had thought about that marvelous day, she'd remembered only the joy of exchanging vows with Curt, entering into a bond that she'd believed could withstand anything life threw at it. She'd remembered not the silly fights with her mother over the silk purse, or the tension she and Curt were sure would flare between Anna, her maid of honor, and Steve, Curt's best man. Steve and Anna's breakup had not been amicable, and for their entire senior year at Brown, Anna and Ellie had never mentioned Steve's name. Yet at Curt and Ellie's wedding two years later, they'd greeted each other with surprising affection at the rehearsal dinner. They'd hugged, they'd sat together, they'd whispered intimately. Steve had offered Anna a lift back to the hotel where many of the wedding guests were staying. Before kissing Ellie good-night and sending her home with her parents for her final night as a single woman, Curt had whispered, "I wonder if Steve's going to be luckier than I am tonight."

Mostly, what Ellie remembered about her wedding was that

it had given her Curt, forever. It had made her his wife and him her husband. For most of their marriage, she couldn't have imagined wanting anything more than to have Curt beside her for the rest of her life, through childbirth and mortgage payments, school concerts and career challenges. Her marriage had made that wish a reality. Together they had taken up permanent residence on Hope Street.

Not so permanent, as it turned out.

"'Ellie was a wonderful nurse,'" a male voice intoned on the DVD. The screen showed a series of scenes from Children's Hospital. "'She was not just top-notch when it came to medical care, but she was also a natural with the children. She could get them to smile and relax even when they were undergoing grueling treatments. They adored her.' Dr. Joshua Steiner, pediatric cardiologist."

"Wow." She let the video pull her away from thoughts of her wedding. "The girls dug up Josh Steiner for a quote? Last I heard, he was spending his retirement sailing around Nantucket."

"I guess he has to make landfall every now and then. They must have caught up with him when he was blown ashore."

"Either that, or they invented the quote," she said. She'd been incredibly lucky to have a doctor like Josh Steiner as her first boss. The hardest part about leaving Children's Hospital had been ending her professional association with him. She'd stayed in touch with him over the years, though. He'd even returned to the mainland for Peter's funeral. That had been the last time she'd seen him.

A group photo of Ellie and two other ward nurses appeared on the screen, accompanied by an unfamiliar woman's voice: "'I loved Ellie, except she was always getting on my case to quit smoking.' Nurse Whitney Rodino."

"Nag, nag, nag," Curt said lightly. He must have sensed that her mood had turned melancholy, and he was trying to recapture their earlier humor.

"I gave her a pacifier from the stockroom once," she said, trying to match his easy tone. "I told her she should suck on that instead of a cigarette."

"I bet she wasn't as sorry as Josh Steiner was to see you go."

"I had only her best interests at heart."

"Nag," Curt grunted. Ellie allowed herself a smile.

She sipped her port and watched as the DVD displayed pictures of her swelling with her first pregnancy. There was a shot of a moving van in front of the house they'd bought just before Katie was born—the house on Birch Lane where they still lived—and a shot of Ellie standing on the front porch of the house, cradling a newborn Katie in her arms. Behind them hung the small shingle Curt had carved and hung above the front door: "Hope Street." Seeing it adorning the entry to their home, so optimistic, so *wrong*, brought the sting of tears to Ellie's eyes, but she blinked them away.

"Katie was the perfect child," a narrator—clearly Katie—recited. "She was a genius, beautiful and always well-behaved. At the age of two months she could speak in complete sentences. At five months she was completely potty trained—although she'd been changing her own diapers right from the day she and her mother left the hospital. By the time she reached her first birthday, she could explain Einstein's Theory of Relativity and sing Wagner operas by heart. Ellie said, 'Raising children is so easy. Let's have another child.' It is thanks to Katie's magnificence that Jessie was born."

"Jessie," the narration continued, in Jessie's voice now, "proved that there is such a thing as *more* perfect. Jessie did everything Katie did, only she did it backwards and in high heels."

Ellie grinned and glanced at Curt. He was chuckling. No matter how badly they'd botched things, she thought, they'd still somehow managed to produce two fantastic daughters.

The movie offered a series of photos of Curt and Ellie and their two little girls—playing on a Slippy Slide in the backyard, posing on the deck of Old Ironsides in Boston Harbor, surrounded by toys and tatters of gift wrap in the living room on Christmas morning with a festively decorated tree looming behind them. Then Ellie began to look plump in the photos.

Not plump, pregnant.

"With two such utterly perfect daughters, Ellie decided there was room for another child in the family," Katie narrated.

"This time it was a son," Jessie continued. "Peter." A photo took up the screen, Ellie in the hospital, smiling blissfully and holding her swaddled newborn son high, her cheek resting against his.

Curt reached for her hand and folded his fingers around it, warm and strong. "You okay?" he asked.

She might have objected to his overprotectiveness, but she didn't. In truth, she appreciated his sensitivity. "I'm okay," she said quietly. "This is my life, the first fifty years. Peter is a part of it." A major part. A crucial part. The rawest, most bittersweet part.

"We could take a break," Curt offered.

"And do what?"

He searched her face. His hand was so warm on hers, his eyes as intense as they'd been the very first time they'd made love, when he'd gazed down at her in his lumpy bed in that ramshackle apartment on the east side of Providence, and she'd seen passion and wonder in their glittering depths.

Certainly he couldn't be thinking about sex now. In her film biography, Peter had just been born. His picture spread across the screen.

Yet why wouldn't Curt be thinking of sex now? The day of his son's funeral, he'd wanted sex. His son in a casket, his son lost forever, his son's spirit hovering like a thundercloud above their heads—and Curt had wanted sex.

Two and a half years later, their marriage dead…was that what his eyes were telling her now? On the eve of their marriage's funeral, was he getting horny?

"The restaurant might still be open," he said. "We could go downstairs and have a snack."

All right, she thought. He wasn't thinking about sex. Which made her wonder why *she* was thinking about sex.

Probably because she was stretched out on a bed next to the only man she'd ever loved, and because she'd just spent an hour reliving her life—a life that had included an intensely beautiful, decades-long love affair with Curt.

She had no appetite—for food or sex or anything else. But she forced a smile and nodded. "A snack would be nice."

SIX

A FEW CUSTOMERS lingered in the main dining room, but the Colonial-costumed hostess, who seemed a bit less fresh and perky than she had when Curt and Ellie had arrived at the inn a few hours ago, explained that no new arrivals could be seated there. However, she informed them, they could order food in the keeping room.

"What's a keeping room?" Curt whispered to Ellie.

"A room with a fireplace off the kitchen," she whispered back. She had no idea why such rooms were called keeping rooms, but thanks to her mother's passion for all things "oldee," she knew a little about Colonial New England architecture.

The inn's keeping room wasn't directly off the kitchen, but it had a brick fireplace with a fire burning in it, and cozy tables set around the room. The hostess seated them at a table close to the fireplace. Ellie inhaled the mellow perfume of burning pine and smiled.

Curt settled into the chair across the table from her. A dessert menu stood in a brass holder at the center of the table and he skimmed it before nudging it toward her. The desserts looked tempting—Indian pudding, deep-dish apple pie, blue-berry cobbler—but she wasn't in the mood for anything sweet. She'd had trouble choking down a taste of the lavish chocolate birthday cake that had been served at her party.

A waiter in knee britches and a blousy shirt approached the table. "Let's split a cheese-and-fruit platter," she suggested to Curt.

He quirked an eyebrow, then nodded at the waiter, who jotted the order onto his pad. "I'll have an espresso, too. Ellie?"

"A cup of decaf," she requested. As if caffeine would make any difference. She didn't expect to sleep much tonight.

The waiter took the menu and disappeared. "You didn't want the apple pie?" Curt asked.

She shook her head.

"You've lost weight."

She pressed her lips together and leaned back in her seat, sur-prised that he mentioned her weight now. She'd lost weight in Africa, but he'd never said a word. She'd just assumed that by the time she'd returned home, he no longer noticed her.

"That wasn't an insult," he added, reading something in her expression. She wasn't sure what. Did she look offended?

She shrugged. "I ate differently in Ghana."

"They didn't have Goldfish there, I take it."

Oh, God. Goldfish—those addictive little fish-shaped crackers, laden with salt and cheddar flavoring. They'd been Peter's favorite snack. When he'd died, Ellie had started eating them. In some subconscious way, she'd felt closer to him while she munched Goldfish crackers by the fistful. She'd sneak into his bedroom, sit in the swivel chair at his desk, play one of his Ludacris or Eminem CDs and devour Goldfish, as if mimicking him would somehow raise his spirit, make him come alive again. Or she'd pick at her dinner, utterly uninterested in the slab of meat and the ear of corn lying on her plate, and then an hour later she'd slake her hunger with half a bag of Goldfish.

She hadn't been eating properly, and she hadn't cared. If she hadn't gone to Africa, she might still be moping around the house, living on Goldfish and vitamins and an occasional cup of tea.

Losing weight had not been her intention in Kumasi, but she'd had no access to Goldfish crackers there. She'd eaten the meals served at the compound—lots of fresh vegetables, pork and chicken, beans and rice and luscious fruits. Between meals, she'd been too busy to snack. There were always children to take care of, always hearts and lungs to listen to, broken fingers to splint, cuts to disinfect and bandage, diseases to treat. Always arms extended by tearful, wide-eyed children who feared needles but understood that the momentary sting of the injection would keep them healthy.

"Tell me about Africa," Curt said.

She studied the man seated across the round table from her. Half his face glowed golden where the firelight struck it; the other half was lost in shadow. She didn't need perfect light to see him, however. She knew every line, every crease, the faint scar above his left eyebrow from when he'd been popped with a bat during a long-ago Little League game, the silver hair that had recently begun to thread through his neatly trimmed sideburns. She knew the slightly crooked tooth that four years of orthodontia had failed to realign and the dimple that dented his right cheek. She knew his eyes, concentric rings of green and gray and amber outlined in black.

She could visualize all his features in the uneven light from the fireplace, but she couldn't discern what lay behind them. What was he after? Did he really want to hear about her experiences overseas, or was he obliquely questioning her about something else?

"You've never asked me to talk about it," she said warily.

"I'm asking now." His tone was low and blunt, almost a challenge.

She wasn't sure she wanted to share those six months with him. Africa was hers, not theirs.

Yet his gaze seemed demanding, almost accusing. What would he do if she refused to discuss her work at the clinic with him? Or if she discussed it and didn't tell him what he really wanted to know? Would he divorce her? She swallowed a bitter laugh.

She was spared from figuring out what to say by the arrival of the waiter with the fruit-and-cheese platter and their drinks. His appearance gave her a moment to regroup, to decide just what parts of her experience in Kumasi, if any, Curt was entitled to hear about. She shifted her attention to the platter, heaped with grapes, wedges of Gouda and Brie, Cortland apples and pale, round crackers. The waiter left two saucers and fruit knives, their coffee and a sugar bowl and pitcher of cream. Ellie plucked a sprig of grapes and set them on her plate.

"Well," she said wryly. "We didn't have Goldfish crackers there."

Something flickered in Curt's eyes. Irritation, perhaps.

"What do you want to know?" she asked.

"What it was like. What you did while you were there. What the people were like. The people you worked with."

She twisted a grape from its stem and popped it into her mouth. The tart skin contrasted with the sweet, juicy pulp. She let the flavors play on her tongue and prayed for them to keep her calm.

As soon as he mentioned the people she worked with, she understood what he was asking. And damn it, she didn't want to answer. Today was her fiftieth birthday, she was on the verge of dissolving her marriage and she just didn't feel like opening up her soul and letting him stomp all over it.

"I sent you e-mails," she reminded him, keeping her tone non-committal. "I wrote you about the clinic and the patients and the weather. And the food."

"Right." The word crackled like static electricity, dry and stinging. He cut a small slab of cheese, laid it on a cracker and devoured it in two bites. Ellie knew he would rather have crushed the cracker to powder in his fist. Anger simmered in his eyes.

Good. Let him stew. He was the one who'd shattered their marriage. He was the one who'd broken his vows. He was the one who'd moved away from Hope Street. If he wanted to be resentful, let him resent himself.

She sipped her coffee, then munched on another grape and wondered whether she'd be able to return to their *très* romantic room with him once their snack was gone. Just minutes ago they'd been stretched out side by side on the bed. They'd held hands. They'd gazed at the photo of their infant son on the TV screen and shared the pain of his death. For a few poignant moments, Ellie could have convinced herself she still loved Curt and their marriage bond was too strong to be severed.

Now... Now it didn't matter what she felt.

"You went to Africa wearing your wedding band," Curt finally said. "You came home not wearing it."

She turned to stare at the fire. Lively yellow flames licked the air, tiny tongues of aromatic heat. All these months, he hadn't said a word about her missing ring. Now that they were actually planning to divorce, he had finally acknowledged her naked ring finger.

"Yes," she said, turning back to him. "I had to wear latex gloves a lot of the time, and the rings weren't comfortable. The edges of the diamonds on the eternity ring would tear the plastic. So I stopped wearing the rings."

"And you didn't start wearing them again when you came home."

"What was the point? We were just as far apart when I got home as when I left. It seemed pretty clear nothing had changed."

"Things changed," he argued quietly. "You changed."

True. She'd come home believing that even though she'd lost her own son, she had saved the lives of a few other children. She'd understood that she was worthy, that she was competent, that she was a healer, that she could sometimes, in some circumstances, make things better. She'd discovered that if she kept moving forward and stayed focused on helping others, she might not slip back into the black hole that had been her life from the moment Peter had died.

She'd come home understanding that healing herself wasn't the same thing as healing her marriage. The first thought that had entered her mind when she spotted Curt and the girls waiting for her by the baggage claim at Logan Airport was, *When I needed him most, he was with another woman.* That hadn't changed.

So she hadn't put the wedding band back on.

She sighed. "I don't want to talk about my rings."

"Why not? We're reliving your life, Ellie. For a long time, those rings were a part of your identity. Why can't we talk about it?"

Because he had no right to ask. Because it was no longer his business.

Annoyed, she pushed away from the table and stood. If she opened her mouth, she'd say something awful, something spiteful, something to remind him of the role he'd played in destroying their marriage. So she kept her lips pressed together and stalked toward the door.

By the time she'd reached the hall, Curt had caught up to her. He clamped his hand on her shoulder, turned her around and pressed her against the wall. She was vaguely aware of its butter-yellow shade, the brass sconce just inches from her ear—and then he leaned in and kissed her.

It was an angry kiss, hard and possessive and forcing; a hostile claim, almost an assault. Yet the instant his tongue touched hers he grew gentle, his hand easing from her shoulder and his breath escaping in a quiet moan. He cupped her cheeks with his palms and she felt the tremor in his fingers—and a matching tremor inside herself. His kiss was suddenly so sweet, so yearning she wanted to weep.

This was the man she'd loved. The man she'd wed. The man who, twenty-seven years ago, had promised her hope.

The warmth of his mouth on hers melted her. It had been so long since he'd kissed her, so long since she'd felt anything but enraged or numb or hateful. So long since she'd looked at Curt and seen the man she'd counted on to prop her up—but who had instead walked away and let her fall.

He wasn't letting her fall now. In fact, he was literally holding her up. She was certain that if he let go of her, she would slide down the wall until she was nothing but a pool of seething desire on the faded rug beneath her feet.

But he didn't let go—and neither did she. She lifted her hands to his chest and felt the fierce drumming of his heart. Her lips pressed his, moved with his. When he ran the tip of his tongue over her teeth, she sighed. Tooth enamel didn't have nerve endings, did it? Yet she felt the stroke of his tongue in her throat, her chest, the cradle of her hips.

She wasn't sure how long they stood in the hall beside the doorway to the keeping room, just kissing, kissing, clinging to each other and kissing. Eventually, Curt relented, easing his mouth from hers, tracing his fingertips down her cheeks until they met at the edge of her chin. She opened her eyes before he did, and she watched as his gaze came into focus on her. In the bright hallway light she had no difficulty reading his emotions in his face: Sorrow. Lust. And, God help her, hope.

He bowed his head and brushed his mouth against her brow. "Let's go upstairs," he murmured.

Wait. They were getting a divorce. He'd betrayed her. Their love had died along with their son.

She shook her head, partly to clear it and partly to reject his invitation. No way was she ready to waltz back upstairs to their *très* romantic room to finish what he seemed to think they'd started. Just because Curt could ignite her with a kiss—he'd always been able to, damn him—didn't mean she should let that blaze consume her.

Not trusting her voice, she turned and walked back into the keeping room, where their fruit-and-cheese platter awaited them. She sat, took a sip of her coffee—which had grown tepid—and waited, wondering if he would follow her or leave her alone.

Alone was something she ought to get used to, she thought, gazing at the creamy wedges of cheese and the apples polished to such a high sheen that their red skin mirrored the flickering flames in the fireplace.

Never kissing Curt again was something she ought to get used to, too.

HE STOOD JUST BEYOND THE doorway for a long minute, trying to compose himself.

Hell. He'd been so furious with her—why couldn't she just *tell* him what she'd done in Africa? It wasn't as if he'd hate her for having a fling. He deserved as much. He'd strayed. Let her stray. Then they'd be even. Then, maybe, they could move past this anger.

But no, she had to play games with him. No more rings, no more marriage—yet she couldn't just tell him, "Yes, I slept with someone else." Or even, "Yes, I fell in love with someone else."

He was a big boy. He could handle the truth. What he couldn't handle was not knowing.

No matter how bad things were between Ellie and him, they'd always been honest with each other. When he'd had his bout of neediness or horniness or just plain insanity with Moira, he'd told Ellie. He'd done it, he'd regretted it and he'd confessed. For the sake of honesty, which had always been the essence of their marriage, he'd kept nothing from her.

She refused to show him that same courtesy. Perhaps this was her way of punishing him. Deny him the truth. Keep him guessing. Leave him never knowing some vital thing about the woman he'd married.

She wanted a divorce? He'd give her a divorce. She wanted financial support? Fine—he earned a lot more as a partner in his law firm than she did as a public-school nurse, so alimony wasn't out of the question. She wanted the house? They could work it out. She couldn't have his BMW, but everything else was negotiable.

First, though, she had to tell him the truth. Until their divorce was signed and sealed, he was still her husband and he had a right to know. And she wasn't going to get her damn divorce until she told him.

He drew in a deep breath, squared his shoulders and marched back into the keeping room. When he saw her seated at the table, flickers of gold firelight illuminating her pensive expression and a feast of fruit and cheese arrayed before her, he experienced a sharp tug in his gut—and lower. The hell with the truth. The hell with the divorce. He wanted her.

Just like the first time he'd seen her in college. She'd been linked to some other guy then—and, God help him, she might be linked to some other guy now. But that didn't change the wanting.

His desire was stronger now than it was then, because now he knew what having her was like. Just minutes ago, he'd had his mouth fused to hers. He'd been drinking from her like a parched nomad who'd just stumbled upon an oasis after two and a half years in the desert. She'd tasted like grapes and coffee and Ellie. Like home. Like love.

She'd wanted him, too, for as long as he'd been kissing her. He shouldn't have stopped. He should have kept his lips locked on hers and carried her up the stairs to their room. He shouldn't have given her a chance to think.

Too late. She sat at their intimate little table, a wedge of apple pinched between the thumb and forefinger of one hand, one leg crossed over the other and the flowing black skirt of her dress primly covering her knees.

He shrugged off his disappointment. Now he knew what he wanted—his wife in his arms, in his bed. He had a mission, and he'd figure out how to achieve it. Her purse was upstairs. She'd have to return to the room for that, and for the DVD. He had the room key, so she wouldn't be able to get into the room without him. Once he had her inside...

He'd make love to her. The hell with her birthday, the movie, their divorce plans. He'd love her, love every inch of her, bring her every kind of pleasure he could think of. And then she'd tell him the truth. She'd never been able to hide anything from him in bed.

He lowered himself onto the chair across from her and offered a conciliatory smile. "All right," he said. "Forget about your rings. Tell me something else about Africa. Something besides the weather and the food."

She eyed him warily, then took a delicate bite of the apple wedge in her hand. "Can you be more specific?"

"Tell me about your patients," he asked.

"I worked mostly with children," she said.

"You work with children at home," he reminded her. "How were these children different from the ones you deal with at the school?"

"They didn't have iPods," she said, then chuckled sadly. "Sometimes they didn't have shoes."

"Tell me," Curt said, and realized that he really did want to hear about this—maybe even as much as he wanted to hear why she'd chosen to remove her rings.

SEVEN

Eight months ago

"I THOUGHT WE'D BE SEEING all our patients at the clinic," Ellie said.

"Most of them, yes," Adrian assured her, helping her climb into the passenger seat of the clinic's open Jeep before he slid in behind the wheel. "Sometimes we make house calls. The families in the outlying villages don't always have transportation into town. And it can be helpful to observe the children in their natural environment. Housing, family dynamics—all of that plays into their health. So off we go to visit them in their own homes. Atu and Rose can manage the clinic for a few hours without me hovering over them."

Ellie glanced over her left shoulder at the back of the Jeep. There was a large black satchel on the floor behind Adrian's seat. A doctor's bag. She hadn't seen one since she was a little girl, in the days when doctors in the United States still made house calls. She remembered when she and her brothers had shared a wretched case of the measles, and Dr. Feldman had come to the house rather than insisting they travel to his office on an Arctic-cold January day when they were all spiking fevers. Ellie had been enthralled by Dr. Feldman's bag, the way its top flaps hinged back to reveal its magical contents: stethoscope, otoscope, tongue depressors, diagnostic hammer and sample vials of drugs. She'd seen the same items in his office, but in his bag they seemed more mysterious somehow, more potent. That might have been the moment she thought she should become a doctor. If she did, she could have a bag like Dr. Feldman's.

That Adrian Wesker owned such a bag intrigued her. Did it signify that Ghana was forty years behind the United States when it came to medical treatment, or simply that Ghana hadn't jettisoned the practices that had once made doctors seem so special, at least to a nine-year-old girl with a fever and a blotchy red rash?

"How many patients will we be visiting?" she asked as he steered across the dirt lot adjacent to the clinic building and out onto the street.

"At least two. More if time allows. Remember, we won't just be seeing patients, Ellie. We'll be checking out their homes and families. We'll be scrutinizing their contexts."

The wind blasted them in their roofless vehicle and blew Adrian's long, wavy hair back from his face. Sunglasses hid his eyes, and she slid her own sunglasses up the bridge of her nose as the morning sun glared through the windshield. The Jeep had to be at least a few decades old. It lacked seat belts, let alone air bags. Adrian wasn't the most cautious driver she'd ever ridden with, either. She gripped the window frame and held on tight as he careered around turns and zigzagged past cars, bicycles, motor scooters and pedestrians milling through the neighborhood's busy roads. More than a few of the people clogging the sidewalks waved and shouted a greeting at him. Dr. Wesker was clearly a popular figure in town.

"My fans," he muttered with mock humility when a couple of dimple-faced children shouted, "Hey, Dr. Wesker! Ya, Doc!" at him, their voices distorted by the wind as he cruised past them.

"Amazing how they recognize you, even with those sunglasses on," she teased.

He shot her a sly grin. "Celebrity is such a bloody burden, isn't it? Stick around, Ellie. You'll have your own fan club soon, too."

She actually liked that idea. Not that she wanted fans idolizing her, but she'd be thrilled if, after she'd spent six months in Ghana, the children she'd treated would feel she was truly a part of their community, and would remember her fondly once she was gone.

The village shrank behind them, and they found themselves on a roughly paved road that cut through farmland. "That's cacao," Adrian told her, gesturing toward the rows of dark green shrubs spreading back from the side of the road. "Chocolate beans."

She stared at the shrubs in fascination. "I love chocolate."

"It releases your endorphins, does it?" He smiled. "According to recent studies, chocolate is a hormonal experience. Women are very susceptible to it."

"I wouldn't say I'm susceptible," Ellie argued, feeling as if she had to defend her entire gender against such absurd generalizations. She smiled to assure him she wasn't outraged.

"You were the one who used the word *love,*" he argued back, his smile as challenging as hers was apologetic.

"Being passionate about chocolate is not the same as being susceptible to it," she insisted. "You can love something and still say no to it."

"Only if you are endowed with a willpower mightier than most of us." He steered onto an even bumpier road. "I have a dreadful time saying no to anything I feel passionate about."

Ellie was tempted to ask him what he felt passionate about, but she stifled the urge. She'd been in Kumasi only a couple of weeks. She'd eaten dinner with Adrian a few times, assisted him in setting and splinting a five-year-old girl's fractured ulna, reviewed the clinic's inventory of supplies and medicines with him and Rose and allowed him to introduce her to a local beer that was dark and heavy and deliciously sour. But she certainly didn't know him well enough to ask him about his passions.

They drove for nearly an hour under the relentless sun, passing fields of cacao interrupted by groves of trees. Occasionally, a rattly truck drove past them in the opposite direction, or an old car so covered in road dirt and dried mud Ellie couldn't identify its color or make. Now and then she spotted a field worker bowed over the plants. Broad-winged birds glided above them, puncturing the late-morning peace with loud caws.

Finally, they arrived at their first destination, a small farm-house built of stucco and wood and roofed with scraggly shingles, set back from the road at the end of a rutted dirt drive. "This was once a prosperous farm," Adrian told her as he turned off the engine. "Unfortunately, the husband died a year ago and his widow can't manage the place alone. She's been searching for a new husband. So far, no luck, in spite of the fact that she owns property. She's rather stuck here, running things and keeping her children in line. Her youngest has cerebral palsy."

"Does the child receive any therapy?"

"Not nearly enough. But he gets along. Sometimes I wonder if it's a good thing he doesn't have therapists fussing over him. He has to learn to cope. But then I worry that he's the reason she can't find a husband. If a man has to take responsibility for some other man's children, I don't suppose he wants any defective ones."

Adrian climbed down from the Jeep and Ellie followed, not bothering to challenge him on his use of the word *defective*. She understood that he was verbalizing the biases of potential husbands for the widow who lived here, not expressing his own views.

Two children barreled out of the house before Adrian and Ellie had reached the screen door, which hung crookedly on rusted hinges, the mesh torn in parts. "Dr. Wesker, Dr. Wesker!" they hooted, their dark faces shiny with excitement and sweat. One of them began boasting about how much his running speed had increased since Adrian's last visit, and the other grabbed Adrian's free hand and singsonged that their mother had fixed him a cake. Ellie wondered whether she might have selected Adrian as a prospective husband. Ellie couldn't imagine him giving up his medical practice to farm cacao in the hinterlands, but she could easily imagine a widowed mother viewing him as a prize catch, even if he was a light-skinned expatriate whose one true love was his clinic.

He wasn't catchable, though. Rose had warned Ellie of that her first day in Kumasi. Not that Ellie had required the warning. She wasn't looking for a husband. She already had one, and he'd torn her heart to shreds.

Inside the farmhouse, the air was warm and stagnant, the furniture rudimentary and as in need of repair as the screen door. No curtains draped the windows, and the pallid walls were marked with water stains that indicated the presence of leaks. But the house was clean, and a dense, sweet aroma filled the main room. The cake, Ellie guessed.

The next hour sped by in a blur. With Ellie's assistance, Adrian examined each of the widow's five children, spending the most time with the youngest, who was about five and had outgrown his leg brace. Thanks to a bit of tinkering and tampering—besides medical supplies, Ellie learned that Adrian carried a few basic carpentry tools in his black bag—Adrian was able to elongate the metal bars so the child could get a few more months' use out of the brace. While he extended the metal rods and loosened the straps, surrounded by yammering children, he requested that Ellie retreat to the kitchen with the widow and find out how her health was.

She was fine, she told Ellie, even though she looked haggard and her eyes were so heavily framed in shadow she resembled a raccoon. "Really, yes, I am fine. No problems. Nothing wrong with me," she said, her voice so lilting and her words so rhythmic she sounded as if she were singing rather than speaking.

"Are you taking any vitamins?" Ellie asked. The kitchen was as clean as the living room, and as dismal. Cracked Formica counters rested on splintering shelves and cabinets. The oven would have qualified as an antique back home, and the refrigerator was much too small to hold all the fresh food she and her children needed.

"Vitamins, yes. Yes, I take them."

"Iron supplements?"

"Oh, sure, that, too."

Ellie smiled at the woman, whose hair was pulled back under a scarf in a way that emphasized how thin and wan her face was. The whites of her eyes had a yellow tinge to them. Ellie didn't believe she was taking vitamins or iron. She wondered if Adrian had brought any supplements in his bag.

"Would you let me examine you?" Ellie asked carefully, hoping not to spook the woman. One thing she'd learned within days of her arrival in Kumasi was that the health of children was inextricably linked to the health of their mothers. The mothers here—like mothers everywhere—would gladly sacrifice their own lives for their children. But whatever sacrifices they made were often passed like weights to their children. A woman might forgo food so her children could eat more, but if she became sick, her children invariably became sick, too.

A woman like this one probably didn't check her breasts for lumps. She probably hadn't had a blood test since her youngest was born. If she felt ill, she most likely doctored herself or suffered.

"I'm healthy," the woman insisted.

Another thing Ellie had learned was that many mothers would prefer not to know if something was wrong with them. If they knew, they'd have to deal with it—perhaps at the expense of their children. Ignorance was better. "Is there anything I can do for you?" Ellie asked, keeping her tone light. "Anything that would make you feel better than you already do?"

"I require a man," the widow said bluntly.

"That would be nice, wouldn't it," Ellie agreed. "It's hard to run a farm by yourself."

"Yah, that. And I require a man to let me be a woman."

Ellie could have interpreted that to mean she longed to let someone else do the farm work so she could spend her days tending to the house and raising her children. But she suspected the widow was talking about sex.

She smiled faintly. What was she supposed to say? She could discuss the mechanics of sex without hesitation. She could discuss pelvic exams and birth control and even ways to achieve physical satisfaction. But love and fear and the deep, gnawing ache of loneliness, the desire to be a woman... No, she didn't feel comfortable talking about that. Certainly not now, given where she was in her own life.

When was the last time she'd had sex? Two years ago. Before Peter had died. Maybe she wasn't a woman, either.

She used to love sex. Then her son passed away and she couldn't bear the thought of it. She couldn't convince herself she missed it. What she missed was being who she used to be—a normal woman, fully alive, a woman who enjoyed sleeping and waking, working and eating, laughing through bad movies and singing along with whatever song was on the radio…and making love. She missed that.

Sex was the least of it.

"All done in here?" Adrian's voice wafted through the doorway from the living room.

With his face in full view, not half concealed by his sunglasses, and the sleeves of his thin cotton shirt rolled up, his sheer masculinity startled her. It wasn't that he was better looking than any other man. It was just that she'd been thinking about sex and whether going without it made a woman less of a woman…and suddenly, there Adrian was, with his silver eyes and his windblown mane and his lean build.

Ellie truly didn't want sex. But she was still enough of a woman to think about it in the presence of a man like Adrian Wesker.

FROM THAT FARM, THEY DROVE to another, maybe ten kilometers away—Ellie was beginning to get used to thinking in kilometers instead of miles. The family there was marginally more prosperous than the widow, but their three-year-old suffered from chronic ear infections. Adrian painstakingly explained the surgery that would implant tubes in the child's ears to reduce pressure, but his mother was adamantly opposed to surgery. "You cut open a child and the evil spirits can enter through his skin," she declared.

"That won't happen," Adrian assured her. "When we do surgery, Mrs. Braimah, everything is very clean and sterile. This is a simple procedure. A surgeon would perform it at the university hospital in Kumasi."

"There are evil spirits in the city, too," Mrs. Braimah argued. "The university is full of evil spirits." Ellie suppressed a laugh. If the universities in Kumasi were anything like the universities at home, she could see why some people might believe they were full of evil spirits. Alcoholic spirits, anyway.

"If you don't let Enam get the operation," Adrian said earnestly, "he will continue to have ear infections. He'll develop a resistance to the antibiotics I've presecribed for him. That means the drugs will stop working. He could lose his hearing."

Mrs. Braimah remained stubborn. "No one will cut open my child."

"It's a tiny little cut," Adrian said. "It's not big enough for evil spirits to get in."

Ellie heard the impatience in his tone and touched his arm. "Let me," she said. She was seated on a wooden bench next to Adrian. Enam, a plump, dimpled toddler with thick curls crowning his head like black bubbles, had climbed onto her lap. She wrapped her arms around him, savoring his weight on her knees. So many years had passed since her own children were small enough to fit on her lap.

She turned to Enam's mother, who sat rigidly on a chair facing her visitors, her fingers knotted together in her lap and her gaze fastened to her child. "He's a sweetheart," Ellie said gently. "Do you know that term? *Sweetheart?*"

"It's something nice," Mrs. Braimah guessed.

"Yes. It means he's gentle-natured and loving. You're a lucky woman to have a son like this."

"He's good," Mrs. Braimah boasted. "No evil spirits in him."

"Actually, there *is* an evil spirit in him. It's the infection that makes his ears hurt. If you let him get the surgery, the little cut inside his ear will let the evil spirit escape. It won't let the evil spirit *in*. It will let the evil spirit *out*. But if you don't let Enam have the surgery, the evil spirit will stay inside him and hurt his ears."

"There's no evil spirit in him," Mrs. Braimah said, clearly fuming.

"Yes, there is. It's called an infection. We have to get that evil spirit out of him. That's what the surgery will do."

Mrs. Braimah rocked in her chair, her gaze drifting and her hands clasped even more tightly as she fretted over whether the surgery would let the evil spirits in or out of her beloved son. Finally, she relented. "How much this surgery cost?" she asked.

"Our clinic will make the financial arrangements," Adrian said. "Don't you worry about that. It won't cost you anything."

"And it lets the evil spirit out?"

Adrian gave Ellie a smile that brimmed with gratitude and admiration. Then he addressed Enam's mother. "Yes, Mrs. Braimah. We will get those evil spirits out of Enam."

"You're a miracle worker," he praised Ellie a few minutes later, as they climbed back into the Jeep. Their hours driving on back roads had layered the vehicle with dust, and Ellie wiped the cracked leather of her seat clean before settling into it. Adrian didn't bother. Now she understood why he dressed in khaki whenever he wasn't wearing surgical scrubs. The tan fabric hid the dust.

She smiled modestly. "I'm not a miracle worker."

"I've been trying without success to get Mrs. Braimah to agree to the surgery for six months. You got her to say yes."

Ellie shrugged. She didn't believe she'd worked any miracles, but she liked the idea that Adrian thought she had. He was the one working miracles in the villages surrounding Kumasi. That he would consider her single triumph with Enam's mother enough to elevate her to his level filled her with warmth.

Back home, her job as a school nurse demanded no miracles of her. Sometimes youngsters remembered to thank her before they galloped back to their classrooms after having a splinter removed or a scrape bandaged. Sometimes, when they were ill and had to be sent home, the parent who picked them up thanked Ellie. But no one ever called her a miracle worker.

Then again, back home she was never called upon to rid a child of evil spirits.

She and Adrian didn't talk much during the long drive back to the clinic. But he wore a faint, devilishly appealing grin throughout the trip, and Ellie—rightly or wrongly—decided that she was in some way the reason for that smile.

She shouldn't have been so pleased with herself. Getting a man to smile wasn't that difficult, most of the time. Lately, she hadn't gotten Curt to smile, but she hadn't gotten herself to smile, either. Cheering everyone up was usually a woman's task, and Ellie had abdicated that responsibility the day Peter died.

Getting Adrian to smile was...special. He was in love with his clinic—and his smile had nothing to do with love anyway— yet he'd called her a miracle worker. She'd accomplished something he hadn't been able to do on his own. She'd come through for him, fulfilled a need for him and maybe, just maybe, saved a little boy's hearing. She hoped Enam would have his surgery before Ellie had to leave Ghana. She wanted to be present, to see him through it, to celebrate with that adorable little butterball of a child once he was liberated from his evil-spirit ear infection.

And shame on her for being proud, but she wanted Adrian to turn to her once Enam was out of the hospital and recovering at home with his doting mother, and say, *You did this. I couldn't have made it happen without you....*

EIGHT

"So you saved a little boy's hearing," Curt said.

Ellie had never before told him about the children she and the doctor had visited in the hinterlands of Ghana. When she talked about those children now, her eyes glowed with a kind of ecstasy he hadn't seen since... God, since the good days of their marriage, when the kids were all asleep and she would lure him upstairs to their bedroom and have her way with him. It was the glow of a woman who'd reached a pinnacle, a woman who'd mastered her universe. He hadn't realized that something other than sex could light up her eyes like that.

Then again, he wasn't convinced she was telling him everything. Yes, he believed she'd traveled from farm to farm with the doctor in a squeaky, dilapidated Jeep with nonfunctional shock absorbers and an open roof that sucked all the road's dirt in on her, and that she'd gotten this superstitious rural woman to trust her with her baby's infected ears. She'd e-mailed him and the girls photos. The Jeep existed. So did the dirty roads. So did the doctor.

But he knew there was more, something beyond simply curing a kid's chronic ear infections. Ellie was editing herself.

If he pressed her, she'd shut down and seal herself off from him. So he simply drank his coffee and munched on grapes and encouraged her with nods and brief comments at appropriate places.

"I didn't think it was such a big deal," she said with a shrug. "I suspect the mother listened to me because I was another woman. But Dr. Wesker acted as if I'd done something astonishing."

"In his eyes, you did." Curt studied her face, loving how radiant she looked as she recounted the incident and wishing he'd been the source of that radiance. "Remember when you saved that guy's life at Walt Disney World?"

She shrugged again, and brushed the notion away with a wave of her hand. "I didn't really save his life."

"You really did." The moment crystallized in Curt's memory, a warm, slightly muggy February afternoon during the kids' winter-break vacation from school. They'd stood in line for what seemed like a year to ride on the Space Mountain roller coaster—a three-minute thrill worth the wait, they'd all agreed—and staggered out of the building into the blinding sunlight. A few steps ahead of them, a portly older man had been walking a meandering path over to a bench. Curt had scarcely noticed him—just one more dizzy roller-coaster rider trying to regain his bearings after an exhilarating ride. But Ellie had immediately noticed that the man was struggling to breathe, his face was deeply flushed and he had his right hand pressed to the left side of his chest.

"Oh, no," she'd muttered just as the man had tipped over sideways and sprawled out on the bench. The woman with him let out a scream, and suddenly, there Ellie was, bowed over him, unbuttoning his shirt and beginning CPR while she shouted to Curt to find a park employee. She kept up the compressions for several long minutes until an ambulance arrived and EMTs took over. Someone from Disney security took her name, and the next day a huge bouquet of flowers arrived for her at their hotel, along with a note that read, "Thank you for saving my husband's life."

Curt remembered that note vividly. Yes, Ellie had saved the man's life. She hadn't had to travel all the way to Africa to be a hero.

"You've always done that," he remarked, wondering why he'd never called her on it. "You make light of all your accomplishments. You say you didn't really save the guy's life, or that kid's hearing in Ghana. You say all you do at the school is wipe noses and take temperatures."

"That *is* what I do," she argued.

"You wipe their noses and take their temperatures and make them feel better. Damn it, Ellie—you do a lot of good in the world, everywhere you go. Africa, Disney World, here at home. You save people's lives."

She made a face. "Believe me, I wish I could save lives. But I can't. When a third-grader has a sniffle, I'm hardly saving his life if I hand him a tissue and tell him to blow."

Curt shook his head. "Sometimes I think your parents brainwashed you into believing that being a nurse instead of a doctor meant you couldn't possibly be healing people," he said. "You do heal people. You make them better. You convince the mother of a little child halfway around the world that the child should have surgery to save his hearing. Don't put yourself down, okay? You save lives. Accept it."

She stared at him dubiously. He hadn't launched into that speech in an effort to win her heart—or even to win himself a bit of predivorce physical pleasure tonight in the *très* romantic room. He'd said it because it was the truth. He'd been listening to Ellie belittle her work ever since she'd quit her job at Children's Hospital and accepted a position as a school nurse at the Felton Primary School in town. "So I can be home in the afternoon, when the children get home from school," she'd said, justifying her decision, but it had required no justification. Suburban children got sick just like city children, or village and farm children in Ghana. Ellie used her expertise to make those suburban children feel better. She deserved a few medals and a ticker-tape parade.

He wondered what she saw in his face. Pride? Admiration? Longing?

Or perhaps regret that he'd never praised her accomplishments, never assured her that she was every bit the miracle worker her Ghana buddy, Dr. Wesker, had declared her.

She lowered her gaze to the nearly empty fruit platter, then turned to watch the fire. How had they traveled from fighting to kissing to tension and anger to this moment of honesty in so little time? Were fiftieth birthdays supposed to be full of introspection and analysis and emotions with as many peaks and dips as the Space Mountain roller-coaster ride at Disney World? His birthday hadn't been. It had been full of rage—rage at Ellie for denying him the chance to feel fully alive, to recover completely from the grief. Rage at himself for wanting what she remained unable to give him. Rage at the brutality of fate, at the cruel whimsy of a world that could snatch his son away from him and destroy his marriage.

Rage and a hot car.

He'd bought his BMW and spent his birthday testing the engine's limits on a barren stretch of Route 2, hoping no state troopers happened to be waiting on that same stretch with their radar guns aimed in his direction. He'd driven until he'd burned off enough anger to trust himself not to erupt in another fight with Ellie when he got home.

Not the happiest birthday of his life.

The keeping room had grown darker, and he realized that the fire was burning down. He glanced at his watch. Nearly midnight.

How many hours until they could go home?

How many hours could he keep Ellie here at the inn and convince her…to make love with him? To forgive him? To call off the lawyers?

To tell him the damn truth about the time she'd spent with that noble doctor in Africa?

He kept his tone light when he said, "What do you say we go back upstairs and watch some more of your life on TV."

Her eyes flashed, shadowed with doubt. "Curt, what happened outside…" Her voice faded into a sigh.

Outside the building or outside the keeping-room doorway? The blush that rose to her cheeks told him she was thinking about their kiss. "You were as much a part of that as I was," he reminded her.

She pressed her lips together, then leveled her gaze at him. "I'm a human being. And you're a good kisser. But we can't— I mean, we've already decided…"

To get a divorce. To treat each other with chilly civility until then. To avoid anything the least bit pleasurable, the least bit sexual, anything that might remind them that they'd once been crazy in love with each other. "I won't do anything you don't want me to do," he said, filtering the resentment from his tone. It was a promise he could keep. He'd never forced himself on Ellie. Never. She'd always been willing.

Except maybe for what had happened in the hallway outside the keeping room. But she'd been willing then, too. Surprised at first, perhaps, but she'd kissed him back. God, how she'd kissed him.

Her hesitation rankled. "The hell with it," he muttered. "Why don't we just go home and tell the girls what's going on. We don't have to be prisoners at this freaking hotel. If you don't want to stay, we'll leave."

"No." The word slipped out of her mouth before she could have given much thought to her response—and her cheeks grew rosy again. She managed a crooked smile. "I want to see the rest of the movie."

"Okay." Hoping he didn't look too pleased, he pushed his chair back from the table. Glancing around the keeping room, he spotted their waiter, who hurried over with a check. Curt signed it to the room, stood and extended his hand to Ellie.

She peered up at him for a long moment, then slipped her hand into his and let him help her out of her chair.

That simple gesture shouldn't have felt like some kind of victory, but it did.

BACK IN THE ROOM, Curt settled into the easy chair. Ellie was grateful; his avoidance of the bed was clearly an attempt to let her know he wasn't going to make any unwelcome overtures. Not that she'd expected him to pressure her. He was Curt, for God's sake.

Still, when he'd grabbed her in the hallway and spun her around and kissed her... Even then, he hadn't pressured her. He'd startled her, certainly, and she still wasn't sure how she felt about that kiss as she kicked off her shoes and resumed her seat on the bed, leaning back into the pillows she'd propped up against the brass headboard. That she'd responded to his kiss was only natural—he was her husband, the only man she'd ever loved. But she hadn't expected to feel such need in him, such yearning. She'd thought they were beyond all that by now. He had his car, after all. She had Ghana. They'd agreed to go their separate ways.

Yet a treacherous desire gnawed at her, a desire for Curt to join her on the bed, to arch his arm around her and offer his shoulder to lean on. It would be more comfortable than pillows against a headboard. It would be more...

Loving.

Fortunately, he distracted her from that thought by turning on the TV and hitting the play button for the DVD. The video biography of her life would keep her from dwelling on any idea that included both Curt and loving.

"Don't cry for me, carpool mother," crooned a man's voice on the soundtrack, accompanied by a montage of pictures that illustrated the frantic scheduling of Katie's, Jessie's and Peter's various activities. A photo of a soccer ball appeared, followed by a photo of Jessie in a green leotard and a headdress of large, floppy yellow petals, the costume Ellie had sewn for her when she'd landed the role of a sunflower in a dance recital. A photo of all three children in swimsuits at the community pool. A photo of Peter climbing the jungle gym at the town's toddler playground. A photo of Katie playing the piano at another recital. A photo of Jessie holding a soccer trophy. A photo of the three at day camp, displaying clay models of horses they had made in arts and crafts—although Peter's horse looked more like a Salvador Dali nightmare vision of a melting giraffe. A photo of Peter in his T-ball shirt and a Red Sox cap. A photo of Katie holding a soccer trophy. A photo of Peter holding a soccer trophy. A photo of the bookshelf in the family room, the top surface of which was covered with soccer trophies, several dozen of them.

"I never bought into that philosophy of handing every kid in the league a trophy," Curt remarked.

"It built self-esteem," Ellie argued mildly. "It made every participant feel like a winner."

"Yeah, but most of the kids weren't winners. Why make them feel like something they aren't? It devalues the trophy."

"I remember how excited our children were whenever they got a trophy. They were more excited by the trophies than by the game."

"Yeah…well, it was soccer," Curt said, then laughed. "How can you get excited about soccer? All you do is run around and kick a ball. Big deal."

She knew he was teasing, so she didn't bother replying.

"Now, this…" He gestured toward the screen, where the girls had spliced in some video footage of Peter, a few years older, hitting a double at a Little League baseball game. Ellie and Curt had been experimenting with their new video cam, and the shots weren't exactly brilliant. But even though the film was as jumpy as a silent-era movie and Peter wasn't always centered in the frame, it was clear that by the time he was eight he had a natural swing and he ran like a jaguar, every bone and joint in his body moving in perfect synchronicity. "Baseball is a real sport."

Tears beaded along Ellie's eyelashes, but she refused to cry. Peter had been such a beautiful, talented child. That he'd died was so wrong. It made no sense. Why couldn't she have died, instead, and he have grown into manhood?

Don't think about it, she ordered herself. She took deep breaths and stayed focused on the screen, as Peter tagged a runner out at second base and a country-sounding song, about sitting in the cheap seats and watching the boys hit it deep played on the soundtrack. Ellie had never heard the song before, but she remembered sitting on the hard bleachers at so many games. The winter Peter was seven, Curt had bought her a bleacher cushion for Christmas. She'd used that padded seat until the seams wore out, then mended it with duct tape and got a few more seasons out of it.

Oh, yes——that Christmas. The bleacher cushion was one of the best gifts she'd ever received, more practical than jewelry, more satisfying than a new food processor, as comfortable as a bathrobe but better, because she could use it while watching her children. They'd all loved sports, the girls graduating from soccer to field hockey and softball while Peter played baseball all spring and summer and basketball through the fall and winter. She'd loved watching her children play, especially once she had her padded bleacher seat.

But that was still an awful Christmas. So many years ago, yet the pain of it swept over her, as fresh as a night breeze. The Christmas disaster that year had been about a gingerbread house. And about Peter.

NINE

Ten years earlier

"CAN I HELP?" Peter asked.

Ellie surveyed the mess that had once been her kitchen and decided nothing her seven-year-old son did in the room could make it any worse. Flour had spilled across the table and drifted onto the floor like incredibly fine snow. The shrink-wrapped turkey thawing on the counter had leaked a puddle of pink water that dribbled down into the sink. Jessie and Katie had left their school backpacks on two of the chairs, and a jumble of damp boots lay heaped by the mudroom door. Someone's scarf had been slung over the pantry door, which stood open to reveal the usual clutter of food and utensils crammed onto the shelves. The room smelled of wet wool and dishwasher soap.

The day before Christmas, people's houses were supposed to smell of cinnamon and cloves, evergreens and eggnog. They were supposed to be clean and tidy, ready to welcome the visits of neighbors and relatives. New tapers were supposed to stand in candlesticks and chains of holly were supposed to coil around the staircase railing. People were supposed to be filled with peace. Wasn't that what Christmas was all about?

Ellie was never filled with peace before the holiday. Most years, the frenzy of shopping and baking and planning and budgeting frazzled her so thoroughly that she fantasized about converting to Judaism, just so she could turn her back on the season's insanity.

Things were slightly more insane this year because the girls had prevailed on her to make a gingerbread house. Katie had found elaborate instructions on the Internet. Ellie could bake a serviceable cake using a mix—she was quite capable when it came to adding eggs and a tablespoon of oil—and she believed that whoever invented those sausage-shaped tubes of cookie dough deserved the Nobel Prize. However, baking gingerbread from scratch posed an enormous challenge to her culinary skills.

"I could break the eggs," Peter volunteered.

She peered down at her son. His blond hair was hidden beneath his ever-present Red Sox cap, and his sweatshirt also featured the Red Sox trademark, a gothic red capital *B* emblazoned across his narrow chest. His blue jeans hung loose on his skinny frame, but they were already too short. He must have experienced another growth spurt when Ellie hadn't been watching.

"We don't need any eggs in the dough," she told him. "But if you want, you can whip the cream and vanilla. Would you like to do that?"

Stupid question. Whipping the cream involved the use of her electric eggbeater—a power tool that made noise and moved fast. Of course he would like to do that.

"This is gonna be the best gingerbread house ever," he said a minute later, kneeling on one of the empty chairs and steering the eggbeater through the foamy white cream in a bowl on the table. "Is this done yet?"

"No." She glanced up from another bowl, into which she was measuring sifted powdered sugar. Who sifted powdered sugar, other than the folks who'd come up with this recipe? Ellie didn't even own a sifter. She'd had to race next door, dodging the snow flurries that swirled out of the late-afternoon sky, to borrow her next door neighbor's sifter. "You've got to whip it until it stands in peaks."

"What does that mean?"

"I'll tell you when it's done," she assured him.

"Danny Barrone is such an idiot," Peter declared as he stared at the cream he was frothing with the beater.

"Oh?" Who was Danny Barrone? And where had she put the molasses? She spun around, searching the counters until she spotted the dark brown bottle near the microwave.

"He said there's no such thing as Santa Claus. He thinks he knows everything because he's the oldest kid in the class. But I think he must be stupid, because if he's so old he should be in third grade, right?"

"That depends," Ellie said, carrying the molasses and her measuring spoons to the table. "Just because he's older than everyone else doesn't mean he's stupid."

"He's gotta be stupid if he thinks there's no such thing as Santa Claus. Who does he think brings all the presents?"

Was seven too young to learn the truth about Santa Claus? The girls had been diligent about keeping the myth alive for Peter. He was so young, so trusting, so eager to believe. Every year he was the first one out of bed on Christmas morning, shouting throughout the house that the cookies and milk Ellie had left on the table near the fireplace for Santa had been consumed, which proved beyond a doubt that the jolly old man existed. Of course, all those presents under the tree proved he existed, too.

Why not let him live with the fantasy a little longer?

"You know," she said carefully, "different people have different beliefs. Some people don't celebrate Christmas at all. Some celebrate it differently than we do. And some celebrate it the way we do."

"So Santa only comes to people like us?"

Ellie nodded. "He only comes to houses where people believe in him."

"Well, I sure believe in him. Is this peaks yet?"

Peter grew tired of beating the cream well before it stood in peaks. His hand hurt, he insisted. The eggbeater was too heavy. After lifting the appliance out of the bowl while the beaters were still spinning, and splattering vanilla-flavored cream all over the table, he bolted, evidently concluding that viewing television cartoons in the family room was more important than making gingerbread.

Ellie sighed as the kitchen settled into stillness around her, and then read the recipe again. It seemed awfully complicated. She should have gone with one of those prebaked kits or substituted graham crackers for gingerbread. But the girls had pleaded with her to make the genuine article from scratch. It would be nice if *they'd* offered to help—this was their idea, after all—but they were shut inside their bedrooms upstairs, no doubt wrapping gifts or jabbering on the phone. Their school's winter break had begun at three-thirty that afternoon. They'd been on the phone with their friends ever since they'd emerged from the middle-school bus and burst into the house, shedding boots and backpacks and then vanishing up the stairs.

Ellie glanced at the window above the sink. The sky was growing dark and the snow was falling harder. She hoped Curt would get home soon. His firm was having its holiday party that afternoon, and as a partner he had to be a dutiful host and stick around at least until all the associates and support staff received their year-end bonuses. He and the other partners also had to make sure no one consumed too much of the holiday punch to drive safely, and had to summon cabs or arrange carpools for those employees who'd exceeded their limits. Ellie wasn't sure what, besides guzzling holiday punch and distributing bonuses, went on at the firm's annual party, but Curt assured her nothing more tawdry than some harmless flirting took place. "If there's anything X-rated going on," he added, "I don't know about it. And I don't want to know."

Fine. He was nursing a cup of holiday punch and flirting harmlessly while Ellie confronted her culinary limitations without even a glass of wine to bolster her. She abandoned the dry ingredients for the cream, whipping it with the beaters until it was stiff. She considered hollering for Peter to come back to the kitchen, just so he could see what peaks looked like. But he probably didn't care. He'd helped her with the gingerbread only long enough to confirm that Santa Claus existed.

Eventually, the dough looked and felt right. Following the recipe's instructions, she rolled it into two sheets that weren't quite uniform in thickness but were the best she could produce. Once they were baking in the oven, she searched the kitchen for the templates she'd cut out—four wall pieces, two roof pieces. Why couldn't she have built a gingerbread tent, instead? A pup tent—two sheets shaping an angle, propped up by stale sticks of licorice.

Through the ceiling she heard the thump of footsteps. The girls were clomping back and forth between their bedrooms above the kitchen. Ellie considered summoning them to help her clean some of the mixing bowls and utensils, but it was Christmas Eve. Shrewishness and nagging were not suited to the spirit of the holiday.

So she scrubbed the bowls and utensils herself. Once she had everything balanced in the drying rack, she reread the recipe for the tenth time in preparation for tackling the frosting.

What crazed person had invented gingerbread houses? she wondered. The Brothers Grimm? They wrote all those sadistic German folktales about witches devouring children and mothers giving their daughters poisoned apples to eat. Didn't the witch in *Hansel and Gretel* live in a gingerbread house? And look at what had happened to Hansel and Gretel: they'd died. Or killed the witch. Or something.

Where the hell was Curt?

By the time he arrived home, the sky had gone black and an inch of snow covered the ground. Wearing a big grin, he swept into the kitchen from the mudroom, his tie loosened and his hair damp. "Whoa, it smells good in here!" he boomed before sweeping Ellie into a hug.

The baking pastry had managed to fill the air with a holiday fragrance. Her frosting was lumpy, and the unevenness in the gingerbread sheets appeared obvious now that they were cooked. When she'd pulled the trays from the oven, she'd seen that the edges of each sheet had turned a dark, tarry hue and the centers were puffy. Somehow, she didn't think her gingerbread house was going to be up to code.

She hoped it would taste better than it looked—the parts that weren't burned, anyway. And if it didn't, at least she could assure herself that she'd tried her best. Certainly her effort had to be worth a few mommy points, regardless of the outcome.

She felt a lot mellower about the project once Curt closed his arms around her. She relaxed against the soft cashmere of his coat, which was chilly from the outdoors. The scent of baking mingled with the scent of him, of snow and the night air and his aftershave and…another smell. A flowery smell.

Perfume?

"How was the party?" she asked, easing out of his arms.

"The usual," he said as he pulled off his coat and carried it to the coat closet by the front door to hang up. Unlike his children, he didn't leave his crap all over the kitchen. "Everyone had fun. A few people got a little tipsy." He returned to the kitchen, peered at the sheets of gingerbread and then at the recipe. He looked impressed—and ridiculously handsome with his tie dangling loose, his hair mussed and a shadow of beard darkening his jaw. "People were thrilled with their bonuses. That always fills them with holiday cheer."

Ellie caught another whiff of the unfamiliar perfume, faint yet obvious because it didn't belong. "Who threw herself at you?" she asked. She wasn't jealous. She had absolute faith in Curt. She just didn't like the idea of a female colleague drinking too much and nuzzling him. Didn't that qualify as sexual harassment?

Curt chuckled. "Four secretaries, two paralegals and Gretchen." One of the founding partners, Gretchen was in her sixties and resembled a mastiff. "Moira Kernan just couldn't resist me, and Lindy Brinson made passes at all the partners and also a potted plant. Oh, yeah, and Bill Castillo put the moves on me. Whenever he has a few drinks his true bisexual nature emerges."

Ellie scowled. "Does he wear perfume?"

Curt slung his arm around Ellie. "Everyone was throwing themselves at everyone. That's what happens when people get big bonuses and consume a lot of Christmas punch." He pressed a kiss to Ellie's temple, which he knew was one of her most sensitive spots. A reflexive heat whispered through her. "Nobody at the party was as beautiful as you. Did you know you've got flour on your nose?"

"I do?" She rubbed the tip of her nose.

She must have missed the spot. He moved his thumb gently along the side of her nose, just below the bridge. "So, you're really going to build this thing into a house?"

"The girls asked me to. It's Christmas eve. How could I say no?"

"Like this." He released her, gazed down into her eyes and murmured, "No." Then he bowed and kissed her, a real kiss on the mouth. "I wish you could've joined me at the party, but we've got that damn no-guests rule. If I brought you, everyone would want to bring their husbands and wives, their boyfriends and girlfriends and their cousin from Quincy."

"I'd be bored at your party," she said, although being wrapped up in Curt's arms, the taste of his kiss lingering on her lips, was anything but boring.

"Believe me, there's nothing boring about listening to Sue Pritchard sing 'Good King Wenceslas.' She sings it really slow, like a torch song. I think in another life, she had the hots for the good king."

Ellie grinned. Sue Pritchard was the firm's senior-most secretary. She'd been there longer than Curt, and in that time she'd been through three marriages. All her divorces had been handled by Gretchen the mastiff, and Sue had emerged from each one exponentially wealthier.

"Well, some of us actually had to work today," she said, giving Curt a parting hug before she turned back to the table to arrange her templates on the gingerbread. "I saw two kids with upset stomachs, one with what looked like conjunctivitis and one with a splinter. Then I came home and baked."

"Santa will reward your hard work," Curt promised as he

headed toward the stairs. "You've been good, for goodness' sake." With that he was gone, announcing to his children that he was home.

Ellie didn't construct the gingerbread house until after dinner—a snack of cold cuts on rye bread. Tomorrow her parents would be coming for dinner; she'd be preparing the turkey, along with stuffing, winter squash, corn bread and steamed beans, and brownies and Christmas cookies for dessert. That plus the gingerbread house seemed like more than enough food preparation to earn her a sleigh full of presents.

The kids didn't mind a supper of sandwiches, anyway. Ellie suspected that they preferred the light meal to a roasted turkey.

After dinner, the children were giddy. Twelve-year-old Katie considered herself the epitome of cool sophistication, but she couldn't conceal her excitement about the holiday. Ten-year-old Jessie veered wildly between preadolescent aloofness and child-like glee. She insisted that the family watch a DVD of *Frosty the Snowman,* which even Peter considered infantile, followed by a showing of *A Christmas Story,* which they'd all seen so many times they could recite most of the script along with the characters.

Before bed, the children brought the gifts they'd bought for one another downstairs to the living room and arranged them under the tree. Ellie had explained to Peter a few years ago that while Santa brought most of the presents, people also gave gifts to their loved ones, because Christmas was all about giving. Peter had a tendency to give the sorts of gifts he would love to receive: packages of Gummi Bears for his sisters, baseball cards for his father and—usually because he'd run out of money—a crayon drawing in a Popsicle-stick frame for Ellie. She treasured his drawings and counted her blessings that he never gave her Gummi Bears.

"All right—bedtime," Curt announced at around nine-thirty. He'd changed from his suit into a pair of jeans and a flannel shirt, and he looked tired and comfortable and glowing with the serenity the holiday was supposed to bring.

The kids exerted themselves to shatter that peace. "It's too early! We're not babies! We can sleep late tomorrow!"

No one was going to sleep late tomorrow, not with Peter rampaging through the house, shrieking that Santa had once again consumed the cookies and left a ton of packages under the tree. "Santa doesn't visit houses where the kids stay up late," Curt warned, and all three reluctantly kissed him and Ellie good-night and trudged up the stairs.

An hour would pass before they were asleep, Ellie knew. She and Curt couldn't arrange the presents under the tree until the children were in dreamland—especially Peter, since he still believed fervently in Santa, his classmate's statement notwithstanding.

But that hour of settling-down time was fine with Ellie. It would probably take her close to an hour to assemble the gingerbread house.

"I'll help," Curt offered, rolling up his sleeves and surveying the pieces of gingerbread she'd cut using her templates. "What do you want me to do?"

"Shovel the snow from the driveway," she joked, then shook her head. "Actually, I could use your help. If you can hold these two walls like this, at a right angle, I can glue them together with the frosting."

"Are you sure we shouldn't be using concrete?"

"Don't get smart with me. Either you help or you clean the driveway."

"Okay. Right angles." He hovered over the table, his large

hands dwarfing the slabs of gingerbread. Ellie used a narrow spatula to seal the corner with icing. She managed to get some of the icing on Curt's pinkie. He let go of the wall to lick it off, and the house nearly collapsed.

"No licking till we're done."

"You're a slave driver."

"You partied all afternoon. Now I get to boss you around."

"Hmm." He nudged the top of her head with his chin. "Are you going to discipline me with a velvet whip? Maybe use some fur-lined handcuffs?"

"If I handcuffed you, you wouldn't be able to hold the walls up. *Right* angle, Curt," she emphasized when he shifted the wall slightly. "Ninety degrees."

"I forgot to bring my protractor," he joked, but he adjusted the walls and Ellie was able to cement them with the icing.

More than an hour passed before they had the house standing reasonably solidly and decorated with candy canes, M&M's, jelly beans and gumdrops—a few of which disappeared into Curt's mouth instead of becoming part of the house's decor. "It'll do," Ellie said wearily. The gingerbread houses she'd seen in magazine photographs looked a hell of a lot better than this one.

"Not done yet," Curt interrupted, fishing a toothpick from the box on the table. He dipped it into a smear of frosting and dabbed it against the house's front wall, above its white-icing door. Another dip and a dab, and another. When he was done, Ellie could see the faint white shape of two letters in the slightly bulging gingerbread that rose toward the peaked roof: "H.S."

Hope Street. Just like the shingle he'd made for this house and attached to the front wall above the door. She remembered the day he'd emerged from his basement workshop carrying that shingle, just a few weeks after they'd moved into the house, when she was eight and a half months pregnant with Katie and looked as if she'd swallowed a watermelon whole. Curt had hung the shingle, then taken her in his arms and said, "I promised you we'd always live on Hope Street. This house might be on Birch Lane, but we're living on Hope Street, too."

Now the gingerbread had officially been granted a Hope Street address. Suddenly, the crooked little structure seemed more beautiful to Ellie than any gingerbread house in any magazine.

She carried it on a foil-covered tray into the living room and set it on the coffee table next to the cookies Peter had left out for Santa. "Do you think we can do the presents?" Curt whispered.

They glanced toward the stairs. No sounds emerged from the kids' rooms, no activity, no signs of life. Ellie nodded, and they tiptoed down to the basement and retrieved the gift-wrapped parcels from assorted hiding places. Katie's gifts were all wrapped in red foil, Jessie's in silver, Peter's in green, Ellie's in white and Curt's in gold. Ellie had explained to the children, years ago, that Santa liked to sort the packages this way so he'd know who was getting what.

From under the tool bench Curt hoisted a large white parcel, squarish but not rectangular enough to be a box. "What's that?" she asked.

"You'll find out tomorrow," he teased.

"Oh, come on—you can tell me!" She sounded as wheedling as the girls when they were angling for some new privilege.

"It's a very big bracelet," Curt said before tiptoeing up the stairs with a bulky pile of gifts.

After a few trips between the basement and the living room, all the presents were arrayed under the tree. Delicate white lights winked among the Scotch pine's branches and glittered off the tinsel garlands, giving the tree an elegantly icy appearance. The Frost tree should look frosty, Curt always said, so they limited their decorations to white and silver. If the tree were standing outside, it would be even more frosty, glazed with snow.

Curt switched off the living-room lights so only the tree illuminated the room. "Sit," he murmured, nudging her toward the sofa before he vanished into the kitchen. He returned carrying two glasses of port. Then he lowered himself onto the sofa next to her and arched an arm around her.

He no longer smelled of perfume or punch. Only of Curt, a dark, heady, deliciously male scent that made her long to melt into him. She rested her head on his shoulder and wished she looked better. She still had on the baggy sweater and frayed jeans she'd donned once she'd gotten home from work, and her scent carried heavy undertones of flour and molasses and ginger. Not the most romantic fragrance in the world.

Curt didn't seem to mind. "The house looks great," he said.

Ellie took a sip of port, then shook her head. "My mother won't think so. What do you want to bet she walks through the door tomorrow and tells me I should wash the kitchen floor?"

"I meant *that* house," he said, gesturing toward her gingerbread creation. "But our house looks great, too. Your mother will be too busy fussing over the kids to notice the kitchen floor."

"Oh, she'll notice." Ellie's mother wouldn't have cared about Ellie's floor if Ellie had fulfilled her destiny and become a doctor. "If you were a doctor, I wouldn't expect you to have time to scrub the floors," her mother would say. "But you just work at that school. You're home by the middle of the afternoon, and you can't possibly be tired. If you haven't got a demanding career, the least you could do is have a clean house."

It was clean enough. And at age forty, Ellie was no longer desperate for her mother's approval. Maybe in another few years, she wouldn't even mind the criticisms anymore.

Curt sipped some port, then lowered his glass to the table. "I think the kids'll be pleased with their presents."

"They ought to be." Along with the usual books, CDs, games and stocking stuffers, they'd bought Katie some computer software that would enable her to edit videotapes—she'd pretty much taken over the family's camcorder, and her current dream was to direct music videos. Jessie would be getting a Discman, which she'd been hinting about for months. Peter had written in his letter to Santa that he wanted a new baseball bat and glove, and those items now sat beneath the tree, awkwardly wrapped in green paper. "I know I'm eager to try on that very big bracelet," Ellie added, gesturing toward the mysterious white package Curt had carried upstairs.

He chuckled softly and kissed the crown of her head. Then he eased her glass from her hand, placed it beside his and pulled her half onto his lap. "It'll look gorgeous on you. You'll have to model it for me—wearing just the bracelet and nothing else."

"Do you think that's what Santa had in mind when he got it for me?"

"Santa's a dirty old man," Curt warned before kissing her again—a deep, sensual kiss that stole Ellie's breath. She turned toward him, reaching for his shoulders, and he slid a hand under her sweater and cupped her breast. "A very, very dirty old man."

"We shouldn't do this down here," Ellie warned.

"The kids are asleep."

"They could wake up."

"They wouldn't dare." With that, he twisted out from under her, deposited her onto the sofa cushions and sprawled on top of her. "You know what the best thing about Christmas is?" he murmured as he pushed her sweater up, baring her midriff.

"Being married to you." He punctuated this sentiment with a warm, wet kiss on her belly.

Her exasperation with the gingerbread house went forgotten. The children's prebedtime rambunctiousness faded from her mind. Her parents' impending visit, the now-refrigerated turkey she'd have to dress and roast tomorrow, the early-morning wake-up Peter would subject them to with his exuberant yelling… Her mind emptied of everything but Curt, his weight, his warm hands moving over her skin, his hips pressing into hers. His stubble scratched her cheeks and throat as he kissed her, and she wondered if she'd have beard burns marking her skin tomorrow. Not that she cared. In fact, they might distract her mother from the fact that the kitchen floor wasn't spotless.

Ellie and Curt had been together for twenty years, married for seventeen. They'd done their share of experimentation— although, joking aside, neither of them had a taste for velvet whips or fur-lined handcuffs. But Curt still excited her. He touched her as if each time was an entirely new experience, as if each brush of his fingers or his lips or his tongue represented a unique discovery. His body was as lean and hard as it had been the first time she'd seen it one twilit morning in his apartment on Hope Street. He'd thrilled her then. He thrilled her now.

"I love you." She sighed as he eased her slacks down her legs. "Oh, Curt…"

"We got this right, didn't we." He slid his hand between her thighs, found her wet and trembling. "The love part."

She didn't want to come without him, but he was too deft, he knew her too well. A few strokes and she was gone, gasping into the hollow of his throat as her body throbbed with pleasure.

"I love when you come," he whispered, and his words made her come again.

"Take off your pants," she moaned.

"I'm getting there." He worked his fly with one hand, his other remaining where it was, teasing her, keeping her tense and painfully aroused. He wiggled his hips and she shoved his jeans in the general direction of his ankles, then guided him to her, took him, held him deep inside.

His movements were familiar, so sweet and strong. She loved the hardness of his buttocks against her palms, the caress of his breath against her brow. She loved the rhythm of his strokes, the depth of them, the way he and she possessed each other, trusted each other, anticipated each other's needs and satisfied them. Ellie knew digging her thumbs into the small of his back made him wild. Curt knew tweaking her nipples sent flames of sensation through her. She knew when he was nearing his peak; he knew when she was nearing hers.

Yes, they'd gotten this right. *So right,* she thought as her body convulsed around him, as he groaned and took her in a fierce final surge.

Eventually they wound down, their bodies sinking into the upholstery, Curt's mouth grazing hers with a lazy kiss. "Merry Christmas, Ellie," he murmured.

"Forget the very big bracelet," she murmured back. "I just got my favorite gift."

THE VERY BIG BRACELET turned out to be a padded bleacher seat—and Ellie was as delighted as she would have been by jewelry. She already had more than enough trinkets—bracelets, pendants, a diamond eternity ring Curt had given her in honor of their tenth anniversary, which she wore every day along with her wedding band.

A bleacher seat would keep her bottom from going numb

during the countless hours she sat watching her kids play baseball, softball and basketball. Sometimes, the comfort of a woman's butt was more important than the glitter of diamonds.

Peter squealed and bellowed over his gifts, single-handedly maintaining a noise level high enough to rouse any neighbors foolish enough to leave their windows open. The girls used to behave the way he did on Christmas morning, but now that they were tweeners they were too cool to scream. Instead, they resorted to muted gasps and murmurs of "Awesome!" and "Yes!" as they unwrapped CDs by Destiny's Child and Matchbox Twenty, books from the Sweet Valley High and Baby-sitters Club series, enameled butterfly-shaped earrings for Jessie and ladybug earrings for Katie. All three children oohed and aahed over the gingerbread house, and Curt modestly downplayed his contributions and insisted that Ellie had created the thing by herself. Personally, she thought his having inscribed the house with "H.S." was the most important decoration, but if Curt wanted to give her all the credit, she wasn't foolish enough to argue.

She observed the happy mayhem for a few minutes, thanked Jessie for the tortoiseshell barrette, Katie for the stacking coasters with impressionist paintings reproduced on them and Peter for this year's Popsicle-stick-framed crayon masterpiece, and then holed up in the kitchen to dress the turkey. After a bit more revelry in the living room, Curt and the children joined her, Curt wearing the handwoven wool sweater Ellie had found at a craft fair in October and impulsively bought to give him for Christmas. The slashes of color—green and gold and a rusty brown—were reflected in his hazel eyes. The pattern and texture were kind of artsy for Curt's taste, but he didn't have to wear it to court. Just when he was around Ellie.

Seeing him in it made her want to tear it off him.

But she couldn't do that when Katie, Jessie and Peter were crowded around the kitchen table, whining about how starving they were. With their Christmas stockings drooping from the mantel under the weight of foil-wrapped chocolate Santas and sugar-cookie Santas and Santa-shaped lollipops, they could certainly have found something outside the kitchen to ease their hunger. But no, it was Christmas morning and only pancakes would do.

Ellie mixed some batter and put Curt and Katie to work cooking the pancakes on the electric griddle, then resumed her efforts with the turkey. Her parents would be arriving around midday and expecting to eat by one. If the turkey didn't get stuffed and into the oven soon, they'd be dining on raw bird.

She hummed while she crumbled a loaf of bread into chunks for her stuffing, and listened to the enthusiastic chattering of her children. Peter boasted that he was going to be the best baseball player ever, and Ellie remembered her brothers making the same proud claims when they were Peter's age. One had wound up an accountant and the other a high-school teacher, both of them having ultimately opted for practicality over glamour— or perhaps reality over fantasy. Of course, the small wooden bat Peter had received, while perfectly suited to the double-A Little League team he'd be playing on next spring, wasn't going to power any balls out of Fenway Park. For the time being, though, he believed Santa was the greatest guy in the world because he'd brought Peter such a wonderful bat. The glove was great, too. "But Santa isn't here anymore," he concluded, "so Daddy will have to show me how to make a pocket in my glove."

"I think I can do that," Curt said, shooting Ellie a grin. Evidently, he didn't mind coming in second to Santa.

Ellie was still in the kitchen, preparing her sweet-potato

casserole, cutting vegetables into a salad, scouring the griddle and stacking the syrup-sticky breakfast plates into the dishwasher long after the rest of the family had departed—Jessie to listen to music on her Discman; Katie to phone all her friends to find out what they'd received for Christmas; Curt to rearrange his tool bench to make space for the power drill he'd selected for himself and then asked Ellie to give him; and Peter to run around the house with his bat, shouting, "It's outta here!" as he swatted imaginary homers out of an imaginary ballpark.

"Watch where you swing that thing!" Ellie warned, visualizing all the fragile objects in her house that could wind up in the path of Peter's bat. Lamps, a set of handcrafted ceramic bowls, the TV... "Just *pretend* your swinging it, Peter," she called from her post at the kitchen sink. "It's really an outdoor toy."

"It's not a toy," he shouted back. "It's a bat."

"It's an outdoor bat."

"I'm being careful."

She smiled. All the tension that had built up inside her during the weeks before Christmas was finally ebbing. Her children were home and happy, her husband liked the sweater she'd selected for him, she had a cushioned bleacher seat along with a box of Godiva dark chocolates, a pair of fleece-lined leather slippers, a new barrette, some pretty coasters and original artwork from Peter. She had a beautiful white snowscape to view on the other side of the window above the sink—just enough snow to look pretty, not enough to mess up the roads. She had a husband who could make spontaneous love to her on the sofa when she was wiped out after a long day, and leave her feeling as if she was actually competent in the art of creating a holiday atmosphere for her family.

What more could a woman want?

A mother who was a little less judgmental, she thought a couple of hours later when her parents swept into the house, bearing armloads of gifts for their grandchildren. For Peter they'd brought a Lego set and for the girls some stuffed animals that the girls were polite enough to thank them for, even though Ellie feared they might be a little too old to appreciate fluffy toy Persian cats wearing rhinestone tiaras and dangly earrings.

"The gingerbread house is so cute," her mother said once the frenzy that accompanied their arrival had simmered down and she could join Ellie in the kitchen. "The girls said you made it yourself."

"Curt helped," Ellie admitted, then bit her tongue. She should have taken full credit, just so her mother would acknowledge her hard work and her domestic achievements.

Too late. "Curt is a gem," her mother gushed. "I hope you thank God every day for a husband like him. I can just imagine what your father would say if I asked him to help me bake a gingerbread house." She clicked her tongue and shook her head. "What kind of stuffing did you make?" she asked, opening the oven to peek. The room filled with the heavy scents of garlic and butter and roasting turkey.

"The usual," Ellie said. "Apples, celery, whole wheat bread…"

"You should make oyster stuffing," her mother declared, closing the oven. "Nobody ever makes that anymore, except for me. Your father loves it. Curt would love it, too."

"He likes my apple stuffing."

"You could use a little foundation, Ellie. And some concealer. You're middle-aged. It's starting to show. You've got frown lines sprouting above your eyebrows…"

On cue, Ellie frowned.

But what was the point of arguing with her mother that Curt—the gem—loved her stuffing and didn't seem to care if she had frown lines above her eyebrows? Even if she wanted to defend herself, she would have been hard-pressed to break through her mother's monologue, which touched on Ellie's job—"Don't you find it disgusting having to treat all those strange children with stomach bugs?" And her sweater—"Didn't you wear that sweater last year? It's getting old." And the children—"You shouldn't baby Peter so much. He's getting to be a big boy." And, of course, the kitchen floor—"All those boots piled up by the back door leave water stains. If you're going to be so lacka-daisical about cleaning your floor, you should get darker tiles. Something with a pattern, maybe. That would disguise the dirt, the way your highlighting disguises your gray hair."

Thank you, Mom.

But Ellie got through it, because Curt *was* a gem and her children were magnificent and it was Christmas. Everyone praised the dinner, even though she hadn't made oyster stuffing, and afterward her parents agreed to watch the *Frosty the Snowman* video with Peter, despite the fact that he'd watched it last night. Katie and Jessie cleared the table and placed the dishes in the dishwasher, and Curt wrapped up all the leftovers and wedged them into the refrigerator, leaving only the pot-scouring chore for Ellie to handle.

Peace—or as close to peace as she could hope to get in a houseful of people—descended, along with a fresh dusting of snow.

She didn't notice the threads of tension woven into that peace until her parents were saying their goodbyes. Her father fussed about having to visit Ellie's baby brother—they'd eaten too much, and now they'd be expected to have supper with that whole branch of the family.

Ellie and Curt and the girls assured him that by the time he

arrived at Uncle Mike's house he'd be hungry again. Peter gave
his grandparents as big a hug as he could, not easy since he was
wearing his new baseball glove, but his face was taut and his
eyes, hazel like Curt's, glinted coldly.

"Are you okay?" Ellie asked him once her parents were in their
car and backing down the driveway to the street.

"Sure," he grunted, then turned and stormed away.

"What's that all about?" Curt asked, watching Peter stomp off
in the direction of the family room.

"He's such a jerk sometimes," Jessie muttered before
heading upstairs.

Curt ushered Ellie into the kitchen. It was nearly clean, and
would no doubt look cleaner if she installed flooring with a
pattern like her hair's highlights. Remembering her mother's
litany of veiled criticisms sparked a giggle. "God, my parents
wear me out."

Curt laughed. "Scary to think you swam out of their gene pool."

"And your children swam out of mine. My parents' chromo-
somes live on."

"Thank heavens the kids have inherited all their good traits
from *my* gene pool."

Ellie jabbed him in the stomach with her elbow. "Yeah, right."

"My height, my talent, my intellect," he ticked off. "My
coloring. My sense of humor…"

"Your inflated ego." She crossed to the sink, lifted the roasting
pan from the drying rack and wiped it with a towel. "Your ugly
toes. Your cluelessness."

"My toes aren't ugly."

"Have you looked at them lately?"

Their banter was interrupted by a loud thumping sound and
then a scream from Katie. "Peter! You idiot! Why did you do that?"

Ellie nearly dropped the pan. Curt was already out of the kitchen, hurrying toward the living room. As soon as she'd set the pan back onto the rack, she trailed him down the hall, nearly colliding with him when he stopped short in the living-room doorway. "Peter. Give it to me," he commanded, his voice ominously low, his hand outstretched.

Ellie sidestepped Curt and then froze when she saw what Peter had done: smashed the gingerbread house with his new bat. The confection lay shattered across the coffee table, chunks of gingerbread, flakes of dried frosting and gum drops strewn around it, as if a tornado had descended from the ceiling and demolished it.

Katie shoved Peter away from the table, her eyes glistening with tears. "You stupid idiot!" she roared. "Mommy worked so hard on this, and now you've ruined it!"

"What did he do?" Jessie yelled, racing down the stairs.

"He destroyed the gingerbread house!"

"Can we still eat it?" Jessie asked.

Ellie was too stunned to absorb their words. Her gaze shuttled between the mess on the table and her son, who glowered at her even as he relinquished the bat to his father. Why was he staring at her as if he wished he'd smashed her rather than the gingerbread house? What had she done to provoke his rage?

"You lied," he answered her unvoiced question. "You're a liar." Tears streaming down his cheeks, he ran up the stairs and into his bedroom, slamming the door behind him.

"He's such an idiot," Katie murmured, hurrying to Ellie's side and hugging her.

I lied? she wondered. What had she lied about?

Curt exchanged a puzzled glance with her. The bat looked

adorable in his hands, so small and harmless. Yet Peter had used it as a weapon, wrecking Ellie's hard work. Suddenly, she hated that bat.

"I'll go talk to him," she said, then pursed her lips, squared her shoulders and marched up the stairs. She knocked on Peter's door and, when he didn't respond, inched it open.

He was seated on his bed, red-faced, wet-cheeked, clutching his new glove. "Care to tell me what this is all about?" she asked from the doorway. His forbidding expression kept her from entering the room.

"You lied," he said accusingly again. "You told me Santa exists and Nana told me that's a lie."

Ellie opened her mouth and then shut it, utterly stumped. Why would her mother have said such a thing?

"She told me I was a big boy and I should know the truth. Danny Barrone was right. There's no such thing as Santa Claus, and you told me there was."

Ellie felt her strength draining from her like air from a balloon. How dare her mother interfere? How dare she deny Peter the chance to believe, just a little longer?

"What I told you," Ellie reminded him, swallowing to steady her voice, "is that Santa exists for everyone who believes in him. Maybe Nana doesn't believe in him, so he doesn't exist for her."

"No, she said there was no such thing as Santa, and I was a big boy and I should know the truth." Peter glared at her. "She said all the presents came from you and Dad, except for the Lego set. That came from her and Poppa." Fresh tears spilled down his cheeks.

"Oh, Peter." Ellie ached to hug him, to urge him to hang on to his dreams and myths for as long as he wished.

"You lied," he said. "You treat me like a baby."

Ellie heard footsteps along the hallway behind her, and then the warmth of Curt joining her in the doorway. He still held the bat. "Say goodbye to this bat. It's going into storage for a while," he told Peter sternly.

"I don't care." Peter rolled away from his parents and hid his face in the corner where his bed met the wall.

"Let me talk to him," Curt whispered to Ellie.

She hated to leave Peter when his resentment was gusting toward her like a toxic fume. Just the sight of his slender back, his drooping gray sweatpants and his little feet, the soles of his socks permanently stained a smudgy gray, sent shudders of grief through Ellie. Had she blown things so terribly by allowing Peter to believe in Santa for one more year? Did Ellie's mother loathe her enough to undermine her relationship with her son? Why couldn't her mother get over the fact that Ellie had not fulfilled the promise of her youth? She'd made a good life for herself and her family and she'd never regretted her decision not to attend medical school. Why couldn't her mother accept who Ellie was?

She was so overwrought she realized she'd be useless in any conversation with Peter right now. Relinquishing that task to Curt, she stalked down the hall to the stairs. And decided Curt's taking over was just one more shred of proof that Ellie was inadequate as a mother.

The girls were in the kitchen when she arrived. They'd salvaged what they could of the gingerbread house and stacked the bigger chunks on a plate. "We'll cover it with red-and-green wrap," Katie announced, pulling the holiday-hued plastic wrap from a drawer. "That'll make it look good."

"And Peter can't have a single piece," Jessie added. "He's such a jerk."

"Yeah, Mom." Katie flung her arms around Ellie's shoulders—when had Katie gotten tall enough to stand eye-to-eye with Ellie?—and hugged her hard. "You should've stuck to having daughters," she said. "Boys are creeps."

"Except for Tyler Berlin," Jessie singsonged, teasing Katie. "He's so cool." She issued an exaggerated sigh.

"He *is* cool," Katie said defensively. It dawned on Ellie that her daughter had a crush on this Tyler boy and Ellie hadn't known anything about it until now. "He'd never do anything this asinine."

"Is that a bad word, Mom?" Jessie asked, turning her big, hazel eyes to Ellie.

"No." Ellie sank onto one of the chairs and watched her daughters smooth the plastic wrap around the plate.

"It sounds bad," Jessie said, glaring at Katie. "I don't think you should use bad-sounding words when Mom is upset."

"I'm not upset," Ellie assured her daughters. She'd already been branded a liar; one more lie didn't make much difference.

"Anyway, we loved the house," Katie insisted, patting Ellie's shoulder. "Let's go watch *The Secret Garden.*"

The girls disappeared to the den to view their new DVD. Alone in the silent kitchen, Ellie let her head drop into her hands. Another shudder passed through her.

Peter could be dramatic, she reminded herself. And the holiday excitement, the presents, the food and all the rest of it had wound him tightly. He'd overreacted to the news about Santa. It wasn't Ellie's fault. It wasn't.

Yet guilt rolled over her like a tidal wave with a sharp undertow, dragging her down and pulling her away from shore. She'd betrayed her son. She'd—well, not lied, perhaps, but fudged the truth.

She was a failure.

She wasn't sure how long she sat alone in the kitchen, inhaling the lingering scents of good food and hearing the muffled music and dialogue from the movie playing in the den. When she felt two strong hands alighting on her shoulders, she flinched. She'd been so lost in her thoughts, so busy wallowing in guilt, she hadn't heard Curt enter the room.

She raised her head and peered over her shoulder at him. He massaged the base of her neck gently, rubbing his thumbs over the sore, knotted spots. "How are you doing?" he asked.

"The hell with me. How's Peter?"

"Sulking. He'll survive. You might even get an apology from him before bedtime."

"I should apologize to him," Ellie said glumly. "He's right. I lied to him about Santa."

Curt released her and circled around to the chair across the table from her. He gazed at her, then reached out and covered her hands in his. "Don't be so hard on yourself, babe. You don't have to be perfect."

"Maybe not perfect, but I have to be good enough," she countered. "I'm not."

"Oh, Ellie…" He dragged her hands across the table and lifted them to his lips. He kissed one hand, then the other. "You're good enough."

This was why she loved him—because when her confidence slipped, he shored her up. When doubt gripped her, he pried that monster's claws off her. When she was sure she wasn't good enough, he insisted she was.

She wasn't convinced, of course. Curt was telling her not the truth but what she needed to hear.

Sometimes, though, being lied to was a good thing. Maybe someday Peter would learn that.

In the meantime, Ellie treasured Curt's lie, met his gaze and gave his hands a loving squeeze. The one thing her mother had said today that Ellie could agree with was that she should thank God every day for a husband like him....

TEN

STRETCHED OUT ON THE BED, Ellie appeared wistful, lost in a reminiscence. Her eyes glittered, focused on something he couldn't see. *Let me in,* he begged silently, then realized she wasn't thinking about Africa, about the stuff she didn't want to share with him.

"What?" he asked.

She smiled faintly. "I was just remembering the Christmas when Peter smashed the gingerbread house."

"Oh, God." Curt let out a short laugh. "What a horror show."

"He could be awfully intense sometimes."

"No kidding."

"Remember when he got into a fistfight in the middle-school cafeteria because someone said his Little League team cheated?"

Curt laughed again. "I thought I'd have to represent him in court."

"No one got hurt, as I recall. Sixth-graders don't have big fists."

"Yeah, but someone wound up with peanut butter in his hair."

Ellie nodded. "And Peter's shirt got torn. I wasn't happy about that."

"Then there was the time he went to some friend's house and the two of them drank their way through the kid's parents' liquor stash," Curt reminded her.

"Oh, God." Ellie winced. "Peter and Doug Rauss. They always found trouble. That was the summer before they started high school."

"Peter was sick as a dog."

"A good thing, too. If he hadn't vomited out all that crap, we might have had to take him to the hospital to get his stomach pumped."

"Funny," Curt said, though it wasn't that funny at all, "when I think about Peter, I don't remember the bad stuff, all the gray hair he gave us. My memory just sort of edits it out."

Ellie sent him an odd look. Then she relaxed and picked up her glass of port, which sat where she'd left it on the nightstand, an inch of ruby liquid in it. "That's the way memory works," she agreed. "Selectively."

"Defectively," he corrected her.

"Self-protectively," she corrected him back.

He studied her from his vantage in the wingback chair. The pillows behind her head had mussed her hair, and he wished he could slide his hands through it. He longed to rejoin her on the bed, to have her next to him, to feel the warmth of her and lean into the dip in the mattress caused by the weight of her body. Maybe the reason he wanted her now was that his memory had edited out all the bad things between them, all the reasons divorce had made so much sense when they'd broached the idea a month ago.

"Hit the play button," she said, angling her head toward the TV. "Let's keep going."

He wondered if she'd read his thoughts and decided to use

the movie to distract him. He wasn't so easily distracted—the movie only reminded him of how good things had once been between them—but he wasn't about to pressure her. That he'd gotten her to trust him enough to return with him to their *très* romantic room was some kind of miracle.

He tapped a button on the remote and the movie resumed. The screen went black, and then a written caption appeared in stark white: "They say the greatest tragedy a mother can experience is to outlive her child."

The muscles in Curt's neck tensed. He'd known it was coming—any story of Ellie's life would have to include this part—and he'd been worried about how she would respond. He'd neglected to consider his own response. But damn, it was going to be hard on him, too. To outlive one's child was also the greatest tragedy a father could experience.

A series of photos filled the screen, one fading into the next: Peter at around age four, towheaded and freckled, standing between his two sisters and reaching up to hold their hands. Peter perched on Curt's shoulders, his grin so big it nearly split his face. Peter in front of the Magic Kingdom castle at Walt Disney World, a Goofy sunhat on his head. Peter in a school portrait, stiff and formal against a blue-gray background. Peter with one of his Little League teams. Peter with one of his basketball teams. Peter with Ellie and Curt at his middle-school graduation ceremony, dressed in pressed khakis and a collared polo shirt, one hand clutching the various certificates and citations he'd received and the other arched around Ellie's shoulders. That was the year he'd surpassed Ellie in height. He clearly had an inch on her in the photo. Her smile was as bright as his.

The montage was accompanied by a plaintive Warren Zevon song. Curt recalled how much Peter had loved the old Zevon hit "Werewolves of London." He'd been too young to know what a werewolf was, but whenever Curt sang that song to Peter, he'd howl along: "Aaa-oooh!" He'd sounded as wild as a mystical beast.

Peter had probably never heard the song Jessie and Katie had chosen for this part of their movie, though. Zevon had recorded it when he himself was dying of cancer—a wistful ballad imploring his loved ones to remember him once he was gone. "Keep me in your heart for a while," he crooned in a broken, heartfelt voice.

The images on the screen blurred as Curt's vision filled with tears. He closed his eyes but couldn't shut out his own pictures of Peter, all elbows and knees, all fierce energy. So much love in that boy, so much righteous indignation. Just like Curt, he'd wanted to conquer the world. Just like Ellie, he'd wanted to save it.

The song washed around Curt and he swallowed, struggling against the sorrow that welled up inside him. *The greatest tragedy was for a parent to outlive a child.* Christ, what an understatement.

He hadn't heard Ellie's approach, but suddenly, her hand rested on the back of his neck, caressing. She pried the remote from his fist and the song stopped. She must have paused the DVD. "Are you all right?" she asked.

"I'm fine," he mumbled, ducking his head so she wouldn't see his tears. Damn it. He wasn't fine. He was falling apart.

She walked away—with the movie's soundtrack no longer playing, he could hear her footsteps—and then returned and dabbed at his face with a tissue. He pulled the tissue away from her. He wasn't going to have her wiping his tears as if he were a helpless child.

"I'm fine," he repeated, opening his eyes and gazing at her.

She was kneeling on the floor in front of him, gazing up into his face. "This is the first time you've cried," she said quietly.

She didn't have to finish the sentence. *The first time you've cried since we lost Peter.* "I've cried plenty," he said.

"I never saw you cry."

"I cry in the shower." He meant to use the past tense, but the truth slipped out. He still wept for Peter sometimes—in the shower, or when he was jogging on the treadmill at the fitness center near his office and his tears were camouflaged by the sweat dripping down his face. Or sometimes at night, when Ellie was asleep and he lay beside her in their cold, loveless bed, and grief crashed over him.

Now Ellie knew—not only that he cried, but that he deliberately concealed his tears from her. He'd never wanted to break down in front of her. She'd been such a wreck after Peter's death—withdrawn, out of touch, teetering on the razor-edge of clinical depression. She'd been emotionally mutilated. One of them had had to remain strong, so Curt had remained strong.

"You should have told me," she said.

He heard a hint of reproach in her tone, and it transformed his embarrassment into anger. "Told you what?" he retorted. "That I was hurting, too? You needed to be told that?"

"I only meant, you shouldn't have hidden your feelings from me."

"I didn't." His tears were gone now, his resentment building. "I was quite clear about how I felt and what I needed. You didn't want to hear it, Ellie. Every time I reached for you, you shut me out and retreated into yourself. My feelings disgusted you. So I stopped sharing them."

His outburst vibrated in the air, hot and bitter. Ellie held his gaze for a second, then turned from him. She pushed herself to stand and moved back to the bed, her head held high but her steps uncertain.

He'd drawn blood and it felt good. Maybe he was a son of a bitch—Ellie undoubtedly believed he was—but he took satisfaction in making sure she knew she wasn't the only one who'd been betrayed. She wasn't the only one with ugly scars etched onto her soul, the remnants of wounds inflicted by the person she'd married.

He watched as she sat on the edge of the mattress near the night table, her feet planted on the floor and her hands resting on her knees. She still held the remote control. Fine. Let her control the freaking movie. She liked to think she was the injured party in all this, but the fact was, she'd always been in control.

Curt was passionately in love with her, insanely dependent on her—but she didn't need him. She had Africa, after all. She'd saved a kid's hearing. She'd probably saved a few kids' lives, too. She'd been respected over there, revered. Loved.

Damn it, *he* hadn't sent her to Africa. She'd chosen to go there, eager to put as much distance between herself and him as she could. She'd walked away from him, all the while insisting that he'd walked away from her. If he had, it was only after she'd slammed the door and bolted it.

She'd been in control all along.

She startled him by speaking. "I still miss him. Every day. Every minute. Even when I think about him smashing the gingerbread house or chugging booze with his friend." She glanced toward Curt but didn't meet his stare. "I don't cry that much, though."

"You cried earlier this evening," he reminded her, the rage gone from his voice.

She nodded and lowered her gaze to her hands in her lap, folded around the remote. "I wasn't crying for Peter then," she reminded him.

He frowned, trying to recall what the movie had been dealing with when she'd started sobbing earlier. *Them*. Their courtship. Their love. She was done crying over Peter, but not over their dying marriage.

We don't have to get a divorce. The words hovered on his tongue, so close to slipping out. But her face was shuttered, her thoughts as far away as Ghana. And really, what could he say to change her mind at this point? He'd apologized a thousand times. He'd told her he loved her. She'd told him she could never trust him again. And she hadn't told him she loved him.

In those stolen moments when he wept for his son, he acknowledged, he was crying for other losses, too. He was crying for the woman he'd once been convinced was all he would ever want. He was crying for all the promises their love had held. He was crying because, somehow, he'd been exiled from Hope Street.

ELEVEN

Three Years Ago

LATE MARCH WAS STILL roaring in. When would the lamb part replace the lion part? Curt wondered as he steered up Birch Lane. The road was fringed with dirty mounds of snow, and his front lawn, barely visible in the evening gloom, was crisp and brown. But the living-room windows glowed amber and the lights above the garage doors were on, brightening the driveway and making him smile at the knowledge that he'd soon be inside all that warmth, with his family.

It had taken him several months to get used to Katie's absence. Ellie had suffered full-blown empty-nest syndrome once they'd lugged the last of Katie's things up the stairs to her third-floor dorm room at Wesleyan and kissed her goodbye. That two more children still lived with them had provided small comfort for Ellie. She'd whined and moped and hovered for long stretches of time in the doorway of Katie's unnaturally neat, empty bedroom, unable to accept that her firstborn had truly left home. She'd barraged Katie with e-mails and instant messages. And eventually, she'd adjusted.

This year, Katie's second year away at school, had gone better. But now Ellie was gearing up for Jessie's graduation and her departure for college. Jessie had received an early-decision acceptance to Bates College, up in Maine. Two and a half hours by car. Much too far, according to Ellie. Wesleyan was only an hour and a half away. Why did Jessie need to go so much farther from home than Katie?

At least they would still have Peter. And frankly, Curt thought as he recalled Peter's recent booze-bingeing escapade with his moronic friend Doug, once their son was gone Curt and Ellie might just heave sighs of relief.

He steered into the garage, shut off the engine, grabbed his briefcase and entered the house. The kitchen's atmosphere was thick with a warm, beefy fragrance that negated the chill of the early-spring night outside. A small pile of mail sat on the table, waiting for him. He riffled through it—all junk—and tossed it into the trash can unopened.

"Hi," Ellie said as she swept into the kitchen. Her hair was pulled back in a barrette, and the overhead light caught the streaks of reddish-blond in it. A few years ago, he'd asked her why she was highlighting it that way—he'd always thought it looked great when it was just a rich, pretty brown—and she explained that the highlights helped to cover the gray. Curt hadn't noticed much gray in her hair, but then he didn't really *see* her anymore. She was Ellie, she was beautiful, and if her face had developed a few lines over the years, if her waist had increased by an inch or two, her hair acquired a smattering of gray, the changes didn't register on him.

He opened his arms and she moved in for a quick hug, then drew back. "Peter's in bed," she said, and he realized she was talking more softly than usual. "When he got home from school, he said he was tired and had a headache. I just tried to give him some chicken broth, but he wasn't hungry."

"Peter not hungry? The world must be coming to an end." Curt scowled. "Is he all right?"

"He's fine. Just run-down, I think. They're doing those two-hour practices every day for the freshman baseball team. He really wants to make the team, so he's knocking himself out." She shook her head and left Curt's side to check something in the oven. "Freshmen shouldn't have two-hour daily practices. It's not like they're varsity."

"So he's not having dinner with us?" Curt asked, tugging his tie loose.

"I left him a bottle of Gatorade. He'll drink that."

"Is that good for him?"

She gave him a haughty look. "Who's the medical professional here?" When he held up his hands in mock surrender, she smiled. "Those sports drinks are great, especially if he isn't eating. They'll keep him from getting dehydrated, balance his electrolytes and give him some energy."

"Whatever you say." Curt peeked over Ellie's shoulder at the contents of the oven—all he saw was a casserole dish—and then went upstairs to exchange his suit for some comfortable clothes. Once he was in jeans and a flannel shirt, he walked down the hall, passing Jessie's closed bedroom door, through which he heard her babbling on the phone, and tapped on Peter's before he inched it open. "Hey, buddy," he murmured. Peter was sprawled out under the blanket, his body intermittently illuminated by the swirling colors of his computer's screen saver, flashing beams of light from his desk.

"Hey, Dad," Peter grunted.

"How're you feeling?"

"Shitty." Peter laughed. "Sorry. Just tired."

"Mom said you're planning to sleep through dinner."

"I'll eat something later," Peter promised.

"Okay, pal. You want me to turn off your computer?"

"Nah. It's not bothering me."

Curt left, closing the door behind him. Peter's voice had been dropping in pitch all year, and it now rested somewhere between a tenor and a baritone. Next year he'd probably be shaving, whether or not he needed to. Curt smiled, anticipating that ritual. He remembered his father ushering him into the bathroom and showing him how to whip up a rich lather with a badger brush and a mug of shaving soap, how to stretch his skin to avoid nicking himself, how to trim his sideburns evenly. Not that he'd had sideburns when he was fifteen, or even much of a beard. But he'd felt so close to his father that morning. They'd been two men then, not a father and a little boy.

Soon, Curt thought, he and Peter would be two men together at the mirror, sharing that manly ritual.

Jessie collided with him in the hall near the top of the stairs. "Hey, Dad! Amanda and Kirsten and I are going to the mall tonight, okay?"

She was already halfway down the stairs before he answered, "It's a school night."

"Dad." She favored him with a classically scornful glare, lips pursed and eyes rolling. "I'm a senior, I got into college and I don't have any homework due tomorrow. And we'll be home by ten, anyway."

"All right," he said, aware that he didn't have much clout with her anymore. She was eighteen, old enough to drive, to vote, to enlist in the armed forces if she wanted. He and Ellie had done their job with her as best they could, and she'd turned out pretty wonderful. If she wanted to go to the mall with her friends, Curt couldn't stop her.

Jessie gulped down her dinner and waltzed out of the house, leaving Curt and Ellie to linger over their food, refill their wineglasses and share the news of their days. In only a few more years, all their dinners would be like this—just the two of them, catching up, bouncing ideas off each other, sipping their wine. Ellie resting her feet in Curt's lap under the table. Curt absorbing her words and the glow in her eyes and undressing her in his mind. No worries about kids barging in on them. No demands to be driven here or there, to sign this or that form, to critique an essay on *Anna Karenina* or the Emancipation Proclamation.

Ellie would be devastated, at least temporarily, when all her babies flew the nest. But Curt would distract her. Sex in the kitchen. Sex in the family room. Sex on the stairs, like in that movie she'd loved so much, with the actor who went on to play James Bond in a few 007 flicks. Watching one's children grow up and leave home could make a person melancholy, but there were compensations.

Curt volunteered to clear the table while Ellie went upstairs to check on Peter. She returned after a minute and carried the casserole dish to the refrigerator. "I don't think Peter's going to be eating tonight," she reported. "He's out cold. Or maybe I should say out warm. I think he's running a fever."

"Should we call the doctor?"

Ellie shook her head. "I gave him some ibuprofen, and he rolled over and went back to sleep. There are lots of little bugs making the rounds at the moment. It's the end of a long winter. Kids are run-down. We've got about a dozen cases of strep throat at my school. If Peter's throat is bothering him tomorrow, I'll take him in for a culture." As Curt rinsed the dishes and she stacked them in the dishwasher, she told him about the student at her school who'd been diagnosed with croup earlier that week. "It's got such a distinctive cough," she said. "At least Peter doesn't have that."

Finished with the dishes, Ellie settled at her desk to pay bills while Curt reviewed his notes from a complicated case he'd gotten dragged into at the firm—professors from two different universities suing each other over research they'd collaborated on. It was like a divorce, except that the baby they were fighting for custody over—their research—had a monetary value. Curt's firm and the firm representing the other researcher had to figure out what that value was and how to divide it. No matter what they negotiated, the settlement was doomed to end with hurt feelings and bristling resentment. He hated cases like that.

At nine-thirty, he tossed the file aside and beckoned Ellie to join him on the sofa. They caught the last half of a college basketball game on TV, Ellie nestled against him. After a few minutes she dozed off, her head heavy against his chest and her breathing deep and steady. She roused herself when Jessie bounced in at around ten-thirty, carrying a few bags with boutique logos on them. Curt and Ellie followed Jessie up the stairs, but while she no doubt intended to spend at least another hour exchanging instant messages with her friends, her drowsy parents were ready to tumble into bed.

Curt almost didn't have enough energy to make love to Ellie. Almost. He could always muster the energy for that. Fortunately, Ellie was too drowsy to demand acrobatics and fireworks tonight. All she wanted was what he wanted: the closeness, the release, the gorgeous lethargy that settled onto them afterward and escorted them to sleep.

He climbed out of bed ahead of Ellie the next morning. He

usually rose before she did; since he had a longer commute to work, he got first dibs on the master bathroom. Once he was showered and dressed, he went downstairs to get the coffee started.

Jessie was already in the kitchen, wearing a snug shirt he'd never seen, and even snugger jeans. "Hey, Dad," she greeted him, amazingly cheerful for 7:00 a.m. No one else in the family was a morning person. Curt liked to joke that Jessie was their foundling, having inherited some other family's circadian rhythms. Whenever he said that, she'd always retort, "Yeah, my real family left me in a basket on your porch because I looked exactly like you." Of all three children, she did resemble him the most.

"You want French toast?" she asked, pulling the container of eggs out of the fridge. "I'm making some for myself."

French toast was too much bother this early in the morning. "Plain toast is fine for me. Get out the milk for your mother. She'll probably have cereal," he mumbled, waiting impatiently for the coffee to finish brewing so he could pump some caffeine into his body.

"Curt?" Ellie's voice shot down the stairs. She sounded wide-awake, too—but not bubbly like Jessie.

Her sharp tone was enough to rouse him fully. He bolted for the stairs. "What's up?"

"It's Peter." Ellie stood at the top of the stairway, but as soon as he drew near, she spun and raced down the hall to Peter's bedroom. "He's burning up, Curt. He's spiking a fever. We've got to get him looked at."

"For a fever?" Kids got fevers sometimes, and Peter was a strong, strapping boy. Couldn't they just dose him with some aspirin or something?

"A high fever."

Ellie's terse comment rattled Curt. If Peter had a high enough fever to alarm Ellie, aspirin wasn't going to do the trick.

Curt trailed her into Peter's room. The computer screen saver was still spinning, spraying colors around the room and splashing odd hues across Peter's pale face. He lay in bed, his eyes half-closed and his respiration shallow. Curt didn't have to touch him to feel his fever. Waves of heat rose off his body.

"Hey, buddy—what's going on?" Curt asked gently.

"My head hurts," Peter groaned. "My neck..."

"I can't get him in to see his doctor this early," Ellie whispered to Curt. "We're taking him to the hospital."

The hospital? For a *fever?*

He drew in a deep breath. As Ellie had said last night, she was the medical professional. If she thought Peter needed to go to the hospital, Curt wouldn't argue.

With a nod, he turned and strode from the room. He descended the stairs so quickly he didn't feel his feet touch them. In the kitchen, he grabbed his wallet and keys and switched off the coffeemaker. "Peter is sick," he told Jessie bluntly. "We're taking him to the hospital. Call your mother's school and tell them she won't be coming in today."

Jessie's eyes widened with alarm. "What's wrong with him?"

"Nothing serious, I hope. We're just going to make sure."

"Do you want me to call your office?"

"No, I'll call them."

"What about me?"

He shrugged. "Go to school."

"Curt?" Ellie was yelling for him again.

Jessie looked so worried he hated to abandon her. "Keep your cell phone with you," he said. "I'll call you as soon as we know what's going on."

"Okay." She sounded shaky.

"Hey. He's going to be fine," Curt promised, then he kissed Jessie's forehead and dashed back up the stairs.

Peter was too weak to stand. Curt managed to hoist him over his shoulder, one hundred and forty pounds of muscle and dangling limbs plus the blanket in which he was wrapped. Somehow they made it down the stairs, through the kitchen and out to the garage without banging into anything.

Ellie sat in the backseat with Peter as Curt drove through town in the murky morning light. A cold rain was falling, or maybe it was sleet, tapping like pebbles against the roof of his car. He felt chilled, even with the car's heater blasting. Was heat good or bad for someone running a high fever? Damn it, did they really have to take Peter to the hospital?

What kind of illness caused a kid to spike a fever? Peter had been vaccinated for all those childhood diseases—measles, mumps, whatever. Strep throat? Ellie had said that was making the rounds. She'd also said she thought Peter was run-down— but kids didn't spike fevers from fatigue.

Ellie spoke calmly throughout the drive to the local hospital. Sometimes Curt realized she was talking to Peter, who occasionally emitted a quiet moan. Sometimes she was talking to Curt. "He's okay," she'd say. "It's just some weird virus, I'm sure. We'll get his fever down and bring him home. He drank some of the Gatorade last night. That should have helped." At one point Curt heard her speaking into her cell phone, leaving a phone message for Peter's pediatrician.

At the local hospital, he skidded the car to a halt at the emergency room entrance. "Let's get a wheelchair," Ellie said.

"No, I'll carry him." Curt eased his overheated son out of the backseat, trying not to stagger under Peter's limp weight, and carried him to the broad glass door. It automatically slid open and he rushed inside.

He hated hospitals. Few people didn't hate them, of course, but even when Ellie had been on the staff of Children's Hospital during the early years of their marriage, he'd despised visiting her there. On those rare occasions when they could meet for lunch, he'd ask her to join him at a luncheonette down the block from the hospital. The glaring lights, the squeaky soles of everyone's shoes, the smell of pine and antiseptic heavy in the air, the eerie hush, the aura of mission and menace that surrounded all the employees, from the most revered doctor to the lowliest orderly…he hated it.

And now his son had to be here. His son, arms wrapped loosely around Curt's neck and so much heat simmering through layers of pajamas and blanket that Curt began to sweat… His son was sick.

Oh, God—make this be nothing serious.

A young man in blue scrubs approached with a wheelchair and helped Curt to lower Peter onto the seat. An older man in a security-guard uniform approached and told Curt he had to move his car. "You can't leave it blocking the entry," the guard scolded.

Curt swallowed the impulse to tell the man what he could do to himself. "Go park the car," Ellie murmured in a soothing voice. "I'll stay here with Peter and take care of the paperwork."

Swallowing his rage, Curt nodded. He would rather park the car than fill out forms and recite insurance-policy numbers, anyway.

He stepped through the automatic door and out into the gray morning. The rain and sleet stung his face. He dove into the car, cruised the small lot outside the emergency room for ten minutes without finding an open space then gave up and drove around the building to the visitor's garage. Before leaving the car, he yanked off his necktie—he wouldn't be needing that this morning—and left a message on his secretary's answering machine, telling her to reschedule his meeting with Professor Benzer. "My cell phone's on if you have to reach me," he told her. "Call me if you need me. If things go well, I may get to the office this afternoon."

He reentered the hospital through the front door and took a minute to orient himself. Even the main entry, with its carpeted floor and framed paintings, its tweedy upholstered chairs and the little cart selling gourmet coffee in one corner, gave him the willies. He could still smell that sterile hospital scent. He could still feel the tension humming in the air just beyond the lobby.

He wandered through a maze of halls until he reached the emergency room. Ellie and Peter were gone. He'd expected them to be—he wouldn't have wanted his son sitting around all this time, waiting for a doctor's attention. But the absence of both of them in the brightly lit area, with its sleek desk and fluorescent lighting, plastic chairs and milky curtains, kicked him in the gut.

Where were they? The hospital monster had swallowed them.

He managed a few deep breaths to steady his nerves before approaching the desk. "I'm looking for my wife and son," he said. "Peter Frost is my son's name. He was running a fever." Good. He sounded calm, authoritative, far more confident than he felt.

The nurse behind the desk checked something on her computer and nodded. "Follow me," she said, beckoning him toward one of the curtained-off areas. She pulled back the curtain to discover no one behind it. "Oh, maybe they're here," she said, leading him to another curtained area. Behind that curtain, an elderly man sat on the table, one hand cradling the other wrist. "Hmm," the nurse said, frowning.

You've lost my son. Curt wanted to throttle the woman. *You've lost my son and my wife.*

Before the nurse could peek behind any more curtains, Curt spotted Ellie approaching him from the far end of a corridor. She was alone. "There's my wife," he said, breaking from the hapless nurse and jogging down the hall.

As he neared Ellie, he scrutinized her face for a clue of what was going on. She seemed tired but not panicked. "Where's Peter?" he asked.

"They're running tests." As soon as Curt reached her, she let her shoulders slump, as if she was passing an invisible burden from her back to his.

"You couldn't stay with him while they're doing that?"

"They wouldn't let me. Even when I said I was a nurse." She managed a feeble smile. "The doctor said we should get some breakfast and then check back here. It'll take a while."

The thought of breakfast caused his stomach to lurch. "I'm not hungry."

"Neither am I."

"Maybe some coffee," he suggested.

They followed the signs to the cafeteria. Even though food was being sold and eaten there, the place smelled of antiseptic cleansers, and it was so brightly lit Curt could imagine surgeons performing appendectomies on the long Formica tables. He grabbed a tray and herded Ellie down the aisle of food offerings, pointing out the pastries, fruit, yogurt and omelet sandwiches to her. She shook her head. He didn't blame her; none of the platters sparked his appetite.

He filled two mugs with coffee, handed the cashier a few dollars and carried the tray to a table. They sat facing each other. Did he look as pinched as Ellie? As haggard?

At least she didn't seem frightened. "They figure it's some kind of infection," she told Curt. "They put in an IV to get some fluids into him and they're going to run a bunch of blood tests. While they wait for the results, they'll be cooling his body down with ice baths."

"How was he feeling?" Curt asked, recalling Peter's succinct answer to that question last night: *shitty.* "Is he scared?"

"He was too wasted to be scared," Ellie said. "He was half asleep." She drummed her fingertips against the thick ceramic surface of her mug, stared into the steam for a moment then sighed. "It's probably either something viral or bacterial."

"Which is better?" Curt wanted to know what to hope for.

She shrugged. "If it's bacterial, they can pump him with antibiotics. Viruses are sometimes harder to treat."

All right. He'd hope for bacterial. "He's going to be okay, right?"

Ellie gazed at him. *Come on, Ellie—tell me what I want to hear. Convince me. You're the medical professional.* "He's strong," she said. "He's always been as healthy as a horse. Whatever he has, he should be able to fight it off."

That wasn't as definitive an answer as Curt was hoping for. He forced down a few sips of coffee and tried not to wince at its metallic flavor. A fever? A freaking fever? How sick could Peter be? How serious was a fever?

They struggled to finish their coffee, then hiked back to the emergency wing. As they approached the waiting area, they spied a doctor at the far end of a hall, marching toward them. "That's Dr. Kaye," Ellie said, accelerating.

Dr. Kaye. The name rang a bell. The kids' pediatrician, Curt remembered, abashed that he hardly knew the woman. Ellie had always handled all the doctor's visits for the children. Curt had met the doctor only a few times.

"Hi, Mrs. Frost, Mr. Frost," Dr. Kaye greeted them when they met mid-hall. Dr. Kaye's smile looked a bit forced and pensive. She wore wool trousers and a turtleneck beneath a starched white medical coat. Gold, button-shaped earrings glinted through her curls.

Curt started praying again. *Please, God. Make it something fixable, something curable. This is my son.*

"We're running some more tests on Peter," Dr. Kaye said, dispensing with chitchat. "He's just undergone a lumbar puncture—a spinal tap," she clarified for Curt. "We'll run a culture on that to confirm our diagnosis. But we're pretty sure it's meningitis."

Curt's muscles seized. He couldn't move, couldn't breathe. How bad was that? People didn't die of meningitis, did they?

"Viral or bacterial?" Ellie asked.

Dr. Kaye's smile grew even more pensive. "Bacterial. I'm guessing streptococcal. He's had his HiB vaccine, so it isn't that."

Bacterial was good, wasn't it? Ellie had said bacterial infections were easier to treat, that Peter could be pumped with antibiotics—

"I'm sorry," Dr. Kaye continued, her gaze shuttling between Curt and Ellie. She must have seen something in Ellie's face—recognition, comprehension—because she turned fully to Curt. "Bacterial meningitis is, unfortunately, the more virulent version of the disease. Viral meningitis usually resolves itself in a matter of days. With bacterial meningitis, we've got to bombard him with antibiotics and try to keep the swelling in his brain down."

Swelling in his brain. No. Curt didn't want to hear that. That was not what he'd prayed for.

"So you'll bombard him with antibiotics," he said, his voice as rough as sandpaper. Peter had a problem, a huge problem.

Dr. Kaye and the other doctors at this hospital would solve that problem. Peter's brain was not going to swell.

"We'll do everything we can," Dr. Kaye assured him. "We'll be admitting him to the hospital, of course. Once we've got a definitive diagnosis, we'll have to notify the Department of Health. And I hate to say this, but the media will probably get wind of it. Whenever a healthy young patient contracts this disease, they make a big deal about it..." Her voice faded into a drone, and Ellie responded with nods and comments, taking over the conversation. Curt heard only echoes, distorted sounds. The brittle hospital air filled his lungs. He stared at the beige cinderblock wall next to him, at the stainless-steel wheeled cart, at the empty gurney, the green oxygen tanks stashed on its lower shelf. He held himself motionless, afraid that if he moved he would fall over.

Thank God Ellie seemed to know what to say, what to do. Thank God she was taking it all in, processing it, discussing treatment options with Dr. Kaye and requesting permission to stay with Peter in his room once he was admitted.

Thank God she could handle it. Because Curt sure as hell couldn't.

THANK GOD CURT COULD HANDLE everything.

During the four long, lost days she remained by Peter's side, Curt took care of whatever needed to be done. He dealt with the high school, the health department officials and prying reporters from the local TV news programs. He drove Jessie to and from the hospital, phoned Katie at college and asked her to come home. He kept in constant contact with his parents and Ellie's. He stayed in touch with his office, rescheduling the negotiations on one of his cases and guiding several associates through another one. He read the mail, fielded calls from friends and neighbors, brought Ellie snacks from home and watched Peter.

All Ellie did was watch Peter. Occasionally, she managed to doze off in the reclining chair wedged between the wall and his bed. Often, she found her gaze drifting from Peter's unnaturally still body to the monitors above his bed, beeping with each beat of his heart. She stared at the doses of antibiotic dripping into him and questioned the nurses about whether the penicillin was working or ceftriaxone should be used, instead. She roused herself enough to hug Jessie and Katie when they visited, but for the most part her mind had narrowed to one single thought: *Peter*.

The weekend arrived and with it the first mild day of the year. Morning sunlight soaked through the window and into the room, lending the air a golden glow. One of the orderlies whistled as he pushed a dry mop down the corridor outside Peter's room. A nurse smiled as she gave Ellie a tall glass of orange juice from the nurses' station. "It's gorgeous out," she reported. "Maybe you ought to step outside and get a taste of that sunshine."

Ellie wound up not getting a taste of sunshine. Just minutes after she'd finished the orange juice, and minutes before Curt and the girls arrived at the hospital, Peter was dead.

The girls became hysterical, sobbing that if only they'd arrived in time, they could have grabbed hold of Peter and held on tight enough, and he wouldn't have slipped away. They were desperate for comfort, for reassurance, but Ellie couldn't provide them with what they needed. She folded in on herself, spiraling down and down, slipping into her own darkness. She could give nothing. She had nothing.

Once again, Curt handled everything. He made the funeral arrangements. He convinced Ellie's parents to put his parents up at their house. He consulted with the high school's principal about a memorial service. He picked out a grave site for Peter and chose his burial clothing.

Ellie wasn't sure what she did. She had memories of lying in Peter's bed back at home and staring at the patterns of colors dancing across his computer screen. Had the screen saver been on all this time?

His bedroom smelled of him. His mattress carried the lanky imprint of his body. The bottle of Gatorade she'd given him to drink still stood on his night table, and a half-consumed bag of Goldfish crackers lay on his desk, next to his earth-science textbook and a copy of *The Great Gatsby*.

Where was Hope Street? Curt had promised her they would live there forever. Ellie wasn't even sure she was still alive. If she was, she was trapped inside some ghastly address, a place that looked familiar but felt all wrong.

The house filled with flowers, so many bouquets their clashing perfumes cloyed. Ellie's colleagues at Felton Primary School sent chocolates and wine along with the flowers, and at her request the principal offered her a leave of absence for the remainder of the school year. Curt eventually went back to work and Katie returned to college after her spring break. Jessie returned to school, too. It was her senior year. Supposedly the happiest year of a teenager's life.

Ellie had nowhere to return to. The first day she found herself completely alone in the house, she stormed through the rooms with a huge trash bag and threw out all the flowers, most of which had begun to droop and wither. Then she entered Peter's bedroom, sat at his desk and hit a key on his computer. A page from MySpace opened, featuring the photo of an extraordinarily cute girl and some text about how crazy she was about baseball players. Had Peter been corresponding with her, or just fantasizing about her? He'd been so young, too young for love but not too young to attempt an online dry run.

She clicked on an icon at the bottom of the screen, and a list of Peter's MP3 music files appeared. She double-clicked on one. She had no idea what the song was—it turned out to be a thumping rap number—but she closed her eyes. *This is what Peter would be doing right now if he were here,* she thought: listening to hip-hop, dreaming about a cute girl…and munching on Goldfish. Ellie dug into the bag and scooped out a handful of the small yellow crackers. The music was awful, the crackers stale, but she didn't care. This was as close as she could get to Peter.

"Hey." The low voice broke into her reverie.

She swiveled in Peter's chair and saw Curt standing in the doorway. How long had she been in a trance, listening to Peter's music and munching on stale Goldfish? All day?

Flustered, she silenced the tune with a click of the mouse and pushed away from the desk. "I was just…" Just what? Acting unhinged? Losing her grip?

Grieving?

If Curt was home, it must be close to six o'clock. Jessie must have arrived home from school, too. Ellie hadn't heard them enter the house. She'd been in her own little world. In Peter's world.

Curt entered the room, extended his hand and helped her to her feet. His arms felt strange around her. Touching Curt meant touching reality, and reality was where all the pain existed.

"We can do some takeout for dinner," he was saying as she tried to relax in his embrace. "Pizza, Chinese, whatever you want."

She'd been eating Goldfish all day. She wasn't hungry.

But Curt apparently was, and Jessie would expect to eat

something, too. "Takeout. Okay," she said. Her voice sounded miles away.

Curt arched his arm around her shoulders and led her out of Peter's room. Did he think she was deranged? Maybe she was.

All she knew was that, for the first time in her life, Curt's touch made her want to scream....

TWELVE

SHE STARED AT THE REMOTE control until she'd memorized every damn button on it. When she lifted her eyes to Curt, their gazes collided for an instant before he looked away.

She had never before seen such anguish in him, or such anger. Curt didn't have a temper. That was part of what made him a successful attorney; he could argue his position coolly, rationally. He was always the most reasonable person in the room. This trait often exasperated her, in part because she envied it.

He'd certainly been reasonable after Peter died. For months afterward, she'd been a wreck. She'd spent most of that spring and summer in therapy and popping antidepressants. Prozac had wreaked havoc on her digestive system. Xanax had not only upset her stomach but created problems with her vision. Valium caused no side effects, but it didn't do much to ease her depression, either.

She'd felt as if she were living in a glass bubble. Inside was her pain; outside, the world just kept rolling along. Jessie had announced that, despite her sadness, she would be attending her senior prom, and that her friend Kirsten's mother would take her shopping for a prom dress because Ellie clearly wasn't up to the task of helping Jessie select a gown.

Curt had resumed his regular schedule at the firm. He'd negotiated deals, handled some civil litigation, met colleagues for lunch, put in time at the fitness center. Judging by his behavior, one would assume that life was normal.

While he and Jessie had behaved like rational, healthy human beings, while Curt had run up billable hours and Jessie had studied for her exams and the two of them had discussed the latest news out of Washington or watched *South Park* together, sometimes actually laughing at the comedy show's perverse humor, Ellie had spent hour after hour, day after day, sitting in Peter's room, listening to his CDs and MP3 files—Ludacris, the Beastie Boys, 50 Cent and someone named Nellie who turned out to be a man, not a woman—and eating Goldfish crackers, and wondering how on earth Jessie and Curt could be functioning so well when Peter was gone.

Curt had never cried, not in front of Ellie. He'd been quiet and steady, fixing simple suppers on evenings when Ellie hadn't managed to get a meal prepared, and answering phone calls when Ellie had recoiled from the shrill ringing. He'd made apologies to their friends and relatives when she couldn't bring herself to attend social gatherings. He'd covered for her and reclaimed his place in the world.

She hadn't. She couldn't.

If only she'd known that he'd been weeping in the shower. If only he'd told her. Maybe she wouldn't have felt like such a failure for her inability to resume her own routines.

Sighing, she swung her legs back up onto the bed and peered at the television. She'd paused the movie on a photo of Peter seated at his desk, leaning back in his chair and grinning at the camera. One of the girls must have snapped the picture, because Ellie didn't recognize it. Peter's hair was shaggy and he wore an oversize blue T-shirt with Rock The Boat printed across it.

He'd been so alive until the moment he died. Seeing him smile like that, when in a matter of months he would be dead, caused a boulder-size ache to lodge in Ellie's chest.

She pressed the play button, eager to erase that bright, happy image from the screen. The photo faded, replaced by a picture of the front of their house, the azaleas in scarlet bloom, the red maple on the side of the porch lush with burgundy leaves. An orchestral rendition of "Don't Cry For Me, Argentina" played on the soundtrack, and Ellie realized what a simple, pretty tune it was when Curt wasn't lampooning it with silly words.

"It took time, but Ellie rebuilt her life," Katie's voice intoned on the soundtrack. "She cheered at Jessie's graduation—" the photo of the house dissolved into one of Jessie in her cap and gown, flanked by Ellie and Curt "—and by the following September, she was back at her job." The graduation photo vanished, replaced by a shot of the Felton Primary School. "Slowly, and with great courage, Ellie got back to the task of living."

"I didn't have any courage," Ellie muttered.

Curt glanced her way but didn't dispute her. He was still stewing after his outburst. Had she actually believed he never got angry? Maybe he'd just been hiding his anger all along. Maybe he'd been burying it for the past fifty years, ignoring it, burning it off at the fitness center. Or maybe he'd never experienced anger, just as Ellie had never experienced depression, until they'd lost Peter.

She was no longer depressed. But damn, Curt was still angry.

Fourteen months ago

THE EMPTINESS OF THE HOUSE unnerved Ellie. Everyone was gone—Katie and Jessie in college and Peter...

Gone.

Her footsteps didn't literally echo when she walked through the house, but she heard an imaginary echo, the sound of no one. When she arrived home from work each afternoon, no voices shouted a greeting. No smell of microwave popcorn or cocoa greeted her. No backpacks lay on the kitchen counter, no pile of boots and cleated athletic shoes huddled by the back door, no babble of music or telephone conversations drifted down the stairs.

Her nest would have emptied anyway. But not this soon. And not when she and Curt were having so much difficulty dealing with each other.

She'd managed to make a nice dinner tonight, at least. She was getting better at that—not just preparing decent meals but downsizing the amount she made to feed only two. For months, she'd found herself filling her shopping cart at the supermarket with Peter's favorite snacks and then having to place those items back on the shelves, everything but the Goldfish crackers, which had become her own personal addiction. Some nights, she'd accidentally cooked enough food to last her and Curt several days—a quantity Peter would have scarfed down in a single sitting. Some nights she'd lacked the will to prepare anything more complicated than sandwiches and sliced pickles.

She'd gotten it right tonight, however. Roast chicken, baked potatoes, steamed broccoli and a tossed salad. Given that she'd spent the past few days working with faculty representatives on a curriculum unit that covered diet and nutrition, she was pleased to have assembled a healthy, balanced meal for herself and Curt.

He appeared genuinely pleased when he saw what she'd fixed for them. "Wow, this looks great," he said, perhaps a bit too enthusiastically, as he settled across the table from her in the kitchen. "I love the way you make chicken."

The way she made chicken was to shake some seasonings onto it, dab it with butter and stick it in the oven. Hardly worth the high praise. She knew what Curt was really complimenting, though: her effort. Her baby steps in the direction of resuming a normal life.

As they ate, he told her about the negotiations he was about to begin. "Remember Professor Benzer? That guy from MIT?" he asked her. "He came up with a bunch of patents, and we were able to assign the better ones to him and not the guy from Tufts who'd collaborated with him. I handled that negotiation a year and a half ago."

A year and a half ago, Peter had died. Ellie hadn't been aware of any negotiations Curt was involved in at the time. She smiled blandly so he'd think she remembered. He seemed so jazzed about this latest development at work.

"Anyway, we helped him set up a corporation to license the patents, and now a major player from Silicon Valley wants to buy the corporation. They're dangling big, big bucks over his head."

"Lucky him," Ellie said.

"He wants to retain control over the patents," Curt went on. "The Silicon Valley folks want to buy the patents outright, give Benzer a lump sum and send him on his way. So we're about to enter into some complicated negotiations." Curt's eyes sparkled, silver and gold. He loved complicated negotiations. "And here's the best part. Moira Kernan is representing the Silicon Valley people."

"Moira Kernan?" Ellie frowned. The name sounded vaguely familiar.

"She used to work with me. She made partner a year after I did. I'm sure you met her at parties. Short woman with straight black hair. She had a blunt personality, sometimes kind of tactless. She was scary smart."

"Oh. Right." A picture materialized in Ellie's mind. She'd gotten to know most of the partners at social events, and she recalled a petite dynamo who favored bright red lipstick and told dirty jokes without blinking. "She's representing the other side?"

"She moved out to San Francisco a few years ago. One New England winter too many, and when a Bay Area firm started sending out feelers, she packed up and left. So now she and I get to butt heads."

"You know all her moves," Ellie pointed out. "You should be able to run rings around her."

Curt chuckled. "Unfortunately, she knows all my moves, too." He nudged away his empty plate and smiled contentedly. "It's going to be fun."

Fun. Ellie tried to recall what that was. Something you enjoyed, something that made you smile. Something you could experience only if you weren't viewing the world through a gray veil of sorrow and regret.

Something Curt didn't seem to have any trouble with. His veil of sorrow had lifted off him and blown away a long time ago. He waltzed through his days as if everything was as it was supposed to be, as if the worst thing that might befall him was a traffic ticket or a computer virus.

Ellie had always believed she and Curt were in sync, their thoughts and emotions perfectly matched. She'd been wrong. Eighteen months after Peter's death, Curt was having fun. Actually, he'd started having fun just weeks after Peter died.

Ellie couldn't imagine having fun ever again.

He helped her to clear the dishes from the table. She rinsed, he stacked, and their rhythm seemed almost natural. When she turned her attention to the roasting pan, he moved behind her, rested his hands on her shoulders and kissed the crown of her head.

No, she thought, but she couldn't bring herself to shake free of him. A light kiss on her hair—it didn't mean anything. She shouldn't shrink from him. He was her husband, after all.

But his hands remained where they were, and he used his chin to brush her hair away from her neck. When his mouth touched the skin beneath her ear, she flinched.

"Don't," she said. Her body went stiff, as if it had been instantly freeze-dried. She couldn't handle this. She couldn't.

"Ellie." His voice was warm and soft. His body, pressed close behind her, was warm and hard. He slid his hands down her arms, stroking, heating her chilled skin. "Let me just…" He circled his hands forward and eased her against him, then nuzzled her throat with another kiss. She felt his arousal through their clothing, the flexing of firm male flesh.

"No." She jerked away, sudsy water splattering from her hands as she dropped the roasting pan into the sink. "Don't do this, Curt. Please." The last word emerged on a sob.

He stepped back and sighed. "Ellie, it's been so long. A year and a half—"

"I know exactly how long it's been since Peter died," she snapped.

He closed his eyes, drew in a breath and then opened them again. "It's been a year and a half since we made love." She heard the tension in his voice, saw it in the jut of his chin and the curling of his fingers into fists. "I want that back, Ellie. I want to make love to my wife." He drew in another deep breath and let it out. "I want my life back. *Our* lives."

She was shaking, queasy. She wanted her life back, too. She wanted Peter's life back. She wanted to be able to have fun. But she couldn't. The grief was still too thick around her, a dense, cold fog that refused to release her. Grief and remorse and a crazed longing to go back in time, to revive the past, to make everything come out differently.

That she could get through a day without weeping, that she could put together a nutrition curriculum at work, that she could cook a well-rounded dinner—she considered these tiny successes nothing short of phenomenal. Curt couldn't ask her for more. Not yet.

"Damn it, Ellie…" He sighed again. "What is it? Are you punishing me?"

"I'm not punishing you," she retorted. "I just can't…I can't feel these things. I can't make myself want this. I can't…" Another sob threatened, and she swallowed it down. "I'm not ready."

"*I'm* ready," he said. "What the hell do I have to do to make you ready?"

He'd been ready the day of the funeral. She remembered that horrible night, hours after they'd buried their youngest child. They'd climbed into bed together and she'd sobbed in his arms, and he'd held her, consoled her. And his comfort had evolved, his caresses changing from soothing to sexual. "My son isn't even cold in the ground," she'd moaned. "How can you even think about that?"

"It would make us feel better," he'd explained. "Maybe we could just forget, for a few minutes…"

"I can't forget," she'd argued. "I don't want to forget."

He'd backed off that night, and made no more overtures for a while. But then, a few months later, he'd brought home a bottle of an expensive Bordeaux and refilled her glass several

Judith Arnold

times over dinner, and when her mind began to get fuzzy he'd tried to seduce her again. "Not yet," she'd begged, bursting into tears. "Not yet."

He'd comforted her then. He'd hugged her and rocked her gently and murmured, "Okay, it's okay, Ellie," while she'd bawled like a baby.

It wasn't okay now, and he clearly had no intention of comforting her tonight. "Maybe you should try some more therapy," he suggested, doing his best to sound reasonable.

"I went through plenty of therapy," she reminded him. "The therapist said mourning has no timetable. There's no set schedule that says I'm supposed to be over it by now, or I'm supposed to be ready for sex after a certain amount of time. She said we all heal at our own pace." *And your pace is pretty damn fast,* she thought bitterly. *You were all healed by the time we left the cemetery. Peter's dead, what a pity. Let's distract ourselves with a little hanky-panky.*

"Ellie..." He wiped a hand over his face, but the gesture didn't soften his scowl. "How long? Just tell me how freaking long I'm going to have to wait for you to come around."

"If I had some disease you could name—cancer or MS or something like that—you wouldn't be pressuring me for sex," she railed. "I'm sick, Curt. I'm coping the best I can, I'm dragging myself through each day, but my son is dead and I can't just make that horrible truth disappear. You can, and good for you. I can't."

He stared at her for a long moment, then scooped his keys from the counter and stormed out of the kitchen, through the mudroom to the garage. She heard the muted roar of his sporty new BMW as he revved the engine. The sound retreated as he backed out of the garage, down the driveway and away.

She told herself she didn't care where he was going. At that moment, she wasn't even sure she loved him. Love was something alien to her. It meant joy, didn't it? It meant strength. It meant faith. It meant confidence. She didn't possess any of those things right now. Joy, strength, faith and confidence had all abandoned her one sunny Saturday morning a year and a half ago.

Curt didn't get it. He didn't feel as deeply, didn't mourn as deeply, didn't suffer Peter's death the way Ellie did. A bad thing had happened, but now he was over it. Sex felt good, and why shouldn't he do something that felt good? Why couldn't she be a good sport and spread her legs for him?

He had no idea what she was dealing with. No idea how sorrow could wrap around a person and smother her, how it could steal hope. He had no idea how much she hated the fact that he was over it, no longer crippled by the pain. He had no idea how much she resented him for having recovered—and herself for being unable to recover.

THE Z4 FELT LIKE A ROCKET beneath him, so smooth he might as well have been soaring through the air rather than racing down Route 2. It still had that new-car smell—a sweet, crisp scent that mingled with the aroma of leather from the seats. The dashboard was sleek, the sky beyond the tinted windshield moonless but sprayed with stars.

When he'd told Ellie he wanted the BMW for his fiftieth birthday, she hadn't objected. Of course she hadn't. The only thing she objected to was sex.

He cursed, banged his fist against the steering wheel and then let up on the gas a little. He was in no hurry to reach a destination—or to return home, for that matter. He just wanted to get his rocks off. Driving this baby was as close as he'd come to that.

Honest to God, he was going crazy. A year and a half, damn it. He was a physical guy. Ellie knew that. When Peter was still alive, she'd been a physical woman. She'd loved sex. Wild sex, tame sex, warm sex, hot sex. All he had to do was touch her and she was ready to rock and roll. Hell, half the time she was the one who initiated things.

But now…nothing.

As he'd told Ellie, he wanted his life back. It hadn't been easy for him to return to work, to force himself to care about his clients, to accumulate his billable hours and regain his awareness of his colleagues. But he'd done it. Like plodding up the world's highest mountain barefoot, he'd progressed one painful step at a time. He'd made it to the summit. The air was cleaner here, the sun brighter.

He wanted Ellie on that summit with him. But she refused to hike the path. She sat at the bottom of the mountain, shivering in its shadow, afraid to let even a hint of happiness into her soul.

Maybe they should try marriage counseling, he thought. But why the hell should he have to go through counseling? He was fine. Ellie was the one who was screwed up.

He loved her. He ached for her. But he couldn't save her. She had to save herself. She had to take that first step on the trail to the top.

And meanwhile, all he could do was stand in the shower and jerk himself off like a horny teenager. Or drive and drive, fly through the night in this raging sports coupe and let the engine do his howling for him.

By the time he got home, Ellie was in bed. The bedside lamps were off, and the only light in the room was what spilled in from the hallway. He didn't know if she was asleep, and he told himself he didn't care.

He wouldn't sleep at all. Cruising sixty miles up and down Route 2 hadn't unwound him. He was tuned as tight as a guitar string, and if someone plucked it the feedback would be deafening.

He crawled into bed next to her and listened to her breathe for a while. It didn't sound like the deep, steady respiration of sleep. So—keeping his arms rigid at his sides to prevent himself from accidentally touching her—he said, "Look, Ellie. Peter wouldn't want you to be like this."

She didn't respond immediately, and he thought he'd guessed wrong about her being awake. Just when he was about to roll away from her, she startled him by saying, "Like what?"

"Wallowing in your misery."

"Peter doesn't get a vote," she said coldly. "Neither do you. Neither do I, for that matter. I'm not choosing to be in this much pain."

"A little cuddling might ease the pain a little."

"A little cuddling?" She laughed wryly at his euphemism. "You want sex that badly? Go ahead and do it. Just do it." She threw back the blanket and hiked up her nightgown.

Jesus. He *didn't* want sex that badly. He wanted his wife. He wanted her whole again, and happy, and loving him. "Stop it," he said, sickened by her bitter invitation. "I don't want sex. I want our marriage back. I want us to be good together, the way we've always been. That's what I want."

"And I want my son to be alive. You know how the song goes, Curt. You can't always get what you want. Neither of us will ever be what we used to be. It's too late. I'm too damaged. The scars are too deep."

"What are you saying? We're never going to make love again?"

"Of course we will." She sighed. "I hope we will," she said less certainly. "I wish I knew what the future held, but I don't. I used to think we'd grow old, surrounded by our three children and their children. Now that's not going to happen. I'm afraid to make predictions."

"You're afraid of everything," Curt muttered.

"Yes," she agreed, sounding so sad his anger relented a little. "I'm afraid of everything."

There was nothing more to say, other than good-night. He turned onto his side, his back to Ellie, but as he'd expected, sleep eluded him.

MOIRA KERNAN GREETED HIM with a hug when he entered the conference room the next morning. "Curt! Great to see you! Look at you New England Yankees," she teased, her gaze passing from Curt to Jonelle, the associate assisting him with the Benzer case, and his secretary. "You're all so pasty. Too little sun and too much snow."

"We've just had a gorgeous summer," Curt argued. "Highs in the eighties every day, and never a drop of rain. And anyway," he added with a taunting smile, "I bet you miss the blizzards. Admit it, Moira. You fantasize about the snow."

Moira laughed. "Sure. Sometimes I stand in the open door of my refrigerator, just to feel an icy breeze." Her skin was a golden hue, and her hair had bronze highlights, something he didn't remember from when she'd been working in Boston. Her suit was profoundly stylish, beige and black, all angles and slanting lines. She still wore her trademark red lipstick.

She looked terrific.

Maybe Curt ought to take Ellie to California. Or someplace else—the Caribbean, Hawaii or any other warm, romantic paradise. They'd lie in the sun together and sip sweet, frothy drinks with paper umbrellas sticking out of them, and the tropical winds would lull them. They'd get massages and dance in the moonlight. Ellie might let go of some of her pain.

What a terrific idea. As soon as this Benzer deal was settled, he'd research some spa resorts.

"So tell me," he asked Moira once his secretary had started up her laptop and then left the conference room to get coffee for everyone, "it's not just a coincidence that you're here, is it?"

She laughed. "Are you kidding? They hired me because I used to work with you. They figure I'll know how to game you."

"It didn't occur to them that I used to work with *you*, too?" Curt felt the first hot rush of competitive energy in his veins. He used to enjoy sparring with Moira when they were on the same side of a case. Sparring with her when they were on opposite sides ought to be even more entertaining.

The sparring began. While they sipped their coffee, they analyzed Dr. Benzer's patents one at a time, Moira lowballing the earning potential of each patent and Curt highballing it. They evaluated Benzer's agreement with his former colleague to make sure Benzer wasn't trading in any patents that weren't his. They discussed the value of Benzer's company and just how far Moira's clients could take that company with their superior marketing and fabrication facilities. Several times, Moira left the conference room and shut herself inside an empty office, where she could confer with her West Coast clients by phone. Several times Curt called Benzer at MIT to clarify a point or obtain a technical explanation.

At twelve-thirty, Curt's secretary phoned out for sandwiches. At one, the sandwiches arrived, along with fresh coffee. They ate, they drank and they argued.

If only Ellie felt the kind of passion in her work that Curt felt in his. As a school nurse she did essential work—more important work than what most attorneys did, even if attorneys got paid a heck of a lot more—but he doubted she ever felt surges of adrenaline when a fourth-grader entered her office with a scraped knee or when she lectured a class of second-graders on the importance of eating leafy green vegetables. Where was the thrill in that? Where was the excitement, the challenge, the triumph? Perhaps she didn't need a tropical vacation to snap out of her depression. She needed something exhilarating, something that got her heart pumping faster. It didn't have to be debating over how much a prosperous high-tech firm in Silicon Valley should pay an MIT professor for his tiny research corporation. But if there was something, *anything* that could get Ellie psyched…

Damn if Curt knew what it was. And really, it wasn't his job to solve Ellie's problems for her. He'd tried, God knew. He'd been trying since the day Peter died. He'd been patient. He'd been supportive. He'd offered suggestions, cheered her on, accepted the crumbs she tossed his way—a cheek kiss here, a hand squeeze there. But if she wanted to get better, she was going to have to do the hard work herself.

Meanwhile…what else could he do but wait? And wait. And wait.

Moira reentered the conference room after one of her phone calls to California, tossed her head to flick her bangs out of her eyes and said, "Where'd you go, Curt? I was only gone five minutes."

"I didn't go anywhere," he said, automatically standing at her entrance and then dropping back into his chair once she was seated.

"You were zoned out. Now's my big chance. Time to lunge." She flashed him a smile and introduced a new payout schedule. Hardly a lunge, but Curt ordered himself to forget about Ellie and stay focused on his hand-to-hand combat with Moira.

The negotiations continued until five-thirty, but by the time his secretary closed her laptop and Jonelle had scribbled her last note onto a legal pad, most of the issues had been resolved. Moira had a satisfactory package to take back to her clients in California, and Curt had an even better package to take to Professor Benzer, one that would ensure him a decent payout up front and continuing royalties and licensing fees for the next twenty years. Everyone shook hands, congratulated one another and themselves and filed out of the conference room.

Curt felt drained but enormously pleased. He was *good,* damn it. With a deft mixture of charm, stubbornness, legal finesse and verbal dexterity, he could win, even against an opponent as sharp as Moira Kernan. And he'd won today. It took all his willpower not to raise his fists into the air and do a victory dance.

He paused outside his office to issue some final instructions to his secretary, then shoved open his door. Feeling a hand on his sleeve, he stopped and turned around.

"Curt." Moira gazed up at him, her confident grin replaced by a solemn expression. "I heard about your son. I'm so sorry."

Curt shrugged. "Not as sorry as I am," he said, then forced a smile. "Thanks."

"I remember when he was born. You gave us all blue bubblegum cigars. Not only did the gum taste vile, but it made my tongue blue." She shook her head. "I'm really sorry."

Curt shrugged. No clever response existed for expressions of sympathy. He'd learned to simply accept them in silence.

"You look like hell, you know," Moira added.

That made him laugh. "I wish I could say the same about you, but unfortunately, I can't. You look fantastic."

"Yeah. Ever since I stopped shoveling snow, I dropped ten years off my life. Maybe the Botox helped a little, too." Her smile was gentle. "You want to talk? We could get a drink and you could cry on my shoulder."

"You don't want to see me cry," he joked, afraid to admit how tempting her invitation was.

"My shoulder would be honored to hold your tears, Curt. Seriously. We're old friends. If you want to talk, here I am."

The truth was, he hadn't cried on anyone's shoulder. Not on Ellie's—her shoulders were much too fragile to bear the weight of a single teardrop. Not on his parents'; they'd just moved to Arizona, hoping the desert climate would alleviate the arthritis in his father's knees and hips.

Not on any of his colleagues' shoulders, either. Unlike Moira, they tiptoed around the subject of Peter's death. The firm had sent him and Ellie a huge bouquet of flowers and several of the partners had sent smaller bouquets individually. When Curt had returned to work a few days after the funeral, his coworkers had anticipated his every need, bringing him coffee and documents he hadn't even gotten around to requesting. They'd given him poignant smiles and spoken to him in muted tones, as if he were feeble.

Because he'd despised the kid-glove treatment, he'd deliberately projected strength and hardheadedness. *I'm back,* he'd communicated with his attitude. *I'm strong and I'm coping. Treat me normally.*

The idea of, well, not crying on someone's shoulder but unburdening himself a little and accepting some heartfelt sympathy… God, that would be nice.

"I'm staying at the Westin at Copley Place," Moira told him. "Why don't you close up shop here and meet me at the lounge there. I think it's called Bar 10."

"Okay. Give me twenty minutes."

She nodded, smiled and vanished down the hall.

He entered his office, closed the door and took a deep breath. A drink with an old friend. That was all this was. A chance to catch up with Moira, laugh over old times and—hell, why not?—cry on her shoulder. Wasn't that what friends were for?

He lifted the phone, punched in his home number and waited. *Just a drink with a friend,* he repeated to himself as he waited for Ellie to answer.

"Hello?"

"Hi, Ellie—it's me. Listen, I'm not coming straight home." *A drink with a friend.* "Some people involved in the negotiations today are getting together for a drink, and..." *Some people? Just two people. Why was he lying?*

He wasn't lying. "Some" could be two. He and Moira were "some people involved in the negotiations."

"No problem," Ellie said. "I didn't fix anything for dinner. I guess I shot my load yesterday."

She'd fixed a delicious meal yesterday, he recalled. They'd eaten, they'd chatted, they'd enjoyed their meal—and then she'd all but slapped him and sent him away. He'd had to drive sixty miles to burn off his rage.

A bolt of fresh anger shot through him, a reminder of everything that was wrong at home. "I don't know when we'll be done," he told her. "Don't wait up."

Twenty minutes later, after parking the Z4 in the Westin's underground garage, Curt rode the elevator upstairs to the lobby and asked for directions to Bar 10. He found Moira waiting for him there, seated comfortably in a pink armchair at a small, round table, still dressed in her chic suit but looking fresh. He himself felt wilted, and as soon as he joined her he loosened his tie. A waitress appeared instantly to take their orders. Moira asked for a cosmopolitan, Curt a Scotch on the rocks. Once the waitress was gone, Moira leaned back in her chair, looking a little like a queen on her throne, and smiled. "Now," she demanded, "tell me everything."

"Everything?"

"I've been gone five years. Catch me up. Fill me in. Spare no details."

Grinning, he relaxed in his own chair and launched into a description of his life over the past few years, considerably sparing her most of the details. He told her about the projects he'd been involved with at work, about the growing size and reach of the firm and the increase in the number of partners. He filled her in on all the gossip: Yes, John Delgado still drank raw eggs for breakfast and never got salmonella. Yes, Ruth Steinberg still played matchmaker and had not a single marriage to show for her efforts. Claude Forrest retired last year and moved to an island off the coast of Maine. Lindy Brinson still dressed like a tart, but she had surpassed Gretchen the mastiff and could now claim the title of Best Divorce Attorney in Boston. Partner bonuses were obscenely high this past year. The firm was working out the economics of expanding its Washington office.

He told her about his new car. He told her that Katie had majored in film-and-television production, and that Jessie was concentrating in political science with the possibility of becoming a lawyer like her father. And he told her about Peter, about how suddenly he became sick, how suddenly he was gone.

Moira sighed and shook her head. "You know me, Curt. Never married, no kids. People think it's because I'm tough, but it's really the opposite. I'm too weak. I could never survive that kind of loss. I know I couldn't. So I've avoided it by not letting myself get too attached."

"You never know what you can survive until you face it," he

said. "I wouldn't have thought I could survive losing Peter. Frankly, I don't know *how* I survived it. But here I am."

"How is your wife doing?" Moira asked. "Emily, was it?"

"Ellie. And she's not doing well."

"I'm sorry to hear that. Is she ill?"

Last night, she'd claimed she was—as ill as someone with cancer or multiple sclerosis. "She's depressed," he explained. "She still hasn't figured out how to get past Peter's death."

"She's his mother," Moira pointed out. "It's different for mothers than for fathers."

"That's a sexist remark," Curt chided.

Moira laughed. "Well, you know me. I'm allowed to be sexist. I've got bigger balls than most of the men in this room." She reached for her drink and he noticed her nails, short but polished a bright crimson, the same color as her lipstick. She might have big balls and a sexist attitude, but she exuded a distinct femininity. Her suit flattered her curves. Her shoes had pointy toes and high heels.

Even though she'd avoided marriage and children, she clearly felt empathy for Ellie. "Your wife carried that boy inside her body. His death must be like having a chunk of her flesh cut out of her. A chunk of her soul, too."

"I ache for her, Moira—I do. But. . ." He silenced himself with a sip of Scotch. He didn't want to sound self-pitying.

"But what?"

"It's like I've lost her along with Peter. She's just not there for me. I need a wife, and I haven't got one anymore."

Moira's eyebrows arched in surprise. "She left you?"

"No. She goes to work, she comes home, she has dinner with me, she sleeps next to me. But she's not *there*." He spared Moira those details, too. Out of loyalty to Ellie, out of his desperate need to believe his marriage wasn't really as dead as his son, he refused to spell out in what ways Ellie wasn't *there*.

"That must be hard on you."

Curt snorted at the understatement.

Moira tapped one red fingernail against the surface of her glass. "Have you gone for marriage counseling?"

He was surprised that she'd give him marital advice. He'd been trying not to let the conversation grow too intimate, but if Moira wasn't afraid to discuss Curt's problems, why not?

She'd offered her shoulder. He should make use of it.

"Ellie was in therapy for a while. Her therapist told her she had to heal at her own pace. I don't think she can begin to fathom what her pace is doing to me. God, that makes me sound so self-centered," he muttered, shaking his head and taking another sip of Scotch. "She's in pain. I understand that. I want to help. But...Christ, Moira, I keep fearing she'll drag me down into the abyss with her."

"You can't let that happen," Moira said gently. "You've got to help yourself before you can help her. Like on airplanes, you know how they say you should put on your own oxygen mask before you assist others?"

"You think an oxygen mask would help?"

"I think you need something, Curt. Maybe Ellie can't give it to you, but your needs are important, too."

He eyed her speculatively. Had she guessed that his sex life was moribund, that Ellie had denied him—denied them both— that most basic human act, that simple, loving grace? Did Moira believe his need for Ellie was as important as whatever the hell it was Ellie needed?

"You were always one of the good guys," Moira recalled. "So faithful. So obviously in love with your wife." She smiled nostalgically. "I don't know if it's still true, but when I was at the firm, half the women working there had crushes on you."

"What?" He laughed.

"You didn't have a clue, right? We all used to talk about you in the ladies' room. We ogled you at meetings and parties. And you never even noticed. You only had eyes for your wife."

"You ogled me? Really?" He chuckled at the thought of tarty Lindy Brinson leering at him, or Sue Pritchard considering him as a potential husband number four, or Ruth Steinberg scheming to match him up with one of the firm's women. "I'm flattered. If only I'd known."

"If you'd known, you wouldn't have done a damn thing about it."

He nodded and laughed again. "You're right."

She leveled her gaze at him. She was smiling, but it was an enigmatic smile, a questioning smile. "What do you want, Curt? Right now. What would it take to make you feel whole?"

He sensed a change in atmosphere, unspoken ideas churning just beneath the surface. "My son?"

"Besides that."

God. She knew. She knew what was wrong in his marriage, in his life. She knew what he needed, what it would take to make him feel whole—and unlike Ellie, she didn't believe his needs made him a despicable person.

"You can figure out what it would take," he said, his voice low and broken. He ought to be ashamed of himself for thinking what he was thinking, for having a woman he respected witness his desperation.

Moira's gaze was sharp and direct. "I'm here," she said, reaching across the table and covering his hand with hers. "I'll be gone tomorrow, but I'm here now."

"Moira. I can't ask——"

"You didn't ask." She gave his hand a light squeeze. Her fingers were strong but soft. It had been so long since a woman had touched him with affection. Since a woman had touched him at all. "I hate seeing you like this, Curt. Let me be your friend."

He told himself how wrong this was.

Then he told himself it wasn't. He couldn't exist in Ellie's no-man's-land anymore, that strange, dark place where she was neither fully alive nor as dead as Peter. He'd stayed there with her as long as he could, done everything in his power to lure her out into the light. He'd begged her to rediscover what it meant to be alive. Nothing he'd tried had worked.

But he was alive. That wasn't a sin. He had no reason to be ashamed. All he wanted was to live.

And Moira—his friend—was giving him that chance.

No more words were necessary. He tossed a twenty-dollar bill onto the table, and he and Moira left the bar.

ELLIE WASN'T SURE WHY he had to go to California. The negotiations on that deal he was handling for the MIT professor had been all but completed in Boston a week ago. Just a few details still had to be ironed out, he'd told her. Couldn't details be ironed out long-distance? Wasn't that what phones and faxes and overnight-delivery services existed for?

Curt had insisted that the ironing would go more efficiently if he flew out to California, and so he went. He'd left on Wednesday and would be back in time for dinner Sunday. Four days.

Ellie had grown inured to the emptiness of her house during the day. But nighttime was different. She and Curt had rarely spent a night apart before Peter's death, and never since then. True, they had huge problems looming between them, but as long as they shared a bed, Ellie was convinced that those problems would eventually work themselves out. Curt had been so patient, and she was trying, really trying, to get back to where she'd been.

Even though they hadn't made love since the day Peter had fallen ill, Ellie depended on Curt's presence in bed. His warmth soothed her. His respiration lulled her. His weight balanced the mattress. With him off in California, the bed seemed as vast as the Sahara, and just as lifeless.

"I'm a big girl," she told herself. "I can handle his absence."

And to her amazement, she discovered that she could.

She returned home from work Thursday, entered the silent house and decided to fix herself a real dinner. She pulled a pork chop from the freezer—God knew how long it had been there; it was as hard as a rock—and defrosted it in the microwave. She measured rice and water into a pot and set it on the stove to steam. While the pork chop broiled, the phone rang.

Curt had become the official phone answerer after Peter's death. For so long, Ellie was afraid to speak to callers; she feared she'd burst into tears if someone dared to ask how she was. So Curt had gotten into the habit of answering the phone when it rang, and all these months later, they were still in that routine.

The sudden, shrill chime of the phone jolted her now, and it took her a moment to remember that Curt wasn't around to answer it. She squared her shoulders, marched across the kitchen to the wall phone and lifted the receiver. "Hello?"

"Hi, Ellie, it's me."

Curt's voice sounded metallic through a crinkle of static. He was probably phoning her on his cell rather than the hotel phone. The lousy connection notwithstanding, she was glad he'd called. "Hi. How are things going?"

"Pretty well. We've worked out nearly everything. Just a few more tweaks and we'll be there." He fell quiet for a moment, then said, "How are you?"

"I'm fine." She realized he might take that as an automatic response. "Really, Curt. I'm good. I'm just fixing myself some dinner."

"Great." Another pause. "I had a free minute and thought I should check up on you."

"You don't have to check up on me," she said, hoping she didn't sound testy. "I'm okay."

"All right." Pause. "I'm not sure if I'll have a chance to call tomorrow. It's just…we're on kind of an odd schedule."

"They've got your time booked up. I understand. If you can squeeze in a call, that would be nice, but if you can't, I'll assume you were too busy."

"Right." He sighed. "I've got to go, Ellie. I'll be back on Sunday."

"I hope the rest of the negotiations go well. I'll talk to you if you have a free minute. If not, have a safe flight home."

They said goodbye and she hung up. He must have been pressed for time, calling her from wherever the negotiations were taking place. California was three hours behind Massachusetts, so he'd phoned her in the middle of his afternoon, which meant he'd probably still been at work. He'd sounded brusque and cool, the way he talked when people were nearby and could eavesdrop on his end of the conversation. She would have liked to ask him how his flight out had been, and whether he would have a chance to travel around San Francisco. She'd never been there, but she'd heard it was a spectacular city.

He'd get to tour the area on Saturday, she acknowledged. Surely the negotiations would be done by tomorrow evening, and then he'd have a day to play. When he'd scheduled his flight, he'd told her he was giving himself that extra day so he could visit the Golden Gate Bridge and Fisherman's Wharf.

She reviewed their conversation in her mind and sighed. Even if he'd been at some law firm, even if business people were within earshot, he could have told her he loved her, couldn't he? He could have told whoever was around that he was checking in with his wife. They would have understood if he'd said something affectionate and personal to her.

Then again, things had been awfully chilly between them at home ever since that night, a little over a week ago, when she'd rebuffed him. Maybe sounding chilly and distant on the phone was his way of letting her know he was still pissed at her.

The silence in the house gave her too much freedom to fret over whether his terseness reflected his professional mind-set or his annoyance with her. She went to the den and put a CD on the stereo—not Peter's rowdy hip-hop music, but Bonnie Raitt. Curt had been such a big fan of Raitt's after he'd seen her perform in Harvard Square during his first year in law school, and he'd turned Ellie into a Raitt fan, too.

Some of the songs were bluesy, but some were upbeat and confident. Ellie poured herself a glass of wine and lingered over her meal, tasting every mouthful, inhaling the wine's bouquet before she sipped. Once she was done and the dishes had been put away, she realized she was feeling a little less morose about Curt's absence.

Friday went better than Thursday. She felt stronger, somehow, more awake and aware. Instead of contemplating the hush that enveloped the house when she got home, she piled a stack of CDs onto the stereo—the Doobie Brothers, Bruce Springsteen, Sly and the Family Stone, music that would make a normal person want to dance.

Ellie was far from normal, but the music energized her. She turned up the volume so it blasted through the house. Then she climbed the stairs, walked down the hall and stepped into Peter's room.

"It's time," she said. Time to empty the bottle of Gatorade that still sat on his night table. Time to throw out the bag of Goldfish crackers on his desk—not the same bag that had been there when he died; since that day, Ellie had consumed countless bags of Goldfish while sitting at his desk and trying to channel his spirit. "It's time," she told herself as she crumpled that Goldfish package and tossed it into a trash bag.

Time to strip the sheets off Peter's bed and launder them. Time to reshelve *The Great Gatsby* in the den bookcase. The earth-science textbook, she discovered with chagrin, belonged to the high school. She should have returned it to the school a year ago.

She found more textbooks in his backpack and made a neat stack of them to take to the high school on Monday. She emptied the rest of his backpack, including a peanut-butter sandwich so stale it could have been used as a roofing slate, and tossed the battered, stained bag into the trash. She left his clothing alone— the girls might want some of his old flannel shirts or sweaters. His other belongings—knickknacks, toys he'd never quite outgrown, his comic books, his globe, the model of the Wright brothers biplane, which he'd constructed from a kit—all that could wait, as well. She intended to keep his numerous sports trophies. He'd been so proud of them. And the baseball signed by all his teammates after he'd pitched a no-hitter in Little League. And his beloved stuffed panda—Peter Panda, Peter had dubbed him, convinced that he and his panda ought to share the name. And his CDs, and the helicopter he'd constructed with his Lego set, and the kitsch lava lamp the girls had given him for Christmas when he was thirteen. It wasn't yet time to deal with all those things.

But the homework papers and old math tests crumpled and stuffed into assorted drawers of his desk—those could go. The smelly gym socks on the floor of his closet—into the trash. The pencil stubs. The scraps of paper with video-game codes scribbled onto them. The ball constructed of rubber bands. The mud-caked cleats. The toothbrush still propped into the stand in the bathroom.

All of it, into the trash.

By the time Ellie had tied the garbage bag and lugged it to the garage, the front of her sweater was damp with tears. But she felt good. So sad she shivered from the pain, but good, as well, as if a sore had been lanced and drained.

She slept well that night, despite the strangeness of not having Curt in bed with her, and she awakened feeling even more energized. When she peered into Peter's bedroom, it didn't look much changed, but it smelled of freshly washed linens instead of stale dust and muddy cleats, and a bright October sun spilled light through the window.

She decided to take a walk.

When was the last time she'd taken a walk? Not just walked somewhere she had to be, but walked *nowhere?*

Dressed in jeans, comfortable sneakers and a hooded sweatshirt, she ventured into her neighborhood, breathing the cleansing autumn air and delighting in the blazing colors of the leaves. She strolled all the way to the town green—a couple of miles at least—and gazed at the rectangle of grass surrounded by the Unitarian church, the fire station, the town hall building and a few preserved historical buildings. The green's grass was half-hidden beneath a carpet of brown and orange leaves shed by the oak, maple and birch trees that punctuated the lawn. The air carried the scent of smoke and tart apples.

Poor Curt, stuck in California during the most beautiful New England fall weekend of the year.

As she reversed course and hiked back home, she thought about how much she missed him. Even though things had not been good between them, she loved him. He was her anchor, her support, an essential element in her reality. She wished he was with her, appreciating the gorgeous foliage and the refreshing breeze. She wished he could see the job she'd done on Peter's room.

He would see Peter's room tomorrow when he got home. He'd be pleased and grateful. He'd put his arms around her.

She'd put her arms around him.

I want you, Curt. I want you home. I want you with me.

Tomorrow, she thought, and a hesitant smile curved her lips. Curt would be home tomorrow. And she would be ready for him. She would never be whole again, but she was healing, finally. Maybe she'd needed a few days away from him to reach this point, but she'd reached it.

Once home, she tackled the living room, the den and the master bedroom, vacuuming, polishing, neatening up. She treated herself to take-out Thai food for dinner—pad thai was a definite improvement over Goldfish crackers—and then settled into the recliner in the family room and watched a Monty Python movie on the VCR. And laughed. Out loud.

Yes, she was ready for Curt.

He was scheduled to arrive home around dinnertime on Sunday. She thawed some strip steaks for dinner, prepared roasted red bliss potatoes with olive oil and herbs and tossed a salad. She carried a bottle of Rioja up from the wine rack in the basement and opened it so it could breathe—she wasn't sure what that meant, but she figured it wouldn't hurt. Then she soaked in the tub, an indulgence she hadn't let herself enjoy since Peter's death, and dressed in the laciest underwear she owned. It wasn't flagrantly sexy—Curt had never been particularly interested in sexy lingerie—but it was feminine and flattering, and wearing it made her feel womanly. She completed her outfit with a beige cashmere sweater and her snuggest pair of jeans. Actually, all her jeans were kind of snug these days, thanks to her Goldfish binges.

She brushed her hair until it glistened, slid the diamond eternity ring Curt had given her for their tenth anniversary onto her finger and poked her diamond studs through her ears. She was nervous, but happy. She was ready. Ready to reclaim her life. Ready to let her husband reclaim her.

He arrived home at around seven. Peeking through the living-room window, she spotted the cab idling at the curb and remained where she was, watching Curt climb out, haul his wheeled suitcase from the seat and close the door. He would be tired, she knew, jet-lagged, bleary. She'd fix him a drink, let him unwind, follow his lead. Wasn't that what he'd been wanting her to do all along?

He came up the front walk and she swung the door open for him. Clad in faded jeans, a wrinkled shirt and his navy-blue blazer, his hair mussed and his mouth set, he didn't look as happy to see her as she was to see him. He probably expected to get turned away tonight. He probably thought nothing had changed since he'd left.

So much had changed. Ellie had cleaned Peter's room. She'd thrown away the Gatorade and the Goldfish. He would be pleased.

"Hi," he said wearily, tilting his head as she rose on tiptoe to kiss his cheek. That she'd kissed him didn't seem to register on him. He smiled briefly, then wheeled his suitcase to the stairs and lifted it by the handle. "Let me wash up, okay? Then we'll talk."

She accepted his reserve as a result of cross-country-flight fatigue. And maybe a touch of apprehension. He probably assumed she was the same Ellie he'd left five days ago. Maybe while he washed up, the importance of her having kissed him would sink in. He'd figure it out.

While he was upstairs, she grilled the steaks, lit the candles she'd arranged on the dining-room table and gave the salad dressing a final stir. He hadn't come back downstairs by the time everything was ready, and she realized that in addition to washing up he'd opted to unpack his bag. She decided that was a good thing. When he joined her, he'd be done with all his tasks and ready for a glass of well-breathed wine.

And as he'd promised, they would talk. He would tell her all about San Francisco. He'd gloat about the negotiation—she had no doubt it had gone his way—and complain about the hassles of flying across the country. And they'd eat, and she'd reach for his hand and say, "Let's go upstairs," and they'd blow out the candles and leave the dishes and make love. She could do this. She swore to herself she could. She wanted it. Her desire would guide her through her inhibitions and hesitations, her fears.

As soon as she heard his footsteps on the stairs, she zapped the steaks in the microwave for a few seconds to heat them. When he appeared in the kitchen doorway, she smiled and said, "We're eating in the dining room tonight."

"We are?"

She led the way, carrying the steaks on a platter. She'd already put the salad and potatoes on the table, and poured wine into two crystal goblets.

"What's this all about?" he asked as he took in the festive table.

"Welcome home?" She shrugged. "You were away and I missed you. And now you're home and I'm glad." She turned to him, searching his face for a sign that he recognized the profound change in her, that he was willing to forget for now how difficult she'd been, how emotionally crippled. She was better now. Surely he could see that. Surely he could forgive her for whatever pain she'd caused him.

"Ellie." He sounded pensive.

Couldn't he tell? Things were good now. He should be smiling. "Sit," she said, pulling out his chair and then settling into the chair across from him. "Let's drink a toast."

He lifted his glass, then lowered it and sighed. "Ellie. We have to talk."

Her festive mood had failed to infect him. The candles, the wine, the delicious meal she'd prepared, her smile... None of it registered on him. Had his flight been that awful? His entire trip a bust? "Fine," she said, refusing to drop her smile. "Let's talk."

"I had sex with another woman."

Ellie had been lifting her wineglass, but her hand twitched so hard she nearly snapped the stem in two. She lowered the glass and stared at Curt. The candles fluttered, their golden light dancing across his face. He looked bleak.

I had sex with another woman. The sentence assaulted her, each word a blade slicing into her. Curt. Her husband. The only man she'd ever loved. He'd had sex with another woman.

She tried to wrap her mind around the idea. It was preposterous. So unlike him. Didn't he love her as much as she loved him? In sickness and in health, in good times and bad? Wasn't that the vow they'd made to each other?

"You weren't in California?"

"I was." He averted his eyes, grabbed his glass and gulped

some wine. Setting the glass back down, he grimaced, shoved away from the table and stormed into the kitchen. Ellie heard the clink of ice in a glass, the slosh of liquid being poured. He returned with a glass of Scotch. Evidently, wine wasn't his drink of choice when he was annihilating his wife.

"You were in California," she said. She could hear an accusation in her voice, a heavy layer of distrust.

"Yes." He drank some Scotch, then met her gaze. "So was the woman."

"Oh, my God." She felt nauseous, but there was nothing in her stomach, nothing but a sip of wine. Closing her eyes, she flashed on a picture of her husband, naked, his beautiful, rugged body stretched out alongside—*who?*

Another woman.

"I'm sorry," he said.

"You're *sorry?*"

"I am. Really."

Her steak knife lay temptingly close to her right hand. She nudged it away. "What is this, an act of contrition? Do you expect me to exonerate you? Cleanse your soul? What?"

"I'm telling you because I love you," he said. "Because we've always been honest with each other. I didn't want to have sex with her. I wanted you. But I couldn't have you for so long—"

"So you went looking for someone else?"

"I didn't go looking. She was there, and she offered."

"Oh, my God." The image of Curt flickered through her imagination again, only this time she visualized the woman— petite, dark-haired, with bright red lipstick. "Moira? Your old law partner?"

He closed his eyes and exhaled. "I'm sorry," he said again.

"I'll bet you are," she muttered. Her mind spun, her

thoughts flying out in all directions, as if her brain were a centrifuge.

"It wasn't what I wanted."

"It wasn't? What happened, did she force you? Did she rape you? What do you mean, it wasn't what you wanted?"

He cursed under his breath. "Okay, yes, I was willing. What I wanted was *you*. But you made it very clear over the past year and a half that that wasn't an option."

"Don't lay this on me," she retorted. "I didn't betray you."

"You locked me out, Ellie. I was going crazy."

"You were horny."

"Yes, I was horny," he retaliated, his anger rising to match hers. "I felt as if I had no wife anymore."

"You had a wife who was hurting, who was broken—"

"I had a wife who shrank from me whenever I touched her. How do you think that made me feel?"

Tears burned Ellie's eyes. She'd been so hopeful about his homecoming. But this man who came home, this man who looked like Curt and sat at her dining-room table—he couldn't possibly be the man she'd trusted with her heart and soul, the man she'd promised to love as long as they both lived.

"Why are you even telling me this? Why didn't you just lie to me?"

"I couldn't lie to you. I love you, Ellie."

"You sure have a funny way of showing it." She shoved away from the table and stormed into the kitchen, carrying her wine. Not that she could taste it, but if she drank enough of it, maybe it would numb the pain a little.

Pain. She'd grown so used to it that not suffering had been like waking up to a new world. Now she was back in the old world, the pain world. She'd climbed out of the hole and Curt had shoved her back in.

He didn't follow her into the kitchen. Standing by the sink, staring at her ghostly reflection in the dark window above it, she heard muted thumps and movements. He was moving around the dining room, taking care of things. Blowing out the candles, stacking the plates. She closed her eyes, clung to her wineglass and hugged her ribs with her free hand, as if that arm could hold her together.

Moira Kernan. His old colleague, his friend, that aggressive bitch.

Ellie knew her assessment wasn't fair. She'd met the woman a few times and she hadn't been bitchy at all. She'd been smart and funny.

And she'd been in Boston when the negotiations on this deal had begun.

She heard footsteps behind her and opened her eyes. Curt's ghost had joined hers in the window's reflection. He stood behind her, keeping his distance. No hugs tonight, no affectionate nuzzling.

"Did you sleep with her in Boston, too?" Ellie asked. Why she was pressing him for more information, she couldn't say. Hearing the details only made the pain worse.

"Yes."

His answer told her why she'd had to ask. She needed to know that he'd been unfaithful to her right here, in her territory, on her turf. He'd sneaked behind her back while she'd been at home, in this house, in their bed.

"Do you love her?"

"No."

"Then what? You used her?" Could he be that selfish?

"I didn't use her. She doesn't like attachments. It was just...a thing."

"A thing."

"Sex. No strings attached. No emotions."

"Like hiring a prostitute, only no money changed hands," Ellie said bitterly.

"It was not like hiring a prostitute. She's an old friend. She saw I was in bad shape. She offered to help."

"How charitable of her." Each word snapped from her, like brittle twigs breaking off the branch of a dead tree. "I know, you're trying to be mature and civilized about this, and you want me to be mature and civilized, too. We're having this charming little chat, you're telling me you slept with another woman and I'm supposed to—what? Thank you for your honesty? Congratulate you for scoring? I don't know. I don't know what to say. I don't know how to deal with this, Curt—except to tell you this hurts as bad as losing Peter. Something else has died—and you killed it."

Unable to say another word, she abandoned the kitchen, walked up the stairs, entered Peter's clean, tidy bedroom and closed the door.

She didn't feel safe in here. The pain was just as excruciating. But she figured that as long as she remained in that room, Curt wouldn't come after her....

THIRTEEN

Curt stared at the screen without really absorbing the images that paraded past his eyes. A few photos of Katie's graduation from college. A scene from Ellie's parents' fiftieth anniversary party a month later. A photo of him perched on a ladder outside the house, cleaning the gutters along the roof's edge, while Ellie held the ladder steady below them.

Moments in a marriage, he thought. Judging by the evidence Katie and Jessie's movie presented, no one would guess that Curt and Ellie were drifting further and further apart, that the foundation of their marriage was developing cracks that would soon expand into chasms, jeopardizing the entire structure. If Ellie had known that less than two months after that afternoon when he'd cleaned the gutters, he would have sex with another woman, would she have knocked the ladder out from under him?

The screen went black, and large white block letters appeared: Eleanor Frost's Excellent Adventure. The sign faded, replaced by footage of Ellie's parents, seated next to each other on the peach-hued brocade sofa in their living room.

"Africa!" Ellie's mother sounded astounded. "All of a sudden, out of the blue, Ellie decided to go to Africa!"

Beside her, Ellie's father shook his head. "She never seemed interested in Africa before."

"All of a sudden, she told us she was going to go to some medical center in—what was the name of that city? Kinshasa?"

"Kumasi," Ellie's father corrected her. "It's in Ghana."

"Ghana. Right. Where is that, anyway? Somewhere in Africa, I know. When she told us she was going, I was so shocked you could have knocked me over with a feather. I know that's a cliché, but that's how I felt. Absolutely shocked."

"She never said a word about Africa," Ellie's father chimed in. "Never in her whole life that I was aware of."

"But you know Ellie. She gets an idea in her head and there's no talking her out of it." Ellie's mother reflected for a moment, then added, "Maybe she went to Africa because she was bored here at home."

"I think she went because she wanted to save the world. You know Ellie."

"Yes, maybe that was it." Ellie's mother smiled. "Either she wanted to save the world or she was bored. One of those two things, that's my guess."

Ellie chuckled, and Curt found himself grinning at her parents' inanity. Of course her parents couldn't have guessed the real reason Ellie had gone to Africa—to save the world, sure, but also to get away from Curt, from the shambles he'd made of their marriage. Ellie had gone to Africa to put thousands of miles between herself and the husband who'd betrayed her.

Not that she'd ever said so to Curt. A few weeks after he'd come home from California, she'd stunned him with her announcement. He'd been waiting for her to take some appropriately dramatic action: demand that he move out of the house, perhaps, or that they see a marriage counselor, or that they get a divorce. She'd issued none of those expected demands, though.

He'd sensed that something had gone cold inside her. But she hadn't slipped back into her depression. No retreat into moping, compulsively gobbling Goldfish crackers or staring moodily at the screen saver on Peter's computer while she listened to his hip-hop music. She'd appeared full of vigor and purpose, as energetic as she'd been before Peter died.

She'd gone to work each morning, come home each afternoon, fixed supper, watched a little TV with Curt and then retired to bed, she on her side, he on his, like tolerant, well-behaved strangers. She'd kept their conversations focused on impersonal matters—the sprinkler system needed to be winterized, and she wanted to get her car in for a tune-up before the season's first snowfall, and did Katie need any financial assistance from them? Those New York rents were insanely high, and her internship at the TV station paid ridiculously little.

Then one evening, she'd said, "I'm going to Africa."

She'd learned about the program through an old friend of hers from Children's Hospital, researched it further online and submitted an application. Of course she'd been accepted. A woman with her credentials—they wanted her yesterday. How soon could she get there?

She'd had to arrange for a sabbatical with her school, but the superintendent had found a replacement and given her the semester. In mid-January, while Jessie was still home from college on her winter break, she and Curt had driven Ellie to Logan Airport and waved her off.

Sure enough, the TV screen displayed one of the photos Jessie had taken of Ellie at the airport, standing near the security checkpoint, wearing khaki slacks, a sweater and a fleece jacket and holding up her passport. In the picture she looked happy, but also a little scared. Or else maybe Curt was reading into her expression the fear he'd felt that day, that she would never come back. That fear had remained with him the entire time Ellie was gone, and with good reason. She'd returned to the United States the last day of July that past summer, but she never really did come back.

"Ellie traveled to Kumasi, Ghana, to work at a pediatrics clinic in an outlying village." Katie's voice emerged from the television's speakers while a map of Africa appeared on the screen, followed by a map of Ghana, followed by a street map of Kumasi. The civics-lesson illustrations ended with the appearance of photos that Ellie had sent home via e-mail while she'd been in Kumasi. Curt had seen all these photos—she'd sent them to him as well as the girls, attached to brief, cheerful notes describing her work and living situation. One photo showed the clinic where she'd worked, a bland, boxy white building constructed of stucco or cinderblock—hard to tell from the picture. Another showed the residence adjacent to the clinic, where she'd lived with the other volunteers. Another showed her in an open-sided, roofless Jeep, her hair held off her face by a colorful scarf and her eyes shielded from the bright sun by dark glasses. Another showed her sitting on the concrete front steps of the clinic, dressed in cargo shorts, a tank top and sandals, with a chubby brown toddler perched on her lap and several other children seated around her on the steps. She'd cut her hair at some point, and in that photo it was short and breezy.

Jessie's voice took over the narration. "After a few weeks in Ghana, Ellie learned to coexist peacefully with snakes—" a photo of a green snake slithering up the side of a palm tree appeared "—and exotic insects." Another photo showed a brightly hued butterfly resting on a palm frond. "She developed a taste for mango——" the next photo depicted her with several other volunteers in the residence kitchen "——and since Kumasi is located in a major cacoa-producing region, she also enjoyed a lot of chocolate." The next photo showed Ellie and a starchy older woman with thick gray hair proudly displaying a chocolate sheet cake. A single candle protruded from its center, and "Happy Birthday, Adrian" was written across it in white icing.

"Most important, of course, Ellie had the chance to help children who weren't like the privileged middle-class children she treated back home. She assisted in surgeries, gave physical examinations, vaccinated children and worked with their families on general health issues." A series of photographs showed Ellie in various poses with her patients. In one, a toddler hugged her leg. In another, she held a thumb-sucking youngster high in her arms. In another, she leaned over a bed, where a toothy little boy lay waving at the camera. In yet another, she sat on the floor in a play area filled with toys and children, several of whom were climbing on her while she laughed.

"Ellie also developed close friendships with her fellow volunteers," the narration continued, accompanied by a series of photos of adults: the starchy older woman with whom she'd presented the cake in the earlier photo; in this photo, the woman stood beside a desk in a cramped office. A trio of college-age girls, vamping for the camera. A tall, thin African man in scrubs. A sixty-something white woman with wiry gray hair and a bulldog face. A white man with sun-bronzed skin and long hair framing his face in rippling waves, standing beside the Jeep, a stethoscope dangling around his neck and his face set in a serious pose. The same man, standing with Ellie in front of the residence, his arm resting on her shoulders. In that photo he was smiling. So was Ellie.

Curt leaned forward, his pulse drumming inside his head. "Pause the movie," he said.

"What?"

"Hit the pause button."

Ellie did. Curt stared at the photo. *Tell me, damn it,* he wanted to shout. *Just tell me if you fell in love with the guy.* All he said was, "That was the doctor, right?"

"Adrian Wesker," Ellie said.

Curt took a deep breath, and another. Why did he need to know? What did it matter? Ellie was leaving him. Whether or not she loved some other man—whether or not she was still in love with him—was irrelevant. Once she and Curt were divorced, she would be free to fall in love a million times, with a million other men. He couldn't do a damn thing about it.

But…he had to know. Call it a compulsion. Call it the same masochistic urge that made a person touch a sore again and again, just to determine if it still hurt. He'd already lost Ellie before she'd gone to Kumasi. He'd probably lost her the day Peter died. If she fell for some other man—someone who hadn't been by her side, trying to prop her up during the long, dark days of her overwhelming grief, trying to reach her, trying to nudge, push or drag her back to sanity—he had to know.

"Tell me about him," he said. "Tell me about Dr. Wesker."

Five months ago

"ADRIAN NEEDS YOU," ROSE announced, barging into an examining room, where Ellie was scrubbing an infected sore on a little girl's hand. The girl was sniveling and flinching, even though Ellie was rubbing the wound as gently as she could.

"Why don't we soak this for a bit, and then I'll come back and dress it," Ellie said, half to Rose and half to herself. "That won't hurt you, sweetie. We're just going to stick your hand in a bowl of warm water—" she prepared the bowl as she spoke "—and you can suck on this lollipop while you soak, and when I come back I'll put some ointment on it and bandage it up." She placed the girl's hand in the bowl and glanced at Rose. "She'll need a dose of amoxicillin, too. How's our supply?"

"Adequate. Adrian's in the surgery. Go." She waved Ellie out the door.

Ellie raced down the hall to the clinic's small operating room. Any surgery that required general anesthesia was performed in one of the hospitals in the city, but Adrian could perform minor procedures that required only local anesthesia.

Ellie stopped outside the room to scrub at the sink, then shouldered through the swinging door. She was greeted by the frantic screams of a boy of about nine, who sat on the table, wearing only a pair of briefs. Adrian stood beside him, his face gleaming with perspiration. "Calm the boy down!" he shouted to Ellie above the boy's howls.

Ellie immediately moved to the table and hugged the boy. "What's going on here?" she asked in a soothing voice. "What's your name?"

"Abrafo," the boy whimpered, hiding his tearstained face against her shoulder.

"Abrafo." She stroked his wiry black hair, then peered past him at Adrian. "What are we doing for Abrafo today?"

"Removing a mole from his back," Adrian told her, his terse tone reflecting his exasperation. "If he deigns to let us."

Ellie turned back to Abrafo, easing his head away from her chest so she could gaze into his terrified eyes. "That's nothing, Abrafo. You won't feel anything. Just a little pinch when Dr. Wesker gives you a shot."

"He's cutting an animal!" Abrafo wailed.

"No, honey. Just a little piece of skin. He'll give you a shot to numb the area—that means you won't feel anything else—and then he'll use a little tool called a scalpel to remove this skin, and then he'll sew a stitch or two and put a bandage on it. That's all."

"It's an animal," Abrafo said. His skinny shoulders trembled against her hands.

"No, it's a…oh!" She let out a laugh. "It's not that kind of mole, the little furry animal that burrows in the ground. A mole on your skin is a dot of discolored skin. Sometimes it forms a little bump. Look—here's a mole." She extended her arm and displayed the small brown mark that had adorned the side of her wrist for as long as she could remember. "When it's in a place where it won't get inflamed, doctors leave it alone. But if it's raised, or it can get irritated, doctors sometimes remove the mole so it won't cause you any trouble."

"This mole—not an animal?"

"No, Abrafo. It's just a little dot, like this." She let him touch her wrist.

He issued a final, shuddering sob, then relaxed in her arms. She grinned at Adrian above Abrafo's head. "Let's lie down, now, so Dr. Wesker can get rid of that little dot of skin. Okay?"

Clinging to her hand, Abrafo lay on his stomach. A few hiccups emerged from him as Adrian swabbed antiseptic on the mole—larger than Ellie's, slightly raised and located near where the waistband of his trousers would likely rub it raw. The actual surgery took no more than five minutes, and while Adrian sutured Abrafo Ellie placed the excised mole into a sterile envelope to be sent to the hospital for a biopsy. It looked benign to her, but the biopsy was a routine procedure whenever a mole was removed.

Once the surgery was completed, Abrafo shook the sterile towels surrounding the surgery site from his back and jumped happily down from the table, announcing that he was going to get dressed. Ellie could barely contain him as he bounded toward the door. As he swung through it, Ellie caught him, scooped him into her arms and carried him down the hall to a waiting area where his mother sat, holding his clothes. "Everything's fine," she assured the mother as she lowered Abrafo to his feet. Her arms had developed some extra muscle over the past few months from carrying children around.

After accepting thanks from Abrafo's mother, Ellie pivoted and jogged back down the hall to the surgery, where she found Adrian peeling off his gloves. "If I didn't stink of iodine, I'd give you a hug right now," he told her as he tossed the gloves into a trash receptacle. "I intend to give you one later. Maybe your magic will rub off on me."

"I have no intention of letting you rub anything off me," she teased. They'd been working together too long, in too close quarters, not to be able to tease each other.

"I want your magic, Ellie. I don't know how you do it. But I shall sing your praises—and perhaps rub some part of you— later. Right now, I have to go and give Abrafo's mother her post-op instructions."

SHE DIDN'T SEE ADRIAN AGAIN until dinner. Gerda had left Kumasi in May, replaced by a cheerful young Canadian couple, both physician's assistants. The trio of college girls would be departing soon and a fresh batch of college volunteers arriving. Ellie would miss the girls more than she missed Gerda. They reminded her of Katie and Jessie, and they were always laughing, yammering, bubbling with enthusiasm. They'd shown Ellie the best places to shop for local handcrafted jewelry and apparel. Ellie supposed she would have to pass all that vital information along to the next crew when they arrived.

Adrian swept into the dining room at the compound five minutes later than everyone else, as usual. "There she is," he bellowed, gesturing grandly toward Ellie before he joined her and the others at the table. "All ye, sing her praises. She soothes the savage breast."

"A good brassiere can do that," she joked.

"I had an hysterical little boy in the surgery today. Absolutely frantic because I was going to remove a mole from his back. It took Ellie to wrest from him the fact that he thought I was planning to cut an *animal* from his back."

This news was met with gentle laughter.

"I would have called it a nevus, but I thought he might find the sound of that far more alarming. So medical, that term."

"Was it cancerous?" Rose asked.

Ellie shook her head and Adrian said, "I think not. It looked innocuous, but it was raised and had the potential to become problematic. We'll get the pathology report next week, but I believe the child will be fine."

A conversation ensued about how much rarer skin cancer was in Africa than in other parts of the world, despite the intensity of the sun in equatorial regions. "Melanin protects the skin," Atu boasted, displaying his dark forearms. "Mother Nature's sunblock."

As the others discussed skin pigmentation, Adrian leaned toward Ellie. "I need to talk to you," he murmured. "Are you free tonight?"

Why wouldn't she be free? Most evenings after dinner, she and the rest of the staff saw more patients and completed paperwork for which there hadn't been time during the day, and then they retired to bed early. Their days were so full no one had the energy to carouse all night. "Sure, I'm free," she said.

After dinner, she, Adrian and the others returned to the clinic. Fortunately, it was a calm evening: a child with a splintered toenail that had to be removed, another child who'd jammed her finger and required an X-ray, a new mother worried about whether she was producing enough milk for her chronically hungry infant. No emergencies, no crises.

By nine, all the patients had been seen and the sky had faded to a canopy of black dappled with stars and tacked in one corner by a lemon-colored crescent moon. Adrian found Ellie in the clinic's modest pharmacy, where she was filling out an order form for drugs. "Come, Ellie," he beckoned. "I've finished making the evening rounds, and our overnight guests are all comfortable and cozy. I've got two very cold beers waiting for us at my house, if you're interested."

"That sounds great." Ellie smiled at him, then signed the order form and dropped it on Rose's abandoned desk before she left the building with him. The night air was hot and sticky, and fireflies danced above the dry tufts of grass lining the road.

Adrian's house was a two-room cottage a short walk from the clinic. He rarely invited his colleagues there, since he spent so much of his time at the clinic working, eating and socializing with the staff. Ellie had visited his cottage only a few times—once to drop off a file of documents on a day when he'd been planning to meet with some of the clinic's British benefactors at one of the fancy hotels in the city, another time when he'd hosted a birthday party for a former patient of his who'd been diagnosed with leukemia four years ago but had defied the odds and remained in remission. For the most part, though, Adrian's cottage was his private refuge, and folks from the clinic stayed away. That he'd invited Ellie to have a beer with him there was an unusual privilege.

The cottage included a screened porch with a long-bladed fan in the ceiling, circulating the steamy air. He'd decorated it austerely, with a few wicker pieces and a ceramic urn on the floor in one corner, a comically glowering face painted across its curved surface.

He motioned for her to sit on one of the wicker rocking chairs, then vanished inside and emerged a minute later with two chilled bottles of beer. He lit the citronella candle that sat on the rattan table between their chairs. Dispensing with glasses, Adrian clicked his beer bottle's neck against hers in a toast, then drank. Ellie drank, too. The icy bubbles bit her tongue and cooled her entire body.

"Ellie," he said, smiling. "I have a proposition for you."

"It better not have anything to do with rubbing," she warned.

"It has to do with your magic," he told her, then leaned back and nudged his chair, starting it rocking. The motion drew her eyes to his feet. He'd left his shoes inside. She rarely went barefoot, concerned about picking up a parasite or some other skin problem, but she supposed Adrian's bare feet were reasonably protected in his own house. "I'd like you to stay," he said.

"Stay?" An undefined emotion sizzled down her spine. Apprehension? Excitement? She wasn't sure. She tried not to glance at his naked feet again. "Stay where?"

"Here at the clinic. You signed up for six months. I'd like you to stay longer. What's the word you Yankees use? Re-up, I believe that's it. I'd like you to re-up."

"Oh." Another ripple of mixed-up emotions passed through her. She was relieved, flattered and, for no good reason, a touch disappointed.

"You're scheduled to leave us at the end of July. That's a little over a month from now. Surely you're not ready to say farewell yet."

She considered his statement. She was happy in Kumasi, much happier than she'd been at home. Partly that was because the work was so rewarding, partly because she was too busy to mope. Partly because she'd needed to get away from Curt and from a house haunted by excruciating memories. She liked living where people knew about her only what she wished for them to know, where they didn't gaze at her with pity or treat her as if she were frail and helpless. She liked feeling that she was doing something worthwhile, making a difference in a few children's lives, healing them.

But she was merely a visitor here, a legal alien on a visa. Every morning when she woke up in her narrow bed in her barren little room, and when she ate fried bananas for breakfast and drank local coffee so strong, one cup could power her through the entire day, she knew this was not her home. She knew it when she heard the local radio station playing unfamiliar music. She knew it in her conversations with the locals, with their accented English and their Twi slang and their superstitions.

"I can't," she said, shaking her head. "It's nice to be asked, Adrian, but I can't."

"Why the bloody hell not?"

She laughed. Adrian had a tendency to assume that any opinion contradicting his own was utterly wrong. His obstinacy helped to keep the clinic functioning and funds flowing in, but it also occasionally made him seem mule-headed and unsympathetic.

"I've got a job waiting for me back in Massachusetts," she reminded him. "I've got a home there. I miss my daughters."

"And your daughters' father? You don't miss him, then?"

She hadn't discussed her marital troubles with anyone at the clinic. They knew she had a husband, even though she'd stopped wearing her wedding band and eternity ring shortly after her arrival. She'd told herself that was for practical reasons: given her work, she was simply more comfortable without them.

Sometimes, though, she wondered whether feeling more comfortable without her rings had anything at all to do with her work.

Adrian had no right to ask her about her husband—except that everyone at the clinic formed such a tight community, and they were all always nosing around in one another's business. When their wireless Internet connection jammed and no one could e-mail home, as happened once a week on average, they would all bitch and moan about the people they absolutely needed to reach. The college girls all had boyfriends. Gerda had a daughter and two grandchildren. Although he was a local, Atu had friends all over the continent, and he claimed he met most of the women he socialized with through dating sites on the Web.

Ellie was as eager as anyone for news from home, and the girls always supplied her with plenty. Katie wrote delicious e-mails crammed with details about her new job in Manhattan, her efforts to furnish the apartment she shared with two roommates on a minuscule budget, her success at discovering discount theater tickets and free concerts. Jessie had landed a summer internship at a legal-aid clinic in downtown Boston, and she filled Ellie in on the clients she interviewed and the cases the clinic took on.

Curt's e-mails, unlike the girls', were generally cautious and measured. He mentioned that the lawn service had raised its prices, that her father asked him to remind her to bring home some interesting Ghanaian postage stamps, that he'd gone golfing with a few of the guys from the firm, and while he shot a respectable 110, he still thought golf was one of the most boring games ever invented.

The most romantic he ever got in his missives was, "Looking forward to seeing you," and, "I hope you're having a good time." He didn't sign his notes "love." Neither did she.

Did she miss him? Adrian was awaiting an answer he didn't deserve.

But she was five thousand miles from home—and home was a place where her son had died and her husband had broken their wedding vows.

"No," she heard herself say, even though she wasn't certain it was true. She missed the man Curt used to be, the man she'd trusted with all her heart. But she would have missed that man just as much if she'd stayed home as she did here. "I'm afraid I don't miss him."

"Ah." Adrian mulled that over in silence. Beyond the screened walls of his porch, insects peeped and chirped in the shadows. Occasionally a car or bicycle meandered down the road. Above her, the fan hummed. "Well, you aren't the first person who came here to get away from a sticky situation."

"I came here to find myself," she reminded him.

"And to lose yourself, too. I remember." He shot her a grin, his teeth glinting white in the evening's gloom. "When I took over the clinic, it was shortly after I'd endured an ugly divorce. I don't suppose there's any other kind of divorce, is there?"

She smiled wistfully. "I don't know."

"I've never heard of a beautiful divorce. Or a lovely one. Rumors exist of a few so-called friendly divorces, but surely if the involved parties were all that friendly, a divorce would be unnecessary. In any event, this is a good place to lose oneself after a divorce, be it beautiful, ugly or otherwise."

"I'm not divorced, Adrian."

"Just in a bad spot with the man, then."

"I guess." She sipped some beer. "But that's not why I came here."

"Oh, of course not," he said, sarcasm layering each word. In a blander tone, he added, "Your reasons are your own. I'm happy to share my reasons for wanting you to stay, however. You are a wonder with the children. You and I work well together, better than I've worked with Atu or most of the nurse volunteers who've been in and out over the years. When you encounter a frenzied little boy, you have the wit to figure out that he's in a state because he thinks I'm going to remove an animal from his back." Adrian leaned forward, his eyes startling in their intensity. "I need you here, Ellie. We rub along quite well together. Ah, there's that word again—rub."

"'Aye, there's the rub,'" she quoted.

Adrian chuckled. "Think about it, love. You could stay as long as you wanted. You could fly home, see your daughters and then return. All I ask is that you think about it."

"That's not all you ask, Adrian," she argued with a smile. "But okay, I'll think about it."

FOR THE NEXT COUPLE OF WEEKS, she thought of little else. Of course, she thought about what she was doing with her patients. She thought about prescribing steroids for a boy's itchy rash, and about whether or not to urge a young girl to wear a sling to protect her fractured wrist, and about explaining the facts of life to a ten-year-old girl who'd raced to the clinic one morning afraid she was dying because blood was oozing from her private place and no one had ever told her that this was normal.

But Ellie also thought about staying in Kumasi, and about going home. She wasn't sure what was waiting for her back in Massachusetts. She'd been gone nearly six months. Had Curt been indulging in multiple flings in her absence? Or maybe found one special woman and started building a relationship with her?

Did Ellie really want to go back and find out?

Did she want to hide from her reality? Would remaining in Ghana be about continuing to do some good for the children of the villages bordering Kumasi, or would it be about trying to avoid the painful truths about her life? Were those truths all wrapped up in Curt and her marriage, or were they somewhere inside her? If they were inside her, wouldn't they emerge regardless of whether she continued to work at the clinic or returned home?

"I can't stay," she finally told Adrian one evening. She'd found him in his office at 9:00 p.m., reading through some papers. He looked worn out from a typically long, demanding day, but not tired. He always seemed to have more energy than anyone else at the clinic. It radiated from him, a corona of vigor spreading around him in invisible waves.

"No need to stay," he assured her. "I'm just proofreading a grant proposal. Bloody bore, but it's got to be done. I can lock up here."

"I meant, I can't stay in Kumasi beyond the end of July."

He lowered the sheaf of papers he'd been reading, rotated in his chair and stood to face her. "I've failed to persuade you of your indispensability, then?"

"I appreciate that you think so highly of me, Adrian, but…" She sighed. "I realized that if I stayed, it would be because I was afraid of facing my problems at home. I may be a coward, but I've tried to develop some courage while I'm here."

"Good heavens, Ellie, you're one of the most courageous people I know. I've never seen you flinch from a snake or a suppurating wound. You've driven around the countryside with me in the Jeep, and I've been told by other passengers that riding with me can be a near-death experience. Yet you've done it without a moment's hesitation."

"Riding in a Jeep with you is easy," she said with a sad laugh. "Coming to terms with an estranged husband is hard."

"Then don't do it," Adrian suggested. Ellie hadn't realized how close he stood to her until he extended his hand, snagged hers and pulled her toward him. "Forget about him for a while. Stay."

He touched his lips to hers, and she felt a strange rush of sensation, fear and desire twining through her. She'd been aware of Adrian's sex appeal from the moment she'd met him—even before she'd met him, since Rose had warned her not to fall for him. And she hadn't. He was a friend, a partner, a comrade-in-arms. A brilliant doctor. A man who lavished her with praise and made her feel more confident than she had in years. A man who inspired her to do her best, to embrace new challenges—to be unafraid.

And damn, being kissed by him felt wonderful. Even after a long day he smelled clean and fresh, of hospital soap and laundered cotton. His mouth tasted of mint. He was warm and limber and...God, it had been so long since she'd felt like a sexual being.

She kissed him back. At first her lips seemed stiff, as if she'd forgotten how to kiss. She hadn't, though. What she'd forgotten was what being kissed felt like—the warmth, the pressure, the eroticism of a man's breath mingling with hers. She'd forgotten, but now Adrian was reminding her.

She wrapped her arms around his neck and he wrapped his around her waist, and they swayed in a subtle dance as their mouths merged and opened and claimed. Standing in his tiny office, in the glare of a buzzing fluorescent light, surrounded by heaps of paperwork and steel file cabinets, Ellie reveled in Adrian's heat, his strength, his obvious passion for her.

She wasn't sure how long they kissed, or who broke from whom. But eventually they leaned away from each other, both of them breathing hard. Adrian pushed her hair back from her face, his fingers long and graceful as they combed through the strands. "You could forget about him for a while," he repeated, his voice a seductive murmur. "I could make you forget."

He could. His invitation tempted her.

But as she gazed into his face, she understood that she couldn't accept it. "No. I can't do this."

"Why not?"

Because she didn't *love* Adrian. Because she'd given her heart to Curt and he'd broken it into pieces and flung it back at her—except that he'd clung to some of the pieces. She couldn't make love with another man as long as Curt still had a hold on her. And to her great regret, he did.

"I just can't," she said desolately. "I'm sorry." She rose on her toes to kiss his cheek, then turned and left the office....

FOURTEEN

"I'VE ALREADY TOLD YOU about him," Ellie said, her tone flat. "He was a brilliant doctor. British. A bit monomaniacal. He had a good sense of humor. Other than that, there's nothing to tell."

Curt stared at the television, still displaying the image of the monomaniacal, humorous doctor with his arm around Ellie. What was that old slogan about Las Vegas? What Ellie had done in Kumasi stayed in Kumasi, right?

Yet he couldn't get past it. He couldn't look at that picture on the screen and *not know.*

He shoved out of the chair, crossed to the bed and lowered himself to sit on it, careful not to crowd her. She held her ground, refusing to shift away from him. "Ellie," he said, then swallowed the catch in his voice. "I know things have gone south for us. We're getting a divorce. What we had is gone, and if you want to place all the blame on me, I'm not going to fight you about that. But damn it, I was honest with you. We always had honesty. And I can't bear the thought that we don't have that anymore."

She studied him, appearing both curious and defiant. "I haven't lied to you."

"You haven't told me the truth, either. Did you sleep with him? Did you fall in love with him?"

She shifted her gaze to the television, then back to Curt. "That's none of your business."

"Your sex life isn't my business. Your honesty is. Don't take that from me, Ellie. Please."

Her eyes went soft, like dark chocolate melting. Her lips turned in a faint smile. "No," she said. "I didn't sleep with him. I didn't fall in love with him."

Curt hadn't realized he was holding his breath until it emerged from him in a sigh. Just because she hadn't slept with the brilliant doctor didn't mean she loved Curt. She hadn't slept with *him,* either.

Her smile grew. "For all you know," she pointed out, "he wasn't interested in me."

"He was interested," Curt argued, glancing at the two of them posed on the TV. "Look at him. You can tell."

Ellie aimed the remote control at the TV and poked a button with her thumb. The screen went black.

If only getting rid of one's past could be that easy. If only he had a remote control with a button he could press to make all his mistakes disappear. "You should have slept with him," he said glumly. "If you had, we'd be even."

Ellie snorted. "It's not a contest, Curt. A marriage isn't a game where you score points and hope for a tie."

Curt agreed with a shrug. "But maybe if you'd slept with him, you wouldn't hate me so much. You'd understand why I did what I did, even though it was incredibly stupid."

"I understand why you did what you did," she said, her tone surprisingly gentle.

"But you can't forgive me for doing it."

She ran her thumb along the edge of the remote control, her eyes focused inward on her own thoughts. Maybe he'd hoped she would finally relent and offer her forgiveness, but she didn't. She just moved her thumb back and forth on the black plastic, gazing at nothing, ruminating.

No forgiveness. Fine. Curt moved on. "So you didn't sleep with him. But you came home a different person."

"By the time I came home, I wasn't a basket case anymore."

"You were cool and collected. No—you were cold and reserved." He forced the words out. "You weren't wearing your wedding band. Something happened over there that made you decide you wanted a divorce."

"The only thing that happened over there was that I realized I could function on my own. I could accomplish things. I could take care of myself. I could live some good days and go to bed feeling as if my life was worth something." Her gaze sought his. "And the divorce was something we both decided."

He conceded the point, reluctantly. He recalled checking out her hand every day for weeks after she'd gotten back to see if her ring had made a reappearance. When it hadn't, he'd confronted her. Over one of their cold, reserved dinners, he'd asked, "Are you ever going to wear your wedding band again?"

She'd touched her bare finger and closed her eyes. "What's the point, Curt? We can't go back to where we used to be."

"Do you want a divorce?" He'd had to force the words out, yet they'd emerged low and even, as if they'd possessed some inherent logic. Perhaps they had. He and Ellie had lost a son. They'd lost each other. They could never get Peter back; maybe they could never get each other back either.

She'd stopped rubbing the naked base of her ring finger and

gazed steadily at him. "That would probably be the most sensible thing."

If Ellie could discuss such a devastating emotional step in terms of how sensible it was, he'd supposed, she must have given the subject plenty of thought already. That late-summer night over dinner had been the first time he'd allowed himself even to think the word *divorce,* let alone speak it. Yet she hadn't seemed surprised. She'd already reached a conclusion. She'd decided to be sensible.

He loved Ellie. He'd wanted her happy. That was all he'd ever wanted, for her to be happy and whole. "All right, then," he'd said. He could have fought her—he'd always loved a good fight—but this fight wouldn't have been good. They would have been fighting over whether Ellie deserved to live the rest of her life the way she wanted to. He couldn't deny her that right.

Yet he'd never wanted a divorce, and he definitely didn't want one now, even though he wondered if he could remain married to a woman unable to forgive him. "What if I told you I was opposed to divorce?" he asked carefully, watching her and bracing himself. He had no idea what her reaction would be.

"Curt…"

The hell with being careful. He was in a battle for his future, for his family, for everything that mattered to him. He was a natural-born fighter, and he had to shoot for a victory. "We've just watched a movie of your life—and a lot of it is our lives together. We've lived so much, shared so much. There's so much affection on that DVD, Ellie. So much joy. I don't give a damn if you can't forgive me. I don't care that you think I'm some kind of monster for what I did. I don't want a divorce."

Her eyes widened. "I never thought you were a monster."

"A sex-crazed beast."

She opened her mouth to dispute him, then shut it and gave him another enigmatic smile. "You want to argue semantics?"

"I want to argue about putting our marriage back together, Ellie."

"We've been discussing a divorce for the past two months. Why didn't you say something earlier?"

"Because *you* wanted the divorce. And I thought, if that's what it would take for Ellie to be happy, then that's what we'd do. Because I can't stand the thought of you going through the rest of your life as sad as you've been."

"And now...what? You *do* want me to go through the rest of my life sad?" The absurdity of her statement made them both smile. Then, simultaneously, they stopped smiling. "Why are you telling me this now?"

"I saw that movie." He gestured toward the television. "And I realized my happiness is important, too." He shifted on the mattress, turning to face her fully. "I crossed a line. God knows I did, Ellie—but it was because I felt as if we were both slowly dying. I struggled to keep you from going under, but nothing I tried worked. So I finally figured I had to save myself. I wasn't looking for fun. I wasn't looking for excitement or passion or love. All I wanted was to feel like I wasn't dead." He sighed, scrutinizing her, wishing she were easier to read. What was she thinking of this overwrought confession? Was she even listening to him? Did she care?

"What I did was wrong. I admit it. I bared my soul to you, told you what I'd done, apologized as many ways as I could. I didn't want another woman. I didn't want an affair. All I wanted was you, Ellie. All I've ever wanted was you."

Her eyes glistened, and she lowered them to stare at her hands in her lap. He lowered his eyes, too. She might not have been wearing her wedding band and eternity ring when she'd stepped off the plane at Logan Airport a couple of months ago, but she was wearing them tonight. Only because she'd been faking it for her parents, but the reason didn't matter as much as the fact that those two bands—one gold, one set with diamonds—circled her finger.

He eased the remote control out of her hand and tossed it onto the night table. Then he lifted her hand to his lips and kissed her ring finger. He felt the hard edge of the diamonds against the inner skin of his lip, the smoothness of the gold band, the silken softness of her skin.

"Forgive me, Ellie," he murmured, then rotated her hand and kissed her palm. Her fingers curled reflexively, and he heard the whisper of her breath. "Forgive me," he implored, pulling her toward him as he leaned forward. "Please. Forgive me."

He touched his mouth to hers.

SHE FORGAVE HIM. AS HER body softened and her breath deepened just from the gentle warmth of his lips on hers, she realized that she'd forgiven him a long time ago.

She waited for his kiss to build in intensity, like the kiss he'd given her outside the keeping room downstairs. But he held back, lightly grazing her mouth with his, a brush of skin against skin, no tongue, no teeth, no wild passion. Quiet and subtle, he seduced her with patience and self-control. No demands, no fire. Only this: a man who wanted her.

She wanted him, too. She'd wanted him all along, from that first night on Hope Street when he'd convinced her that her dreams and goals were noble, and that refusing to mold herself to other people's expectations didn't make her a failure. She'd wanted him when she'd fallen asleep beside him that night, and when she'd awakened in his arms the next morning, and every day since then. She'd wanted him when they were apart—Curt in law school, Ellie still finishing college—and when they were together, and when they got married, and when they had children.

She'd wanted him even after one of those children had died.

She'd been unable to acknowledge the want then. All she'd felt had been crushing grief. And so much time had passed, she'd assumed she would never be able to feel anything other than crushing grief again.

But she *could* feel other things. Right now, she felt her body stirring, awakening from a long hibernation and realizing how hungry it was. Like pins and needles that flooded a sleeping limb as sensation returned to it, the sensation hurt, but she reveled in the hurt. It was a good hurt.

She reached up with her free hand and cupped Curt's cheek. She had touched his face a million times, but its warmth and texture seemed new to her. Even though he'd shaved before they'd left the house to meet her parents for what was supposed to have been a quiet birthday dinner, his jaw was slightly scratchy from his beard. How long had they been at the inn, eating, talking, recovering from the surprise party and watching the movie of her life? How long had they been trapped in this romantic prison of a room, trying to figure out where they would go once they checked out?

Long enough, she decided. Long enough for her to admit she still loved her husband.

He must have detected a change in her, a surrender, because he deepened the kiss. Only a little bit, only a tilt to his face, a gentle nip on her lower lip, a tightening of his fingers around her hand. For long minutes, that was all—just teasing, coaxing kisses, full of promise.

Was he waiting for another signal from her? Was she supposed to make the next move?

She wasn't sure she could do that.

Fortunately, she didn't have to. He guided the hand he held to his shoulder, then released it and dug his fingers into her hair. And opened his mouth over hers.

Their tongues touched. When he'd kissed her downstairs, their tongues had fought aggressively, almost angrily. But this was just sweetness, a tender invitation. He stroked her tongue with his, traced the surface of her teeth, withdrew and slid his tongue lazily across her lower lip. His languid pace served only to arouse her more completely. Her thighs clenched and a pool of heat spread low in her belly.

If she'd had any breath in her, she might have asked him to speed things along. But her lungs seemed to have ceased working, and perhaps her brain as well. She had no choice but to float along on his current, accept it, enjoy it—if she could let herself.

Still kissing her, he moved his hands through her hair and down the sides of her neck to the jacket of her outfit. The fabric was gauzy and light, and when he eased it off her shoulders it floated down her arms to her elbows. She let go of him and the jacket fell free of her hands. Curt stroked the newly bared skin, his palms warm against her.

He pulled back, then dipped his head to kiss her throat. She heard herself sigh. She knew where they were going with this—however slowly—and she told herself she was willing to travel that road with Curt. They could figure everything out afterward. Right now... She sighed again. Right now, all she wanted was his mouth exploring the ridge of her collarbone, his fingers playing over the fabric of her sleeveless top and under her arms. Were armpits an erogenous zone? Tonight, hers were.

"Oh, Ellie…" That was all he said—her name, spoken reverently. Just her name and his mouth and his hands, moving down her sides to the hem of her blouse and slipping beneath it. "Ellie…"

She traced his forearms, sinewy muscle and bone and a downy layer of hair, and then reached the bunched cotton of his sleeves where he'd rolled them up. Was she supposed to tear off his shirt? His hands were on her midriff and she wanted her hands on his. She wanted to feel the broad, supple surface of his chest. But his kisses seemed to drug her. She didn't think she could handle his shirt. Buttons were beyond her.

He bailed her out by leaning back again and unbuttoning his shirt for her. He shrugged out of it and tossed it onto the floor. She gazed at his chest—like his face, familiar yet new. He'd been spending a lot of time at the fitness center, probably because over the past couple of years jogging on a treadmill and sweating through a Nautilus workout were more fun than hanging around the house with her—or hanging around the house by himself while she'd been in Ghana. His efforts showed. His biceps were clearly defined, his abdominal muscles sculpted slabs.

He was so beautiful. And he wanted her. After everything, he still wanted her.

He lifted her blouse and she dutifully raised her hands so he could pull it off. Her bra wasn't anything special; she'd replaced frills and lace with discreet engineering as her breasts went soft with age. Curt appeared enthralled by the plain garment, smooth and beige. He rose onto his knees and kissed a path over the swells of flesh above the cups, at last settling his mouth in the hollow between. He made a sound—of pleasure, of frustration, maybe both. It took more courage than Ellie knew she had to grope behind her back for the clasp and undo it. The bra fell slack and Curt moaned.

She leaned back into the pillows as he kissed her breasts, languidly, delicately, taunting her with his leisurely progress. When his mouth closed over one nipple she felt her womb tighten and throb. When he rubbed his thumb over the other, she felt dampness between her thighs.

She wanted him. Wanted him madly. Wanted everything she knew he could give her, every exquisite pleasure he could bring her. She wanted her skirt removed, and his pants. She wanted him on top of her, inside her, giving them both what she'd denied them for so long.

"Curt—"

He raised his head and peered at her. "Should I stop?" he asked, so solemnly she knew that if she said yes, he would.

"No."

"Tell me what you want."

Happiness. Love. My life. My husband. "You," she said.

He leaned back on his haunches, undid his belt, yanked down his zipper. Before she could blink, his trousers and briefs were gone. His efficient search of her skirt located the waistband button, and within a minute the skirt was gone, too, along with her nylons and panties. But instead of taking her, he stretched out on his side, rolled her onto her side facing him and gazed into her face while his hand roamed up and down her body. "I don't want to rush you," he said.

Go ahead, rush me, she longed to plead. *Rush me so I don't have to think.*

He seemed to be doing plenty of thinking. He didn't smile, didn't look away from her. His expression was pensive as he let his hand dip into the slope of her waist. He skimmed her shins with his toes, lured her knee between his legs, stretched to caress her bottom. And just kept kissing her.

Please don't make me take the lead, she silently begged. *I'm not up to that. I can't.*

Kisses. More kisses. His hands on the backs of her thighs, his fingers brushing over the creases behind her knees. Kisses on the bridge of her nose, on the bottom edge of her earlobe while his thumb dug through her hair to her nape. Kisses as he inched closer to her, as she felt his heat vibrating in the narrow space between them, as his erection pressed into her belly.

At last he guided her onto her back and eased her legs apart. Even feeling how wet she was, he didn't smile. He played his fingers over her, slid one into her, watched the twitch of her hips, the curl of her toes, until she was sure she'd burst. So long since she'd felt that pulsing heat inside her. So long since she'd felt anything other than numb.

"Are you ready?" he asked, even though the answer was pretty obvious.

"Yes." She barely had the strength to speak. All her energy had gathered down below, where Curt was touching her.

"Because I could—"

"Yes," she groaned.

He allowed himself a hint of a smile at her impatience, then stretched out above her. She felt him against her, testing, and then slowly—oh, God, so slowly—he locked his body to hers.

In spite of her arousal, his invasion hurt. Years had passed since the last time she'd done this. But she welcomed the discomfort and willed herself to relax as he rocked above her, his thrusts controlled but deep, so deep. He propped himself on his elbows and continued to watch her, searching for signs of—what? Climax? Anger? Regret?

Did he fear that their entire marriage hinged on what was happening right now? Did *she* fear that?

She closed her eyes and lifted her hips. She loved this, loved the lush rhythm of it, the friction, the way her body gradually remembered, recognized Curt and accommodated his movements. She loved his weight, his fingers tangling into her hair, the pumping of his abdomen against hers.

This was enough, she told herself. Accepting him, his body, his love—it was enough. She didn't need or expect more than what she felt right now.

"Come for me, Ellie," he whispered.

She opened her eyes and looked up at him. She saw the strain in his face, his need for release rising inside him. He didn't rush, though, didn't force. Just asked.

"Let go, honey. Come for me."

She couldn't. She'd gone this far. It was enough.

He shifted, changing his angle, increasing the contact between them, and suddenly *enough* was no longer relevant. Heat built inside her, burned through her resistance. Instinct took over and she arched to meet him. She couldn't stop her response, not anymore. It thundered through her, leaving her shattered, exhausted, in tears. She'd let go—of herself, her fear and her fury. It was wonderful. It was awful.

She was demolished.

Curt groaned and shuddered. A tremor racked his body. His arms shook as he held himself steady above her, and his breath emerged brokenly. "Oh, Ellie... Don't cry, baby. Don't cry."

Just as she couldn't keep herself from responding to his love-making, she couldn't keep her tears from spilling over. He eased onto his back and gathered her in his arms, letting her sob against his chest. She wept for what she'd found in this bed, and for what she'd lost. She wept for the years her marriage had been all but dead. She wept for Curt's betrayal, and for her own.

He stroked his hand through her hair, soothing. "Talk to me, Ellie. This wasn't so bad, was it?"

"It was good," she said, her lips tasting the salt of her tears on his skin.

"It was good," he agreed, only when he said it the words sounded like a ridiculous understatement. "We've got this. We can work out the rest."

"I don't know."

"I *do* know. If you're not ready to forgive me, I'll wait. You know I love you. As long as it takes, I'll wait. There's no deadline here. We'll get through it."

"No." She wished she had the willpower to pull out of his embrace. His arm was so strong and protective around her, his chest so firm beneath her cheek. If she could close her eyes and lie with him on this grand brass bed in this charming room forever, maybe she'd never have to confront the truth.

Curt's voice was soft and lulling. "Tell me," he urged her. "Why can't we get through it?"

"It's me," she said, at long last allowing the truth out. "I forgive you, Curt. It's *me* I can't forgive."

"You did nothing you have to forgive yourself for," he argued. "You were so depressed, remember? You were a wreck. It's not your fault you didn't bounce back. That's what you told me, and you were right. Whatever happened between us wasn't your fault."

"You don't know, Curt." She swallowed down her final sob and inhaled deeply to calm herself. "I don't deserve your love. I don't deserve—this." She gestured vaguely at the bed. "It is my fault. All of it."

"Give me a little credit, Ellie. I had something to do with the mess we made of our marriage."

"I'm not talking about what you did, Curt. I'm talking about what I did." *Say it,* she ordered herself. *He wants your honesty.* "I'm talking about Peter."

"What about him?"

"I killed him."

FIFTEEN

For a moment, Curt couldn't move. As if someone had injected him with one of those poisons that paralyzed a person, he couldn't breathe, couldn't lift his hand, couldn't blink his eyes. His heart stopped beating.

Just moments ago, it had been beating so hard, he wouldn't have been surprised to see it burst through his ribs. The sex—damn, it wasn't sex. It was love. What he and Ellie had just experienced transcended sex. It transcended their bodies. It was the most intimate, the most personal, the most emotional connection he'd ever felt with a woman.

Sex was what he'd experienced with Moira. They'd enjoyed each other, satisfied each other, but his soul had been light-years removed from the act. The evening at her hotel room in Boston, he'd been half-crazed with hunger and self-loathing. The few days they'd spent together in California, he'd been a little less crazed and a lot more riddled with guilt. When he'd volunteered to travel to California to finish up the Benzer deal, he'd known the real reason he wanted to fly to the West Coast. Whatever happened between him and Moira during that trip had been intentional. Curt had known what would happen. He'd hoped it would happen.

But once it *had* happened, he'd been riven with guilt, not just about Ellie but about Moira. Had he been using her? Taking advantage?

Late that Saturday night in her elegant Pacific Heights condo, he'd tried to push back the guilt. That had been about as effective as pushing back the ocean with his hands. He'd done a deplorable thing to his wife and his marriage. He'd broken vows. No matter how desperate he'd been, how angry, how alienated from Ellie...he'd inflicted damage that was probably irreparable.

"What happens tomorrow?" he'd asked Moira.

"You go to the airport and fly home," she'd replied bluntly. "I meet a boyfriend for brunch." He must have seemed startled, because she'd added, "Come on, Curt—we both know what this was. Fun, friendship, something to tide you over until you figure out what you want to do about your marriage. Don't turn mopey on me."

He hadn't turned mopey. He'd been relieved to learn that Moira was as detached as he was, that her emotions hadn't been involved and no commitment, acknowledged or unspoken, had been made.

As she'd predicted, he'd gone to the airport and flown home the next day. He'd spent the entire flight thinking about what he'd done and what he wanted.

Not Moira. Not loveless sex. His body had appreciated the workout, just as it appreciated a five-mile jog on the treadmill at the fitness club. But he'd realized, as the jet carried him back to Massachusetts, that what he and Ellie had was so much richer than a brief fling with an old friend. It was profound, precious, essential.

What they'd had. Could they ever have it again?

Tonight, on Ellie's fiftieth birthday, he had his answer. They *could* have it again. They'd had it just moments ago.

Except for Ellie's confession afterward. *I killed him.* She might as well have plunged a knife into Curt's chest.

"What are you talking about?" he asked when he was finally able to make his mouth function.

"Peter's death."

He hadn't misheard. His heart started beating again—too fast. A chill spread through him; even Ellie's body, nestled against his, couldn't warm him. He inched away from her, sat up and stared at her. She looked normal. She looked beautiful, in fact, her skin flushed, her hair tumbling in glorious disarray around her face, her cheeks marked by glistening tracks left by her tears.

She'd killed their son? *No.*

"Ellie. If you unplugged his respirator or something, slipped him an extra dose of medicine—"

She cut him off with a shake of her head. Then she sat up, too. She kept her gaze focused on her hands in her lap, as if unable to meet his eyes. As well she should be, if what she was saying was true.

"I sat by his side that whole time, Curt," she said. "When he was in the hospital. I prayed for him. I held his hand and talked to him. I sang him lullabies. Even if the doctors had told me he was brain-dead, I couldn't have unplugged him."

"Then you didn't kill him," Curt said, feeling his panic begin to drain away.

She shook her head again. "It's my fault he died. He came home from school that day with a terrible headache and a fever, and I sent him to bed. I told him it was nothing. I gave him some ibuprofen and left him a bottle of Gatorade."

"Ellie—"

"If I had recognized the symptoms, if I had erred on the side of caution…" She lifted her face to him, and he saw nothing but despair. "If I'd gotten him to the hospital right away, he would have lived."

"You don't know that."

"They would have started pumping antibiotics into him sixteen hours sooner. It would have saved him."

"Maybe it wouldn't have."

She ignored Curt's remark. "I didn't rush him to the hospital, or even call his doctor. Instead, I told him to go to bed. I shrugged off his illness. I'm a nurse, Curt. I should have known. By the time we got him to the hospital, it was too late to save him. A day earlier, it wouldn't have been too late."

He was about to repeat that she couldn't say with certainty what might have happened if they'd gotten Peter to the hospital sooner. The fact was, she knew better than he did. She was a medical professional.

What if she was right? What if her delay had cost Peter his life?

He turned away. His gaze settled on the black TV screen across the room from the bed, and its blankness provided a frame for his thoughts, a backdrop for his memories. He recalled the evening Peter had fallen ill. Curt had poked his head into Peter's room and Peter had said he felt lousy—although, as Curt remembered, Peter had used a stronger word. And then apologized for using it. He'd been himself that evening—a tired, headachy version of himself, but Curt had certainly seen nothing in Peter's behavior or symptoms to cause alarm.

Ellie hadn't viewed Peter as a patient, either. She'd viewed him as a mother and done just what any other mother would have done: she'd ordered fluids and bed rest.

But what if? What if quicker action on Ellie's part could have saved Peter's life? What if he'd died because they'd gotten him to the hospital too late?

On the other hand, what if they'd rushed him to the hospital that evening and he'd still died? What if in their haste they'd gotten into a car accident and all three of them had died? A person could strangle on what-ifs.

All the twenty-twenty hindsight in the world couldn't bring Peter back. That was the bottom line. Peter was dead. Ellie had done the best she could. So had Curt. And they'd lost their son.

"If I'd gone to medical school," Ellie said, "I would have recognized the symptoms. But I didn't want to be a doctor. I let everyone down. My family, my professors...and my son."

"Ellie." Curt twisted back to her. "If you'd gone to medical school, Peter would never have existed. You would have been in school for years. We would have put off having children until you were established. Different sperm would have met different eggs. Katie and Jessie wouldn't have been born. Neither would Peter. If you'd been a doctor, you might not have wanted three children—or any children at all. You might have decided to devote yourself completely to your career."

"How would you have felt about that?"

If he hadn't had children, he wouldn't have known what he was missing. But... "I wanted children," he confessed. "We talked about that, back at Brown. I always wanted to be a father. If you'd decided you didn't want to be a mother..."

"You wouldn't have married me," she said, completing the thought.

He contemplated that possibility before answering. His own words echoed in his head: *We've always had honesty.* Now wasn't the time to stop being honest. "I probably wouldn't have married you," he conceded. "Part of what made me love you was that you wanted children. You wanted to create a home with me, and a family, and our own special world. If you weren't that way, I wouldn't have loved you."

"Would you have married me if you knew my stupidity would lead to the death of one of our children?"

Again he thought long and hard before replying. "You're sounding a little like a doctor now—like you've got control of who lives and who dies. Like you're that important."

Her eyes flashed. She looked indignant but also intrigued.

"You're not that important, honey. Sometimes fate decides these things for us. Fate or God or whoever you want to blame. Sometimes we can do everything in the world, and we still can't keep a terrible thing from occurring. We're just not that powerful, Ellie."

She seemed doubtful.

"We're only human. We make mistakes. I made a bigger mistake than you."

"You didn't—"

He held up his hand to silence her. "It doesn't matter. We made mistakes. But we loved Peter, we loved him as much as any two parents can possibly love a son, and we'll always love him. You don't get one without the other. If you're human, you make mistakes and you love your children. And we're human."

She sighed, evidently unable to argue. Instead, she sank back into the pillows. Her eyes grew shiny with fresh tears. "Do you know why I stopped seeing the therapist?"

He shrugged. "I assumed it was because she wasn't helping you."

"I stopped seeing her because she was wrong." Ellie sighed shakily. "She told me I refused to let go of my pain because I feared that if I let go of the pain, I'd be letting go of Peter. If I stopped hurting, it would be as if I'd finally lost him for good. But as long as I still hurt, he still existed for me."

"And that was wrong?"

"I held on to the pain because I felt responsible for his death." She sighed again. A tear streaked down her cheek to her chin and dripped onto the curve of her breast. "I couldn't feel happy ever again. I couldn't feel joy. I didn't deserve it. I didn't deserve to have a husband who loved me, and daughters who admired me. I didn't deserve lovemaking. I didn't deserve pleasure. I'd killed Peter, and I had to suffer for my mistake." She aimed her shimmering gaze at him, as if seeking absolution.

Her confession tore at him. Even tonight, when he'd been making love to her, she'd held back. He'd thought she was just rusty after such a long time, or maybe unable to open herself completely to her faithless husband. Now he realized the truth: she didn't believe she was entitled to that kind of fulfillment. She'd fought the ecstasy as long as she could before finally giving in to it.

"You should have told me what you were going through," he said. "All those months, that long, dark stretch when I just couldn't reach you, you should have told me. Instead, I assumed you were satisfied just to shut me out. And I acted like an SOB. I did a terrible thing. If only I'd known—"

"*I* didn't know. How could I tell you what I didn't know myself? I knew I'd done something tragically wrong, I knew I didn't deserve your love anymore—but I don't think I actually figured it all out until this evening, watching the movie."

He glanced toward the black screen again. What in the movie had led her to her epiphany?

"There was a period when I actually thought I was ready to face life again. It occurred to me that you didn't deserve to do penance for my sins. So I tried to pull myself together. I tried to be happy. I even thought I'd make love to you. I'd let human warmth back into my heart."

"What happened?"

"You came home from California," she reminded him.

He cursed.

"Bad timing," she said with a poignant smile.

"Oh, God, I remember. You'd made a fancy, candlelit, welcome-home dinner for me."

"And I'd cleaned Peter's room."

"Yeah." He recalled his shock when he'd carried his suitcase up the stairs that Sunday evening, preoccupied with how he was going to break the news to Ellie about his affair, how she would take it, whether his compulsion to tell her the truth would destroy her for good. As he'd passed Peter's bedroom, he'd paused, his attention snagging on something. Nudging the door wider, he'd realized that the computer was off. The bed was made with fresh linens. All the teenage-boy clutter had been removed from the floor and that damn bottle of Gatorade had vanished from the night table.

The altered condition of Peter's bedroom had disoriented Curt. For a few strange minutes, he'd wondered whether he had entered the wrong house that night, whether the cheerful woman arranging a gourmet feast downstairs in the kitchen was really Ellie, whether his flight had delivered him to some alternate universe. Whether sleeping with a woman who wasn't his wife—sleeping with a woman he didn't love—had transformed him or transformed the world around him.

He'd recovered from his shock. But he remembered how tense and unnerved and desperately afraid he'd been.

"So I decided to go to Africa," Ellie said. "I figured that if I could save enough lives over there, it might make up for what I'd done to Peter here. Pretty ridiculous, I guess—my traveling to a foreign country to cleanse the stains from my soul."

"You did save lives there," he pointed out.

She shrugged. "I saved a boy's hearing."

"I said it downstairs, and I'll say it again. You are not a failure, Ellie." He faced her fully, took her hands in his and held them tight. "You are *not* a failure. You've saved the lives of sick children. You didn't save Peter's life because you couldn't. And you shouldn't have become a doctor because that wasn't your calling. It wasn't your destiny."

She studied him as if he had all the answers, all the wisdom. He didn't. Hell, he knew how to negotiate a damn good deal with other lawyers, how to litigate when negotiation didn't work, how to threaten and cajole and get all the conflicting parties to a mutual understanding and a workable agreement. He knew how to wash dishes and clean gutters and how to maneuver a hot sports coupe down a winding country road. He knew how to howl like Warren Zevon singing "Werewolves of London" and how to bench-press a hundred pounds. He could hold his own on a golf course and at any social event. He knew how to argue politics without offending too many people, and how to charm his in-laws when they were driving Ellie crazy.

He knew how to love. He loved his daughters so much, just thinking about them caused his heart to swell painfully in his chest. He'd loved his son and would continue to love his son for all the days he had left to live.

And he loved Ellie. No matter what. For better or worse. He loved her.

But wisdom?

"What is my destiny, Curt?" she asked.

"To live each day?" He tossed the idea out for her consideration. "To embrace each day? To wring as much pleasure as you can from it? To try your best?" He contemplated, then added one more choice for her: "To forgive yourself, Ellie. To love yourself as much as I love you, and to be as forgiving with yourself as you are with me. That's your destiny."

She gazed at their hands, clasped between them. "That sounds like a good destiny," she said.

"What was it in the movie that helped you to figure everything out?"

"Oh. The movie." She peered past him at the television. "I don't know. Seeing myself at all those different ages. Remembering all my doubts and insecurities. I always thought I had to be perfect, and I always fell short. And this voice inside me whispered, 'You fell short with Peter.'"

"Can you forgive yourself for not being perfect?" Curt asked.

"I guess I'll have to."

He smiled. If she could forgive herself, their marriage would survive. If they could talk this way, if they could always be this honest, whether the honesty was brutal or gentle, they would never leave each other. When Curt had given Ellie his heart, the gift had been forever.

She had been his destiny. She still was.

He turned so he could lean back into the pillows, stretched his legs and curved his arm around Ellie, drawing her against him. Her cheek was damp against his shoulder but he didn't mind. He imagined his cheeks were a bit damp, too.

His hand brushed the remote control on the night table, and he scooped it up and pointed it at the television. He hit the button to turn the TV back on, and then the pause button to restart the movie.

"Don't cry for me, Ghana clinic," crooned the singer in his now-familiar voice. Curt grinned, imagining Katie in a sound booth with some guy, taping him as he sang a dozen different versions of that *Evita* tune. The singer must have considered her nuts. Curt wondered if Katie had had to pay him, or if he'd done it for free, as a favor. Maybe he was a friend.

Or a lover. Maybe he was as in love with her as Curt had been with Ellie at that age. If Ellie had ridden the bus up to Cambridge and asked him to stand in Harvard Square, at the busiest intersection in the city, and belt out a silly song, he would have done it without hesitation.

He was astonished to realize that his daughters were as old as he and Ellie were when they'd met. Now they were embarking on their own lives, seeking their own destinies. And Curt knew there was no way to protect them from the terrible things that might befall them. All he could hope was that they would be able to forgive themselves.

"Ellie returned home from her African adventure at the end of July," Jessie narrated. A video—Katie had brought her digital video camera to Logan Airport to film Ellie's homecoming—showed Ellie waving as she strode toward her waiting family in the crowded baggage-claim area at Terminal E. The camera bounced as Katie ran toward her mother. She filmed Jessie hugging Ellie, and then a wild arc of their surroundings as she kept the camera recording while she herself hugged her mother. Then she filmed Curt's approach.

He'd been apprehensive that day. Had Ellie come home ready to mend things with him, or determined to continue on her adventurous new life without him?

For the sake of the girls, he supposed, she'd smiled at him, given him a brief hug and turned her cheek toward his mouth for a kiss. She'd looked gorgeous, her skin darkened by the sun, her hair threaded with streaks of silver, her body taut and trim, her posture straight and her gaze determined. All he'd wanted to do was fall to his knees, right there in the terminal, and propose marriage all over again. If he had, though, she would have said no. For all her strength and confidence, he'd felt her reserve when he'd kissed her cheek. His lips could have gotten frostbite from the chill.

But the girls hadn't sensed anything amiss. They'd filmed the reunion as if it were the happiest moment in Curt's and Ellie's lives.

"Ellie's African sojourn was a fabulous experience," Katie continued in the narration. "Everyone who saw Ellie could tell. She glowed with a new spirit." The film showed Curt lifting her suitcase from the baggage carousel, and Curt and Ellie walking toward the exit, the suitcase between them, the way her trip to Africa had stood between them.

"Ellie returned to her job at the Felton Primary School," the narration continued, with another photograph of her school. "She worked with renewed passion. Everyone who saw her realized how much she'd changed.

"And yet she was still Ellie Frost, the warm, wonderful woman we love."

A collage of photos appeared out of chronological order, floating in and out of focus. A photo of Ellie fresh from Africa, one of her as a radiant bride, one of her with her three children—Katie around eight years old, Jessie six and Peter three. A photo of the whole family on a beach on Cape Cod; they'd asked a stranger to take their picture. A photo of Ellie seated behind the wheel of that dilapidated Jeep in Kumasi, her hair flying and her smile wide and wild. A photo of Ellie and Curt seated side by side on the front-porch steps at their house, the Hope Street shingle visible above their heads.

Along with the parade of photos came yet another rendition of "Don't Cry for Me, Argentina," with new words. This time it was sung in three-part harmony—a male voice and two females, Katie and Jessie and someone who, had life taken a different turn, would have been Peter:

Now let us sing "Happy Birthday"
To Ellie, our awesome mother
We've always loved you
We'll always love you
And that's our promise
We share this promise.

The song ended, but the photo of Curt and Ellie sitting on the porch steps remained. In the photo, Ellie's head rested on Curt's shoulder and he had his arm around her, just as he did right now. They were both smiling.

When had that picture been taken? They looked ageless in it, as old as they were now, as young as they were the first night they'd spent together on Hope Street. They looked happy, sharing all the promises they'd made and all the promise the world still held for them.

White letters appeared across the photo: Happy Birthday! followed by an inflated list of credits similar to what they'd printed on the label for the DVD. The instrumental version of "Don't Cry For Me, Argentina" played in the background. The credits ended when the song did, and then the screen faded to black.

"Don't cry for me, Curt," Ellie said.

"Don't cry for *us*," he corrected her. "We're going to be okay."

"You think so?"

"For at least the next fifty years. Then we can reassess."

"I love you," Ellie said, snuggling closer to him.

"I love you, Eleanor Brennan Frost." He circled both arms

around her and held her, and prayed that the trust they'd redis-covered, so fragile and delicate, would in time grow more solid and sturdy. He prayed that they would always have their honesty, always have their love—always have hope.

For tonight, he thought, this *très* romantic room at the oldee inn would be Hope Street. Tomorrow they would go home to the house with the shingle above the front door.

THE MARRIAGE BED

To the XRomX gang
With gratitude and love

ONE

WHAT THE HELL WAS he doing here?

Joelle stared at the man standing on her front porch and stifled the urge to scream, slam the door in his face...or pretend she didn't know who he was.

She did know, of course. Thirty-seven years might have passed since she'd last seen Drew Foster—she was aware of exactly how long it had been, considering how drastically her life had changed that night—but she recognized him immediately. His hair was a little sparser and grayer, his laugh lines deeper, his jaw softer. His well-cut pinstripe suit didn't hide the slight paunch that had sprouted above his belt, but despite carrying a few excess pounds, he appeared generally fit for a man only a few years away from his sixtieth birthday.

How had he found her? Why hadn't he called to give her some warning before he appeared on her doorstep? How could she get him to leave? He'd come close to destroying her life once, but she'd painstakingly rebuilt it—and now here he was, perfectly capable of destroying it all over again. Fear gathered in her gut and squeezed.

"Joelle," he murmured, his gaze deep and intense. "God, you look great."

She clenched her dust rag so tightly her fingers began to go numb. She'd been cleaning the house, as she did every Saturday morning, and she hadn't bothered to put the rag down before answering the door. If only he'd arrived a few minutes later, the roar of the vacuum cleaner would have drowned out the doorbell and she'd never have realized he was there.

At her continuing silence, his smile faded. "You don't remember me, do you?"

"Of course I do." She shook her head, then forced a smile. "I'm just…surprised. How did you— I mean, what are you…" She pressed her lips together to stop from stammering.

"It's a long story. May I come in?"

Back then, his voice had been as smooth and sweet as warm honey. It still was. Just like his warm, honey-sweet grin.

She didn't want him inside her house, but she couldn't think of a way to keep him out without leading him to assume she had something to hide. If he suspected her of hiding something, he'd be right. What had happened thirty-seven years ago, the decisions she'd made, the turn her life had taken—he mustn't find out. She couldn't let him.

But if she barred the door, he'd grow suspicious. Reluctantly she stepped back and allowed him to enter. If luck was with her, he'd tell her he just happened to be in Gray Hill, and someone at the gas station had mentioned her name and he'd thought he would stop by and say hello. They'd chat for a few minutes about old times and then he'd be on his way.

"You have a lovely place," he said, surveying the foyer before he peered through the arched doorway into the living room. "Beautiful landscaping, too."

"Yes. Bobby—" She cut herself off. If she talked about Bobby, she might start talking about their children, and she couldn't do that.

"Bobby D. Who would've thought you two would get married?" Drew smiled wistfully. "He's a damn lucky guy. Is he around?"

"No, he's—" Again she cut herself off. Bobby often spent Saturdays meeting with clients who weren't available during the week. But if she said he was working, Drew might assume he did some kind of labor that demanded weekend shifts. She wanted to assure Drew that Bobby's business was a success, that he had clients as far away as Hartford and Bridgeport and even across the state line in New York, that his sons were now working with him, that he and Joelle were no longer kids from the poor side of town. She wanted to shout that Bobby was more of a man than Drew could ever hope to be.

All she said was, "I'm afraid he's out right now."

Drew shrugged. "Well, at least you're home."

"Cleaning the house." She held up the dust rag in her hand and smiled faintly. The air smelled of lemon-scented furniture polish, and through the arched doorway into the living room the vacuum cleaner was visible, its electrical cord snaking across the rug to the socket near the bay window.

"I'm sorry for springing myself on you like this. I was afraid that if I called you, you might tell me not to come."

Good guess, she thought, then reminded herself that acting rude would rile his suspicions. If she could force herself to behave civilly, he'd be less likely to ask questions.

Everything had happened so long ago. Maybe he'd forgotten, or he no longer cared about the mistakes they'd made when they were teenagers. Maybe none of it mattered to him anymore.

"Would you like something to drink?" she asked. "Coffee?

Tea?" He was standing too close, and she backed up another couple of steps. "Wine or beer?" she offered, even though it wasn't yet noon.

"Have you got anything stronger?" His voice was tinged with laughter, but she sensed that he was serious.

"No." Bobby preferred no hard liquor in the house, and she respected his wishes.

"Coffee's fine."

Nodding, she pivoted and headed down the hall to the kitchen, her footsteps muffled by the runner rug. She was barefoot—the house was hot, despite the air-conditioning units Bobby had installed—and she always worked herself into a sweat when she cleaned. Dressed in one of her son Danny's ratty old Colgate University T-shirts and a pair of denim cutoffs, with her hair pulled into a sloppy ponytail, she'd been warm until she'd opened her door and discovered Drew Foster on the other side. From that moment on, she'd felt chilled.

He followed her into the kitchen, where she tossed her rag onto the counter and busied herself scooping coffee beans into the grinder. She could feel him prowling around the room behind her. Was he assessing the quality of her appliances? Peeking through the window in the top of the back door, which opened onto the flagstone patio that Bobby had built? She refused to turn and watch her guest. She hated that he was here, hated that his presence made her hands tremble and her fingers fumble as she arranged a filter in the basket of the coffeemaker.

"You have grandchildren?"

His question jolted her. Flecks of brown powder spilled from the grinder's cup and scattered across the counter. *No,* she silently begged, *don't ask me about my grandchildren.*

She glanced over her shoulder and saw him standing in front

of the refrigerator, admiring the crayon scribblings she'd fastened to the surface with magnets. He knew she was too old to have children drawing like toddlers. Obviously she had grandchildren. She couldn't lie about it.

"Yes," she said. "How about you?"

"No." The word was hard and blunt. He softened it by adding, "You don't look old enough to have grandchildren. I mean it, Joelle. You look fantastic. You must be drinking from the fountain of youth."

His flattery made her scowl.

"Do you work out?"

She emptied the grinder into the coffeemaker's basket and wiped away the grounds that had spilled. Drew was buttering her up for a reason, and sooner or later he'd tell her what it was. *A long story*, he'd warned. She hoped he'd tell her the abridged version and then disappear.

"The only workouts I do are dusting and vacuuming," she said, pulling the ceramic pitcher and sugar bowl from the cabinet above the sink. The sugar bowl was full, but she had to pour some milk into the pitcher. She wished he'd move away from the refrigerator so she could open it without standing too close to him. She also wished he'd stop staring at the primitive artwork Jeremy and Kristin had created. Those precious scribbles could ruin everything if the conversation drifted to questions about Jeremy and Kristin's mother.

Fortunately, Drew backed away as she approached the refrigerator. "I gather you and Bobby have never gone back to Holmdell for high-school reunions," he said as she filled the pitcher. Hands shoved in his pockets, he leaned casually against the counter while the coffeemaker chugged and wafted a rich aroma into the air.

Joelle surprised herself by laughing. "God, no."

"I've managed to avoid them, too."

"Do you still live there?"

"New York City. We've got a weekend place out in Amagansett, on Long Island, but we call Manhattan home." He flashed her a grin. "Manhattan and Connecticut—who would have thought you and I would wind up practically being neighbors?"

Joelle would hardly consider Manhattan and the hills of northwestern Connecticut the same neighborhood. Although throughout the years she and Bobby had lived in Gray Hill, more and more New Yorkers had bought up the ramshackle old farmhouses and barns and turned them into weekend retreats. It was in part because of all those rich city folks that Bobby's business had flourished. They all wanted stone walls around their properties, brick patios with built-in hot tubs, elegant plantings and pools with waterfalls. They paid DiFranco Landscaping huge fees to tame the wild beauty of their surroundings.

"You said *we*," she noted. "You have a wife?"

Drew held up his left hand to display his wedding ring. "Helen. A wonderful woman. We just celebrated our thirtieth anniversary this year. You'd like her."

Joelle doubted that. Despite her history with Drew, she'd always known they were from two different worlds. His wife was undoubtedly from his world, not hers.

"So, what are you doing with yourself?" he asked, as if they were in fact trapped at a high-school reunion in the old West Side Motor Lodge down on Rockwood Turnpike, drinking stale punch and standing amid bouquets of helium balloons while a deejay played great hits of the sixties. "Career? Hobbies? Volunteer work?"

"I'm a kindergarten teacher," she told him. "Bobby owns a landscape-design business." Pride made her stand straighter. She and Bobby had done well for themselves, better than anyone in Holmdell, Ohio, would have predicted. Back then, folks had probably assumed Bobby would wind up a mean drunk like his father, tending the grounds of the town cemetery all day and drowning his sorrows at the Dog House Tavern all night. And Joelle...well, people might have believed she'd had prospects, but only because she'd been dating Drew, a rich boy who lived in a mansion overlooking the ninth hole at Green Gates Country Club.

The coffeemaker announced the end of its brewing cycle with a raucous gurgle. "We could sit in the living room," she suggested, "but I'd have to straighten things up in there—"

"This is fine," Drew said, pulling out a chair at the butcher-block kitchen table. He remained standing until she'd carried over two steaming mugs, waited for her to take her seat, then lowered himself onto the chair facing her. He dipped his head toward the cup and inhaled. "Smells great."

He was stalling. "Why are you here, Drew?" she asked.

He stalled some more, stirring milk into his coffee, then lifting it, blowing on its surface and taking a sip. After swallowing, he sighed. "Joelle." His voice had grown soft, his expression pensive. "I'm here because I'm a desperate man."

She wasn't sure if he was serious. His statement was so melodramatic. Yet he didn't seem to be joking. His words hung in the air, unsettling her.

"I would never have gone to all this trouble—hired a private investigator to find you and then intruded into your life like this—if I could have figured out another way, but..." He sighed again and set down his mug with a thud. "Helen and I have a son. Adam. He's the joy of our lives. You're a mother—I don't have to explain what it means to have a child."

Her heart began to pound, sending shards of pain through her chest. *Don't talk to me about my children. Don't.* He had no right to barge into her life and tell her, of all people, what it meant to have a child. If she could think of an excuse, any excuse, to get him out of her house—

"Adam is dying, Joelle," Drew said, his voice even more hushed. "And I'm here because the only person who can save him is your daughter." He paused, his dark eyes meeting hers. "*Our* daughter."

BOBBY NOTICED THE BMW with the New York plates parked out front and wondered who was visiting Joelle. Some new summer person, probably. The only rich New Yorkers they knew were the people buying up all the houses in the northwest hills and turning them into vacation homes. Thank God for those rich New Yorkers, too. Many of them paid him good money to land-scape their property.

The guy he'd spent that morning with was a bond trader or something, one of those Wall Street professions that earned people ten times what they were worth. His wife was heavily into an English-country-manor fantasy. She'd already done up the house with floral wallpaper and frilly pillows on every damn surface, and now she wanted the backyard to look like an English garden, only with a free-form pool in the middle of it. Bobby had patiently explained that English gardens didn't generally include free-form pools and she ought to aim for a nice Connecticut garden, instead. He promised her lots of perennials and a gorgeous pool, and she'd seemed satisfied. The husband required stone walls so the place would look like fox-hunting country. Honest to God, why didn't they just go buy themselves a place outside London?

But they'd signed a whopping contract with DiFranco Landscaping. When Bobby was done with their property they'd be happy, and so would his company's bottom line.

He'd considered phoning Mike and Danny with the news that he'd landed the job, but decided that could wait until Monday. He had to remind himself that when it came to the business, they were his colleagues, not his sons. You didn't phone colleagues on a Saturday morning to talk shop, even if the news was good. Sons you could call anytime, but with business associates, Monday was soon enough.

He had to admit that having both his sons choose to join him in the company made work a thousand times more rewarding. He liked his business, liked the job's demands, liked the praise from satisfied customers, but he loved having Mike and Danny as partners.

You did well, Bobby D, he thought as he steered the truck up the winding driveway to the garage.

He'd done well with the house, too. Maybe it wasn't a palace, but it was spacious and comfortable and Joelle deserved no less. She'd had faith in him when he'd bought it, back when it was so shoddy a nasty blizzard would have knocked it flat, and one weekend at a time he'd rebuilt it. Claudia had helped, he recalled with a grin. Nothing like having a ten-year-old girl assisting. "Can I get your hammer, Daddy?" she'd ask, hovering behind him. "Should I hold the tape measure?" Once she'd hit adolescence, she couldn't be bothered anymore, but during the first couple of years of renovations, while Joelle had had her hands full with one and then another baby, Claudia had been Bobby's loyal assistant.

He eased the pickup into the bay next to Joelle's little hybrid. He wasn't convinced her Prius saved them much in fuel costs, but she'd craved one, so what the hell. As he swung out of the cab, he checked the thick, treaded soles of his work boots. He and the bond trader had traipsed all over the guy's four-acre property, and they'd hit a few mucky areas. Bobby would leave his boots in the mudroom. He wasn't going to track dirt into the house when Joelle had spent the morning cleaning.

Inside, he heard the muffled sound of voices in conversation, Joelle's and a man's. Yanking off one boot, he called out, "Hey, Jo!"

The conversation came to an abrupt halt, punctuated by the clatter of chairs scraping on the kitchen floor. "We're in here, Bobby," she said. She didn't have to tell him where *here* was.

The silence spooked him. He tugged off his other boot, then left the mudroom for the kitchen.

Seeing the man standing at his table was like walking into a fist. He lost his breath, his vision briefly blurred and his muscles contracted into knots. He inhaled slowly and met the man's gaze.

"Bobby," Drew Foster said quietly, his right hand extended.

Bobby nearly blurted out that only family got to call him that. To the rest of the world he was Bob or Robert or Mr. DiFranco. But to say that would make him sound like a psycho. Back in Holmdell, where Foster had known him, everyone had called him Bobby or Bobby D.

He swallowed again. Joelle slipped away from Drew to stand beside Bobby, an unspoken show of support that he appreciated. He wished he'd kept his boots on. It would be easier for Bobby to kick the bastard out of his house if he was wearing shoes.

The brush of Joelle's fingers on his elbow reminded him that he had to shake Foster's hand. He wasn't surprised by the softness of Foster's palm. The guy probably never lifted anything heavier than a pencil.

"Foster," he said brusquely, then gave a nod.

"Let me get you a cup of coffee." Joelle broke from him and crossed to the coffeemaker. He didn't like this—the fact that she hadn't asked how his appointment had gone, that she hadn't kissed his cheek, that no one was explaining the presence of Drew Foster in his kitchen, dressed in a thousand-dollar suit, with every freaking hair in place. Less hair than he'd had in high school, Bobby noted with grim satisfaction.

He wondered what Drew and Joelle had been doing before he'd arrived, and the possibilities made his stomach churn.

They couldn't have been doing much, he tried to assure himself. Joelle was dressed for housework, and despite the cooling hum of the air conditioners, her hair was beginning to frizz into little golden springs around her face. She had on no makeup, no perfume. If Foster had hoped to seduce her, he'd caught her at the wrong time.

Bobby fought off his reflexive jealousy. Joelle had been his wife a hell of a lot longer than she'd been Foster's girlfriend. They weren't in high school anymore. They'd all made their choices and Joelle's choice had been to marry Bobby. Still, his gaze drifted to her left hand, to the simple gold band she always wore on her ring finger, just to make sure it was there.

She handed him his favorite mug, filled with coffee. Claudia had given him that mug for Father's Day a few years ago. It said Number One Dad on it—silly, but he loved it.

Claudia.

Staring at Drew Foster over the mug's rim, Bobby felt the tension in his abdomen increase. Did Foster know about Claudia? Had Joelle told him? After all these years, did she still care enough about her old boyfriend to think he had a right to know?

His eyes never leaving Foster, Bobby moved warily toward the table. Something was bad here. Something was very bad.

"Drew has a problem," Joelle said gently, settling into her chair. "He needs our help."

"It's okay, Joelle. I'll explain," Foster said, resuming his own seat.

Bobby's tension spiked. He didn't like the intimacy between Joelle and Foster, the way they were speaking for each other. He lowered himself into a chair, his hands curling into fists. He rested them in his lap, under the table. If he had to pummel Foster, he would. But he hoped he wouldn't have to.

"I was telling Joelle, you've got a lovely house. Beautiful piece of property, too—"

"You didn't come here to talk about my house," Bobby cut him off.

"No, I didn't." Foster bit his lip, then leaned forward. "You see, Bobby…I have a son. He's twenty-five. A terrific kid, I can't tell you—" His voice cracked.

Bobby waited him out, his fingers flexing against his denim-clad thighs, his teeth clenched so tight his jaw ached.

"When Adam was sixteen, he was diagnosed with acute myelogenous leukemia," Foster said. "He was treated with chemotherapy and the disease went into remission. He finished high school, went to college—for more than six years he was disease free. We really believed he'd licked it. But then it returned. The chemo isn't working this time. His only chance is a bone marrow transplant."

Bobby forced himself to keep breathing, to remain still. He felt as if he was back in 'Nam, waiting for the next explosion. Peril vibrated in the air.

Foster hadn't come here to talk about chemotherapy any more than he'd come to talk about Bobby's lovely house and his beautiful piece of property. And if he didn't get to the point soon, Bobby would bring on the next explosion himself. He'd trip a land mine, just to end the suspense.

"I don't understand all the science," Foster continued, "but neither my wife nor I were a good match to be a donor. None of his grandparents or cousins matched. We worked with the National Marrow Donor Program, searching for a possible match." He studied his coffee for a long moment, then lifted his eyes to Bobby. "For some reason, a sibling makes the best donor."

Boom. No need for Bobby to trip an explosion. The word *sibling* had done it. He understood why Foster was here now— and anger turned his vision red, just the way the land mines in 'Nam used to.

"I always wondered—I mean, that autumn, after I'd left for college and Joelle called and told me she was, well…"

Pregnant, you piece of scum.

"I'm not sure what she told you or what you… Well, that's between you and her. The thing was, I never heard from her again. I had no idea if she'd gone through with…" He faltered.

An abortion. Say it.

"All I heard was that she left town and never came back. I asked my parents if they had any news of her, but—" he glanced at Joelle "—they'd never been crazy about us, and I think they were relieved she was gone. I tried to talk to Joelle's mother, too—this was years ago, Bobby, before I got married, before my son… Anyway, Joelle's mother seemed to dislike me as much as my parents disliked her. She wouldn't give me the time of day. So I let it go—until Adam's leukemia returned, and the doctors asked if he had a sibling."

"He doesn't." This conversation was over. Bobby pushed back his chair, ready to stand, ready to pick Foster up by his fancy silk necktie and drag him out to the street.

At Bobby's movement, Foster sat straighter and spoke faster. "I hired a detective, and he found you. He told me you had a daughter who was thirty-six-years old. I did the math, Bobby."

Bobby shook his head.

"I realize it's not fair, my coming to you like this," Foster said, including Joelle in his gaze. His voice wavered. "Back in Holmdell, when——I mean, I was young, and I was a fool and——"

"Claudia is my daughter," Bobby said, these words sharper than the last, slicing through the air.

"Of course she is. I would never——"

"You can leave now."

Foster flattened his hands against the butcher-block surface of the table, as if clinging to it to would keep Bobby from evicting him. "All I'm asking is to have her tested, to see if she's a match."

"No."

"Bobby," Joelle murmured, reaching for his hand.

His hand fisted again and he yanked his arm away. This man, this creep, was staking a claim on Claudia, and Joelle was taking his side. Explosion after explosion rumbled inside Bobby's skull. Could Foster really invade his home, win over his wife and steal his daughter? Could this actually be happening?

"You wouldn't have to tell her everything." Foster pressed him, pleading. "Just have her take a blood test. If she isn't a match, then it's done."

"No." Bobby refused to look at Joelle. If she wanted to ally herself with Foster, Bobby would fight on his own. "Claudia is my daughter. I'm her father. Now you're asking me to tell her that everything she's ever known, everything this whole family is about, is a lie. You're asking me to tell her some other guy—some son of a bitch who knocked her mother up and abandoned her—is her real father."

Foster sighed. "My son's life hangs in the balance, so yes," he conceded. "That's what I'm asking you to do."

If Bobby drank the coffee, he'd choke. If he sat in this room with Drew Foster for another minute, he'd start swinging. He shoved away from the table so hard his chair fell over when he stood and then he stormed out of the room. Behind him, he heard Joelle call his name and then Foster say, "It's all right, Joelle…"

Oh, sure. It was all right. The two of them—Claudia's *parents*—would figure this whole thing out once hotheaded Bobby D was out of the way.

He stalked through the mudroom to the garage and climbed in behind the wheel of his truck. He wasn't going to drive anywhere, not without shoes. He didn't really want to go anywhere, anyway. He just needed to get away from Foster. Foster and Joelle. Drew and JoJo, the lovebirds of Holmdell High School.

He had to breathe. Had to calm down so he could think. Had to hold himself together. Violent urges simmered inside him, but he was a better man than his father. He wasn't going to snap.

He rested his arms on the steering wheel and his forehead on his hands. Inhale, exhale. Control.

Claudia was his daughter. He was the only father she'd ever had. He'd wiped her butt, bandaged her scrapes, perched himself on tiny chairs in colorful primary-school classrooms to discuss her progress with her teachers. He'd taught her how to use a hammer and a tape measure, how to grout tile and repair dry rot and how to plant a rosebush without getting pricked by the thorns. He'd paced the floors when she'd stayed out past her curfew, and he'd paid her college tuition, and nine years ago, he'd walked her down the aisle in church and delivered her to her groom. Her children called him Grampa.

He and Joelle had a life. They had a family. They had two sons and a daughter, a home, an understanding. They'd put it together and made it work. They'd succeeded, no thanks to Drew Foster.

And now that prick was in Bobby's house, begging for his son's life. An ailing son didn't give him permission to undermine everything that made Bobby's life worth living. His family. His children. His wife.

Drew Foster had no right. Yet Bobby knew, with a sickening certainty, that it was too late. The mines had exploded, and soon everything Bobby held dear would be nothing but rubble.

TWO

May 1970

"'OOH, BABY, BABY, it's a wild world,'" Joelle sang along with Cat Stevens as she brushed blue shadow on her eyelids. The music spilled into her bedroom from the FM radio Drew had given her for her eighteenth birthday last month. Her mother had been annoyed by the gift—"He's been dating you since before Christmas. He should've bought you jewelry"—but Joelle loved the radio. The old hi-fi in the living room wasn't a stereo, and besides, her mother hated when she played Jimi Hendrix or Bob Dylan or the Byrds. She even bitched about Simon and Garfunkel, who had pretty voices but rubbed her wrong. And the Beatles. "They used to be so cute, but then they got all druggy," she complained.

With her own radio, though—the most generous gift anybody had ever given her—Joelle could listen to music in her bedroom. Druggy music, heartbreaking music, dance-till-you-drop music. Jewelry was nice, but you couldn't sing along with a bracelet.

Joelle also couldn't sing along with Cat Stevens while she applied her mascara. For reasons she had never figured out, she found it impossible to put on mascara without opening her mouth like a fish. She'd chosen a brown shade, because black would have looked tarty with her fair coloring. But her pale lashes were invisible without mascara on them.

She blinked a couple of times to dry the lashes, then shut her mouth and stepped back to assess her reflection in the mirror above her dresser. People were always telling her she was pretty, but she didn't see herself that way. She'd been spared the curse of acne, thank God, but her nose was too long and her cheeks too flat, and no matter how much she tweezed her eyebrows, one was higher than the other. Her hair was naturally blond—she didn't even have to use lemon juice in it to bring out the highlights—but without makeup, her eyes were practically invisible.

Tonight they were vivid, though—and not just because of the eye shadow and mascara. Her dress was the same blue as her eyes. She'd picked the fabric just because of the color.

She hoped no one would guess that she'd sewn her prom dress herself. The rich girls had all traveled to Cincinnati to buy their gowns, and the girls who couldn't afford to make that trip had bought their dresses at Beldon's, Holmdell's local department store. Joelle couldn't even afford the prom dresses at Beldon's. She'd gone into the store, read the price tags and realized that the only way she'd wind up with a formal gown was if she sewed one herself. She'd chosen a dress pattern with narrow shoulder straps, a sleek bodice and an A-line skirt that flared as it descended to her ankles. It appeared homemade to her, but maybe people wouldn't notice.

Yeah, right. And maybe they wouldn't notice how awful her hair had come out, either. She'd set it so it would hang in fat corkscrew curls. She'd globbed on the setting gel and drenched her hair in most of a can of her mother's Aqua Net. But the curls hadn't held. They sagged and drooped.

The rich girls all went to Fontaine's beauty parlor on prom day. Their hair would be perfect. She looked like a witch.

Tears stung her eyes, but she batted them away. She couldn't cry, not with all the mascara she'd just brushed on. Sighing, she turned her back to the mirror. She'd done the best she could. And the bottom line was that none of the rich girls, with their fancy big-city gowns and beautiful hair, was Drew Foster's prom date. Joelle was. Drew had chosen her.

"Remember—" her mother had been coaching her ever since her first date with him "—this boy is a catch. You don't want to lose him. He's your route to a better life. Don't screw up."

In the living room, her mother chain-smoked and gossiped with their landlady, Mrs. Proski. A chubby old widow, Mrs. Proski could pass for Santa's wife, although her chronically pink nose was caused not by arctic weather but by drinking too much sherry. Still, she was tolerable. When Joelle had been younger and her mother had had to work odd shifts at the Bank Street Diner, Mrs. Proski had been on call in case Joelle had an emergency. Mrs. Proski was always home because she didn't have a job. She managed to make ends meet between her late husband's pension and what she charged in rent for the first-floor flat that Joelle and her mother occupied in the duplex on Third Street.

Since Joelle and her mother didn't own a camera, Mrs. Proski had brought hers downstairs so she could take photos of Joelle and Drew before they left for the prom. Unfortunately Joelle's hair was going to look like crap in all the photos.

"'Ooh, baby, baby…'" she sang, then held her lips still so she could dab some pale pink lipstick on them. Through the closed door she heard the doorbell ring.

Her mother hollered, "Joelle! He's here!" She sounded more excited than Joelle felt. But then, her mother didn't have to impress anyone tonight. She didn't have to have magnificent hair and a stunning dress. No rich kids from the Hill were going to be checking her out and issuing her a failing grade.

She examined her reflection for one final minute, then pulled her sling-back sandals from their box and slipped her feet into them. She so rarely wore heels that she felt a bit wobbly, even though they were only two inches high. She practiced pacing the room—or as close as she could get to pacing, since her bedroom was so small she could move only two steps in each direction— but that was enough to get her balance and grow used to the flow of the dress.

"Never mind," her mother shouted through her shut door. "It's just Bobby."

Her tension escaped her in a long breath that ended in a laugh. She swung the door open to see Bobby DiFranco swaggering down the hall to her room. In a pair of torn jeans, a T-shirt with a fist stenciled across it and over that a faded, fraying army shirt, his long, dark hair splayed out from his face like a lion's mane and his scuffed boots green with grass stains, he was clearly not dressed for the prom.

"Far out, JoJo." He let out a low whistle as he swept into her room. "You look great."

"Really?" Feeling a bit more secure in her sandals, she pirouetted for him. "I look okay?"

"I'm speechless." He pressed his hands to his chest. "I'm in love."

"Don't you be slowing her down," Joelle's mother yelled from the living room. "She's got to get ready for Drew."

Joelle and Bobby shared a scowl, then snickered. They'd been friends since childhood. Bobby knew Joelle's mother nearly as well as Joelle did—and he knew Wanda Webber didn't put much value on her daughter's friendship with him. Wanda was placing all her bets on Drew Foster, the young man from the Hill who'd taken a liking to her daughter. Drew was Joelle's ticket out of Tubtown—the neighborhood of Holmdell where she and Bobby and all the other poor slobs lived. Everyone called it Tubtown because of the large number of bathtubs planted vertical in people's front yards, with little statues of the Virgin Mary inside them to create shrines. Mrs. Proski hadn't erected a bathtub shrine in front of the duplex where she and the Webbers lived, but she kept a rusting washtub planted with geraniums near the front porch, her idea of decorative landscaping.

Bobby was just another Tubtown boy on the fast track to nowhere. Why Joelle wasted any time on him was a mystery to her mother, one Joelle had long ago quite trying to explain to her.

"You think people will figure out I sewed the dress?" she asked him.

"If they do, they'll be throwing money at you and begging you to sew dresses for them."

Snorting in disbelief, Joelle stalked back to the mirror and frowned. "My hair looks gross."

"Are you kidding? It looks—" he sighed "—wonderful." He touched one of the wayward curls. "Feels kinda sticky, though."

"You wouldn't believe how much hair spray I used."

He shrugged, then sprawled out on her bed. "It looks great, really. You look like a flower child."

"I don't want to look like a flower child." She located her white leatherette purse and gathered everything she needed to stuff into it: lipstick, her keys, a couple of dollars, a few neatly folded tissues. "I want to look like a princess." The kind of princess who belonged on the arm of a prince like Drew Foster.

"Don't expect me to call you Your Highness," Bobby teased. "Your heinie, maybe."

Joelle wrinkled her nose at him. If she'd hoped he would help calm her bristling nerves, she'd hoped wrong. He'd come here to give her a hard time, to tease her as if he were an irritating brother.

She decided to tease him right back. "You should be going to the prom, too," she said, turning back to her dresser and zipping the purse shut. She dabbed a little Jean Naté behind her ears. "You should have asked Margie."

Bobby snorted. "Thirty bucks for the tickets. Another thirty to rent a tux. Then I'd have to buy her a corsage. And find a car. I couldn't drive her to the prom in my truck."

"Do you think she would have cared how you drove her? She's your girlfriend. You should have asked her. I bet she would have loved to go."

"Proms aren't for Tubtown kids."

"I'm a Tubtown kid and I'm going."

"Because you're in with the Hill kids. They'll all be decked out in their fancy threads, acting stuck-up and pretending they're cool. That's not for me." He shrugged. "I'll do something with Margie tonight. Maybe we'll catch a movie. *Easy Rider* is still playing at the Bijou."

"You've seen it already," Joelle reminded him.

"So we'll see it again. Or we'll go to the lake or something."

The lake was where people went to make out. Joelle didn't know if Bobby and Margie were having sex, but she suspected they were. She sometimes believed she was the only high-school senior in Tubtown—in all of Holmdell, probably—who was still a virgin.

She imagined that everyone at school assumed she was putting out for Drew. Why else would a boy like him, who had money and good looks and was heading to an Ivy League college in September, be dating someone like her?

Because he loved her; that was why. Because he thought she was nice and fun to be with and she wasn't snobby like the other Hill girls. That was what he told her, anyway. And since she wasn't putting out for him, she figured he must be speaking the truth.

Someday she'd make love with him. But she hadn't yet. She loved him with all her heart, yet she couldn't say with absolute certainty that he loved her. She supposed most girls who put out didn't care all that much whether or not they were in love, but Joelle was old-fashioned. She wanted to be sure Drew was hers as much as she was his.

Bobby broke into her thoughts. "Listen, Jo, do me a favor."

"What?"

"Mrs. Proski is taking pictures of you and Foster, right?"

"Yeah."

"Have her snap a picture of just you alone, for me. You never looked this good before, and you'll probably never look this good again—"

Pretending to be insulted, Joelle spun around and threw her purse at him.

Bobby laughed and batted it away. "I want to remember what you looked like the night you were a princess. And I don't want Foster's ugly mug in the picture."

"Drew Foster isn't ugly." She knew that was nothing more than Bobby's teasing, but she wasn't in the mood to be teased tonight. She was anxious—about whether she was truly pretty enough to belong with Drew, whether she was even remotely classy enough to fit in at the prom. Whether after the dance he would drive her to the lake. Whether he'd expect her to go all the way with him because he'd spent so much money on the tickets and flowers and his tux. Whether he would still want her to be his girlfriend tomorrow.

Any other time, she'd welcome Bobby's taunting and give as good as she got. But not tonight.

Bobby seemed to sense that. His smile lost its sneering edge and he pushed himself off the bed. "You're gonna have a good time," he assured her. "Remember, JoJo, you're better than they are."

"No, I'm not." In front of anyone else, she would have hidden her insecurity. But not Bobby. They went back too far, knew each other too well.

She was aware that the Hill kids tolerated her only because she was Drew's girlfriend, not because they thought highly of her. She didn't wear the right brand of jeans, didn't take all the honors classes, didn't participate in glee club or cheerleaders or student government. The rich girls treated her pleasantly only out of respect for Drew—which was why, when she wasn't with him, she hung out with Bobby and the other Tubtown kids she'd grown up with. Some of them had stopped being friendly to her once she'd started going with Drew, though. They thought she was stuck-up.

She wasn't. At least Bobby recognized that.

The doorbell rang again. "Drew's here," Wanda bellowed.

Joelle didn't miss the flicker of disapproval on Bobby's face. He resented the Hill kids because they viewed him as trash. Joelle insisted that Drew wasn't like the others, but Bobby considered him just another spoiled, arrogant rich boy. If only he knew Drew the way she did, he'd realize how wrong he was.

She and Bobby emerged from her bedroom and met up with Drew in the hallway. He had asked her what color her dress was and he'd rented a tux to match—powder blue, his shirt white with blue-trimmed ruffles down the front and his cummer-bund and bow tie a slightly darker, satiny blue, the same color as her dress.

Unlike her hair, his was perfect, parted on the side and slicked smooth across the crown of his head. He kept it relatively short—because it was easier, he claimed, but she suspected he just didn't want anyone to mistake him for a hippie.

"You look beautiful," he said, then glanced at Bobby. "Bobby D."

"Foster," Bobby responded curtly.

Staring at her two favorite guys in the whole world, Joelle had to stifle a laugh. One clean-cut, polished and elegant, the other scruffy and defiant. They were so different, and she loved them both. But Drew was easier on her nerves. He never seemed to struggle. He never suffered a moment's doubt. He understood what he wanted from life, and he knew how to get it. He wore his good fortune as if it were a comfortable pair of shoes.

Good fortune had never favored Bobby DiFranco. Maybe that was why he wore scuffed old boots.

"I gotta go," he said, patting Joelle on the shoulder. "Have fun. And don't forget that photo."

Joelle watched him stride through the living room, mumble a farewell to her mother and Mrs. Proski and then swing out the front door. She wished he weren't so negative about the prom and the Hill kids. He could have gone to the prom with Margie and had fun tonight, too.

If he and Margie went down to the lake, he'd probably have fun, she realized with a quiet laugh. Maybe even more fun than she and Drew would have at the prom.

SHE DIDN'T GO TO THE LAKE with Drew that night. Instead he and two of his buddies and their dates all drove to a nightclub three towns away. Joelle was the only one of the six without fake ID, so she'd ordered ginger ale while they'd all gotten tipsy on cocktails, and she'd felt like an idiot. But to her great relief the question of whether to go all the way with Drew never came up.

Two weeks later, they were high-school graduates. Joelle had a job running the cash register at Harley's, a convenience store where she'd worked the previous summer. She had enrolled in two classes at the community college, which would start in September. Two were all she could afford, and the light schedule would allow her to continue working at Harley's during the school year.

Drew would be heading to Dartmouth at the end of August. He spent the hot, empty days of summer playing tennis and lounging by the pool with the other Hill kids at Green Gates Country Club. He didn't bother to get a job. His parents provided him all the money he needed.

Bobby got his draft notice. He'd scored a low number in the lottery and college had been out of the question for him, so he couldn't apply for a student deferment. "I don't want to go to Vietnam," he confessed to Joelle, "but I'm not gonna shoot my kneecap off or pretend I'm queer just to stay out. I just can't do that." With a philosophical shrug, he added, "At least Vietnam isn't Holmdell. Going there can't be as bad as staying here."

He had a job doing maintenance at the town cemetery, mowing the grass, trimming the shrubs and clearing away the wilted flowers left by visitors. He spent most of his evenings with Margie and Joelle spent most of hers with Drew. But two nights a week she had to work until 10:00 p.m. at Harley's, and Drew considered that hour too late for them to get together. On those nights, Bobby would swing by Harley's in his rattly old pickup truck and drive her down to the A&W. They'd sneak into the woods beyond the parking lot and share a joint. Once it was nothing more than a wisp of lingering smoke, they'd buy root beers and split a jumbo order of fries and they'd talk.

"You think he's gonna ask you to marry him?" Bobby inquired one evening while they were satisfying their munchies with hot, salty fries.

"I don't know. It doesn't make sense to be engaged while he's in New Hampshire and I'm here."

"But that's what you're hoping for, right?"

"Yeah," she admitted, feeling her cheeks warm. The Hill girls were all leaving town for college, and they talked about having careers and waiting until they were established before they got married. But Joelle was never going to be "established"—not unless Drew established her as his wife.

She wouldn't mind having a career, too. She wasn't afraid of work. Before she had a career, though, she'd have to earn a college degree. Accomplishing that might take her longer than normal if she enrolled in only two courses a semester at the community college, but eventually she'd transfer to a four-year university and graduate. Drew wouldn't want to have a wife who wasn't college educated.

Sitting beneath the awning bordering the parking lot at the A&W, Bobby sent her an enigmatic smile and drawled, "You wanna get yourself a big fat diamond on your finger." He always smiled that way after he'd smoked pot, a mysterious I-know-something-you-don't-know smile. "You wanna drive a Caddy and wear a mink and have everyone call you Mrs. Drew Foster." Still smiling, he shook his head. "You should aim higher, JoJo. If you can get Foster, imagine who else you could get. The world is filled with rich guys. Why settle for him?"

"I'm not looking for a rich guy," she insisted, trying not to let

Bobby rile her. "That's not why I love Drew. I don't put Margie
down, Bobby. Don't you put Drew down."

She never smoked pot with Drew that summer. He preferred
liquor to drugs. He seemed to believe booze was sophisticated.
He preferred mixed drinks, and he liked to lecture on which
brands of vodka or Scotch were the best. At least he never got
smashed on a regular basis, like some of his friends.

She wished he would take her to Green Gates some evenings,
but he rarely did. He would complain to her that he'd already spent
the whole day there and didn't want to go to the nighttime swim
or sign up for the lighted tennis courts. Not that Joelle knew a
tennis racquet from a snowshoe, but she would have liked to swim
in the pool. She owned one swimsuit, but it was a black bikini. If
Drew saw her in it, it might make him love her a little more.

They did go to the lake pretty often in his Corvette—but not
to swim. Making out wasn't easy in that car, since it had no
backseat. She let Drew touch her breasts and even slide his
fingers inside her shorts, which seemed to excite him more than
her. And she touched him, stroked him, let him come in her
hand. That always struck her as incredibly intimate, his spurt-
ing all his fluid onto her palms. After she cleaned up, using
tissues from the portable pack he kept stashed in his glove compartment, he'd always cuddle her and tell her he loved her.

As the summer stretched into August, he began to push for
more. "We're going to be apart for months," he reminded her.
"If we did this, it would make us closer. It would seal our love."

"I don't know, Drew… Maybe I'm not ready yet." Everyone
was always talking about free love, but she didn't get how anything that significant could be free. If she gave in to Drew, would
he love her more or less? If she gave in to him, would she love
herself more or less?

"We're high-school graduates, Joelle. How much more ready do we have to be?"

"Sex isn't exactly like trigonometry," she argued. "You don't just take a course and pass."

Whenever they had these discussions, Drew always worked hard not to get impatient. Joelle could tell; she could see him wrestling with his temper, breathing deeply then holding her hand or wrapping his arm around her. He didn't yell. He didn't force. That told her he must love her.

Toward the end of August, he tried a different approach. "It would be like this gift you gave me to bring with me to Dartmouth," he explained. "This special thing we shared that would keep us close, even when I'm away."

"If I gave you that gift, how do I know you wouldn't just leave and forget I ever existed?"

"Because I love you. You know I do."

The night before he planned to leave for college, she yielded. She still wasn't sure she was ready or if it was right, but when she imagined him traveling all the way to New Hampshire and meeting all those new, smart, sophisticated Ivy Leaguers, she couldn't bear the thought that he wouldn't have something of hers in his possession, something precious, something she would never give to anyone else. So she told him yes.

He borrowed his father's Lincoln for the occasion because it had a wide, well-upholstered backseat, which Drew carefully draped with a towel because he was aware she would bleed. He brought a condom. They drank half a bottle of Chianti, the kind with straw around the base, and Joelle told him to save the bottle when it was empty and stick a candle in it, and every time he lit the candle it would be like a memory of her burning in his soul. He told her she was a poet.

Despite the wine and the towel and the car's wide backseat, it hurt. All she felt was pain and Drew's hot, wine-tinged breath in her face. She'd believed making love was supposed to feel good, but it didn't. It hurt, hurt, hurt.

At least it ended quickly. Drew tore into her and pounded on her for less than thirty seconds, and then he groaned and shuddered and was done. He pulled out of her so fast the condom remained behind. That was probably the worst part of it, so embarrassing, his poking around with his fingers and dragging the condom out.

"I love you, Joelle," he whispered. "I love you so much."

Hearing those words soothed the awful burning between her legs. They'd made love and now they were bound forever. Because she'd given him this, he would never stop loving her.

The next day, he was gone.

THREE

JOELLE STOOD IN THE open doorway, a silhouette in the light from the mudroom, and stared into the garage's gloom. Bobby watched her through the windshield. Even with her face in shadow, he could picture her features—the hollows of her cheeks, the pointed tip of her nose, the faint lines fanning out from the corners of her dazzling blue eyes. He'd fallen in love with her face when he was ten years old, sitting three rows to her left in Mrs. Schmidt's fourth-grade class, before he'd had any idea what falling in love meant. And today, forty-seven years later, he still loved her face.

He wasn't the sort who ran away from a problem, but as long as Drew Foster had been sitting in his kitchen, threatening everything Bobby cared about, everything that had ever mattered to him, he couldn't have stayed. Not because Foster scared him but because he scared himself.

His father had been a violent man, and Bobby had sworn he would be exactly the kind of man his father wasn't. But looking at Foster, listening to him calmly explain why Bobby should tell Claudia the truth about her birth, had made Bobby feel his own father's blood pulsing through his veins. He'd had to get the hell out.

Joelle was alone now. He knew she wouldn't have come looking for him unless Foster had left. She'd probably made some excuse for Bobby, explained that he had a quick temper—which, in general, he didn't—or invented some other justification for his behavior. Or maybe not. Maybe she'd just let his rage sit there in the room, simmering in the air.

He shoved open the door, swung out of the truck and walked toward Joelle. He felt the cold, hard concrete floor against the soles of his feet, right through his socks. Cold and hard suited his mood.

"He's gone," Joelle confirmed.

"I'm sorry," he said. He was sorry not for walking out on Foster but for abandoning Joelle. He should have stood by her and made clear to Foster exactly whose wife she was. Instead, he'd bolted, leaving her alone with a man she'd once loved with all her heart.

She gave him a sad smile. "It's okay."

No, it wasn't okay. Nothing was okay.

He followed her through the mudroom into the kitchen. The air smelled of coffee. He wondered if from here on in he would always associate that scent with Foster, if he would never be able to drink coffee again.

His own cup was resting in the dish rack beside the sink, already rinsed clean. The coffeemaker was turned off. Except for the aroma, he detected no sign that Foster had ever been in his house. Yet the atmosphere felt charged. The sunlight streaming through the windows seemed too bright.

In that glaring summer light, he could see Joelle's face clearly. Her mouth was tense, her eyes tired. Her ponytail hung lopsided, brushing against her left shoulder.

"He can't have Claudia," Bobby said. If that SOB wanted to reach Claudia, he'd have to get past Bobby, and Bobby intended to make that impossible.

"He doesn't want Claudia," she said wearily. She reached for Bobby's hand. Her fingers felt like icy twigs on his skin. "He wants her to take a blood test, that's all."

"That's all," Bobby echoed, then snorted. "How do we ask her to take a blood test without telling her why? And what if she's a match? What do we tell her then?"

"I don't know." Releasing his hand, Joelle sank into a chair, propped her elbows on the table and rested her chin in her palms. "It's not a simple situation."

"It's simple enough," Bobby argued, dropping onto another chair. "You and I had an understanding. We based our marriage on that understanding. Claudia is our daughter. That's the end of it."

"His son is dying," Joelle said, her eyes as overly bright as the sunshine pouring through the windows. "Can't you at least have a little sympathy for the man?"

Not as much as Joelle had, obviously. Sure, he felt sorry for Foster in an abstract way. He'd feel sorry for any man whose child was at risk. Maybe he ought to feel sorry for himself, since right now his own daughter seemed at risk.

"If she had the blood test and didn't match," Joelle argued, "she'd never have to know."

"Of course she'd have to know. What do you think—we can sneak a blood test past her?"

"We wouldn't have to tell her what it was for. We could say she's being tested to find out if she matches a distant cousin—"

"Oh, there's a plan." Sarcasm soured Bobby's voice. "You're an only child and my brother's gay. My father's family gave him up long ago. How's your mother fixed for cousins? How does

Claudia wind up with a cousin?" He crossed to the sink and washed his hands, just because the whole situation made him feel dirty. "Don't you think she'd ask about this cousin she'd never heard of? Maybe she'd even want to meet this miraculous new cousin of hers."

Rather than commenting on his sarcasm, Joelle nodded in agreement. "You're right. Lying isn't going to help. It's just that we've been lying all along. What's one more lie at this point?"

Bobby dried his hands on a dish towel, buying time to consider his response. Had they been lying all along, or had they been trying to create a family? Had they been lying or simply figuring out a way to survive, a way to make life work? Had Bobby been lying from the start when he'd convinced himself he could be the father of another man's child, and the husband of a woman who hadn't loved him the way he'd loved her?

Everything—his home, his work, his family—had sprouted from a lie. Like a plant grown from a poisoned seed, that lie had broken through the ground and blossomed, but the roots were rotten. Sooner or later the plant was doomed to die.

"Nothing can change the fact that you're her father," Joelle said, twisting in her chair so she could look at him. "If I'd conceived her at a sperm bank, it would have been the same thing."

"No, it wouldn't." He flung the towel aside and shoved his hair back from his face. The kitchen was too warm. The streaming sunlight was killing him. "A sperm bank is anonymous. This..." He waved vaguely toward the front door, through which Foster must have entered his house. "This was a guy you were in love with."

"I was a kid then."

She didn't deny that she'd loved Foster. She wouldn't. Now wasn't the time for lies. Yet acknowledging that she'd once

loved that bastard—a truth Bobby had managed to avoid thinking about for years—pained him. He wished he were the only
man she'd ever loved. He'd married her knowing he wasn't, but
still…the truth hurt.

"All right." Her shoulders slumped and she glanced away
from him. "What do you want, Bobby? What do you want to
do about this?"

"I want to tell Drew Foster to go to hell." Actually, what he
wanted was to turn back the clock a half hour. He wanted to
drive home, excited about landing a new contract—even after
years in the business, every new contract gave him a thrill—and
confident that when he got home, Joelle would be waiting for
him. He wanted to arrive and find her finished with her housecleaning, sweaty and heading for the shower. He wanted to pull
off his clothes and slip into the shower with her and screw her
silly while the water sprayed down onto them.

"What do *you* want?" he shot back, dreading her answer even
though he had to hear it.

She turned back to face the table and folded her hands, as
though praying. "I keep thinking about how his son is dying," she
said, her voice muted but steady.

"His daughter would have been dead if you'd done what he'd
told you to do all those years ago." The words sounded brutal,
but he didn't care. "If you'd done what Foster asked back then,
Claudia would never even have existed."

"Here's the thing, Bobby." Her voice remained calm, her eyes
dry, but she clasped her hands tighter, turning her knuckles
white. "Imagine if it was Claudia who was sick today. Imagine
the only thing that could save her was a bone marrow transplant
from a sibling."

"She's got two brothers."

"Imagine they weren't a match." She seemed to be address-ing a molecule of air directly in front of her. "Imagine her life was at stake. If there was the slightest chance that Drew might have gone on to have other children who would be her half brothers or half sisters... You know as well as I do that we'd be hiring a detective to find him. If the shoe was on the other foot, we'd do exactly what he did."

Bobby opened his mouth and then shut it. Joelle was right. He hated her for being right, but he couldn't argue. If Claudia was dying, Bobby would try anything, go anywhere, destroy any family if that was what it took to cure her.

"What happened then happened then," Joelle said. "Now we've got to deal with today. A young man is dying, and there's a chance Claudia can save his life."

Joelle's words and all they implied enraged him. He wanted to hit things, break things. He wanted to confront the doctors treating Drew's son and tell them to come up with some other treatment so he wouldn't have the burden of that boy's life pressing on his back.

He wanted to preserve his family. He wanted to protect his daughter. He wanted to keep on living the lie. It had been a good lie. It had worked for all these years.

He gazed down at Joelle. Seated, she should have looked small. But her spine was straight, her eyes clear, her chin raised. A piece of his soul shriveled inside him as he considered his choice.

If he said no, he'd lose her. If he said yes, he'd lose every-thing his life had been about up to this minute.

Closing his eyes, he saw red.

CLAUDIA LIVED SOUTH OF Gray Hill in Fairfield County. Her husband was an attorney—he made too much money to be a mere lawyer—and Claudia had been a well-paid marketing consultant until she gave birth to Jeremy four years ago. She'd contemplated returning to work when Jeremy was six months old, but she'd been so reluctant that Gary had urged her to be a full-time mother for a few years. They could live well on his income alone. And two years later, Kristin was born.

So Claudia was still a full-time mother, though she often told Joelle she intended to return to paying work someday. "Women who work outside the home can be terrific mothers," she often said. "Look at you. You're a teacher, and you were a terrific mother."

After tonight, Joelle thought, Claudia would hardly think Joelle was terrific. This was probably a huge mistake. She should tell Bobby to turn the truck around and drive home. She should forget that Drew Foster's shadow had ever darkened her front porch.

It was too late to turn around. Seated beside her in the driver's seat of his truck, Bobby appeared grim and determined as he steered south toward Claudia's house. Joelle had done too good a job of convincing him that this was the correct thing to do, that Drew's son didn't deserve to die just because Drew and Joelle had been young and stupid.

"Claudia has a right to know the truth," she said, wishing she could convince herself the way she'd convinced Bobby. "We probably should have told her years ago."

"Told her what?" He stared through the windshield at the headlight beams illuminating the road. "That I'm not her father?"

"Stop saying that, Bobby. You *are* her father. Even Drew understands that."

"If Drew understands it, then I guess it must be true."

His sarcasm implied just how bitter he was. She hadn't meant to cause him pain—not now, not ever. But she didn't see how continuing the lies would help, especially when a young man's life hung in the balance.

Claudia should have learned about her genetic heritage years ago, for her own benefit. Better for her to find out from her parents than from some doctor should a crisis arise, like the one Drew's son was facing.

But Joelle and Bobby had never told her. The secret had simply gotten buried by daily life. One year had rolled into the next until the truth had grown invisible, just one blade of grass in a thick green lawn.

"She'll never stop loving you," Joelle reassured Bobby. "You're her daddy. She's named after your mother, for God's sake."

He glanced at her. His hair was too long, but she liked it that way, a remnant of his rebellious youth. Strands of silver had infiltrated the dark waves and the outdoor work he did had weathered his face. Unlike Drew, Bobby hadn't gone soft at all. His body was still sinewy, his jaw defiant. He'd started using reading glasses a few years ago, but even when he was wearing them, he looked tough and brimming with energy, ready to take on the world.

"Are you going to explain everything?" he asked. "Or should I?"

"I will."

"What if she kicks us out of her house?"

Joelle didn't want to consider that possibility. "I'll tell her it's all my fault. Let her blame me, Bobby."

"I don't want her blaming you," he muttered. "You're her real mother."

And I'm not her real father. The words lingered unspoken in the snug cab of the truck.

Joelle had already told him countless times that he was Claudia's father. She wasn't going to say it again. She felt sick, her stomach clenching, her head thumping. *Turn around*, she thought, but she couldn't force out the words.

Just as Drew's son deserved a chance to live, Claudia deserved her parents' honesty.

Bobby pulled into Claudia's driveway, which led to a spacious colonial in a ritzy subdivision. The porch lights had been left on for them. Joelle wondered if this would be the last time Claudia ever welcomed them into her home. Even braced for the worst, she wondered if she'd survive her daughter's reaction.

Gary opened the door for them. A tall, affable man, he greeted them with a warm smile. "You're lucky you caught us home tonight," he said as he ushered them into the house. "Saturday night we're usually out carousing."

"Ha!" Claudia commented from the kitchen. "We can barely keep our eyes open after 9:00 p.m. The kids wear us out." She waltzed down the hall and hugged Joelle. Claudia resembled Joelle—the same slender build, the blond hair, the elegantly hollow cheeks—except that she had brown eyes. She'd always claimed she had her father's eyes, but now, as Joelle peered into them, she saw Drew as much as Bobby in those mocha-brown irises.

"I've got to admit, we were surprised you asked to stop by so late," Gary said. "Usually you don't even want to see us. You just come to play with the kids."

"That's not true," Joelle said, her tone more defensive than she'd intended. She knew Gary was joking. He and Claudia always kidded that their sole value to Bobby and Joelle was as the people who'd supplied them grandchildren.

Tonight, though, Joelle had told Claudia they would be stopping by after Jeremy and Kristin were in bed. This was not a visit for which the children should be awake. Lowering her tone, she said, "I'm sorry we're keeping you awake past your bedtime."

"Not a problem," Claudia insisted, wrapping Bobby in a hug. Claudia's hair was cut in a chic, angular style and her outfit, a wrinkly cotton shirt of turquoise, with slacks the same vivid fabric, probably cost more than Joelle's entire summer wardrobe. "Dad, you look terrible. Are you feeling okay?"

"It's been a rough day," he said cryptically.

"Why don't we sit down," Joelle suggested, gesturing toward the living room. "We have to talk, Claudia."

Claudia eyed Gary. "I don't like the sound of this," she said through a tight smile.

"Hey, it's Saturday night. No bad news allowed." Gary grinned at Joelle and Bobby. "Can I get you something to drink?"

Bobby answered for both of them. "No, thanks." He sat in the wingback chair in Claudia's impeccably decorated living room.

Gary took the other wingback chair and Joelle settled on the couch with Claudia. She wanted to be close to her daughter. In fact, she wanted to gather Claudia up, hold her on her lap and hug her, the way she had when Claudia had been a little girl. She wanted to cling to her baby and assure her that nothing bad would ever happen to her. Her own mistakes had brought so much pain to Bobby, and now they would bring pain to Claudia, too—and this wasn't a pain she could kiss away, like the scrapes and bruises Claudia had suffered as a child.

Just get it over with, she ordered herself, then added a stern mental reminder that Claudia deserved the truth. "We had a visitor today," she said. "Someone Dad and I went to high school with. In fact, he was my boyfriend senior year."

"I thought Dad was your boyfriend," Claudia said.

"I adored Dad. He was my best friend." She felt Bobby's gaze on her, cool and condemning. Swallowing, she pressed on. "This old classmate of ours is married now, and he has a son. His son is sick with a kind of leukemia. He has to receive a bone marrow transplant."

Claudia's smile faded. She glanced away—at Bobby or Gary, Joelle didn't know—and then turned back to her mother. Her eyes were filled with questions. "How tragic."

"Yes. It's tragic. Claudia…that man, that old boyfriend…" Joelle drew in a deep breath. She tasted the salt of tears at the back of her throat and swallowed. "He believes you might be a match for his son as a donor."

Claudia's mouth tensed. Her eyes hardened. She didn't need Joelle to spell it out. "Oh, my God," she whispered.

"We probably should have told you years ago, but… There never seemed to be any need. We're your parents, you're our daughter and nothing else mattered. So we just never said anything. But now, with his son so sick—he begged us to discuss this with you."

Claudia spun away, seeking her husband. Gary started to rise, but before he was standing, Claudia had twisted back to her mother. "Who is this man?" she demanded. "Who is this old boyfriend of yours?"

"He was someone from our hometown, Claudia. A classmate of ours."

"What's his name?" Claudia's voice was as cold as stone.

"Drew Foster."

Claudia mouthed his name, as if testing the syllables. She closed her eyes and shook her head. "I can't believe this. I can't believe…" She glanced at Bobby. "You knew about this?"

From the corner of her eyes, Joelle saw him nod.

"But you never—you always—" Again Claudia shook her head. Her eyes glinted with moisture. "How could you?" she asked, directing her question into the air rather than toward

Joelle or Bobby. "How could you keep this from me? How could you let me think…" Her voice trailed off.

"Think what, Claudia?" Joelle asked.

Gazing desperately at her, Claudia gestured toward Bobby. "Think *he's* my father."

Joelle felt her heart crack in two. She couldn't bear to look at Bobby, to witness how badly Claudia's words wounded him. "He *is* your father. He's the only father you have."

"But this other man—this Drew Foster—"

"Asked me to get an abortion. I wanted you so much, Claudia. I couldn't do that. And your dad—" she dared to peek at Bobby, whose face was frozen except for his dark, turbulent eyes "—wanted you, too, every bit as much as I did. So we raised you, and we loved you and we still love you, more than you can imagine."

"But you never told me this." Claudia's anguish carried an undertone of hysteria. "You never told me some other man was my father. My God. I don't even know who I am anymore."

The sobs in Joelle's throat threatened to choke her. She wouldn't let herself cry, though. Not in front of Claudia and Gary, not in front of Bobby. Yes, she'd made mistakes in her life. But she would never believe that giving birth to Claudia had been a mistake. Not even now, when she felt as if the pain in her heart would kill her.

Abruptly Claudia stood and stalked out of the living room. In the stillness she left behind, Joelle could hear the tread of her footsteps as she climbed the stairs, followed by the click of a door closing.

Gary shoved to his feet and glowered at them. "You can show yourselves out," he said as he stalked out of the living room. In less than a minute Joelle heard that upstairs door open and shut again, sounding miles away.

IN THE SUMMER, BOBBY slept nude. If Joelle's body were as sleek and youthful as his, she might sleep nude, too, but she was too self-conscious about the droop of her breasts, the way the skin of her abdomen sagged between the points of her hip bones, the damage left by fifty-six years of living. So she slept in an oversize T-shirt. Her sons had outgrown so many T-shirts over the years that she had several wardrobes' worth of castoffs from them.

Tonight she was wearing a striped cotton shirt Mike had worn constantly throughout high school, until in one of those odd adolescent spurts he'd awakened one morning to discover that he'd grown two inches and his shoulders were straining the shirt's seams. The cotton fabric felt soft against her skin, but she couldn't find a comfortable position between the sheets. When Bobby finished washing and joined her, he eased himself onto the bed, making sure not to touch her.

Usually he stretched out on his side facing her and slung one arm around her. Their bed was their refuge, their haven. In bed they were united. Husband and wife. No disagreements, no resentments, no bullshit. Just the two of them, JoJo and Bobby D, unbreakable.

Tonight he kept his distance.

She lay in the darkness until his silence began to feel like an actual presence, a stranger in their bed. Damn it, she wouldn't allow Drew to tear her and Bobby apart. No matter what had happened today, no matter how Claudia dealt with what Joelle had told her, she was not going to sacrifice her marriage.

She breached the chasm between her and Bobby—only a couple of inches, yet wide enough to contain the ugly truth they had carefully avoided until today—and stroked her hand down his chest. His skin was warm, the hair on his chest springy.

When he didn't move, she shifted closer to him, snuggled up to him, skimmed her lips against the underside of his jaw.

He lay as still as a stone.

Sitting, she yanked off the T-shirt. She needed Bobby tonight. She needed him to know how much she loved him. She needed proof that they could survive this as they'd survived so much else in their lives.

She grazed his chin again, caressed the length of his torso, raised herself to kiss his cheek. He seemed to struggle against her invitation, against his own reflexes, but he was able to resist her only so long. When her hand slid downward to stroke him, she found him fully aroused.

With a curse, he pushed her fingers away—then cupped his hand around her head and pulled her down to him. His kisses were hard and angry, his tongue subduing her, his hand fisting in her hair so tightly she could feel his knuckles against her scalp. There was nothing tender or seductive in his kiss, in the way his free hand clamped onto her hip, his fingers digging into the soft flesh. After a moment, he tore his mouth from hers. Breathing heavily, he swore again.

"Bobby," she murmured. They'd gotten through bad times in the past by reaching for each other, using their bodies to communicate when they had no words. She knew that when Bobby was uneasy or afraid, he withdrew—and when he withdrew, she could bring him back this way, through touch, through sex. He wasn't much for talking. He was a physical man. He could close himself off, but she knew how to open him up again.

She brushed her fingertips against his lips, as if she could wipe away his coarse language and the emotion behind it. He jerked his head, recoiling from her gentle touch, then reared up and pushed her onto her back against the mattress. Her vision had adjusted to the darkness and she could make out the rage and sorrow in his eyes, the resentment tightening his jaw. He ran his hands down her body, his motions rough, his chest pumping as though breathing was a struggle.

Everything about him seemed to be struggling. She arched her arms around his shoulders and urged him onto her. *It's all right,* she wanted to tell him. *I need this. We both need this.* Not seduction, not tenderness—just connection. Just the knowledge that they were still together, that not even the truth could tear them apart.

He took her, his thrusts fierce and fast. When he came, his groan was tremulous, almost like a sob. She circled him with her arms, holding him on top of her, refusing to let him withdraw as her body pulsed around him. Had this been love or rage? Desperation? Fear?

He let out a long breath and with it another curse. *It's all right,* she assured herself, even though the past few minutes had failed to convince her anything was all right.

After a minute, he rolled away from her and flung an arm across his eyes, as if he didn't want to risk glimpsing her. "Sorry," he muttered.

She cupped his jaw. He recoiled from her touch, and she let her hand fall. "If anyone should apologize, it's me," she said. She'd started this, after all. She'd started the whole thing by telling Claudia about her parentage. She'd started it by allowing Drew Foster to enter her home. She'd started it thirty-seven years ago by foolishly believing she was in love with Drew.

Bobby's breathing was still ragged, his skin steamy, the sheet bunched around his hips. Despite the dark, she could see the sharp outline of his nose, the angle of his chin.

"Talk to me, Bobby," she pleaded.

"And say what?"

Say you're hurting. Say you're afraid. Say you want to make love to me again, gently this time. Love, not sex. Not anger. But he hated to discuss his feelings, to probe and analyze and bare his soul. For thirty-seven years, she'd been trying to get him to talk, and he never did. "Tell me what you're thinking."

He lay quietly for a stretch, his rib cage rising and falling beneath his skin, his eyes shielded from her. After a while he moved his arm away from his face, but only to stare at the ceiling. "When you build a stone wall," he said, "you've got to pick each stone out and put it in exactly the right place. If you want the wall to be stable, you have to do it right. The size of the stones. The shape."

She wasn't sure what he was getting at, but at least he was talking. She waited for him to continue.

"We didn't lay the foundation down right," he murmured. "We're standing on that wall and it's shaking beneath our feet. It's going to collapse. And we're going to fall."

"We'll get through this, Bobby. I know we will."

He shook his head. "We're falling, Jo. And it's a long way down."

Lying in a bed now cold, with her husband beside her yet a thousand miles away and that awful silence once again settling into the space between them, Joelle wondered how long the fall was and how broken they would be when they landed.

FOUR

October 1970

BOBBY PREFERRED THE part of the cemetery farthest from his mother's grave. When he worked over in her section, near Bailey Road, he found himself lingering at her site, paying too much attention to each weed that dared to poke through the grass, dusting smudges of dirt from her headstone. Reading the stone: *Claudia Ricci DiFranco, February 27, 1930–May 6, 1964. Beloved wife and mother. She is with the angels now.* As if he didn't have the damn thing memorized. As if there was any question in my mind where she was.

Where she wasn't was with him and his brother, Eddie, who were certainly no angels. And she wasn't with their father, who had as much angel in him as the headstone had diamonds.

It was better when he was mowing the lawn on the Jackson Street side of the cemetery. He didn't have to think about angels and his mother as he tidied up the landscape around the older graves, some of them dating back to the late 1800s. Old families in Holmdell had designed little family parks within the cemetery, with the graves all clustered and marble benches where visitors could rest. People rarely left flowers on the old grave sites, although the town always planted a little American flag by each veteran's grave on Memorial Day, the Fourth of July and Veteran's Day. Bobby had had to clear away all the American flags twice this season, but he would be gone by the time Veteran's Day rolled around, on his way to becoming a veteran himself.

Autumn was late arriving in southern Ohio this year. The midafternoon air was hot and heavy, but he wasn't allowed to remove his shirt while he worked. A bare chest was disrespectful to the dead, his boss had scolded him when he'd yanked off his T-shirt and looped it around his belt one scorching afternoon a couple of months ago. He'd learned to bring an extra bandanna with him——one to use as a headband and the other to mop the sweat off his face.

Only two more hours and he could punch out for the day, he thought as the mower's engine made a stuttering noise and spewed some black smoke out the exhaust pipe. Only ten days and he'd be done with this job and on his way to Fort Dix in New Jersey.

He paused under an oak dense with summer-green leaves and pretended the shade was cooler than it actually was. Staring down the hill toward the more recent graves, he saw a few people ambling along the paths. Thursday afternoon wasn't a busy time at the cemetery. Funerals were usually held before noon so that afterward the mourners could eat heartily or drink heavily, depending on how they felt about the dearly departed. Bobby was sometimes assigned to fill in a grave after a funeral service, although that was supposed to be a union job, not a task for the kid who mowed the lawn and pruned the shrubs. But when his boss was shorthanded, or if it was raining and the interment had to be done before the hole filled with muddy water, he wound up shoveling.

He spotted a visitor heading up the hill toward him, walking in long, purposeful strides. Sun-streaked blond hair swung below her shoulders and her white peasant blouse and denim bell-bottoms hung wilted on her slender frame. He knew that walk, that hair. He knew those beautiful blue eyes.

He shut off the lawn mower. If Joelle had come to see him—and she didn't have any loved ones buried in the cemetery, so Bobby figured he was the reason she was here—he could take a break.

He leaned against the tree and pulled a crushed pack of Marlboros from the breast pocket of his faded blue work shirt. By the time he'd shaken out a cigarette she was within shouting distance. Her face was pale and her smile was one of those brave, quivery things women wore when they were about to burst into tears.

He slid a book of matches from where he'd wedged it inside the cellophane wrapper of the cigarette pack. "You okay?" he asked.

"Have you got a minute?"

"Five minutes at least," he said, gesturing toward a memorial bench near the tree. She sat on it and propped her purse in her lap. It was a patchwork fabric sack with velvet drawstrings, and she'd told him some time ago that she'd designed and sewn it herself. Bobby was in awe of her talent.

He wondered if she'd traveled here straight from school. She was enrolled in classes at the community college, trying to make something of herself. She had so much going for her—brains, school, a rich boyfriend at Dartmouth and all that gorgeous blond hair—while Bobby cut grass and counted the days until he got shipped overseas. He would have thought that by now she'd have become friendly with her college classmates. She had no reason to hang out with him anymore.

Yet she did. No matter that she was on the path to bigger and better things; she clearly valued their friendship. Just one more reason he loved her.

He lit the cigarette while he waited for her to speak. "I need a favor," she finally said, gazing at the ornately carved headstone of Abigail Charney, who'd died in 1914 and was spending eternity in a grave a few feet from the bench.

"Sure."

She glanced at him, then turned back to stare at the gravestone. "Can you drive me to Cincinnati?"

He almost laughed—that was such a small thing to ask. He'd been expecting something a lot more demanding, given her obvious distress. "You can't borrow your mother's car?"

"No." She shook her head, just in case he hadn't understood her answer. "I could take the bus, but I—" Her voice broke.

Hell. Just as he'd predicted, she started to cry. He pulled the blue bandanna from the hip pocket of his jeans and handed it to her, glad that it wasn't too sweaty. "Screw the bus," he said. "I'll drive you down. When do you have to go?"

Tears rolled down her cheeks. She dabbed at them with his bandanna. "It has to be a weekday. I'm sorry. That probably messes up your work schedule."

"Big deal. I'll call in sick." For Joelle, he'd call in dead.

"It's just that…" She swallowed hard. "I have to see a doctor."

Despite the afternoon's heat, fear rippled like ice down his back. Holmdell had doctors. She must be seriously ill if she had to travel all the way to Cincinnati to meet with one. A specialist, maybe. At one of the big hospitals.

He eased closer to her on the bench and bent so he could peer into her downturned face. "What's wrong, Jo?"

She lifted her chin and gazed at him, her eyes puffy and her cheeks streaked with tears. "I'm pregnant."

SHE COULDN'T BELIEVE THIS had happened to her.

Of course, she *could* believe it. This sort of thing happened to girls all the time. And in her case, it was clear Drew hadn't known what he was doing with that damn condom. She remembered the humiliation of having him pry it out of her with his fingers, how nauseating the entire experience had been.

Little had she known then how much worse it would become.

Fresh tears spilled out of her eyes and she squeezed them shut. When the nurse at the college clinic had told her the results of her pregnancy test, she'd managed to hold back her tears until she was outside the building. Then she'd collapsed onto a bench and wept, and thought: *I have to talk to Bobby.* Not her mother, who would immediately view this ghastly mistake as a way to capture Drew. Not even Drew.

Bobby was her friend. They were honest with each other. They trusted each other. In a crisis, he was the one she wanted by her side.

Once she'd calmed down, though, she'd realized she had to tell Drew first. She'd phoned him at his dormitory and forced out the words: "I'm pregnant, Drew. I'm sorry. I'm pregnant."

"Okay. Don't panic, Joelle. I can't talk now," he'd said, though he hadn't explained exactly *why* he couldn't, what pressing matter he had to deal with that was more important than his girlfriend's pregnancy. "I'll get back to you soon, though. Don't worry, okay? We'll deal with this."

He'd gotten back to her, all right. The creep.

Now, belatedly, she'd approached Bobby. She prayed that he would live up to her trust and help her do what had to be done. She could get through this disaster alone if she had to—at least, she hoped she could. But if Bobby could help, if he could hold her hand through the ordeal and offer her a shoulder to lean on… Maybe it wouldn't be quite so bad.

Seated next to her on the bench, he leaned back and dragged on his cigarette. Gray smoke streamed between his lips as he sighed. "What kind of doctor are we talking about?"

"You know what kind," she said, her voice hoarse from her tears.

"Shit, Jo. You don't want to do that."

"Why not?"

"It's against the law."

"Don't lay that on me." She heard the anger in her voice and immediately felt contrite. Bobby didn't deserve her anger. He was only saying what she'd been thinking about nonstop ever since she'd received Drew's letter. "I have the name of a doctor who does this. He's supposed to be safe."

Bobby scrutinized her, squinting as if he thought that would bring her into clearer focus. *Please,* she begged silently, *please don't judge me. Please don't hate me for doing what I have to do.* "Who gave you the doctor's name?" he asked, and she understood his disapproval then. It was aimed at Drew, not her.

He'd obviously guessed, but she answered his question anyway. "I called Drew," she said. "I reached him at his dormitory and told him. He said he'd get back to me, and he did." Her breath hitched from all her crying and she fidgeted with the ties of her purse. "I got a letter from him today. He sent me the name of a doctor and some money. Enough to pay for everything. The doctor and transportation, too."

"I'm not going charge you carfare," Bobby muttered. He rubbed out his cigarette on the sole of his boot. "How much did he send?"

"A thousand dollars."

Bobby flinched. "A *thousand* dollars? What—is he buying you off?"

She had to admit that possibility had crossed her mind, too. "I have no idea what these kinds of doctors charge. Drew sent me a check. I can't cash it in town. Everyone would know. I guess there would be a bank branch in Cincinnati, or somewhere along the way..."

Bobby shook his head and cursed again. "Do you want to do this? Is this your choice, or are you just doing it to make Foster happy?"

"What else can I do?" Her voice began to wobble again. "I can't spend nine months pregnant and then give my baby away. I just couldn't do that. And I can't raise the baby myself. I know what that's like, Bobby. It's the story of my life."

She'd told Bobby years ago about the father who'd briefly, mysteriously drifted through her life. Dale Webber had been a cross-country trucker who used to detour off the highway to avoid weigh stations. He'd met Joelle's mother during one of those detours and they'd gotten involved, enough that every time he was passing through Ohio he'd stop in Holmdell to spend time with Wanda, the cute waitress at the Bank Street Diner. During one of those stops, he'd knocked her up.

Joelle had vague memories of Dale's visiting and bringing her a coloring book and a shabby little doll when she was a toddler. But after a while the visits ended, and when Joelle was about five, her mother had received a letter from a woman who claimed to be Dale's sister in California. The woman reported that Dale had been killed in a highway accident, and she'd enclosed some money from an insurance settlement and they'd never seen Dale again.

Joelle's mother had used the money to buy a car. A Rambler. "It seems appropriate," Wanda had said. "Your dad was a rambling man."

Whether her dad had married her mother, Joelle couldn't say for sure. But one day in fourth grade, Tommy Travers had called her a bastard child. She hadn't even known what that meant, but she'd denied it. She'd stood up to that sniveling bully and told him she wasn't a bastard child, because she understood innately that a bastard child was not a good thing to be.

"I don't want a life like my mother's," she told Bobby now. "And I don't want my child to grow up the way I did."

"So Foster mails you a check and tells you to deal with the problem? He can't even come back and get you through it?"

"He's in college," she pointed out. It was no excuse, but she'd rather defend Drew than admit that he'd given her money with the hope that she'd deal with her problem and disappear from his life.

Bobby pulled another cigarette from his pocket and a book of matches. She watched him bend a match inside its cardboard folder with his thumb and scrape its tip against the flint. It flared into flame and he lit the cigarette, inhaling deeply. "What about adoption?" he asked.

"I can't do that," she said. "Like I said, I can't spend nine months with this baby inside me and then give it away. I just couldn't do that."

He smoked in silence, staring at the sunlight-dappled gravestone in front of them, though his eyes seemed focused somewhere else. He said nothing until his cigarette was gone and he'd stubbed it out. Then he turned to her. "I'll marry you."

She gaped at him, too shocked to speak.

"I'll be your baby's father," he elaborated.

Was he nuts? He would take responsibility for her and a baby that wasn't even his? When she'd screwed up so royally, when she'd pretty much ruined her life with her own stupidity? When she'd told him all summer long that she dreamed of marrying Drew? Bobby was her best friend in the world, but what he was offering went way beyond what anyone should do for a friend. It was crazy.

She couldn't insult him by saying so. Instead she said, "You're about to leave for basic training."

"That's what'll make it work, Jo. It's not like we'd have to live with each other or anything. I'd be away, you'd be my wife, you'd have your baby and then when I got home, we could figure out where we stood."

"Bobby." He couldn't be that generous. Not to her. She didn't deserve such kindness, such a sacrifice on his part.

"If something happens to me in Vietnam," he continued, sounding calm and logical, "there are widow's benefits. You could use those to support yourself and the kid."

No. She'd been an idiot. She'd gotten pregnant, like some careless, dim-witted slut. Bobby DiFranco was too good-hearted, too decent, to be stuck cleaning up her messes. "Bobby, I—"

"To tell you the truth, having a wife and baby waiting for me back home would help me. It would, you know—keep my spirits up."

That brought her up short. Maybe he wasn't offering to marry her strictly out of charity. He saw something in it for him, too. A wife waiting at home for him. A wife who would write to him, who would send him home-baked cookies and dry socks and reminders of all the good things he'd be returning to once he finished his service. She'd be at home, praying every day for his safety. That might be enough to get him through his year in 'Nam.

"I'd have something to come back to," he explained. "I need that, Jo."

"What about Margie?" she asked. "Aren't you going to come back to her?"

He snorted. "There's nothing there," he said. "We're just… You want to know the truth? We're both just waiting for me to leave so we can break up without going through the fights and the hurt feelings. She thinks she's doing her patriotic duty, going out with me until I leave for basic."

"I'm sure she loves you," Joelle argued, even though she had no basis for that assertion.

He shook his head. "We're already history. Just waiting for Uncle Sam to make it official." He gazed at Joelle's hands, folded tensely atop her purse and then at her face. "I could give your baby a name, Jo," he said quietly. "And then, if I got home and we decided this wasn't what we wanted, we could get a divorce. But your baby would have a name."

Without thinking, she moved her hands to her stomach and pressed. So flat, so smooth. A baby she couldn't even feel was in there, and Bobby was willing to give it his name. Fresh tears welled up in her eyes. "Wouldn't it bother you, knowing that the baby…"

"Was Foster's?" He turned back to stare at the gravestone again. "If we do this, the baby is mine. Your baby would be a DiFranco. Could you live with that?"

She opened her mouth, then shut it. Tears beaded along her lashes and blurred her vision. She didn't deserve this. She didn't deserve him. But as stupid as she'd been two months ago, in the backseat of Drew's father's Cadillac, she wasn't stupid enough to reject what Bobby was offering her.

Had she thought a radio was the best gift she'd ever received? No. *This* was. Bobby's help. His friendship. His hand and his name.

"I would consider it an honor if my baby was a DiFranco," she said.

FIVE DAYS LATER, SHE STOOD in her cramped bedroom at the back of the first-floor flat on Third Street one final time. She felt a little queasy, but that was from the pregnancy, not from panic or doubt about what she was doing.

She was running away with Bobby, her best friend, the most trustworthy guy she'd ever known. She was sad, she was grieving over the fact that her life wasn't turning out the way she'd planned—but she had no regrets. For as long as she lived, she would do whatever she could to make sure Bobby never had any regrets, either.

Yesterday morning, she'd mustered her courage and visited the local branch bank. She'd told the teller she was planning to move her account to a bank closer to campus, an explanation the teller had accepted without question. She'd let Joelle empty her account, then cashed Drew's check and counted fifty twenty-dollar bills into Joelle's palm. Joelle had stuffed the money into an envelope, which was now zipped inside an inner pocket of her suitcase.

She'd packed most of her clothing, even though she understood that within a month or two it would no longer fit her. After the baby was born, she hoped she'd get her figure back quickly. If not, maybe she could sell the clothes. The money would come in handy.

She left her prom dress behind, even though she loved it. She left her radio behind because it reminded her of Drew.

One stupid time. She'd given herself to him one stupid, stupid time, and he'd told her it would seal their love. Had he always been such a liar? Had she been dumb enough to love him?

That's the past, she reminded herself. If she looked backward, she'd trip and fall. She had to look forward, to the future, to her baby. Her baby and Bobby DiFranco.

Since she didn't have any classes at the college that day, her mother had taken the car to work. Wanda's absence simplified Joelle's departure. If Wanda hadn't had a shift at the diner, Joelle and Bobby would have had to wait until nighttime to leave, and Joelle would have had to climb out her window— not that difficult, but walking out the front door was a heck of a lot easier.

Still, she lifted her suitcase over the sill and behind the yews that grew beneath her window and then hoisted out the carton of stuff she was sure she couldn't live without—her hairbrush and rollers, her makeup, the polished marble egg Bobby had given her for Christmas, her sewing-pattern books, the teddy bear she'd had as a baby, her flashlight, her jewelry box, which had a built-in music box that played "Edelweiss" when the lid was raised and her college textbooks, which had cost a fortune and might prove handy if she could find a school to attend near wherever she and Bobby wound up.

Passing her belongings through the window was prudent. She didn't want Mrs. Proski to put down her sherry long enough to peer out her living-room window and catch Joelle marching through the front door with a suitcase and a carton.

Bobby arrived at around ten in the morning. While he carried her things down the alley to his truck, she circled her bedroom one last time. It wasn't as if she'd never come back. Of course she would. Her mother would want to see her and the baby. But when she returned to Holmdell, it would be as

Joelle DiFranco. Maybe married, maybe divorced—Bobby had seemed pleased by that escape hatch, and if he wanted to leave her, she'd never do anything to stop him—but one way or another, she'd be home again. This wasn't goodbye forever.

She reread the note she'd written to her mother:

Dear Mom,

   I'm aware that isn't what you hoped for me, but Bobby DiFranco and I have gone to get married. We wanted to do this before he left for Vietnam. I tried to love Drew, but Bobby is the finest man I have ever known. Please be happy for us. I'll call you once we're settled in. Love, Joelle

It was funny to think of Bobby as a man. Almost as funny as thinking of him as her husband. Thinking of herself as a wife— a pregnant one—was so funny she started sobbing.

She wiped her eyes, blew her nose and left her bedroom. After propping the note against the salt and pepper shakers on the kitchen table where her mother wouldn't miss it, she left the apartment, locking the door behind her.

Neither she nor Bobby spoke until they'd crossed the town line. The morning was cloudless, the sky an intense Day-Glo blue. Ahead of them lay acres of pale brown fields, occasionally interrupted by clusters of dried yellow cornstalks left over from the September harvest. Bobby switched on the radio, got static and turned it off.

"You know how to drive a stick, right?" he asked.

"I'll figure it out." *You can teach me,* she thought, although she doubted he'd have enough time to show her how to drive his truck before he reported for basic training.

"I was going to leave the truck behind for Eddie," he said, "but he's got another year before he can get his license. You'll use it for the year, and then when I get back, we'll see."

We'll see. They would see if they still wanted to be married—if they could even stand to be together in the same room. They'd see if Bobby truly wanted to be a father to someone else's baby. In another year, God alone knew who they'd be, what they'd want, how they'd feel. The fate of Bobby's truck was the least of it.

They stopped for lunch at a McDonald's east of Columbus. Joelle's hamburger tasted funny, but pretty much everything had tasted funny ever since the nurse at the college clinic had told her her urine test had been positive. Bobby apparently had no trouble wolfing down two burgers and a sack of fries. He paid for lunch, as if the two of them were on a date.

All summer long, she'd had no trouble talking to Bobby while they'd nibbled on fries at the A&W. But now she didn't know what to say, what they were to each other. Seated across from him on a bench at a redwood table with a big plastic umbrella over their heads, she struggled to force down at least half her burger while she stared at him. His thick, dark hair would soon be gone—the very thought of some army barber shearing him like a sheep was enough to make her want to weep. They'd train him to kill and dress him in khaki and then ship him halfway around the world. *We'll see,* she thought, realizing for the first time that the next twelve months might change him a lot more than they changed her.

What if he was shipped home maimed? What if he came back deranged? The news was full of stories about soldiers coming back to the states crazed or strung out on drugs. What if the Bobby DiFranco who returned to her after a year in Vietnam was someone she couldn't love?

She would love him anyway. That was her vow to him. She hadn't spoken the promise, but she'd stitched it into her heart. Bobby had offered her this chance to be a mother, to keep her baby and give it a home. Whatever he wanted—if she could do it for him, she would.

A group of teenagers drove into the parking lot in a rumbling Camaro. The windows were open and music blasted out of them, Led Zeppelin whining, "Way, way down inside…"

The song made her scowl. The singer whined about giving some woman a whole lotta love, but the loud, thumping music wasn't what love was about—at least, not in her mind.

She peered at Bobby and told herself love was about *him*, his dark, brooding eyes and his hard jaw and his broad shoulders. She told herself that giving his name to another man's baby was a whole lotta love.

He ate without speaking. She wondered if he was having second thoughts, regretting the whole thing, resenting her. He could have stayed home a few more days, spent a few more nights with Margie…

Unless he'd agreed to marry Joelle to get away from Margie. And his dad.

"Did you tell your father what we're doing?" she asked.

The sound of her voice seemed to startle him. He wiped his mouth with a napkin and lifted his cola. He took a long drink, then shook his head. "I told him I got a call from the draft board asking me to show up earlier for basic."

"I left a note for my mother. She'll be phoning your father soon enough."

Bobby emptied the final fry from the paper wrapper and popped it into his mouth. "My father'll be relieved that he didn't have to dress up in a monkey suit and spend a morning in church watching me get hitched. Your mother'll yell at him until he hangs up on her."

"My mother's going to blow a fuse." She would, too. She'd be devastated that Joelle wasn't marrying Drew. If only Joelle had played things more shrewdly, she could have had a big wedding in the Episcopal church—no matter that Joelle and her mother were Catholic—and a reception at Green Gates Country Club, and then Wanda's little girl would be set for life, free of Tubtown and poverty forever.

"What's up?" Bobby asked as he gathered their trash. "You look worried."

"Do you think we're doing the right thing? Or are we just two dumb-ass kids?"

He swung his long legs over the bench to head to the waste bin with their trash, and his eyes darkened. "Who the hell knows?"

THEY DROVE STRAIGHT THROUGH Pennsylvania, pausing only to buy gas, use the bathroom and eat a quick supper at a rest stop along I-80. By ten at night they'd reached the outskirts of Trenton. Bobby pulled in to the parking lot of a motel with a vacancy sign glaring in pink neon in the office window. He parked and shut off the engine.

They'd hardly spoken all day and now they were faced with spending the night together. Bobby cleared his throat. "It's not like we're legal or anything yet," he said, addressing the windshield more than her. "I mean, Joelle, I—"

"Call me JoJo," she said. She longed to have her friend back, not this quiet, brooding boy.

He glanced at her. "This marriage…once we do it, it's for real."

She nodded. "That's how I see things, too."

"You'll be my wife. It's not going to be like it used to be with us."

She suffered a pang in her soul. She had treasured Bobby's friendship for so many years. She had no desire for their relationship to change. But it would. Once she was his wife, maybe they wouldn't be friends anymore.

"I think—" he gazed past her "—I think we should wait until we're married, if you know what I mean."

Oh. She noticed the flush reddening his face—they were too far away from the vacancy sign for her to think its glow had caused him to blush. Once they were married, they'd share a bed. They would sleep together. Have sex together.

Sex with Bobby. God, she'd always loved him; he was her best friend—but sex?

Grow up, Joelle, she scolded herself. If he wanted sex, of course they would have sex. That was what marriage was all about, right? Sharing a bed.

"I think we should wait, too," she agreed, hoping he didn't hear apprehension in her voice, hoping that once they shared a bed he wouldn't hate her, or hate himself for having married her.

THEY HAD PLENTY TO TALK about during the next couple of days, but mostly it involved logistics: blood tests performed at a clinic in Trenton, papers filed at city hall, a futile search for an apartment for Joelle. Bobby mentioned that there might be base housing at Fort Dix, but she couldn't imagine anything more depressing than living on an army base, especially once Bobby had shipped out. "Don't worry, I'll find something," she said, sounding more positive than she felt.

They bought rings, the cheapest they could find. The store wouldn't engrave them—their skimpy width offered no surface to engrave on—but they were genuine fourteen-karat gold and they came in pretty plastic boxes lined with velvet. Finally, the day before Bobby had to report to Fort Dix, all the paperwork was done, the blood test results were normal and she and Bobby returned to city hall to get married. She would have liked to buy a new dress for the occasion, but she couldn't fritter away her money on a dress that wouldn't fit her by December. So she wore a ribbed white turtleneck and a short gray skirt.

Bobby wore his cleanest jeans, a button-front shirt, an ugly striped tie and a brown corduroy blazer. "I stole the jacket from my father's closet," he confessed. "He never wears it, anyway."

Over Joelle's protests, he'd insisted on buying her flowers. Nothing big, nothing like what a real bride would carry, but a small bouquet of daisies and carnations. She broke the stem of one of the carnations and tucked the flower through the buttonhole in his stolen jacket's lapel. Then they entered city hall. When they emerged an hour later, it was as Mr. and Mrs. Robert DiFranco.

They ate dinner at an Italian restaurant a few blocks from city hall, a small place with red-and-white checkerboard tablecloths and mandolin music piped through ceiling speakers. Bobby assured her they could afford a restaurant meal, and she wouldn't deny him a hearty dinner when, starting tomorrow, he'd be stuck eating army food for the next year.

He seemed cheerful. Joelle wasn't cheerful at all. When she gazed across the table at Bobby, with his long, shaggy hair and his drooping boutonniere, she felt…dread. She was *married* now. To *Bobby*. Oh, God, what had she done? Was this an even bigger mistake than giving in to Drew in the backseat of his father's Cadillac two months ago?

"Eat," Bobby ordered her. "You're supposed to be eating for two."

She occupied herself coiling long, marinara-soaked strands of spaghetti around her fork. "I wish you didn't have to leave tomorrow," she said.

"Don't worry." He smiled gently, then tore a hunk of Italian bread from the straw basket and smeared butter onto it. "I'll be back soon enough."

"I don't know, Bobby, I just—"

"JoJo." He set down his bread and reached across the table, covering her right hand with his left. She stared at the gold band circling his finger. The ring looked so delicate in contrast to his labor-roughened hand. "Yeah, this whole thing is crazy. But we can make it work. I'll go, I'll come back, I'll get a job. We'll be a family."

Moisture gathered along her lashes—pregnancy made her much too weepy—but she batted her eyes to keep the tears from falling. They were tears of gratitude, not joy. Wasn't a woman supposed to feel joy on her wedding day? What was wrong with her? Why did she feel as if she'd lost something terribly precious today?

During the rest of their dinner, he reviewed everything she had to do once he was gone: find a place to live, find a doctor to monitor her pregnancy, find a job. "I think there are some colleges in the area, if you'd like to take some classes," he said.

"I can't afford college."

"Well, it was just a thought. Remember—the gas gauge in the truck isn't always accurate. The minute that needle points to three-quarters empty, fill the tank. Otherwise you might wind up getting stranded somewhere."

"Okay."

"And the clutch pedal is tight. You have to press real hard on it."

"Okay."

He continued talking about the damn clutch pedal the whole drive back to their motel. Honestly. He would be leaving tomorrow, shipping off to Vietnam in a matter of weeks, and they'd just gotten married, and all he could do was babble about his stupid clutch pedal. She wanted to scream at him to shut up.

He parked the truck in front of their door near the rear of the motel and she swung out, inexplicably furious. She fumed while he unlocked the door and shoved it open—and then he surprised her by hoisting her into his arms.

She let out a gasp.

"Isn't this how it goes?" he asked, one arm securely under her knees and the other under her back, leaving her no choice but to wrap her arms around his neck. "I carry you over the threshold, right?"

"I guess." That was when she realized she wasn't furious at all. She was petrified.

The truth settled deep into her bones. This was their wedding night. Bobby DiFranco, her buddy, her confidant, her dearest friend, was carrying her over the threshold and into her new life as his wife. Their room had two beds in it, but tonight they would be using only one of them.

She steadied her breath. She could handle this. It would just be one night, and then he'd leave. She could figure out how she felt after he was gone.

Besides, sex with Bobby couldn't possibly be as awful as sex with Drew Foster had been. And it was too late for her to worry about getting pregnant. And this was the deal they'd made: once they were married, the marriage would be real.

He kicked the door shut behind them, carried her across the small, stale-smelling room and lowered her to her feet next to one of the beds. His smile melted away as he gazed down at her. "You okay?" he asked, evidently struggling to read her expression.

She nodded and bit her lip. *You can do this,* she lectured herself.

"A little nervous, huh," he guessed.

"A little."

"Me, too." He smiled then, and brushed her lips with his. "Relax, Jo. I'm not going to hurt you. I would never hurt you. You know that, don't you?"

Yes, she knew that. Hearing him say the words convinced her, not in her brain but somewhere else, some part of her where knowing was a visceral thing. When Bobby kissed her again, a little less gently, she closed her eyes, parted her lips and let him in.

She had never been kissed like this before. She hadn't kissed all that many boys, but none of them had kissed like Bobby. His mouth was so strong, so sure. His tongue was so aggressive. She felt his kiss through her entire body, which felt as if it was unfolding inside, opening like a flower's petals to the sun, warming and softening and wanting.

He undressed her first, and then himself. His body was different from Drew's—bigger, more massive...*older,* somehow. He had hair on his chest; not much, but it made him seem like a man. So did the thickness of his shoulders, the swells of muscle in his arms and legs, the contours of his torso.

When he urged her onto the bed and then lay down beside her, he didn't go straight for her crotch. Instead, he kissed her neck, her shoulders, her breasts. He ran his hands all over her, every now and then murmuring her name. He caressed her feet, her knees, her belly, and when he finally touched her between her thighs, she was embarrassed by how wet she was there.

He didn't seem embarrassed at all. He only murmured her name again and then climbed onto her and pressed her hand to his erection. She stroked him the way she used to stroke Drew, until he covered her hand with his and slowed her down, showing her how he liked it.

She desperately wanted to please him. Whatever he wished, she would do it. This was Bobby, and he hadn't made fun of her for being so wet or for stroking him the wrong way. This was Bobby, who'd done her the immeasurable favor of marrying her.

This was Bobby, her husband.

When at last he entered her, it didn't hurt at all. It felt... good. Better than good. He moved in a steady, seductive rhythm, and his stomach rubbed hers and he sighed her name again and again. She thought she would die from the sweet sensations surging inside her. "Oh, Bobby..."

"Yeah," he whispered.

Lush pulses swept through her, endless spasms wrenching her and then soothing her. She closed her eyes and sank into the soft mattress, astonished by what she'd just experienced. Above her Bobby thrust hard, then groaned and trembled and lowered himself into her arms. Given his size, he should have crushed her. Yet his weight and warmth felt as good as everything else he'd done.

Was *that* what sex was supposed to be like? So intimate, so tender, such an excruciatingly lovely mix of glorious sensations still throbbing deep inside her, wringing her body and massaging her soul, filling her with the urge to laugh and cry at the same time?

If being Bobby DiFranco's wife meant experiencing sex like this, she yearned to spend the rest of her life in his bed.

She opened her eyes and gazed up at him. His hair fell forward to brush her cheeks and his eyes were dark and beautiful as they searched her face.

Her husband. Dear, God, he was her husband.

"I don't want you to go," she said.

He kissed her. "I'll come back," he vowed.

FIVE

"Hey, Dad?"

Bobby slammed his desk drawer shut and glanced up. He'd been staring at an old photo of Joelle that he kept stashed in the top drawer, the picture he'd asked her to pose for before the senior prom. In it she was radiant, her hair rippling around her face, her eyes bluer than the blue dress she wore. He'd carried that photo with him through Vietnam and pretended, whenever he'd looked at it, that she'd been his girl the night she'd worn that blue prom gown. He'd pretended that she'd loved him. In time, she'd sent him other photos—of herself pregnant, of herself very pregnant, of herself holding Claudia, a little pink peanut of a girl. But the photo of Joelle before the prom had been his treasure.

The color had faded from it over the years. Three of the corners were bent, the fourth torn. It didn't matter. Some important part of him was in that picture, a slab of his life, his memory, his dreams.

But he didn't want Mike to catch him mooning over it and wondering whether Joelle was any more his girl today than she'd been the night that photo had been taken, thirty-seven years ago. He shaped a smile for his elder son. "How's it going?"

"Good. We're ahead of schedule on the Griffin job."

"Great." He continued to gaze at his son, continued to fake a smile. At twenty-six, Mike resembled Bobby, with thick dark hair a bit curlier than his father's and dark, deep-set eyes. Those eyes were studying Bobby. "It's four-thirty, Dad. What do you say we quit early and celebrate the job you nailed this weekend."

Bobby had spent most of the day making arrangements for that job: a conference call with a swimming pool company he worked with, an order placed with a granite quarry, more calls to area nurseries, a review of his staff assignments to determine who'd be available when, plenty of paperwork and number crunching. As much as he enjoyed outdoor work, he also enjoyed the mental demands. Until he'd taken business classes, he'd never known he had a gift for negotiating and strategizing.

He'd gotten a lot done that day—an amazing amount, considering what a train wreck his personal life was. Bobby had learned how to focus, how to ignore distractions. In 'Nam, distractions could kill a soldier, so he'd developed the ability to tune them out.

Mike wasn't a distraction, though. He was Bobby's son, and if he wanted to celebrate, Bobby would put on a happy face and do his best.

He locked his desk and followed Mike out of the office, which occupied a corner of the small warehouse building that housed trucks and equipment and supplies. Most of what he needed—construction materials and plants—was shipped directly from suppliers to work sites, cutting down on DiFranco Landscaping's storage requirements. But the trucks and tractors had to be parked somewhere at night.

Exiting to the gravel parking lot outside the building, Bobby blinked in the glaring late-afternoon sun. "The Hay Street Pub shouldn't be too crowded," Mike suggested. "Why don't you meet me there."

"Sure." The Hay Street Pub was a relatively subdued place where the TVs were adjusted to a low volume and young singles didn't crowd the place, prowling for pickups. Bobby would steer the conversation toward Mike and survive the next hour without revealing the mess his life was in. He'd gotten through worse; he could get through a drink with his son.

As Mike had predicted, the pub was calm and not too busy and they were able to snag a quiet booth along the back wall. A lamp with a stained-glass shade hung above the table, casting half of Mike's face in red and half in amber.

"I'll have an iced tea," Bobby told the waitress who materialized before them.

"Oh, come on, Dad. Live a little. Have a beer."

Bobby reluctantly ordered a Bud. He enjoyed beer, liked the foam and the sour flavor. But growing up the son of a drunk made him cautious around liquor, so he rarely drank it.

Mike requested a microbrewery lager Bobby had never heard of, and the waitress departed to get their drinks. Bobby gazed at his son through the wash of colored light from the stained-glass lamp. Mike wore a dark green polo shirt with DiFranco Landscaping stitched in white above the breast pocket. All the employees wore those shirts except for Bobby. Collared polo shirts weren't his style. They looked like something a man would wear on a racquetball court or a sailboat, or at the Green Gates Country Club.

"So, would you like to hear about this English-garden job?" he asked.

Mike's smile faded. He tapped his fingers together, then let his hands rest on the table. "As a matter of fact, no. Dad…" He took a deep breath. "Gary called me yesterday."

The waitress chose that moment to reappear with their drinks, denying Bobby the opportunity to bolt for the door. Not that he could run away from his son. The truth lay squirming on the table between them. It had to be dealt with.

He waited until the waitress was done arranging cocktail napkins, beers, frosted-glass mugs and a bowl of pretzels on the table. He watched her walk away, not because she was worth looking at but because he needed a minute to collect his thoughts. He and Mike shouldn't be having this conversation alone. Joelle ought to be a part of it. Revealing the truth to Claudia had been not his idea but hers—hers and Foster's. Let her do the heavy lifting.

She wasn't here, though. Bobby would have to struggle through it himself.

"Did you talk to Claudia?" he asked.

Mike shook his head. "Gary said she was too upset."

"How about Danny? Did you talk to him? Did Gary mention whether he—"

"Danny's been up at Tanglewood all weekend. Lauren got them tickets to some symphony thing."

"And he went?" Danny's current girlfriend had grown up in Manhattan, surrounded by museums, theater and the Lincoln Center. "He really must love her."

"Either that or she's good in bed," Mike muttered cynically. He was between girlfriends right now. Maybe he wished that, like his younger brother, he had a woman in his life willing to drag him off to symphony concerts. "I saw him for ten minutes this morning, before he headed down to Trumbull for that strip-mall job. We didn't really talk." Ignoring the mug the waitress had brought him, he hoisted his bottle to his mouth and drank. Then he set the bottle down and leaned forward. "What the hell is going on, Dad? Is this for real? Some other guy is Claudia's father?"

"Yes." Bobby took a sip of beer, hoping it would keep him from choking.

"I can't believe it." Mike shook his head. "How could you—" Apparently the question stymied him, because he left it dangling.

"How could I what?"

"Raise Claudia like she's your daughter."

"She *is* my daughter. I love her every bit as much as I love you and Danny. You're my children. All of you."

"Right. She's my *sister*. I can't believe you let her live her whole life in ignorance about this."

Bobby sighed.

"And me and Danny. We're her brothers. I mean—my God, what she must be going through right now…"

"It's not easy, Mike." As hard as it was for Claudia, it was every bit as hard for Bobby. He didn't want to come across as self-pitying, though, so he silenced himself with a sip of beer.

"So…what's the deal? Mom had an affair?"

"She was pregnant when I married her," Bobby said. He could have argued that what had happened all those years ago wasn't any of Mike's business. But telling Claudia about her parentage had been like poking a hole in a dam. Once the truth started leaking through, it flooded everything and everyone in its path.

Besides, if Gary had called Mike, it had to be because Claudia wanted to share the news with her brothers. "Your mother didn't have an affair."

"You knew she was pregnant with some other dude's baby?" Mike looked appalled.

"That's why I married her, Mike. I loved her, and she was in trouble."

"Jesus." Mike shook his head again and drank his beer. So did Bobby. "I guess back in the days of hippies and free love, the details didn't matter."

Mike's sarcasm rankled. "It wasn't like that," Bobby retorted. "We were young. She got in trouble. Stuff happens."

"But you married her. Even though her baby wasn't yours. What were you—a candidate for sainthood or just a chump?"

Anger bubbled up inside Bobby, spraying in so many directions he wasn't sure where it came from or what it was aimed at. "Mike. This is your mother you're talking about."

"And my sister, who I love. And who, it turns out, is actually the sister of some other guy we never even heard of." He plucked a pretzel from the bowl, flipped it over in his hand a few times, then tossed it onto his napkin. "Do you know Claudia's father?"

More anger, spinning faster. "*I'm* Claudia's father."

"I mean, her *real* father."

Too enraged to speak, Bobby chugged some more beer. It slid down his throat, cold and bitter. "I think we're done, Mike."

"No, we're *not* done. This is my family, too. You and Mom kept this secret from us for all these years. It's *our* family— Claudia's and Danny's and mine. How could you not tell us? How could you let us all live a lie for so long?"

Bobby drained his bottle in two long swallows. He'd known the aftershocks from telling Claudia the truth were going to be bad. He just hadn't realized how much hurt there was to go around, or how wide it would spread. He hadn't realized how much trust would be lost between him and his children, between him and Joelle. Between him and the whole freaking world.

"Here's all you have to know," he said, his voice muted. "You and Danny are my sons. Claudia is my daughter. The past is the past."

"Great," Mike muttered. "If that's the past, I'm afraid to think what the future is."

JOELLE HAD COOKED LASAGNA for Bobby. As if she could make things right by fixing one of his favorite dishes for him.

Sunday had been wretched for them both. She'd arisen early after a restless night and told him she was going to church, something neither of them had done in aeons. She'd asked him to join her. He'd said no. She'd really hoped he would go with her, but she wouldn't beg him. Partly pride, partly fear of making him feel even worse than he already did—she left the house without him.

Morning mass at Our Lady of Lourdes hadn't helped. The local priest was a bland suburban type, so careful to avoid offense or controversy he wound up coming across as plastic and remote. She couldn't imagine asking him for his counsel. Still, she'd prayed—not for herself but for Bobby, for her children and for a young man named Adam Foster, whom she'd never met but who was critically ill. Her prayers seemed to bounce off the vaulted ceiling rather than passing through the rafters and up to God.

When she'd returned home, the house was empty. Bobby had stuck a Post-it note to the mudroom door, saying he'd gone fishing. He didn't even own a rod and tackle, but she accepted his statement as an indication that he needed some time alone.

She'd spent the day doing the housecleaning that had never gotten done yesterday. She'd scrubbed the bathroom floors until her knuckles were chapped. She'd pulled out the refrigerator and vacuumed behind it. By the time Bobby came home—

carrying a pizza rather than a fresh-caught trout—the house was cleaner than it had ever been.

When she'd asked him what she could do to make him feel better, he'd said nothing.

She'd decided to make lasagna today after the flowers had arrived. A spiffy young man in a green uniform had delivered them shortly after Bobby had left for work, and they'd sat on the kitchen table all day, a magnificent array of roses, orchids and lilies, ferns and baby's breath in a curving glass vase. Bewildered, Joelle had opened the card that accompanied them:

Joelle and Bobby,
I can't tell you how grateful I am that you let me into your home on Saturday. I'm aware my visit might have been difficult for you. I hope and pray you can forgive the mistakes of the past and find the compassion in your hearts to help my son. Sincerely, Drew

She must have reread the card a dozen times throughout the day. The flowers were an apology, a peace offering—maybe a bribe. But the callous, selfish Drew Foster she'd remembered, the boy who had mailed her a check and the name of a doctor in Cincinnati, had been replaced in her mind by the sad, desperate man who'd appeared at her front door Saturday morning. He was a father and his son was dying. He'd sent these flowers with the best of intentions.

She hoped Bobby would view them that way, too. But just in case he wouldn't, she'd decided to prepare one of his favorite meals.

She'd bought fresh vegetables for a salad at a local farm stand and a loaf of Italian bread at a bakery in town. All afternoon, as she'd browned the meat and mushrooms and whipped eggs into the ricotta and crushed cloves of garlic for the bread, she'd thought of Bobby, of pampering him, assuring him that she loved him and so did Claudia. He was hurting and she yearned to ease his heartache.

She also hoped a day of productive work at DiFranco Landscaping would cheer him up, or at least remind him that their life today was a universe away from their lives back in 1970, when she'd found herself pregnant and Bobby was heading off to war. They'd believed in each other back then, she recalled. They'd believed no mistake was so bad that doing the right thing wouldn't help. Was fixing this feast the right thing to do? Had cleaning the house yesterday been the right thing? Had telling Claudia the truth been the right thing?

Telling Claudia had definitely been right. So why did the truth leave so damn much pain in its wake?

She heard the rumble of the automatic garage door opening and raced to the first-floor bathroom to check her reflection in the mirror. A flushed, sweaty face gazed back at her. It wasn't as if she hoped to entice Bobby with her beauty, which had lost its youthful gloss long ago, but she fussed with her hair anyway and splashed some cold water on her cheeks.

She was surprised to hear Mike's voice rather than Bobby's echoing in the mudroom. Why had Bobby brought Mike home with him? She had more than enough food to feed an extra mouth, but after her visit with Claudia on Saturday night, she wasn't sure she was ready to deal with her sons.

She was even less ready to deal with what Mike brought her. "He's drunk," he said, steering Bobby ahead of him into the kitchen and handing her Bobby's keys.

"I'm not drunk," Bobby growled. His eyes looked bleary, his posture unnaturally rigid.

Joelle had never seen him drunk. He didn't *do* drunk. She fell back a step. "How much did he drink?"

"Not enough," Bobby snapped, then shoved past her and headed for the stairs.

She leveled an accusing gaze at Mike. "A beer," he said.

"One beer?"

"And three whiskies. I drove him home because I didn't think he should drive himself. He's really pissed."

Joelle didn't need Mike to point out the obvious. Her husband was pissed, he was drunk—and as the son of an alcoholic, Bobby would rather smash his head through a pane of glass than drink to excess. If he'd gotten himself blitzed, things were worse than she'd imagined.

"Where's your car?" she asked.

"I left it at the Hay Street Pub. I can take Dad's truck home and pick him up for work tomorrow. Somewhere along the way I'll get my car."

Mike's voice was cold and clipped, his gaze filled with contempt. She realized he must have heard about Drew Foster. Perhaps Bobby had told him between his second and third whiskey. Or perhaps Claudia had brought Mike up to speed.

It didn't matter. He knew the truth and it filled him with hatred. He was her son; she could read him easily.

"I'll drive you over to the pub so you can get your car," she said, not yet ready to confront Bobby.

"That's not necessary."

"Your dad will be using his truck tomorrow. I'll drive you." She turned off the oven so the lasagna wouldn't burn, then grabbed her purse and keys from the storage table near the mudroom and preceded him out to the garage.

The pub was less than ten minutes away in the center of Gray

Hill. Ten minutes of silence would be unbearable. Mike clearly didn't wish to speak to her, but that didn't mean she couldn't speak to him.

"How could you let him drink like that?" she asked. "He never drinks. Why didn't you stop him?"

"He's a big boy. He wanted those drinks, so he had them."

A potent blend of sorrow and fury churned inside her. "Your father never wants drinks."

"Yeah, I used to think that, too." Mike's voice reeked of hostility. "Funny how the truth is sometimes completely different from what we used to think."

"I gather you and your father discussed Claudia," she said in as level a tone as she could manage.

"Yes, we discussed that particular subject."

"Life is not always black and white, Mike. There are things you don't know about your father and me."

"Here's what I do know. Our family is a lie. Everything I assumed, everything I thought we were... All a lie."

She wondered whether he really believed that or was just trying to bait her. Either way, his words sliced deep. "I wish you didn't feel like that, Mike. Your father and I love you and we love Claudia. We did the best we could under some difficult circumstances."

"Keep telling yourself that, Mom," he grunted. "Maybe it'll make you feel better. It doesn't do much for me."

She'd barely braked to a halt in the parking lot before he had the door open. Not bothering to say goodbye, he swung out of her car and slammed the door behind him.

She remained in the parking lot, watching him cross the asphalt to his own car, climb in and peel away. A shudder wrenched her as she considered her beloved elder son. She'd been so worried about how Claudia would respond to the truth, she hadn't even considered how the boys would react. Claudia was their sister. This was their family. Their parents had lied for thirty-seven years, and their father had for the first time in his life gotten drunk and everything she valued in the world was dissolving into dust.

With a shaky sigh, she ignited her engine and drove out of the lot. Who was the moron who'd said "The truth will set you free"? The truth had set her daughter and at least one son free to hate her. It had set her husband free to stonewall her, hiding behind his sullen silence and three glasses of whiskey. Saturday night in their bed, the truth had brutalized them both, even as they'd made love.

Right now, she considered the truth a pretty nasty business.

She drove home, her head aching and her ribs weighing heavily on her lungs, making each breath an exertion. Entering the kitchen, she found the flowers scattered across the floor and broken pieces of the vase lying in puddles of water. Drew's note lay crumpled in a ball beside the trash can.

Her instinct was to curl up on the floor, close her eyes and howl. But she'd been through too much in her life to give in to such impulses. When there was a mess, you cleaned it up. Closing your eyes didn't solve anything.

With a ragged sigh, she gathered the crushed blossoms and tossed them into the trash. She picked up the shards of glass carefully to avoid cutting herself and then mopped up the water. By the time she was done, she became aware of the sound drifting down from upstairs, a muffled moan.

She raced up the stairs, hurried through the master bedroom and found Bobby in the bathroom, hunched over the toilet. His shirt lay in a heap in one corner, and the broad, muscular expanse of his back glistened beneath a sheen of perspiration.

He held a damp washcloth in one hand, and he took deep, rasping breaths.

All right. He'd drunk himself sick. He'd shattered the vase and destroyed the flowers. He was crocked and he was violent and he was puking. If he were sober right now, he'd be horrified. He'd see how close he'd come to acting like his father.

She was horrified, too—frightened more for him than for herself. She eased the washcloth from his fist, rinsed it out in the sink and ran it gently over his face, which had a grayish cast. "You shouldn't drink like that," she said quietly. "Your body isn't used to it."

"I shouldn't drink at all." He shut his eyes and leaned away from the toilet so she could reach the rest of his face. Then he flushed the toilet, rose shakily to his feet and moved to the sink. Joelle sat on the ledge of the bathtub, watching while he brushed his teeth and scrubbed his face. He avoided her gaze as he grabbed for a towel. Only when he was dry did he look at her. "That son of a bitch sent you flowers."

"He sent them to both of us."

"Yeah. Flowers are the quickest way to *my* heart."

"Bobby. He meant them as a peace offering."

"A peace offering." Bobby hung the towel back on the rod and bent over to pick up his shirt. The movement must have hurt his head, because he paused before straightening up. A few long seconds passed before he turned to her. "They were very nice flowers. Expensive. Top of the line."

"Bobby—"

"Remember the first time I gave you flowers? A two-dollar bouquet on our wedding day."

"That bouquet was beautiful," she said.

"It was cheap. It was all I could afford." He limped toward the door, then halted, gripping the doorjamb as if afraid he might stumble. "You could have done better for yourself, Joelle. You could have held out for a guy who could buy you fancy flowers."

"I didn't want fancy flowers, Bobby. I wanted you."

"Right." Disbelief underlined that terse syllable. "Flowers were a better bet." Bobby swayed in the doorway, then pushed himself out of the bathroom. She listened to his footsteps, heard the creak of the bedsprings and knew he had lain down. She considered joining him in bed, just holding him, stroking his head and reassuring him—but what reassurance could she offer? Could he even bear to have her in bed with him?

He was *drunk,* damn it.

After all these years, after all she and Bobby had endured, all they'd shared, he had done something he'd vowed never to do: he'd acted like his father. He'd gotten drunk and broken things.

Her soul felt as splintered as the glass vase she'd found in pieces on her kitchen floor, as dead as the flowers Bobby had crushed.

SIX

May 1971

THE AIR WAS LIKE A STEW, HOT and wet and heavy with the smell of seething plant life. For once Bobby didn't notice the oppressive atmosphere. He was too busy staring at the photo in his hand.

Joelle. Joelle holding a football-size parcel of pink in her arms. *I named her Claudia,* she'd written. *I hope you don't mind.*

He settled back on his cot and gazed at the photo. His sheets were wrinkled, his blanket lumpy. He recalled how obsessed with tight sheets the commanding officers had been during basic training, but no one gave a damn about tight sheets in-country.

He'd written to Joelle that life in Vietnam was boring. That was half-true. When life in 'Nam wasn't boring, it was terrifying, but he saw no reason to alarm her. He wasn't much for letter writing, and when he wrote, he kept it simple. "I made twenty bucks playing poker last night," he'd tell her, or, "The food sucks," or, "This country doesn't need soldiers. It needs air conditioners."

Yesterday had been one of the terrifying days. His platoon's

assignment was to keep a road passable, a task that reminded him
of cutting grass. You cut grass, and it grew back again. Then you
cut it, and then it grew back. His platoon's job was almost the
same, except instead of cutting grass, they had to scout for
snipers. They'd kill or capture a few, then go back to base. Then
a few days later, someone would get shot at and they'd have to
go out and beat the bushes for snipers again. No matter how
many snipers you got rid of, more always arrived to replace
them. Like well-watered grass, they kept growing back.

Unfortunately, while Bobby and his buddies were visible on
their patrols, the snipers stayed hidden, so they got off better
shots than the Americans did.

But the platoon had done their sweep yesterday, and today was
one of the boring days, a day to relax under the sagging canvas
roof of the tent that Bobby had called home for the past six
months. A fine, hot drizzle fell from the stone-gray sky. The tent's
walls were rolled up to allow in any breeze that stirred the air,
and those too-rare breezes brought the dampness in with them.

This place was worse than hell.

But Bobby had a daughter and he didn't care.

A few feet from him, Deke Jarrell and Ramón Ruiz were
playing chess, using a footlocker for a table. Two cots down, Joe
Kelvin was listening to *Workingman's Dead* tape for the millionth
time. "We've got some things to talk about…" the Grateful
Dead sang, their harmonies too buoyant for the hot, murky air.
A couple of guys sat on the plank floor, divvying up the contents
of a plastic bag of weed.

Mail call had occurred three hours ago, but Bobby wasn't
done with this letter yet. This letter and this photograph.

Labor wasn't bad, Joelle wrote. *I had the midwife and all my housemates with me.*

After he'd left for basic, she'd taken up residence in a house with a bunch of women. Bobby didn't get it, but she'd insisted the setup was perfect. They all chipped in on expenses, took turns cooking and watched out for one another. Two of the women were attending college full-time, and Joelle had managed to squeeze in a class along with her hours as a teacher's aide at a nursery school. She'd told him how much she loved working with little children—a lucky thing, given that now she had her own little child to work with.

Her living arrangement sounded kind of like a hippie commune to him, with heavy overtones of feminism, but if it made her happy, he wouldn't complain. He actually liked the idea that she wasn't all alone, pregnant and struggling to make ends meet.

The midwife, however... Joelle had been entitled to hospitalization through the army, but she'd claimed that since her pregnancy was progressing well, she saw no reason not to give birth at the house with a midwife. He didn't approve, but he was twelve thousand miles away and couldn't do a hell of a lot about it.

It didn't matter now. She'd delivered a healthy baby girl. A beautiful girl, as he could see in the photo one of the women she lived with had taken with her Polaroid camera. A girl Joelle had named after Bobby's mother.

"Hey, DiFranco, you wanna take the winner?" Ruiz called to him from the footlocker, where the chess game seemed to be racing toward checkmate.

"I'm a father," he called back. He couldn't think of anything else to say, anything that had meaning. The only words he seemed capable of pronouncing were: *I'm a father.*

"Wow! No shit?" Ruiz shouted above the eruption of voices.

"Hey, DiFranco!"

"Far out!"

"Girl or boy?"

"Watch it," Bobby warned as the guys jostled one another around his cot in order to view the photo. "Don't touch it. This is the only picture I have."

"Oh, man, she's a heartbreaker," one of the guys said, then sighed. Bobby wasn't sure if he was talking about Joelle or the baby.

"Pink. Must be a girl."

"Man, that thing is tiny! You sure it's not a doll?"

Bobby laughed. Someone slapped his right shoulder. Someone socked his left arm. "We need cigars. Go find Sergeant Weaver. He's always smoking those things."

"His cigars smell like turds, man."

"They look like turds, too."

"No cigar for me," Bobby said, raising the photo above his head, out of reach of the grasping fingers swatting at it. With his free hand, he groped in the breast pocket of his T-shirt and pulled out his cigarettes. "Here, who wants these?"

"That ain't no cigar," Deke complained.

"I'm not smoking anymore," Bobby said. "I'm quitting. Do something with these." He tossed the pack at Deke. "Give 'em away or smoke 'em yourself."

"Hey, gimme one of those," Ruiz demanded, and the swarm abandoned Bobby's cot for Deke's, where they wrestled for possession of his cast-off smokes.

No more cigarettes for Bobby. No more weed. No more sips of that swill Schenk kept in a rusty canteen—Bobby had no idea what that stuff was or where Schenk got it, but it smelled like paint thinner and knocked a guy flat on his ass after one good swallow.

Bobby wasn't going to drink that stuff anymore. He was a father now. He had to live right, be strong—be the man his own father had never been. He had to keep his lungs healthy, his body whole, his mind clear.

He had to stay alive. He had to get through the boredom and the terror, the steamy days and the sticky nights, the explosions and the even scarier silence. He had to survive, because there was a baby girl waiting for him back in America.

JOELLE AND BOBBY HADN'T discussed names for the baby—just one of many things they hadn't discussed—but names were important. Joelle had written him a letter a couple of months ago in which she'd asked if he had any preferences. Two weeks later she'd heard back from him, a single tissue-thin sheet of paper telling her about how muddy the base was from all the rain they'd been having.

She'd grown used to his ignoring her questions. Some of them he probably couldn't answer—"What is your mission? Is it dangerous?" Some he likely didn't want to answer—"The newspapers report that everyone's doing lots of drugs over there. Is that true?" He'd developed the habit of writing whatever was on his mind rather than responding to the issues she'd raised.

With no input from Bobby, she was on her own in naming the baby. If she had a boy, would Bobby like her to name him Robert Junior? She couldn't imagine naming a boy Louie, after Bobby's father, since Bobby hated his dad. Nor would she name a son Dale after her own father. She loved the name Michael, but would Bobby approve?

Boys' names went forgotten when, after ten hours of labor— which had seemed like a century to her, but the midwife said was quite fast, especially for a first child—Joelle gave birth to a perfect little girl. Surrounded by her housemates in the rickety old Victorian a mile from the Rider College campus,

Joelle wept as the midwife placed the damp, squirming infant in her arms. Gazing into that scrunchy pink face crowned by a tuft of pale hair, she murmured, "Claudia." The baby gazed back at her, and Joelle swore she saw a smile on those puckered little lips.

Bobby's mother had never made a vivid impression on Joelle. Claudia DiFranco had been a vague presence in the background when Joelle was playing in Bobby's backyard, a tangled lot of weeds and scruffy shrubs and old tires that had seemed like a magical world compared with the tiny, fenced-in square of yellowing grass behind her own duplex. Bobby's backyard had trees to climb and junk to explore, room to move—and his front yard had a bathtub shrine.

Occasionally Mrs. DiFranco would stick her head out the kitchen door and say, "How about some cookies?" As they clambered up the back-porch steps, she'd say, "Wipe your feet before you come in." That was pretty much the sum of Joelle's contact with her.

The winter Joelle and Bobby were in sixth grade, his mother grew gaunt and her skin appeared waxy. "She's got cancer," Bobby confided to Joelle. "Don't tell anyone." Joelle wasn't sure why he should keep his mother's illness a secret, but she honored his request.

Claudia DiFranco died in May. With her death, Bobby's secret became public knowledge. Dozens of sixth-graders showed up at St. Mary's Catholic Church for the funeral. Bobby sat in the front pew with his father and his younger brother, Eddie, three sad, solemn figures in dark jackets and ties. Bobby's and Eddie's classmates filled the rear half of the church. Some cried openly. Joelle wondered if they could possibly have known Bobby's mother better than she did, but then she realized those kids were crying because they were thinking of their own mothers, of how horrible it would be to lose a mother to cancer.

Bobby missed a few days of school afterward, and when he finally showed up, no one dared to mention his mother. Joelle asked once how he was doing and he said fine, but his tone was clipped and forbidding. It was clear he didn't want to talk about his mother and his grief, and Joelle would never press him. In art class, she painted a sunset with watercolors and gave it to him, hoping it would cheer him up. He took it and said thanks, and then never mentioned it again.

One night at around ten, just days after school had ended for the summer, Joelle heard a tapping on her window screen. Her room was dark, the air too hot and stagnant for her to fall asleep. She'd been lying in bed, listening to the cricket song through her open window and wondering if she might die from the heat.

She heard the tapping again. She sat up, glanced toward the window and saw a shadow through the thin voile curtains, Bobby's silhouette backlit by the moon. "JoJo?" he whispered.

"Yeah, I'm up." She slid out of bed, tiptoed to the window and drew open the curtains. She didn't care if Bobby saw her in her nightgown. It fell nearly to her knees, and besides, this was Bobby, not some creepy boy who'd go around boasting that he'd seen Joelle Webber in her nightie. Not that there was anything worth seeing. She was skinny and flat chested, her arms and legs too long and her hips nonexistent.

Through the screen she heard Bobby breathing hard, as if he'd run all the way from his house. Once her vision adjusted to the gloom, she made out his face. His eyes were wild, his T-shirt stained. Who washed his clothes now that his mother was dead?

"I'm in big trouble," he confessed. "I have to run away."

Forcing herself to keep her voice as soft as his, she asked, "What happened?"

"I hit my dad. I…I hurt him, Jo."

"Oh, God."

"I didn't want to." A sob seemed to clog Bobby's throat, but he wasn't crying. Just struggling to get the words out. "He was beating on Eddie. I couldn't let him do that."

"Why was he beating on Eddie?"

"I don't know. He was drunk and Eddie's little. I was just trying to get him to stop. I think I broke his nose. Or maybe worse." In the silver moonlight, she glimpsed the shine of tears in his eyes. "There was blood everywhere. If they catch me, I'll go to jail."

"No, you won't," Joelle promised. As if she was any kind of a legal expert. "You were just protecting your brother."

"When my mom was around, he didn't touch us. She wouldn't let him."

Bobby had never before told Joelle that his father was violent. He'd mentioned that his father liked to drink, that he usually started getting loaded when he arrived home from work—unless he went straight from work to the Dog House Tavern and got loaded there—and his temper would flare and his mother would steer him into the bedroom to cool off, or he'd fall asleep in front of the TV. But she'd never heard anything about beatings.

"We don't have my mom anymore." Bobby was still breathing hard—from his emotions, probably. He should have recovered from his run by now. "She used to protect us. If they arrest me, who's gonna protect Eddie?"

"They won't arrest you," Joelle insisted. "You're just a kid. And anyway, all you have to do is tell them he was beating your brother."

"Then they'll take us away from him and put us in an orphanage or something."

Joelle wondered if that might not be an improvement over living with a father who beat his kids. But she didn't want Bobby sent away—either to jail or to an orphanage—because he was her best friend. "Is your father still at your house?"

"I don't know."

"Maybe you should go back and find out if he's okay. Maybe he wasn't hurt as bad as you think."

"He was hurt bad. There was so much blood… What if I killed him? I can't go back there. The police could be waiting for me."

She thought some more. He looked so scared. "I'll go with you," she resolved. "You can hide while I try to find out what's happening. If the police are there, we'll figure out what to do then."

"Okay."

"Close your eyes," she ordered him, then hurried across her room to her closet and removed her nightgown. She trusted Bobby not to look.

She donned a pair of shorts, a T-shirt and her canvas sneakers. Then she crept back to the window and unhooked the screen. Bobby hinged it away from the window frame so she could climb out. The moonlight struck the back of his right hand. His knuckles were swollen and bruised.

How hard had he hit his father? What if he really had killed him?

She refused to consider that possibility. After nudging the screen back into place, she and Bobby scrambled over the fence and through the adjacent backyard and the one after that, down an alley and across another tiny yard. They couldn't risk showing their faces out on the street at this hour.

Bobby's house was only a few blocks away. No police cars lined the road. The driveway held only Bobby's father's old truck, with its dented rear fender and rust scabs and bug-crusted windshield.

They sneaked past the truck and around to the backyard. Bright yellow light spilled through the kitchen windows and the screen door and voices could be heard—Bobby's father and another man. *Please, not a cop,* Joelle silently prayed.

Bobby hunkered down in the shadows of an overgrown forsythia while Joelle inched closer to the back porch, straining to make out what the men were saying. She heard a burst of laughter. If Bobby had hurt his father that badly, he and the other man wouldn't be laughing, would they?

She crouched as she approached the porch, then straightened enough to spy through the vertical slats in the railing. "So, I'm thinking that sumbitch owes me a raise, one way or the other," Bobby's father was saying. "I work harder than he does, don't I? So— Ouch! No more ice."

"It'll keep the swelling down," the other man said.

"The hell with it." She heard the thump of a glass against the table.

Gripping the railing, she inched higher, hoping to peek through the window. Unfortunately Bobby's father saw her as soon as she saw him. His nose was covered with white gauze and tape. "What the hell?" he muttered, rising from the kitchen table and crossing to the porch, his friend right behind him. Both men wore sweat-stained undershirts and work pants worn to a shine at the knees and frayed at the hems. Both were unshaven, and both had tousled hair. Louie DiFranco also had a puffy cheek and a purpling eye and all that bandaging on his nose. "Who is that?" he demanded, swinging open the screen door.

Joelle hadn't heard Bobby come up behind her, but he said, "It's me, Dad. Me and Joelle Webber."

"Bobby?" Louie seemed to falter for a moment. Then he

managed a feeble smile. "What are you doing out this late? Ya missed all the excitement, buddy."

"Your daddy walked into a door," his friend said, then laughed. "Looks like the door won, huh?"

Bobby and Joelle exchanged a glance. Apparently Bobby's father hadn't told his friend how his face had gotten busted up. If he wouldn't tell his friend, he sure wasn't going to tell the police.

"It's kinda late for you kids to be running around, don't you think?" Louie asked. "A little past your bedtime?"

More than a little. "I gotta take her home," Bobby told his father. "Then I'll go to bed."

Something flickered across Louie's face—anger, maybe resentment that Bobby hadn't apologized for being out late and then meekly entered the house. Maybe fear. But he said, "Fine, you take your friend home and then you get your butt up those stairs and into bed."

Neither Bobby nor Joelle spoke as they walked back to her house. No need to run—Joelle's mother never checked up on her after she went to bed, and now that they knew Bobby's father hadn't called the cops, the urgency of the night had vanished. Bobby hadn't killed his father, he wasn't going to jail and in all likelihood no one but Bobby, his father, his brother and Joelle would ever know what had happened that night. The rest of the world would be snickering about the night Louie DiFranco drank too much and collided with a door.

Unlike the DiFranco house, the first-floor Webber apartment was dark and quiet when they reached Joelle's bedroom window. Bobby jiggled the screen loose from the frame, then let his hands drop to his sides and turned to Joelle. "Thanks."

His voice had deepened this past year. It was still a boy's

voice, but lower and thicker than it used to be. When he whispered, he sounded almost like a man.

"Will you be okay?" she asked.

He nodded, but his eyes said no. Joelle opened her arms and he let her hug him. Surrounded by the hot summer air, the screech of crickets and buzz of mosquitoes, she held him tight. She felt his rib cage and spine right through his shirt, through his skin. His shoulders had begun to widen, but he was only an inch or so taller than her, and not much broader.

She couldn't tell if he was crying. She hoped he was. He needed to and he didn't have to be embarrassed in front of her. She would never tell anyone.

For a long time they just held each other. Eventually he leaned back. His cheeks were damp, and she knew if she touched her hair she'd feel his tears in the strands. "I miss my mom," he murmured, his voice hoarse.

"Of course you do."

He let out a broken sigh. "She wasn't—you know, beautiful or funny and she didn't talk a lot, but... She believed in me."

"I believe in you."

He searched her face, then turned to stare at the moon. "Sometimes I don't know how I'm gonna survive without her."

"You're strong, Bobby," Joelle assured him. "You'll survive."

"What if my dad starts in again?"

"You're almost as big as he is," Joelle pointed out. "He can't push you and Eddie around. You showed him that tonight."

"He breaks things," he told her. "When he gets mad, he breaks things."

"They're just things. As long as he doesn't break you and Eddie, you'll be okay." She reached up to wipe a stray tear from his cheek. He ducked his head away, but not quickly enough to avoid her touch. His skin was warm and fuzzy, like suede. In another year or two, he'd be shaving. "If he tries to hurt you or Eddie, grab Eddie and come here. We'll figure out what to do."

"This isn't your problem."

She shook her head. "I'm your friend, Bobby. That's all that matters."

He peered down at her. Another tear streaked down to his chin, and she brushed her hand against his face. "Yeah," he murmured, then lifted the screen. "You better go in."

She hoisted herself over the windowsill. Bobby held the screen in place while she hooked it shut inside. Then he sprinted across the small backyard to the fence and vaulted over it.

She stood at her window, watching the night outside. The dampness of Bobby's tears lingered on her palm.

GAZING AT THE SQUIRMING bundle of pink in her arms, she remembered that night. Bobby never mentioned his father hitting him or Eddie again, but sometimes she'd sensed a tension in him. And every now and then, when they were hanging out at the A&W or some other place, he'd have Eddie with him. No explanation, no discussion about why a kid three years their junior was tagging along. Joelle suspected that those were nights when Bobby's father had drunk too much and was breaking things.

She had learned that night how much Bobby's mother had meant to him. Maybe the woman had been quiet, maybe she'd made no more of an impression on Joelle than a passing breeze, but she'd protected Bobby and his brother. She'd kept them safe for the years it took Bobby to grow up, to become big enough to fight back. Joelle didn't really believe in guardian angels, but if they existed, she liked to think Claudia DiFranco was watching over Bobby now, keeping him safe while he faced dangers greater than his father's fists.

She was only vaguely aware of all the bustle around her—Maggie, the midwife, gently washing her off with warm, wet cloths, Joelle's housemate Lucy snapping photos with her camera, Suzanne—at forty, the owner of the house and the grande dame of their community—gathering towels and linens into a laundry basket, Renee combing Joelle's hair back from her sweaty, teary cheeks and Lenore giggling and cooing and generally being useless. "Try giving her a breast," Maggie advised. Before Joelle could respond, Renee and Lenore eased down the strap of Joelle's nightgown to free her breast.

She lifted her squirming little daughter and guided her nipple into the baby's mouth. With an eager tug, the baby started to suck. It was all such a miracle—this glorious little girl feeding from Joelle's body. Joelle a mother. This precious life. This tiny angel.

"Claudia," she whispered. "You'll be my Claudia." *Our* Claudia, she added, praying that Bobby would accept her as his daughter, that he would return from Vietnam and still wish to be Joelle's husband. What if he looked at Claudia and saw Drew Foster in her pale, feathery hair, in her round, gray-brown eyes, her little pink hands and her fingernails like tiny seed pearls? What if, when he confronted the reality of what he'd done, he decided to flee? He'd been the one to point out that they could always get a divorce.

He'd also been the one to say this baby would be his, a DiFranco.

Maggie approached Joelle with a clipboard. "Oh, she's nursing so well! She's probably not getting full-strength milk yet, but that'll come soon. I hope she does everything as beautifully as she does this."

"So do I." Joelle was unable to look anywhere but at the baby in her arms, her cheeks pumping and her feet kicking eagerly against the soft cotton blanket in which she was wrapped.

Maggie picked up the clipboard. "We have to fill out a few forms for her birth certificate. Father's name?"

Joelle drew in a deep breath and said, "Robert Louie DiFranco. Capital *D,* capital *F.*"

The midwife left about a half hour later. Suzanne went downstairs to fix dinner and Lenore volunteered to run a load of laundry. Lucy left a stack of instant photos on the bedside table and Renee, at Joelle's request, brought her stationery box over to the bed. Claudia had already emptied one breast and was drinking from the other, although a lot less enthusiastically. Her eyelids fluttered and her legs didn't move so much. All the excitement of getting born and eating seemed to have tired her out.

She had the most delicate eyelashes Joelle had ever seen.

"Would you like to rest?" Renee asked.

The peace in the room, after all the tumult of the birth, soothed Joelle. She suspected moments of peace would be rare now that Claudia was in her life. "Thanks," she said, nodding at Renee.

Renee left the room, one of five cozy bedrooms in the rambling Victorian. Through the floorboards Joelle could hear the sounds of her housemates moving around downstairs, the muffled drone of the TV, Lenore's giddy laughter. In her arms, Claudia made a slurping sound, then nestled her head into the bend of Joelle's elbow. Her eyes were shut—she was obviously asleep, although her mouth kept making sucking motions. Maybe she was dreaming about milk, Joelle thought with a smile.

Trying not to jostle the baby, she grasped with her free hand for her stationery. She also gathered up the photographs. A couple were blurred and one hadn't developed very well. But one showed her and Claudia clearly. She set it aside, then took a sheet of letter paper from the box. *Dear Bobby,* she wrote, *I gave birth today to a baby girl. I named her Claudia. I hope you don't mind.*

SEVEN

BOBBY KNEW MORE ABOUT GARDENS than Joelle did, but after thirty-seven years of marriage, she'd learned a few things. A few years ago, she'd asked him to help her plant a vegetable garden in the backyard. He'd carved her a plot with as much care and professionalism as he would for any DiFranco Landscaping project. He'd cut a nice-size rectangle, surrounded it with marigolds and trimmed it with scalloped wire fencing buried deep enough to hinder burrowing critters. He'd filled the enclosed area with enriched loam. He'd supplied her with frames to tie her tomato vines and some sort of organic antigrub soil treatment.

When her children were young, her summers had been filled with mothering. She'd spent every July and August shuttling the kids to day camp, Little League, swimming lessons and play dates. When they'd grown older, she'd chauffeured them to assorted summer jobs.

But now they were gone and Joelle's summers were her own. A lot of teachers picked up supplementary income working as camp counselors or tutors, but Joelle and Bobby didn't require the extra money. And since summer was his busiest season, she was happy to spend those months free of paying work and available to take care of chores he had no time for. She sewed, she puttered, she grew fresh vegetables and she fixed special meals to greet him with at the end of his long days.

Like lasagna, she thought churlishly, recalling the overcooked meal she'd wound up throwing away last night.

Gardening wasn't merely a hobby today. It was therapy. She needed the grit of the warm soil against her knees and between her fingers. She needed the hot sun roasting her. She needed the satisfying rip of roots as she tore weeds from the dirt. She needed something to tame, something to inflict her anger upon.

How could Bobby have gotten drunk last night? How could he have come home and smashed a vase? Was her family as broken as that vase? Had she demolished the family by telling Claudia the truth about her birth, or had the lie, the basis of her marriage, been like a flaw in the glass, an invisible crack just waiting to split apart?

Lost in her ruminations and drugged by the morning heat, she wasn't at first sure she heard Claudia's voice: "Mom?" Silence, and then she heard it again. "Mom."

She glanced over her shoulder and saw Claudia standing on the patio, using her hand to shield her eyes from the sun's glare as she gazed at Joelle. She wore white cotton shorts and a lime-green camp shirt and she was alone.

Where were the children? Did Claudia intend to deny Joelle access to her grandchildren because of what she'd done so many years ago? If she did…Joelle would die. Without her beloved grandbabies, she couldn't imagine how she would go on.

She stood, tossed down the garden claw she'd been using to loosen the weeds' roots and dusted the dirt from her knees.

"Hello, Claudia." No sound of Jeremy's or Kristin's laughter drifted from the side of the house. Not that Claudia would have let them out of her sight if she'd brought them with her. They would have been standing right beside their mother on the patio—or, more likely, racing across the grass to Grandma, arms outstretched as they clamored for hugs.

Claudia must have read her question in her eyes. "I left the kids at a neighbor's house," she said. "This isn't a friendly visit."

Of course not. Joelle supposed that meant she shouldn't hug Claudia, either. Clearly Claudia meant to punish her for…what? Giving birth to her? Marrying a man who promised to be a father for her? Raising her and loving her and sending her off into the world?

"I want to know about my father," Claudia said.

"He's at work right now," Joelle said, her voice taut. "You have his number." *Maybe you can meet him for a beer and a few whiskies after work,* she thought bitterly. *Maybe you can get him so drunk he'll get sick, the way your brother Mike did, and by the time I join him in bed he'll be passed out.*

"I meant my birth father," Claudia said quietly.

Joelle sighed. She heard an undertone of worry along with indignation in Claudia's voice. Sadness, too, and fear. "What do you want to know?"

"I tried Googling his name," Claudia told her, then laughed dryly. "*Drew Foster.* I got thousands of hits about foster programs for children, plus a few that seemed to be about drawing pictures and a couple about duels."

"Duels?"

"People drawing their guns. Maybe I would have found some information about him online if his name was weird— Vladimir Binglehoffer or something." Claudia's lingering smile, although faint, gave Joelle a touch of hope. Her joke was a door opening a sliver.

Joelle dared to smile back. "He was one of the rich kids in town," she explained. "A purebred Wasp with a Waspy name." Leaving her tools, her gloves and the bucket of weeds by the garden, she strode across the lawn to the patio. "What do you want to know? I'll tell you everything I can."

Claudia ruminated. Evidently she didn't know what she wanted to know. Finally she asked, "Was he smart?"

"He was a good student. He went to Dartmouth College. People at our high school were so excited about his going there. Ivy League colleges were a big deal in those days."

"They still are." Claudia's eyes remained on Joelle. "Did he have any talent? Was he musical?"

Joelle realized Claudia was trying to figure out what gifts Drew's genes might have bestowed upon her. "I don't recall him playing any instruments," she said. "He played tennis, though. I remember he played soccer, too. Our school had a team, but it wasn't such a popular sport back then. Not the way it is now."

"What did he look like?"

Joelle struggled to conjure a picture of a teenage Drew. Whatever memories she'd had of him from high school had been overtaken by his appearance inside her house a few days ago. He'd looked prosperous and middle-aged that morning, not like the boy she'd fallen for in high school. "I've got my Holmdell High School yearbook somewhere," she said, swinging open the back door into the kitchen.

Claudia followed her inside. The kitchen was pleasantly cool after the oppressive heat of the backyard. Joelle paused at the sink to wash her hands and face. She toweled herself dry, then headed for the basement door.

Bobby had finished a rec room in the basement a few years after they'd bought the house, once he'd had the rest of the place in reasonable repair. The rec room was nothing fancy—Sheetrock walls, cheap brown carpeting covering the concrete floor, built-in shelves and drop-ceiling fluorescent lighting. It had been a haven for the kids, a place for the boys to scatter their toys and play video games, a lair where Claudia and her teenage friends gathered for sleepover parties. By the time the boys were in high school, Joelle had added some style to the decor, painting the walls a cheerful yellow, spreading a few braided rugs on the floor and sewing new slipcovers for the sofa and chairs. Last year Bobby had splurged on a wide-screen TV. Joelle considered most TV shows just as inane in wide-screen as on the old set, but Bobby adored the oversize screen. So did Mike and Danny, who spent many Sundays in the fall watching football with their father. If the TV lured her kids home for visits, she was glad Bobby had bought it.

The carton she was searching for was in the unfinished half of the basement, where the furnace and the hot-water tank, Bobby's tool bench and a wall of steel storage shelves were located. The shelves were stacked with boxes of Christmas decorations, old athletic gear, luggage, tax records and junk that, for whatever reason, Joelle wasn't yet ready to discard. She shoved a few boxes around until she located the carton at the back of one of the shelves.

She lugged the carton into the rec room, Claudia shadowing her. After dropping the box onto the coffee table, Joelle settled on the couch. She wrinkled her nose at the sour scent of the dust that rose from the flaps as she pulled them apart.

She hadn't opened this carton since the family had moved to Gray Hill, and she told herself its contents no longer meant anything to her. But when she lifted out the polished marble egg Bobby had given her for Christmas so many years ago, in high school, she felt a pang so painful it brought tears to her eyes. "Oh, God," she said, her hand molding to the smooth curves of the egg. "This was a present from your dad."

"My birth father?"

Joelle started. "No. Your *real* father." She held the egg up for Claudia to see.

Claudia frowned. "What is that?"

"An egg. A marble egg. There was this little head shop in town that sold them."

Claudia took the egg from her and studied it, her frown deepening. "What were you supposed to do with it?"

"I don't know. Display it. Hold it." She sighed. "There was no 'supposed to' about it. All I cared about was that Bobby DiFranco gave it to me."

"Even though you were in love with some other guy," Claudia said, her tone laced with suspicion.

"I always loved your father," Joelle insisted, silencing the quaver in her voice. Last night when Bobby was lost in a drunken slumber, had she loved him? Had she loved him when she'd thrown away the ruined flowers and the broken glass and the dinner he'd never eaten? Why couldn't he have stayed calm and reasonable and *talked* to her? Why, when they were both so sad, did he get to act out, while she got stuck cleaning up after him?

Sighing, she reached back into the carton and pulled out her old jewelry box. She opened its lid. The box was empty—the few pieces of jewelry she'd owned before she left Holmdell with Bobby had since been moved to a much nicer jewelry box, which sat on her bedroom dresser. After all these years, she hadn't really expected the old box to start playing "Edelweiss," but the silence jolted her.

She flipped the box over and cranked the key protruding from the underside. Then she righted the box and opened it again. The crystalline notes of the song emerged.

"Hey." Claudia's eyes grew wide as she sank onto the sofa next to Joelle. "I know that song."

"It's from *The Sound of Music*," Joelle said.

"No, I mean—I *know* it." She eased the music box out of her mother's hands and placed it on her knees, letting the music rise like a vapor in front of her. "I know this music box."

"It's been stored away forever," Joelle said, gesturing toward the carton.

Claudia frowned, shook her head and twisted the key to make the music continue. "When I was really little, before we lived here, Daddy would play this music box for me. He'd sit me on his knee and open the lid. I thought it was magic, the way the music just rose out of the box like that."

Daddy. Claudia wasn't referring to Drew Foster now. Her daddy was Bobby, the man who'd raised her, who'd made her believe in the magic of a music box.

Joelle didn't remember Bobby playing the music box for Claudia, but the early years of their marriage had been filled with a lot of tag-team parenting. She'd worked while he was in physical therapy. Or she'd brought Claudia with her to the preschool where she was employed. Or he'd cared for Claudia in the evenings while Joelle attended college. Those first few years after Bobby came home from the war were a blur of exhaustion, determination and discovery. They'd had to learn how to be a husband and wife at the same time they were learning how to be parents. They'd had to learn how to create a family while actually doing it.

Apparently during those times when Bobby and Claudia were on their own, Bobby had amused his daughter with the music box. Together they'd experienced things that Joelle had never been a part of.

If Claudia could remember "Edelweiss," her relationship with Bobby couldn't be torn apart by the intrusion of Drew Foster into their lives. It simply couldn't.

While Claudia opened and shut the music box, lost in her own memories, Joelle dug deeper into the carton. There was her old childhood piggy bank, long empty. There was her teddy bear, which she'd let Claudia keep until she'd had enough money to buy her a brand-new stuffed animal. And there, underneath the black plastic folder holding her high-school diploma, was her yearbook.

She hoisted out the heavy album and nudged the carton away so it wouldn't cast a shadow on the glossy pages. Claudia set down the jewelry box and lifted the yearbook onto her own lap. "I don't think I've ever seen this," she said, spreading the book open across her thighs. She sped through the first part of the book, full of candid shots and faculty photos, and then slowed when she reached the portraits of Joelle's classmates. "Foster," Claudia murmured, flipping past the *A*s, the *B*s, the *D*s so quickly Joelle didn't even glimpse Bobby's picture.

Claudia halted at Drew's page. The photo resembled him as much as any yearbook photo would: a black-and-white portrait of a young man gazing dreamily just past the photographer's shoulder, his eyes aimed at some supposedly glorious future. His hair was neatly combed and not particularly long for 1970. He wore a dark blazer, a white shirt and a dark tie. His face was smooth and boyish.

"That's him?" Claudia asked, her voice a whisper.

"Yes."

She scrutinized the picture, as if trying to discern his character from that one artificial pose. She traced the photo with her fingertips, as if she could feel the shape of his nose, the curve of his chin. She stared, sighed, drank him in.

"He doesn't look like that now," Joelle reminded her. "He was eighteen when that photo was taken."

"I know, but… It would have been right around when you became—I mean, this is what he looked like when you conceived me."

Unsure what to say, Joelle remained silent. Claudia seemed both horrified and enthralled by the photograph. Joelle was mostly just horrified by it. She'd believed she loved that boy—a boy so selfish, his way of dealing with his pregnant girlfriend was to send her a check and the name of a doctor. Why had she agreed to help him now? He'd been a son of a bitch, just as Bobby said.

His son, she remembered. She was doing this for his son.

For her daughter, too. Observing the intensity of Claudia's expression as she studied the man whose sperm had created her, Joelle had to believe she'd been right to tell her daughter the truth. She couldn't let herself believe anything else.

After several long minutes, Claudia thumbed back a few pages, into the *D*s, until she found Bobby's photo. Unlike all the other students on the page, Bobby lacked the traditional tentative yearbook smile, and he stared directly at the camera, not at some goal hovering just above the photographer's right shoulder. His dark hair was long and wild with waves, his eyes dark and burning, his mouth set firmly. He wore a blazer—a corduroy blazer, Joelle realized as she leaned in to study the photo. His father's jacket, the one he'd stolen when he and Joelle had fled to New Jersey and gotten married.

Claudia had wedged her finger into the book to hold Drew's page, and now she turned back to that page. She inspected Drew's photo, then flipped back to Bobby's page and grimaced. "Dad was so cool. Why didn't you go out with him?"

Studying Bobby's photo, Joelle had to agree that he'd been handsome. But she'd known him so long, she'd hardly even *seen* him by the time they were high-school seniors. When she'd looked at him, she'd seen their shared history. She'd seen his wicked grin, his sense of humor, the smell of his cigarettes, the grief darkening his eyes at moments when he didn't realize she was watching him. Grief over his mother's death, she'd assumed, or over his father's drinking, or over the fact that kids like him were denied the opportunity to escape their fate. No wonder he wasn't gazing into the future in his yearbook photo. The future he'd imagined for himself back then wasn't one he'd wanted.

Objectively, though, he'd been gorgeous. His hair, his eyes, the stubborn set of his jaw, the fierce defiance in his gaze… Definitely gorgeous.

"I didn't date your father because he never asked me out," she answered.

Claudia eyed her dubiously.

"We were friends, but he dated other girls."

"Who?" Claudia began thumbing through the pages. "Who did he date?"

Quite a few, Joelle recalled. Bobby had made the rounds of available Tubtown girls throughout their high-school years. He'd always been popular. He'd dated one in particular toward the end; he'd been going with her when he'd asked Joelle to marry him. "Margie something," she recollected. "I think her last name began with an *N*. Newland, maybe?"

Amid the *N*s, Claudia found Marjorie Noonan's photo. "Her?" She scowled in disapproval.

Claudia looked at Margie's photo. Joelle looked, too. She'd forgotten how beautiful Margie was, with her long black hair, her round cheeks and her large, almond-shaped eyes framed in thick eyelashes. Her lips shaped a perfect pout as she focused on the space beyond the photographer. Why hadn't Bobby stayed with her? She was much prettier than Joelle.

"She was nice," Joelle told Claudia.

"She's tarty. He could have gone out with you."

"He wanted to go out with her," Joelle said simply. The emotion that welled up inside her wasn't simple, though. Bobby had gone out with Margie and other girls because he'd wanted to—and he hadn't wanted to go out with Joelle. Surely if he had, he would have asked her out. Surely if he had, she would have said yes.

But he hadn't loved her, not that way. She'd been his pal. Not the girl of his heart. Even when he'd married her, she'd been aware of that.

And it hurt. After all these years, it still hurt to admit that Bobby hadn't loved her the way he'd loved all the girls he'd been involved with in Holmdell. He'd married her out of friendship and charity, nothing more. Crazy though it was, she suffered a pang of jealousy for all those girls he'd dated, all the girls he'd chosen. He'd never really *chosen* her. She'd been his good deed, nothing more.

"So he was dating her, and you were dating..." Claudia returned to Drew's photo amid the *F*s. "Drew Foster."

"Drew was very nice," Joelle defended him. "He was smart and handsome and considerate." *Until the end,* she added silently. *Until he found out I was pregnant and sent me money.*

"He looks rich."

"He was."

Claudia raised her eyes to Joelle. "Is that why you dated him?" she asked.

"Of course not," Joelle said automatically, then pressed her lips together. Hadn't she told her daughter enough lies for one lifetime? "I didn't mind the fact that he was rich," she confessed. "He lived in a neighborhood called the Hill, where all the rich people lived. It's been so long since you've been in Holmdell, maybe you don't remember. But the part of town where Dad and I grew up, where Grandma Wanda lives and Papa Louie used to live, was where all the poor kids lived. And Drew lived up on the Hill, on the other side of town, in a big house on two acres, with cars and a huge allowance and a membership in the country club. I was dazzled, Claudia. I couldn't believe a boy like him would be interested in a girl like me."

"Did you love him?"

Joelle lowered her gaze back to the yearbook page. "At the time, I thought I did," she conceded. She *had* thought she loved him, and not because he was rich. Because he had confidence. Because he had two parents. Because he knew who he was and where he belonged and what he was entitled to. To a bastard child from Tubtown, his life seemed like a fantasy.

Claudia continued to study Drew's photo, as if trying to memorize it. "You had sex with him?" she finally asked, her gaze trained on the yearbook.

"Obviously."

Claudia sighed. "Why didn't you marry him?"

"He..." It pained Joelle to admit the truth, almost as much as it pained her to acknowledge that Bobby hadn't loved her like a girlfriend. "He wasn't ready for marriage and fatherhood. He was in college. He sent me money to get an abortion."

Claudia shrank from Drew's photo. "God."

"He was frightened," Joelle said, although she had no good reason to defend him. "He wasn't ready to be a father."

"And you were ready to be a mother?"

Joelle laughed sadly. "I was so unready. But I wanted you, Claudia. In spite of how young I was, and how unprepared, I wanted you. And your father—your *real* father—wanted you, too. So we got married."

"Dad's name is on my birth certificate," Claudia said. At Joelle's nod, she asked, "You lied on the birth certificate? Is that legal?"

"You're the one married to a lawyer," Joelle reminded her. "You'd have to ask him. I guess we figured that as long as no one probed, what difference did it make? Your father loves you, Claudia. You are his daughter. The reason I never told you about all this—" she gestured toward Drew's yearbook photo "—is that I was afraid it might make you feel differently toward him. Maybe you'd stop loving him. That would kill him, Claudia. If he lost you, he would die." Or at least, he would drink and break things and stop being the man he was.

Claudia digested this, then steered her attention back to the yearbook. Her face registered revulsion as she stared at Drew's photo. "So this boy wanted you to get rid of me. And now, all these years later, he comes back into your life and says he's my father?"

"He's grown up, Claudia. He's not the kid he once was." Joelle sighed. "God knows, he could have found me years ago and insisted on being a part of your life."

"But he wanted me dead," Claudia argued, still staring at Drew's photo, as if trying to imagine him capable of wishing such a terrible thing. "He wanted you to get rid of me. And now he claims he has a right to——to what? My bone marrow?"

"I don't think he believes he has a right to anything, Claudia. He only has hope."

"And you kept all this from me because you didn't want me to stop loving Dad." She shut the yearbook and shoved it off her lap, onto the coffee table. "Did it ever occur to you that maybe I ought to know who my father is?"

"Yes." Joelle sighed and rubbed her face with her hands. "Claudia, Dad and I were so young then. We were only trying to do what was best. It wasn't like we sat down and said, 'Let's keep this secret from Claudia. She doesn't need the truth.' We only wanted you to grow up happy and loved, with two parents who were crazy about you. Who never, ever wanted you dead."

Claudia's shoulders trembled, as if she were shaking off a chill. "I feel cheated."

"I'm sorry." Those words sounded so feeble falling from Joelle's mouth. "It's my fault, Claudia. I made a mistake. I got into trouble. Your father rescued me. I was a fool and he was a saint. If you want to hate someone, hate me. Your father..." Her voice faltered and she cleared her throat. "He's afraid he's lost you, Claudia, and he doesn't deserve that. Please don't hate him." Tears beaded along her lashes. She ducked her head so Claudia wouldn't see.

"I don't hate him." She sighed. "I hate this man, this Drew Foster...but he's my father. I'm not sure what I'm supposed to think, how I'm supposed to feel."

Once again Joelle ached to touch her daughter, to wrap her arms around her and heal her pain with a kiss, the way she used to use mommy kisses to heal Claudia's childhood scrapes and mosquito bites. But Claudia was an adult, and what was troubling her now couldn't be kissed away.

"Maybe you could feel a little forgiveness, honey," she said. "You're stuck with a bunch of people who did the best we could a long time ago."

"A long time ago," Claudia echoed, raising her eyes to Joelle. "What about now?" She was on the verge of tears, too. Joelle opened her arms, but Claudia leaned away. No, mommy kisses weren't going to cure anything today.

Suffering the sting of her daughter's rejection, Joelle stood and started stuffing things back into the carton. Her musical jewelry box. The marble egg. The book containing photos of a long time ago, of the people who'd made devastating mistakes with the best of intentions.

BOBBY'S HEAD ACHED AND HIS tongue felt like a strip of sandpaper inside his mouth. He'd been drinking water all day, and he'd managed to consume some saltines and half an apple at noon. But the heat and glare of the sun assaulted his brain. Too bad he couldn't spend the day in his air-conditioned office, but a blue-stone patio had to be installed around a free-form pool in Arlington, and Bobby was better than any of his employees at cutting the stone slabs to mesh with the pool's amorphous shape. So he was at the job site, exposed to the elements.

The two crew members working with him were sweating like marathoners, their faces red and shiny. Bobby considered telling them they could take off their shirts, but the customer was home, no doubt spying on them through the windows that overlooked her backyard. Bobby thought having the guys work shirtless might be disrespectful. He had never forgotten the lecture he'd received when he'd removed his shirt while mowing the cemetery lawn in Holmdell.

If he could keep his shirt on, so could his crew. They were

good kids, college boys working for DiFranco from mid-May through the end of August. They could probably hold their liquor better than he could, too.

He lifted a twenty-pound slab of stone from the pile, carried it over to the pool and laid it on the sand-and-pebble bed he'd groomed as the patio's bottom layer. He appreciated the weight of the slab, the way it tugged at the muscles in his back and arms. Sweat burned his eyes. He told himself that a little exertion, a little suffering, might make him less aware of his headache.

As if his throbbing skull was the only thing bothering him. Hell, his hangover was nothing compared with the *real* demons gnawing at him.

Joelle must despise him. Last night he'd turned into someone he'd sworn to himself he would never become: his father. He'd gotten ripped, he'd smashed a vase, he'd crushed a bunch of flowers. He'd let his rage blind him.

Yet he'd been unable to apologize. Last night he'd felt too ill. He'd fallen asleep sometime before eight, and he'd regained consciousness at six that morning, much too early to wake Joelle. He'd remained in the shower a long time, but she'd still been sleeping when he was washed and dressed, so he'd left for work without talking to her.

He wouldn't have known what to say, anyway. "I'm sorry I got drunk yesterday, but I'm not sorry I destroyed those damn flowers."

"I'm sorry I made myself sick, but after all these years, we should have left the past alone. We shouldn't have torn away all the scar tissue and let the old wounds start bleeding again."

"I'm sorry, Joelle, but it's killing me that that guy, the big love of your life, can march into our house and make you see things his way."

In his jeans pocket his cell phone vibrated. He nestled the stone into place, straightened up and dug out the phone. A glance at the tiny monitor informed him it was Mona, his office manager. He flipped the phone open. "Mona?"

"Hi, Bob. You got a call here at the office."

He shrugged. Mona's job was to take messages, not to interrupt him at work—unless the call was an emergency. "From Joelle?" he asked. His anger went forgotten. Was she all right? Had she been in an accident? Had something happened to Claudia or the babies?

Of course, if Joelle faced an emergency, she could have phoned him directly. She knew his cell number. But maybe after last night, she was afraid to call him. Maybe she was annoyed about his sneaking out of the house that morning while she slept, instead of waking her up and having it out with her. Not that he knew what the "it" he was supposed to have out with her was. Apologies? Recriminations? Accusations? Howls of outrage?

"No, it wasn't from Joelle. That's the thing." Mona hesitated. "It was from a woman and she said it was personal. I just—it's none of my business, but you were in a kind of a mood this morning, and...I thought I should let you know about this call."

A woman? Personal? He might have hit a pothole with his wife—or maybe plunged into an abyss—but he couldn't think of another woman who would phone him with something personal.

"She said her name was Helen Crawford," Mona informed him, "and it was important and it was personal. She requested that you call her back. I stuck the message in the top drawer of your desk. I didn't think it should be lying around on your blotter where someone might see it."

"I don't know anyone named Helen Crawford."

"Whatever. I'm just passing the message along." Mona hesitated. "Something's going on with you, and to tell you the truth, I'd rather not know. But I don't want to be taking these kinds of messages, okay? Tell her to call you directly."

Mona could be a sweetheart. She could also be a prig. Right now, she was being a bitch. "I don't know what *kind* of message this is. I've never heard of Helen Crawford. So stop implying things."

"I'm not implying anything," Mona said, sounding put-upon. "I'm just telling you I decided it was best not to leave this message lying on your desk in full view."

"Thanks." He flipped the phone shut, wondering whether she thought she deserved his gratitude for having insinuated that he'd gotten a phone call from... What? A girlfriend? A mistress? A customer who'd hired him for more than just landscaping?

Honest to God. Not only did he have fissures in his relationship with his wife and his daughter, but now the third most important woman in his life—his loyal officer manager—thought he was screwing around with someone named Helen Crawford, whoever the hell she was.

He'd figure it out later. His life was already a disaster, possibly beyond redemption. If his mystery caller wanted to mess things up even more, let her try.

But not now. He had to finish building a patio. He had to get one thing right in this long, hot, miserable day.

EIGHT

August 1971

BY THE TIME SHE FINALLY HEARD from Bobby, she'd already received an official letter from a medical officer:

> *Dear Mrs. DiFranco,*
>   *This is to inform you that your husband, P/FC Robert L. DiFranco, was wounded in the line of duty during a routine patrol. He was brought to a field hospital to be stabilized and then evacuated to a military hospital in Hawaii for further treatment. If you have any questions...*

She'd had questions, tons of them. But when she'd dialed the phone number provided in the letter, the woman at the other end of the line had offered no answers. "I'm sure you'll be kept informed about his condition," the woman kept saying. "I'm honestly not sure about the extent of his injuries, but the doctors will be in touch."

The doctors weren't in touch. Joelle had no idea what had

happened to Bobby, how serious his injuries were—the words *stabilized* and *evacuated* scared the hell out of her—or what would happen next. She drifted through her days in a trance, feeding Claudia, changing her diapers, feeding her again, laundering her smelly little outfits, rocking her, singing to her and all the while wondering whether she would be a widow before she ever saw Bobby again.

He'd told her, when he'd offered to marry her, that if something happened to him, she could use her widow's benefits to support herself and the baby. Now something had happened to him. She didn't want benefits. She wanted *him*. She wanted him home. She wanted him well. She wanted him to be Bobby D, with a cocky smile and a swagger, lecturing her about his truck's sticky clutch pedal and blasting his Doors albums. She wanted him to know she had a daughter—*they* had a daughter. Had his "routine patrol" occurred before he'd received her letter about Claudia's birth?

At least that question was answered when a letter from him arrived a couple of weeks after the letter notifying her that he'd been wounded in action. He must have left his letter behind when he'd gone on his "routine patrol," and someone had eventually found it and mailed it to her.

Like all Bobby's letters, it was brief. Writing wasn't his thing. He scribbled:

Dear Joelle,

I got the photo. You are both so beautiful. I wish I could be there with you and hold the baby in my own arms. Take care of her for me. Take care of yourself, too. Thank you for naming her Claudia.

He didn't sign his letter *Love, Bobby*. He never signed his letters with love. Neither did Joelle. She figured he was avoiding the word for a reason and she'd best avoid it, too. Maybe the idea of love scared him. Or maybe he just didn't love her. She believed she loved him——but they'd spent less than twenty-four hours as a married couple before he'd left. Did she love *him* or did she love what he'd done for her? Did she love him as a friend, a husband or the father of her baby? Did definitions matter when she felt guilty for devoting more time to worrying about him than about Claudia?

She loved him. She felt so many things when she thought of him, but add them all together and they equaled love. She couldn't expect Bobby to love her, but that didn't matter. What mattered was that she loved him.

The weeks dragged. She fretted that she was a terrible mother, so tired all the time, her breasts leaky and aching, her eyes scratchy from fatigue. When she sang to Claudia, the lullabies were out of tune. When Claudia awakened in the middle of the night for a feeding, Joelle staggered to the crib she'd bought for fifteen dollars at the Goodwill thrift store, lifted Claudia out and plugged a breast into her mouth. She didn't coo to her. She didn't babble and nuzzle her daughter's soft, sweet belly. She was too weary, too frazzled...too afraid of what Bobby would be like when he got home. *If* he came home.

Thank God the preschool where she worked gave her a maternity leave. She could barely manage her own child, let alone nine others. Her housemates spoke in murmurs and handled her chores when she neglected them. When day after day passed with no word from Bobby or his doctors, they hugged her and assured her that everything would be all right.

Then, at last, he phoned. The call came at 10:00 p.m. She'd already bathed Claudia, dressed her in one of the terry-cloth sleepers she'd stocked up on at Woolworth's and was trying to get her to nurse before bed when Lenore hollered up the stairs, "Joelle! Hurry! Bobby's on the phone!"

Joelle nearly tripped racing down the stairs. Bouncing against her shoulder, Claudia fussed and whimpered. They skidded into the kitchen, where Lenore held the receiver of the wall phone while Suzanne pulled a chair from the table closer to the wall so Joelle could sit while she talked. She grabbed the phone from Lenore, settled Claudia into the crook of her arm and drew in a deep breath. "Hello?"

"Jo?" He sounded faint. But he was alive. He knew who she was. Whatever his injuries, they hadn't affected his mind.

"Bobby." She said his name just to taste it, to savor the fact that he was connected to her. She wanted to chant it over and over, to croon it, to cheer it—but that would waste precious time. "Where are you?"

"Hawaii."

"You're still in the hospital?"

"Yeah. I can't talk long. A nurse rigged this call. I just…" Claudia began to fuss again, mewing like a kitten. "Oh, God," he said. "Is that her?"

"That's Claudia." Joelle's cheeks were as damp as Claudia's, but she laughed, too. "That's our baby."

"Oh, God," he said again, softly, like a prayer.

"How are you?"

"I'm okay."

"What happened to you?"

"I can't…" Long-distance static filled the line. Then he spoke. "I'm okay. Making progress."

"Did you—" she couldn't think of a tactful way to ask "—did you lose anything?" She watched the news and read the newspaper. Lots of soldiers arrived home missing limbs, in wheelchairs, paralyzed, damaged beyond description.

"A body part? No."

She started breathing again.

"My leg is f—screwed up," he said, considerately editing out the obscenity. "I had surgery. They put me back together again. They're gonna send me home once I'm vertical."

"Vertical?"

"Walking. Or crutching, I don't know. You'll have to find us a place to live with no stairs. I've got to do rehab before I can deal with stairs."

"All right."

"Call Fort Dix. Someone there'll help you with housing."

"Are you in a lot of pain?"

"It's not too bad." He chuckled. "They give me drugs."

She was desperate to know more. What did "screwed up" mean in regard to his leg? What kind of rehab would he need? What drugs was he taking?

If he'd wanted to go into detail, he would have. Clearly, he didn't wish to. "Should I contact your father?"

The laughter left his voice. "And tell him what?"

"That you were hurt?"

"No." His tone was gentler when he added, "I'm okay, Jo. I'm gonna make it, and I'm gonna come home. All right?"

"Come home," she said. Claudia was sobbing now. So was Joelle. She didn't care if Bobby could hear her tears in her voice. "Just come home."

"I've gotta go. Give Claudia a kiss for me. I'll see you soon." She heard a click, and then dead air.

She should have told him she loved him. Maybe he didn't love her, maybe he didn't want to think about love, but she should have said what was in her heart.

OVER THE NEXT SEVERAL WEEKS, Bobby sent her a few short, cryptic notes: *They've got me doing some exercises. The dizziness is gone.*

What dizziness? she wondered.

My hearing's starting to come back.

His hearing? He'd been deaf? If so, how had he been able to talk to her on the phone?

Guy in the next bed is in really bad shape. I'm so lucky, Jo.

How lucky could he be if he'd had to spend months in a hospital, dizzy and deaf and horizontal? When would he be vertical? When would he get home?

He would get home in early September. She spent most of August searching for a first-floor apartment she and Bobby could afford, signing a lease and furnishing the place on pennies and ingenuity. Her housemates helped. She couldn't imagine how she would have coped without them, and she was reassured when Suzanne was able to find a college student arriving in September who could take over Joelle's room and her share of the expenses.

Anxiety unraveled Joelle's nerves as Bobby's arrival date drew near. Renee had urged her to buy some sexy underwear for the occasion, but she was still breastfeeding Claudia, and while she'd lost her pregnancy weight, her breasts were fat and the skin of her tummy was still loose and puckered. She hoped Bobby wouldn't be repulsed by the sight. She also hoped she wouldn't be repulsed by the sight of him. What if he was scarred? How could she be fretting about her bloated breasts and baggy tummy after what he'd been through?

How could she be worrying about appearances, at all? When

he'd left her, nearly a year ago, he'd been her best friend. Now…she didn't know. He'd fought in a war and she'd become a mother. Would they even recognize each other?

The day before his homecoming, she drove his truck through a car wash and filled it with gas—he'd warned her never to let the needle drop too close to empty. At the grocery store, she splurged on a porterhouse steak and fresh strawberries and Suzanne bought her a bottle of red table wine because Joelle was still too young to buy that herself. The morning he was due, she made the bed with brand-new sheets, gave Claudia a bath and dressed her in her prettiest outfit—a pink dress and matching pink socks that Joelle's mother had sent from Ohio. Despite her swollen breasts, Joelle was able to fit into a sundress she'd sewn last year, a simple sheath hemmed several inches above her knees.

Swallowing her nerves, she drove to McGuire, the air force base adjacent to Fort Dix. A dozen soldiers were scheduled to arrive on the same plane, and an officer corralled Joelle and the other waiting relatives into a fenced-in area near the tarmac. The sun beat down on Claudia in her stroller, and Joelle lowered its canopy to protect her.

The other waiting relatives all seemed joyous. None of them appeared to be wrestling with dread the way she was. But then, the other young wives had probably been married for longer than a day before their husbands had left—and they probably were safe in the knowledge that their husbands loved them.

The plane landed on a distant runway, then taxied over. Someone wheeled a stairway to the door. A woman in uniform opened it and the soldiers emerged, clad in their dress uniforms, many of them with medal ribbons pinned to their shirts. Next to Claudia's stroller, a boy of about five waved an American flag. A few people snapped photographs.

The last soldier to emerge was Bobby. She absorbed the sight of him, framed by the plane's doorway. He was standing. His hair was longer than she'd expected, but she supposed he hadn't needed a buzz cut while he'd been in the hospital. He handed a pair of crutches to the soldier in front of him, who headed down the stairs, leaving Bobby to maneuver the descent alone, his hands gripping the railings for support. His left leg was strapped into a metal brace that resembled a medieval torture device. He extended that leg in front of him and hopped down the stairs on his right foot. At the bottom of the steps, he took back the crutches, said something to the soldier who'd been holding them and then gazed at the fence. At Joelle.

All the other soldiers ran once they spotted their loved ones. Bobby couldn't run. Joelle wished she could run to him, but the relatives had been ordered to stay behind the fence. So she only watched him as he made his laborious way across the asphalt.

As he neared, she searched his face. No obvious scars, but his appearance had changed. His eyes were darker, more wary. His easy smile was nowhere in evidence. Maybe he wasn't happy to see her.

He passed through the gate and hobbled over to her. The bone slid in his neck as he swallowed. "Bobby," she murmured, then mustered her courage and rose on tiptoe to kiss his cheek.

"Jo." He didn't kiss her back. His gaze was on the stroller. "Pick her up," he said.

She folded back the canopy, unstrapped Claudia and lifted her so Bobby could see her. He stared at her and his eyes grew misty. She stared right back, then reached out and tried to grab his nose.

He allowed himself a smile as he ducked his head, evading her pudgy little hand. "Hey, there," he whispered. "Hey, little girl. You know who I am?"

Claudia issued a cheerful gurgling sound.

"I'm your daddy," Bobby said. "I'm your dad." He bowed and brushed her cheek with his, then leaned back and met Joelle's eyes. His smile didn't completely disappear, thank God. He'd saved a little of it for her. "Let's get out of here," he said.

Someone lugged Bobby's duffel to the truck. Someone else folded the stroller and put it in the flatbed while Joelle strapped Claudia into her baby carrier. The truck's front seat would be crowded with all three of them crammed in—especially since Bobby had his crutches and couldn't bend his leg. She supposed that was what a family was: everyone crowded together.

The drive back to the apartment passed in silence, and Joelle's nerves frayed until they were nothing but ragged threads. When she glanced at Bobby, she saw him gazing out the window, his face blank. Maybe viewing New Jersey's suburban sprawl was a shock to him after Vietnam and more than two months in a hospital. Or maybe she and Bobby just didn't know how to talk to each other anymore.

His expression remained inscrutable as she led him into the apartment. It wasn't grand, but she'd knocked herself out to make it as pretty as she could on a budget of zero. She'd picked daisies growing along a roadway and stuck them in an empty Coke bottle to create a centerpiece for the coffee table in the living room. She'd sewn curtains for the windows and throw pillows for the couch. She'd bought a small black-and-white TV with a rabbit-ear antenna at the St. Vincent de Paul store. She'd set up a corner of the bedroom as a nursery area, squeezing in Claudia's crib and the changing table she'd created out of an old kitchen table and a colorful plastic pad. When Claudia had been born, the women at the house had bought her a mobile of butterflies, which Joelle had fastened to the crib railing so the colorful butterflies floated above her when she slept.

Bobby thumped around the apartment on his crutches, saying nothing.

"Is it all right?" she asked. "For what we could afford, I—"

"It's fine," he said.

They ate their steak dinner. Bobby didn't want any wine, so Joelle skipped it, as well. He watched TV while she got Claudia ready for bed. Once she had the baby down for the night, she joined Bobby on the couch. "Can you tell me about your leg?" she asked.

He forced a grim smile. "They had to use some bolts to pin the bones together. I'll have another surgery to remove those once it's healed."

"But it *will* heal." She asked more than said it.

"That's what they tell me."

"And your hearing?"

"It's back."

"Anything else?"

His gaze was haggard as he glanced her way. "I don't want to talk about it."

"Okay." She dared to touch his wrist. "If you change your mind, I'm here, Bobby."

He didn't move his arm away, but he didn't twist his hand to capture hers, either. They sat for another hour, her fingers resting on the back of his wrist, and watched *The Mod Squad*. Then he went off to the tiny bathroom to shower, insisting he didn't need any help.

While he was in the bathroom, she undressed, setting aside her boring underwear and putting on the prettiest nightgown she owned, thin white cotton with flowers embroidered on the front and the shadows of her body visible through the fabric. She turned down the blanket and brushed her hair a hundred strokes and prayed that she and Bobby would connect in bed, even if they hadn't connected on the couch. Their wedding night had been so wonderful. She wanted that closeness again. She wanted Bobby back.

He crutched into the bedroom, clad in sweatpants and a clean T-shirt—olive drab, army issue. His hair was wet, and the spicy scent of his shampoo nearly overpowered the sweet perfume of baby powder that filled the air. He made his way to the bed, dropped his crutches on the floor beside him and unstrapped his brace. Then he lay down.

Joelle hurried into the bathroom. It was humid and smelled of soap and toothpaste, of Bobby. She washed, inserted the dia-phragm the midwife had urged her to buy—"People say you can't get pregnant when you're nursing, but that's not true," she'd warned—and returned to the bedroom. He'd turned off the lamp on his side of the bed and pulled the covers up to his waist. If he'd noticed the pretty new sheets, he didn't mention them.

She climbed into bed next to him, switched off her bedside lamp and waited. Nearly a year had passed since they'd been together. Nearly a year since they'd been intimate. Maybe he'd visited prostitutes in Vietnam—soldiers did that—and he'd re-alized that he longed for a more experienced woman. Joelle knew next to nothing about lovemaking, and even after bathing she smelled like baby's milk, and Bobby had been around the world and he'd probably been with all kinds of sexy, worldly women who could satisfy him so much better than Joelle could.

Still, she was his wife.

He made no move toward her. She wondered whether he was in pain, whether his leg just didn't work well enough. Drawing again on every ounce of courage she possessed, she rose and leaned over him. Even in the dark, she could see his face. She touched her lips to his.

He kissed her back, gently, softly. He lifted his hand to her cheek, dug his fingers into her hair and closed his eyes. A shudder passed through him, and she felt him withdraw. Even before he let his hand drop, she realized she'd lost him.

"Bobby——"

"Don't," he whispered. She heard his sigh, and the steady rhythm of Claudia's breathing as she slept across the room. "I don't know where I am yet. I need…"

"Time?" she said helpfully.

"Yeah."

"Okay."

"I'm sorry."

"No, Bobby——don't be sorry. It's okay. Really."

He said nothing more, but shifted on the mattress, retreating.

She rolled away from him and squeezed her eyes shut to keep from crying.

THE NEXT DAY, BOBBY and Joelle drove to a used-car lot and traded in his beloved truck for a five-year-old Chevy Nova with eighty thousand miles on it. It had an automatic transmission, so he'd be able to drive it without a functioning left leg. Joelle had never been enamored of the truck, but Bobby's wistfulness was obvious as he signed the paperwork and handed the truck's keys over to the salesman.

Once he had a vehicle he could drive, he concentrated on organizing his life. Three days a week, he would attend physical therapy sessions at the V.A. hospital. The other two days, Claudia stayed home with him. He carried her around in a pouch Joelle had fashioned from an old knapsack, and together they ran errands and visited the playground. Bobby rigged a device out of pieces of an old bicycle's handlebar that enabled him to push Claudia's stroller with his chest while he propelled himself along on his crutches. .

Joelle was impressed by his determination and focus, and pleased that he was no longer smoking. "Did they make you quit at the hospital?" she asked when he'd been home for nearly a week and she hadn't seen him light up once.

"I quit for Claudia," he said. He didn't elaborate, and Joelle didn't press him. Whatever the reason, she was glad he'd kicked the habit.

He might have demonstrated good judgment about the smoking, and he was without question a devoted father. But still, a wide emptiness gaped between him and Joelle. He loved perching Claudia on his lap and letting her tug on his fingers, which would cause her to squeal with joy. He never gave his hand to Joelle to hold, though. Sometimes he smiled at her, sometimes he patted her shoulder as he maneuvered around her in the apartment's cramped, dark kitchen and once, while playing one of his Doors albums on the portable record player she'd found at a garage sale, he'd smiled at her and crooned, "'Come on, baby, light my fire'" along with Jim Morrison.

But when he climbed into bed, clad in sweatpants and a T-shirt... Nothing. He wouldn't reach for her. He wouldn't talk to her. He wouldn't touch her.

One night in late September, Suzanne invited them over to the house for dinner, claiming everyone missed Claudia and wanted to meet Bobby. He was a good sport about it, even though Joelle guessed an evening spent with a group of women wasn't his idea of fun. Suzanne made lasagna, thank God, and not one of her lentil-and-bean casseroles. Everyone but Bobby drank wine.

Joelle wondered whether he was declining alcohol because of the painkillers he still occasionally took. That she didn't know—that her husband wouldn't discuss with her why he refused to drink wine—only proved that their marriage was a farce.

She drank enough for both of them, figuring she could indulge since he'd be driving them home. Bobby bore up well as her old housemates peppered him with friendly questions. The student who had taken over Joelle's room when she'd moved out tried to explain to him why the Vietnam War was a bad thing, but he was more knowledgeable about the subject than she was, and he didn't need her lecture. "I got drafted," he explained. "Don't blame me."

After dinner, he and Claudia settled in the living room with a few of the women. Someone turned on the stereo and strains of Joni Mitchell seeped into the air. Joelle suppressed a chuckle. Joni Mitchell was such girlie music. Listening to her sweet, trilling soprano as she sang about heartache and romances gone sour was probably torture to Bobby.

Suzanne asked Joelle to keep her company in the kitchen while she cleaned up. Joelle refilled her glass with wine and gathered some plates from the table.

"I think everyone here has a crush on him," Suzanne said. "He's really cute."

"I know." He no longer appeared as drawn as he had the day he'd limped off the plane. His hair continued to grow in, black and thick with waves and he smiled a little more often. He'd always had a strong physique, but propelling himself around on crutches had built up the muscles in his arms and shoulders. As for the rest of his body, she couldn't say. She hadn't seen him undressed since the night they'd gotten married, close to a year ago. He'd been thin when he'd hobbled down the steps from the plane at McGuire; she suspected he'd gained a few pounds since he'd gotten home, which he'd desperately needed.

"You, on the other hand, look like hell," Suzanne said as she squirted dishwashing soap into the deep-basin sink.

"Thanks." Joelle smiled feebly. "I'm just tired, Suzanne. Between work and the baby and taking care of Bobby—"

"Does he want you taking care of him? For a guy recovering from some serious injuries, he seems to be doing pretty well."

"He is. But…" Joelle shrugged and drained her wineglass, then busied herself wrapping the leftover garlic bread in aluminum foil.

Suzanne eyed her sharply. "But what?"

Joelle adored Suzanne. The woman had been the big sister she'd never had, the surrogate mother she'd needed over the past year. Yet how could she tell her the truth—that her husband didn't desire her anymore? That their marriage had never been real, that they'd entered into it with the understanding that they could divorce each other once Bobby's military service was done? That he'd married her only because she'd been in trouble and desperate to keep her baby, not because he loved her?

"It's an adjustment," she finally said, because she had to say something.

"There are marriage counselors," Suzanne reminded her. "And don't tell me you can't afford them. I bet the army provides free counseling. You're not the only couple separated by the war and having adjustment problems." Suzanne shook the water from her hands and clamped them on Joelle's shoulders. "Talk to someone, Joelle. Get this worked out. If you love him, it's worth the fight."

Suzanne's words echoed inside Joelle as she and Bobby drove back to their apartment in the dark New Jersey night. Claudia lay strapped into her seat between them, pulling on one of her bare feet and making gurgling noises. "Bobby," Joelle called across the seat to him.

His gaze remained on the road. His profile could have been carved from granite it was so still.

"Maybe…maybe we ought to see a counselor."

In the glow from an oncoming car's headlights, she noticed a muscle ticking in his jaw. "I don't need a shrink."

"Not a shrink, Bobby—"

"You think I'm a head case?"

"No." She put more force into her voice. "I didn't mean *you* should see someone. I meant *us*. I was thinking of a marriage counselor."

He shot her a look, then turned back to the road. He said nothing.

Was he insulted? Hurt? She knew he wasn't given to deep introspection. She wasn't big on that, either—but their marriage was a disaster. Either they had to fix it or they had to quit.

His silence convinced her he'd just as soon quit.

It's worth the fight, Suzanne had said. If only Joelle had some idea about the right tactics. She wasn't the soldier in this car. She was nineteen years old, a mother, living in the amorphous center of suburban New Jersey because that was where an army base happened to be, not because it was her home. She was married to a man who had proposed to her with the promise that they could get out of this marriage if they wanted, no hard feelings.

"Do you want us to be married?" she asked, hoping he didn't hear the quiver in her voice. She was trying to be strong, tough, fighting for the man who was her husband.

He shot her another look. "Do we really have to have this discussion?" he asked. "You've been drinking wine all night."

"I'm not drunk. And all I'm asking—" *is for you to love me.*

Claudia chose that moment to start crying. Her outburst gave Bobby an excuse not to respond to Joelle. He winced at Claudia's wailing and steered in to the parking lot of their apartment complex. Joelle rubbed Claudia's belly, hoping to soothe her. But Claudia continued to howl all the way to their assigned parking space outside the door of their building.

Bobby shut off the engine and Joelle unstrapped Claudia. She took the baby onto her shoulder and rocked her. "Something happened to you in Vietnam—"

"No kidding," he muttered.

"And now, I just... You said we could split up when you got back. Is that what you want?"

"Joelle." He practically had to shout to be audible over Claudia's shrieks. "Why are we screaming at each other in the car?"

"Because you won't say what's going on with you!" She felt as frantic and frustrated as Claudia. "You never talk to me, Bobby. You never tell me what you're going through, what you're thinking. You won't even tell me what you went through over there."

"I don't want to talk about that."

"Yeah, I've figured that out. You don't want to talk about anything that matters. I'm your wife, Bobby—at least, I am right now. And you won't even—I mean, when you were wounded... You don't act like a husband. You don't..." She was too embarrassed to ask him why he wouldn't kiss her, gather her into his arms, make love to her the way he had on that lumpy motel bed a year ago. "You don't do what a husband does," she finished feebly. "I can't help wondering if maybe, when you were wounded..."

"Were my balls blown off?" His hands gripped the steering wheel so tightly she was afraid he might crush the plastic. "No."

Then the problem was her. He just didn't want her.

Too hurt to respond, she shoved open her door and swung out of the car. Getting out of the car took Bobby longer; his leg didn't move well and he had to retrieve his crutches from the floor of the backseat. Joelle didn't wait for him. She stormed into the building, silently howling along with Claudia.

Inside their apartment, she marched straight to the bedroom, to Claudia's changing table. The baby's diaper was full of poop, and once Joelle had her cleaned up and snapped into a sleeper, she subsided. A few minutes of nursing, and she fell into a peaceful slumber.

Joelle didn't feel peaceful. She couldn't imagine falling asleep. But it was nearly eleven, and she wasn't going to stay awake and chat amiably with Bobby, who had remained in the living room the whole time she was dealing with Claudia. She shut herself up in the bathroom, washed, changed into a nightgown and bundled under the covers, even though the room was too warm for a blanket. The sheets smelled of fabric softener. She laundered them every week, despite the fact that not enough life existed in their bed to warrant that much laundering.

After a while, Bobby joined her. As always, he wore sweat-pants and a T-shirt. As always, he remained on his side of the bed. He might as well have been in Ohio, for all the distance between them. He might as well have been in Vietnam.

He lay motionless, his respiration growing deeper and more regular as he sank into unconsciousness. She stared into the darkness, too agitated even to close her eyes. What should she do? If they got a divorce, where would she go? She couldn't move back to Suzanne's house; her room there was occupied by that new college student. And she sure as hell couldn't go back to Holmdell.

Nor would Bobby pay her alimony if they divorced. She was

earning more money than he received from the V.A. Maybe he was staying with her only because of her salary.

"Shank," he mumbled.

She turned to look at him. Her eyes had adjusted to the gloom, and she could see his face contorted, his body twitching.

"Shank. Shank."

What was he talking about?

He flinched, deep inside a nightmare. "Oh, Jesus—Shank?"

She sat up and leaned toward him. He might not love her—he might even hate her—but the humane thing was to awaken him from his terrifying dream. "Bobby…"

She reached out to shake his shoulder. His body thrashed, his arms flying. Before she could duck, his fist connected solidly with her cheekbone.

She screamed.

BOBBY OPENED HIS EYES IN time to see Joelle leap out of bed and run out of the room. From the crib rose a thin, anxious wail. He cursed. His body was damp with sweat, his head throbbing, his bad leg rattling with pain.

Just when he'd thought he couldn't do any more damage, couldn't cause more destruction, couldn't ruin Joelle's life more than he already had, he'd hit her. That he'd been asleep at the time didn't matter. He'd hit Joelle and he'd hurt her, and he wasn't sure how he was going to live with himself.

He'd had lots of nightmares during his months at the hospital, but they'd tapered off since his discharge. Sure, he continued to suffer from flashbacks, tremors, black memories, but nothing so fierce it made him flail and punch people. Why he'd done that tonight he couldn't say, unless it had something to do with Joelle's accusations in the car.

An evening drinking wine with her girlfriends had given her the courage to take him on, and she'd slammed into him hard. Every word she'd said was true—except when she'd denied thinking he was a head case. He was. The war had messed with his brain, and he was afraid to tell her, afraid for her to think he really was insane.

Maybe he ought to leave, let her go, give her the chance to find someone better than him, someone who wasn't all busted up inside and out. Someone able to love her the way she deserved to be loved.

Claudia had revved up to a full-throttle roar. Bobby reached for his crutches and eased himself to his feet, not bothering with the brace. Two hops brought him to the crib's railing. Leaning against it for balance, he lifted Claudia onto his shoulder. He'd noticed that she liked big shoulders. She calmed down a lot quicker when he was holding her than when Joelle was.

Eventually Claudia wound down, sniffled, pressed her moist, overheated face against his neck and let out a breath. A few more minutes and she was asleep.

He lowered her into the crib, then pivoted and observed the empty bed. The blanket was rumpled, the sheets untucked.

Steeling himself for the likelihood that Joelle had fled the apartment, he hobbled out of the bedroom and into the living room. Relief swamped him when he saw her seated on the couch, pressing a lumpy dish towel to her face.

He worked his way over to the couch, lowered himself beside her and nudged the towel away. The lumps, he realized, were ice cubes. The skin where she'd been holding the compress to her face was cold and imprinted with the towel's texture. A faint red mark along her cheekbone told him where he'd hit her. He'd bruised her. Hell.

"I'm sorry," he said.

"You didn't know what you were doing." Refusing to look at him, she directed her words to her knees. "You were sleeping."

"I'm still sorry." That faint red mark might as well have been a gushing wound. He'd promised her, the night they'd gotten married, that he would never hurt her. Add a broken promise to all the other reasons he was no good for her. "What you said earlier—if you want to leave me—"

"I don't want to leave you," she retorted. "I want you to..." She drew in a deep breath. "Touch me," she whispered, still staring at her lap. "I know you don't desire me. The pregnancy made me all pudgy—"

"Oh, God, Joelle." He closed his eyes, as if not viewing her would make him want her less. But even with his eyes closed he saw her, her soft golden hair, her soft body, her soft blue eyes. He had been watching her since the moment he'd spotted her behind the fence at McGuire, wearing a sleeveless minidress that showed off her graceful arms and legs. He watched her when she washed dishes, her fingers glistening with soap, and when she entered the apartment after a day working at the preschool, her hair disheveled and a smear of fingerpaint on her shirt. He watched her when she fed the baby. She always tried to cover herself with a cloth or the edge of her shirt when she nursed, but he could see. The sight of her nursing Claudia was so beautiful it pained him.

Everything pained him. That was the thing. His body ached, his mind ached, his soul ached. Joelle was lovely, untouched by anything mean and ugly and violent, and he was scarred, so grotesque he couldn't bear for her to get close to him.

And damn it, he *had* touched her—in a mean, ugly way. The bruise below her eye was smaller than one of Claudia's hands, but it was there.

"Why were you talking about a shank?" she asked.

His eyes opened. "When?"

"In your dream. You kept saying 'shank, shank.'"

"Schenk," he corrected her, then closed his eyes again and leaned away from her.

"Schenk?"

"One of the guys in my platoon." His voice went paper thin.

"Tell me what happened, Bobby. Tell me about your dream."

He sighed. If she wanted to know—if she really wanted to know why he'd been such a crappy husband, such a poor excuse for a human being—he would tell her. "Schenk always had a canteen full of booze with him, even during the day, when we were out in the field. He'd share it if you wanted some, but it was vile stuff. He was…kind of wild, but a good guy. He'd give you the shirt off his back. Or the rotgut out of his canteen."

Joelle twisted on the couch, tucking one foot under her other thigh and facing him. Her expression was solemn, expectant.

"We were on patrol, and he was taking a hit from the canteen and he tripped a wire. I was maybe three, four feet away from him. All I saw…" A wave of nausea swept through him and he swallowed, wishing he could speak the memory without living it. "All I saw was red. There was no more Schenk."

She didn't fall apart, thank God, or do anything to indicate she pitied him. She only nodded.

"I was shouting—only, I couldn't hear my voice. I started running toward him—only, I wasn't moving. In my head I was running and shouting, but I was just…just lying there, seeing red."

She reached for his hand, but he drew back. She hadn't heard the worst of it yet.

"It wasn't just my leg. The explosion ruptured my left eardrum, but that healed. I had shrapnel embedded in my back, my

side. The shrapnel didn't only come from the mine, Jo. It..."
Another wave of nausea hit him, but he fought it off. "It came
from Schenk. Pieces of his canteen. Pieces of his rifle, his
helmet... Pieces of *him*."

She reached for him again, this time snagging his hand before he could pull it away. Her fingers were cool and smooth
and gentle. He felt tears sting his eyes; he didn't deserve her
gentleness.

"Did they get all the shrapnel out?" she asked.

He shook his head. "They don't remove it surgically, unless
it's in an organ. If it's just in your skin, they leave it. It comes
out on its own over time." His nausea seemed to fade, mostly
because Joelle wasn't grossed out. She appeared sad, even anguished, but not disgusted. "It's still coming out, Jo. I can't let
you see my body. Can you understand that?"

"I can understand it," she said, "but I'm your wife. If you
want this marriage to work, you can't hide from me. I'm your
wife, Bobby." She rose onto her knees, released his hand and
freed his T-shirt from the waistband of his sweats. Jaw set,
lower lip caught between her teeth, she shoved the shirt up, over
his head and off.

He watched her while she scrutinized his torso, the mosaic
of sores and scars along his side. Some of the wounds had closed
into ropy pink scar tissue. Others were scabbed. He knew how
grotesque he looked. He inspected himself in the mirror every
day after his shower, searching for bits of shrapnel that had
worked their way to the surface of his skin, reading his wounds
as if they were some kind of obscene graffiti.

Joelle didn't recoil. She ran her hand lightly over his side,
then shifted to view his back. Even the nurses in Hawaii hadn't
ministered to him as gently as she did. "Does it hurt?"

"No." Not physically. Emotionally it was excruciating.

"I want to see your leg," she said.

"That's not so pretty, either." The grueling physical therapy was only just beginning to rebuild his wasted muscles, and he had surgical scars running like train tracks near his ankle and knee and along his thigh. But he couldn't bring himself to stop her as she untied the drawstring and eased his sweatpants out from under his butt and down his legs. There he was, naked, mutilated. Not the man she'd married. Not the man he'd been before Vietnam had done a number on him.

Her hand glided the length of his legs, moving her fingers lightly across the scars on his left leg, tactfully not mentioning that the calf of that leg was a good three inches smaller in circumference than its mate. Her palms floated, glided. They were cool, but they made his skin burn. As she skimmed her hands up his thighs, the burning traveled with them. By the time she'd arrived at his groin, he was practically in flames.

She raised her face to him, then inched one hand around his dick and stroked. Slow and tight.

She'd seen him and she hadn't run away. If he hadn't already loved her, he would have fallen madly in love right now, just because she was there, touching him, accepting what he was.

He gripped her shoulders and pulled her to him, sinking into the cushions and bringing her with him. He kissed her, kissed her with everything he had, every bit of strength, every bit of trust and yearning and love the war hadn't wrung out of him. She kissed him back, matching his passion, his desperation.

By the time she broke the kiss and gulped in a breath, he was ready to burst. "The bed might be more comfortable," she murmured.

"It's a friggin' nursery in there," he argued. He wasn't even sure he could make love to her when his leg wasn't working. He sure as hell couldn't make love to her with Claudia snoring just inches away from them and the air smelling like baby powder.

Joelle smiled hesitantly, a little nervously, then leaned back and lifted her nightgown over her head. A surge of lust ripped through him as he gazed up at her. "You are so beautiful," he whispered.

She made a face. "I've got stretch marks, and my breasts are too big—"

"No such thing as too big," he argued, filling his hands with her breasts. He caressed them, then slid his hands down to her belly, to her crotch. She was already wet, and he was dying for her. Clamping her hips, he urged her down onto him.

As bad as he'd been feeling for far too long, that was how good he felt now, inside her. From nightmare to dream, from hell to heaven, it was a change so swift he felt a whiplash in his spine.

She seemed uncertain, and he realized she'd probably never been on top before. What was her experience, anyway? One night with him, and one other guy he refused to think about.

He used his hands to guide her, moving her up and down. His body strained, pressed, wanted. He wasn't going to last— he knew that. His first time with Joelle in nearly a year, his first time since his world had come apart, and she was so soft and warm and snug around him, her skin like velvet, her hair spilling down into his face. He had no willpower, no staying power, nothing. Nothing but the pulse pounding in his head, the fire in his balls, the tension in his muscles as Joelle rode him. Nothing but gratitude and fear and love.

He tried to slow her down, but she was rocking on her own now, emitting hushed, throaty sounds. He wedged one hand between them, and when she rose, he found her with his fingers.

She let out a cry, and that was it. He was gone, his body wrenching, emptying, spilling into her.

She collapsed on top of him, light and limp. He closed his eyes, closed his arms around her and willed his heart to stop hammering in his chest. He didn't deserve a woman as good as she was, a woman so sexy, a woman who could accept his ravaged body, who could accept him when he'd shut her out for so long, when he'd been so sure she would reject him. He didn't deserve this.

But it was his, at least for now, and he'd take it.

NINE

JOELLE LOOKED AT THE SHRIMP, on skewers, swimming in teriyaki sauce and ready for the grill. They'd been marinating for hours, far longer than necessary. Right now, she was ready to throw them into the trash.

She heard a rumble in the garage, the truck's engine echoing off the concrete walls, idling and then shutting off. The understanding that Bobby was finally home caused her hands to clench so tightly her fingertips tingled. Her gaze rose to the clock on the wall oven's facade: seven-thirty.

Would he be drunk this time? Would he break things and puke and act like a jerk? Had she been a fool to spend hours fussing with her shrimp, measuring rice and water into a pot, hoping that her having prepared yet another of his favorite meals would soften him up? Her lasagna hadn't made a difference. Her rosemary chicken hadn't. Nor had her rib-eye steaks.

Grilled shrimp teriyaki? While he'd been out doing who knew what?

She listened to the door opening, and then the clomp of his boots in the mudroom. *Don't throw a tantrum,* she reminded herself. *Don't jump down his throat the instant you see him.* Her will-power was in short supply, though. She'd been building up to this moment ever since she'd gotten that phone call an hour ago. She wanted to scream, to flail, to force that fool husband of hers to tell her what the hell was going on.

He swung into the kitchen, his hair windswept, his skin darker than it had been just a week ago. He'd been working outdoors a lot, building a patio in Arlington and consulting on a plaza at a college down in Bridgeport. Unlike her, he wasn't fair-skinned. A few days in the summer sun and his complexion turned brick-brown.

He didn't seem drunk. But that was the least of her worries.

Without a word, he crossed to the sink and twisted on the faucet. He washed his hands, using soap, lathering up past his wrists. What was he washing away?

"Who is she?" she asked when she couldn't stand the silence anymore.

He gazed over his shoulder, scowled, then tore a few squares of paper towel from the roll. "Who is who?"

"The woman you were having a drink with," she said, her nerves cutting through her voice like jagged bits of broken glass.

He shot her an unreadable look.

"Harriet Briggs from down the street saw you go into the Hay Street Pub with a woman. She followed you inside. You and that woman were at a table for two."

"And then Harriet raced outside and phoned you," Bobby muttered. "She's a bitch. She's always trying to stir up trouble."

"She can't stir up trouble unless there's trouble to stir up." Joelle leaned against the counter and crossed her arms over her chest. That position forced her to relax her fists before her nails drew blood from her palms.

She wasn't jealous by nature. Early in her marriage, she'd been envious of other women—women whose husbands had married them for all the right reasons, women certain that their husbands loved them, women who understood sex in ways she didn't. She'd wondered whether Bobby might have been with other women while he'd been in 'Nam. True, he'd been a married man, but their marriage had barely existed when he'd left her. Just one night, and then he'd been gone.

But he'd come home, and they'd stuck together and her schoolgirl insecurities had gradually faded.

They were back now. Drew's invasion into their lives reawakened all her anxieties, her worries about whether she was good enough, whether she should still feel beholden to Bobby for having married her. And he was obviously so angry with her now. If he could get drunk like his father, what else was he capable of doing?

"The woman," he said slowly, his frown aging his face, "was Helen Crawford."

That name meant nothing to Joelle.

"You don't know her," Bobby continued, parceling out information as if it were more precious than gold. "She's Foster's wife."

Drew's wife? Bobby had been having a drink with Drew's wife? Joelle struggled not to launch herself at him, grip his shoulders and shake him until the whole truth spilled out.

"She called and said she wanted to meet me. So I said okay, and she drove up to Gray Hill."

"And you took her to a bar?"

"I had iced tea. She had a wine cooler." He tossed the paper towels into the trash and turned back to Joelle. "She looks a little like you. Foster must have a thing for blondes."

How could he act so calm, so aloof? Didn't he realize their

marriage was disintegrating? He was the one who'd said they were perched on a stone wall that was about to collapse. That was last Sunday. Now it was Thursday, and the stones were scattering and slipping. She and Bobby were in a free fall with no soft place to land.

And he chose to talk about Drew Foster's taste for blondes?

"Why didn't you call me?" she asked. "I would have met you there."

"Helen didn't want you there. She wanted to talk to me alone."

Joelle stared at him. Even across the room, he seemed to loom above her, tall and sturdy. He hadn't removed his boots, and their thick, ridged soles added an extra inch to his height.

Had Drew Foster's wife noticed what a handsome man he was? Did the women Drew had a thing for have a thing for Bobby?

"Why did she want to talk to you alone? Am I allowed to ask that?" She wished she could behave as detached as Bobby, but she couldn't. Panic churned inside her, searing her stomach with acid.

Bobby didn't comment on her sarcasm. He crossed to the refrigerator, swung open the door and pulled out a can of ginger ale. He snapped the top, took a sip, then dropped onto a chair by the table. That made him seem a little less imposing, at least.

"She said she and I were...how did she put it? The outer corners of a trapezoid."

"What?" Joelle would have laughed if she hadn't been so upset.

"There are four people involved, so we can't be a triangle. But we're not a square, because we've got different investments in this situation. So we're a trapezoid." He must have sensed Joelle's bemusement, because he shrugged. "I'm just quoting her."

"Yes, we aren't a triangle," Joelle said. Besides, a triangle would imply there was something going on between her and Drew.

He shrugged again. "She said she was still in shock from the news that her husband had fathered a child out of wedlock. She just learned about it a few weeks ago."

"So did he," Joelle pointed out. "Until he hired that detective to find me, he had no idea that I hadn't used his money to get an abortion."

"He knew he'd knocked you up," Bobby reminded her, his voice taking on an edge of its own. His words were cold and bitter.

"So...what? His wife decided to get together with you and plot against Drew?" *And against me?* she almost added.

"We didn't plot anything." He swallowed some ginger ale and leaned back in his chair. His eyes were tired, his mouth grim. "She wants her son to have a chance. I felt sorry for her. Her kid is critically ill and her husband is a freaking son of a bitch. So she wanted to drink a wine cooler and vent a little. No harm in that."

Like hell. Bobby had given this poor grieving woman his shoulder to lean on, and all the while Joelle had been home, exerting herself to prepare yet another special dinner for him while she fretted about how to mend their marriage. "You could have called and told me you'd be late. I was worried. I didn't know where you were."

"Yes, you did. Harriet Briggs told you." He drank some more soda. "I had a drink and a conversation with a woman, and you automatically assumed the worst."

"Bobby—"

He peered up at her and she noticed more than weariness in his eyes. "What did you think? I was doing something wrong with this woman? Having an affair? What?" His gaze was stormy. "You have that little faith in me?"

"Of course I have faith in you," she said, but her voice wavered and she averted her eyes. Yes, she'd assumed the worst. Given the current state of their marriage, given that the last time Bobby had touched her she'd instigated it and he'd wound up pounding into her like someone crazed, she'd assumed the absolute worst.

At one time she'd had faith in Bobby, in herself, in their marriage. But tonight…the faith wasn't there.

"What have I done that would make you stop trusting me?" he challenged her.

"Three days ago you came home drunk."

He scowled. "Lots of men come home drunk every day. My father did."

"And I haven't been able to talk to you. There's all this anger. You resent me."

"What makes you think that?"

"It's there, Bobby. In the silence. In everything you don't say, everything you won't tell me. All I feel coming from you these days is hostility."

His scowl intensified, making her feel even more hostility.

"Maybe we should get counseling," she said, then braced herself for his response.

As she'd expected, it wasn't positive. He hammered his fist against the table. "I'm not going to bare my soul in front of a total stranger."

"But we can't talk anymore. Maybe a therapist would help get us talking."

"We're talking now."

"And saying nothing. Nothing that matters. You're stewing inside, Bobby. It's like when you came back from the war and you had all this rage inside you, and you wouldn't let it out. That's what you're like now."

"Who needs a counselor when I've got you?" he snapped. "You've got me all figured out, Jo. Why waste time talking?"

"You consider talking a waste?"

"Talking about this is." He thumped his hand against the table again. "What should I say? All Claudia's life, I was her father. Now I'm not. That's all there is to it."

That wasn't all there was. "What about our marriage?" she asked. "Isn't that about more than Claudia?"

"You married me because you had to," he reminded her, his voice taut and low. "You married me to protect Claudia. Now she doesn't have that protection anymore. The reason we got married—it doesn't exist anymore."

"But our marriage still exists, Bobby. You're saying there's no reason for that?"

He eyed her sharply. "I was Claudia's father, and you took that away from me."

Joelle's legs faltered beneath her. Her vision blurred, then sharpened into painful focus on the man seated at the table in the center of her kitchen. Was that really how he felt, after all these years?

She knew he hadn't married her out of love. Marrying her had been an act of enormous kindness and generosity on his part—and she'd done her best to show her gratitude over the years. She'd confided in him, cooked for him, argued with him, goaded him, cheered him on. She'd shared his bed.

Now their bed was cold and barren, a reflection of their marriage. It was no longer a haven where they could shut out the world and open to each other. It had become a place she dreaded.

"When we got married," she said, struggling to keep her voice level, "you said we'd go into it with the understanding that we could always get a divorce. Now you're saying the reason we got married doesn't exist anymore. Do you want to cash in? Play your get-out-of-jail card?"

"I didn't say—"

"You said I married you only because of Claudia. *You* married *me* only because of Claudia. Now that reason is gone." Could he hear the tremor in her tone? Could he tell she was struggling not to shake? "What's left? What is this marriage really about?"

He turned to stare out the window, avoiding Joelle. "God only knows," he muttered.

"Then what do you want from me? A divorce?" Maybe if she said the word enough, she might begin to accept its weight.

"I want…" He looked at her. "I want what we had before. And I can't have that anymore. You took that away from us. It's gone."

Bobby so rarely allowed her to glimpse his soul. Opening him up was like chiseling through solid stone. When he'd been ravaged by injuries and nightmares after the war, she'd had to drag his feelings out of him. He never would have told her if she hadn't forced him.

She'd forced him now, and his feelings lay plain before her. The foundation of their marriage had vanished, and he blamed her for it.

Holding her face immobile, refusing to let him see the devastation he'd inflicted on her, she carried the tray of shrimp to the refrigerator and slid it onto a shelf. Then she walked out of the kitchen, away from her husband. Away from the man who felt their marriage no longer had a reason to exist.

HE MADE A POINT OF DRIVING home early the next day.

Their bed had turned into hostile territory, as ominously quiet as patrol in 'Nam. He and Joelle slept side by side like strangers. Every night he lay awake, holding himself motionless, wondering where the mines were and how close he was to tripping one. And sometimes not even caring if he did.

Things couldn't go on this way. He had to find his way back

to Joelle. Tonight was Friday, and they had a weekend ahead of them. They would talk. Talking—*real* talking, personal talking—didn't come easily to him, but he'd try.

He'd been an idiot last night. He should have phoned Joelle and told her he was getting together with Foster's wife after work. When Helen Crawford had said she wanted to meet with him alone, because he and she were the two "outsiders" in this situation—whatever the hell that meant—he should have said no, that Joelle ought to be included. But Helen had shown up at his office, slim and pretty and as fresh as an ocean breeze, her face unnaturally smooth and her blond hair containing not a single strand of silver, and when she'd said, "Let's go somewhere and talk," he'd said sure. As they'd left his office, he'd felt Mona's eyes on him, as suspicious as any wife, and he hadn't cared.

Helen had dominated the conversation; he'd mostly listened. She'd told him about how shocked she'd been to learn of Claudia's existence. "Thrilled and appalled at the same time," she'd explained. "Thrilled that my son might have a chance to beat his leukemia, but appalled that Drew had been so careless and thoughtless all those years ago. He'd been young and foolish, of course, but it's one thing to be young and foolish and another to impregnate a girl and then leave her to fend for herself."

Bobby hadn't had an argument for that.

"At least you knew the truth all along," she'd gone on. "I was the only one who had no idea what had happened way back when in your little Ohio town."

Not true. Claudia hadn't known, either. The boys hadn't known. But he'd let Helen vent, let her babble, let her lean toward him and murmur that she was sure he could appreciate why she felt the way she did, that certainly he understood her feelings in a way her own husband couldn't begin to grasp.

She'd been coming on to him. Subtly, not openly, but he'd picked up on it. He wasn't interested—women whose faces were stretched tighter than a bedsheet on a barracks cot weren't his type—but he was a man, and when a classy New York City lady sent signals, he would have had to be dead not to feel a little flattered.

Helen Crawford was distraught. She was resentful. If it made her feel better to flirt, who was he to stop her? He hadn't encouraged her, hadn't reciprocated, but given how unpleasant things were at home, he'd allowed himself to enjoy the moment.

Today he felt guilty. Last night he'd fumed in silence at the fact that Joelle didn't trust him, and today he was prepared to admit that maybe she'd been right not to trust him. He didn't like dredging up old crap, probing his emotions, analyzing things to death, but if Joelle wanted to talk to him tonight, they'd talk.

He'd take her out to dinner. He'd massage her shoulders and neck, if she'd let him. He'd fight his way back to her. This had been the angriest week of his life—worse than any week he could remember in 'Nam, even after he'd gotten blown to shit. It was time to assess the damage, time to reset the broken bones and start rehab.

Joelle's Prius was gone from the garage when he got home, and a note was waiting for him on the kitchen table:

Dear Bobby,

    I need some time to myself, to clear my head and think things through. If the kids have to reach me, I've got my cell phone. The shrimp I was going to cook last night is in the fridge. Fire up the grill and lay the skewers on. When the shrimp is pink, it's cooked. It shouldn't take more than five to ten minutes on each side.

Not a word about where she'd gone or when she'd be back. Just cooking instructions.

He read the note again, crumpled it into a ball and hurled it across the room. Then he retrieved it, grabbed his reading glasses from atop that morning's newspaper on the kitchen table, smoothed out the note and read it once more. His glasses didn't alter a word of her message. She was gone, and he should grill the shrimp.

He crossed the room to the cordless phone and punched in her cell-phone number. After four rings, her taped voice answered: "Joelle can't talk right now. Please leave a message."

A message, he thought frantically. There were plenty of things he wanted to say. Like, *Jesus Christ, Joelle—where are you? How could you run away like this? Here I am, ready to talk.*

All he said, however, was, "Come home. Please."

He knew why she'd run. Four days ago, he'd stormed into the house drunk from a binge, broken a vase on the floor and thrown up. He'd gotten crocked and acted violently. Shamed by his behavior and infuriated by Joelle's refusal to pity him, he'd withdrawn. He'd been nowhere, nothing, way out of reach. More accessible to Foster's wife than to Joelle.

Of course she'd left. Why would she want to hang around with a screwed-up asshole like him?

He swung open the refrigerator and found, along with the tray of shrimp skewers, a few bottles of microbrewery beer. Joelle kept them on hand for when the boys dropped by. They liked gourmet beer, which Bobby considered a contradiction in terms.

He pulled out a bottle and carried it out the back door to the patio. The evening sky was the pink of a dogwood blossom, pale in parts and more richly hued where thin clouds streaked above the horizon. He sprawled out on one of the lounge chairs, tapped his palm against the bottle's cap but didn't twist it off, not yet.

Where would she have gone? She was still close to that woman Suzanne, the senior member of the communal house she'd lived in while he'd been in 'Nam.

Suzanne was living somewhere in the Southwest. She and Joelle still exchanged Christmas cards. He wondered if they kept in touch with e-mail, too.

E-mail. If he could open Joelle's account, he might find evidence of where she'd gone. He had no idea what her password was, but he could probably figure it out. Her maiden name, maybe, or one of the kids' names.

No, he couldn't hack into her software. She'd left him because she didn't trust him anymore. He wasn't going to win her back by doing something untrustworthy.

He lifted the bottle again. Its brown surface was slick with condensation. He closed one hand around the cap to twist it off, then hesitated and balanced the unopened bottle on the arm of his chair.

Damn it, JoJo.

The coppery sun rode along the spiked tips of the pine trees that edged the horizon beyond his yard. Purple shadows stretched across the grass and reached into Joelle's vegetable garden. Her tomato vines were covered in yellow flowers, her zucchini shaped a tangle of dark green along the ground and her chard looked like miniature shrubs leafing out from the soil. He'd created that garden for her. He'd bought the house and rebuilt it for her. He'd bought her the damn Prius she'd run off in because she wanted to save the environment. Everything he'd done, everything he'd become—it was for Joelle. He'd given her everything he could.

Apparently everything wasn't enough. The one thing he couldn't give her was marriage to the man she'd loved.

Thirty-seven years. He and Joelle had had good times, great times, tender times, but the knowledge that he wasn't the man she'd been in love with burned like a pilot light inside him, never extinguished. She'd married Bobby only because she'd had to, because the alternatives had been worse. Bobby DiFranco had been her second choice, her desperation choice.

He sat outdoors long after the light faded from the sky, after the crickets began to chirp and the mosquitoes to bite, and the air cooled down and filled with the pure scent of evergreens and grass. He sat listening to the emptiness of the house behind him and wondering whether marrying Joelle had been the smartest thing he'd ever done in his life, or the stupidest.

Finally, after slapping a mosquito dead on his cheek, he rose from the lounge chair and went inside to wash the bits of bug from his hand and face. He put the unopened beer back into the refrigerator.

Drinking wasn't going to help.

AFTER HOURS OF INSOMNIA, he rose from bed early the following morning. His forehead felt tight, his throat was dry and his empty stomach grumbled. He threw on an old pair of shorts and a T-shirt, staggered down the stairs and entered the kitchen. Opening the refrigerator, he saw the skewers of marinated shrimp and lost his appetite again.

Joelle's absence was like an invisible beast. All night long, lying in their bed alone, he felt that beast's hot breath against his neck. Never in his life had he felt so alone.

He put up a pot of coffee to brew, then wandered into the

living room and crossed to the hutch that held their stereo equipment. Doors, he thought—he needed the Doors. He slid four Doors CDs onto the carousel, punched the "shuffle" button and returned to the kitchen to get some coffee.

Damn. He had an appointment to meet with a potential client that morning. Joelle was supposed to dust and vacuum and scour the sinks, and Bobby was supposed to traipse around yet another estate with yet another proud new home owner and promise to create yet another weekend paradise of flowering shrubs and hot tubs and stone walls.

He couldn't even bring himself to shave. Dealing with a new customer was way beyond him.

Mike could handle it, he decided, grabbing the phone in the kitchen. He punched in Mike's number, apologized for calling so early, said he wasn't feeling well and asked Mike to walk the property with the prospective client and write up his specs. "Bring Danny with you," Bobby suggested. "Between the two of you, you'll get it right."

"Danny's with Lauren," Mike said.

The symphony girl. "Are they at Tanglewood again?"

"No—I think they're at his place."

"Then it's not a problem. He can go with you." Being one half of a couple didn't mean you stopped doing what you were supposed to do.

Being one half of a couple when the other half had vanished, however… That was enough to stop Bobby dead.

"Have you been drinking, Dad?" Mike asked.

Great. His wife was gone, and now he had Mike distrusting him, too. "No," he said coldly. "I only drink when I'm with you."

"Right." Mike sounded just as cold.

"I'm not hungover, if that's what you're asking. I'm just…"

All alone and scared to death. "Not feeling well. Take the client for me, would you?"

"Sure."

He said goodbye to Mike, listened as Jim Morrison ordered him to break on through to the other side and lifted the phone's handpiece again. He entered Joelle's cell-phone number, then pressed the phone to his ear. Four rings and her taped voice requesting that he leave a message.

He'd already left the only message he had for her. *Come home.* He disconnected the call and lowered the phone to its base.

He poured himself a cup of coffee. He'd made it too strong, and it scorched the length of his digestive tract.

He knew he should eat something. Instead he returned to the living room with his Number One Dad mug, sank onto the overstuffed sofa, rolled his head back and closed his eyes. The music washed over him like a warm tide. He wished it would lift him up and carry him to some other, happier shore. A golden beach where Joelle would be waiting for him, smiling, her arms spread wide.

The sound of the doorbell jarred him from his trance. "Riders on the Storm" had been playing, slow and bluesy and mournful. He didn't want to drag himself off the sofa. He didn't want to see anyone. But what if it was the police? What if they were here to tell him something awful had happened to Joelle?

He forced himself to his feet, strode across the living room to the entry and opened the door. Claudia stood on the porch, holding the morning newspaper he'd never bothered to bring inside. "What's going on?" she asked, shoving past him and across the threshold.

"Why are you here?" he retorted, too tired to bother with manners.

"Mike phoned and said something was wrong. He and Danny had to go meet with a client because you said you were sick. Where's Mom?"

Claudia was as brisk and focused as he was hazy. He watched her poke her head through the living-room doorway before stalking down the hall to the kitchen, calling for her mother.

Reluctantly, he followed her into the kitchen. She stood in the middle of the room, hands on hips. "Where's Mom?"

What was the point in pretending? "She left," he said.

"She left? What do you mean, she left?"

He moved to the counter and located the wrinkled sheet of paper with Joelle's note on it. "I mean she left," he said, handing the note to Claudia.

She read it, her brow furrowing. "When did she leave?"

"She was gone when I got home last night." He sipped his coffee. It had cooled off, but its bitterness scorched his throat.

"Did you phone her?"

"Twice. She won't answer."

Claudia pursed her lips. "She's got caller ID on her cell, right? Let me try her from my phone. Maybe she'll take my call." She set her purse down on the table and rummaged through it. "Have you eaten anything?"

"I'm drinking coffee. Don't baby me."

Her lips pursed harder, compressing tighter than a kiss. She dug out her cell phone. "Any idea where she might have gone?"

"She took her car. How far do you think she'd drive?"

"The airport isn't that far," Claudia pointed out. "She could be anywhere." She tapped her thumb against the buttons on her cell, then held it to her ear. After a few seconds, she started talking. "Mom? It's Claudia. Where are you?"

Bobby dropped onto one of the chairs. He no longer had the

strength to refill his mug. The comprehension that Joelle would accept a call from Claudia but not from him cut through him like a stiletto, so sharp it took him a minute to realize how badly he was bleeding.

"Okay, I understand," Claudia said into the phone. "It's just…" She glanced toward Bobby. "No, he's fine," she said, and Bobby closed his eyes and nodded his thanks. "He says he tried to phone you."

"Tell her I want her to come home," Bobby murmured.

"He wants you to come home," Claudia told her mother, then listened some more. "All right. Yes. I'll tell him. I'll talk to you again later." She folded her phone shut, then regarded her father sternly. "She said she needs a little time to herself to think things through. She also said to let you know the Prius got excellent mileage on the highway."

"Where is she?"

"Holmdell." Claudia lifted the coffee decanter, studied the gravy-thick sludge inside it and emptied it into the sink. She rinsed it and prepared a fresh pot. Then she walked to the refrigerator, opened it and pulled out a package of English muffins and a tub of butter. Without a word, she slid two split muffins into the toaster oven and turned it on. While the muffins browned, she returned to the refrigerator, removed the platter of skewered shrimp and dumped its contents into the trash.

Bobby felt a rush of gratitude that she'd disposed of the damn shrimp. When she presented him with a plate holding the toasted muffins, he felt a little less grateful. "You don't have to feed me," he said. "I'm not one of your babies. Where are they, anyway?"

"They're with their father," she said crisply. She set the tub of butter in front of him. Then she filled his mug with the freshly brewed coffee, poured some into another mug for herself and joined him at the table. "Is this all because of me?"

"What do you mean?"

"Mom's disappearing act. Is it because of me?"

He opened his mouth, then shut it and used the time it took to butter his muffin halves to sort his thoughts. "None of this is because of you, Claudia. I don't ever want you thinking that."

"But if my real—I mean, my biological father hadn't made the scene, Mom would be home right now."

"I don't know." Bobby lifted the muffin, then lowered it back to the plate. He ought to eat something, but he couldn't. He was starving, but he wasn't hungry. "Drew Foster opened a door we used to keep closed," he said. "Whatever was behind that door existed, even when the door was bolted shut. Now it's open. That's all."

"What's behind the door, Dad?" Claudia asked, her voice hushed and gentle.

"I don't think that's your business," he said, equally gently. She meant well, but Christ. She was his daughter.

"It *is* my business. The person who unlocked this door you're talking about was looking for me." She folded her hands on the table in front of her, like a schoolgirl praying to do well on a quiz. She was dressed in a flowery sundress. Claudia was the kind of woman who'd put on a dress at eight on a Saturday morning just to check on her father. There was nothing pretentious about it, no attempt to impress. It was just the way she was.

Her lovely grooming made him feel twice as rumpled. He hadn't combed his hair, his cheeks were covered in stubble, the edges of his shorts were fraying and his bare feet were ugly. Thanks to Joelle, he'd learned not to be self-conscious about his scars, which had faded over the years. Along his side and back was a faint graph of pale lines. As for his legs, he could wear shorts and not care that someone might notice the tracks his surgeries had left on his skin.

But even if he'd been left with huge, ugly scars, Joelle had accepted his body, and that had enabled him to accept it.

He managed to swallow a bite of muffin. "Your mother married me so you wouldn't be born out of wedlock," he said. "Is that what you wanted to know?"

"I already figured that out."

"Okay, then. You get the picture. We didn't marry for love."

"But you *do* love each other." Claudia studied his face, searching for reassurance.

"I love your mother. I don't think she loves me."

"Just because she went off to Ohio doesn't mean she doesn't love you."

"I'm not talking about this." He gestured toward the note Joelle had left him. "I'm talking about our lives. She married me because she had to, because she couldn't see any other way to keep you. And we made a go of it for a long time because we kept that fact locked behind the door. If you don't think about something, you can pretend it isn't there."

"She told me…" Claudia traced the rim of her mug with her finger. "She told me she would have gone out with you in high school if you'd ever asked her. You never did."

Bobby sat back, surprised. For a moment he regressed to being a teenager, Joelle Webber's best friend and secret admirer. "We were pals," he said.

"You never asked her out. You were dating some other girl. Mom showed me everyone in her high-school yearbook. I don't remember the girl's name. She had black hair and too much eye makeup."

"Margie Noonan," Bobby recollected. Then he shook his head. "Your mother was out of my league."

"She was a kid from the wrong side of the tracks, just like you."

"She was a Tubtown kid, but she wasn't anything like me." He sipped some coffee. It tasted wonderful after the crap he'd brewed earlier. "She was going places. She was destined for greatness. I wasn't about to stand in her way."

"You were destined for greatness, too," Claudia said. "Look at you, Dad. You own your own business. You own a beautiful house on a beautiful piece of land in a beautiful part of New England. You're an American success story."

"I never thought I'd wind up like this," he admitted. Even scruffy and agitated, his wife gone and his future threatened, he allowed himself a moment of pride in all he'd accomplished. Then he acknowledged the truth: "Whatever success I've achieved, it was because of your mother. I wanted her to have the life she'd dreamed of. When I came back from the war, I was a mess, inside and out. She had two babies to deal with, not just one. You and me. She deserved so much more—and I've spent my life trying to give it to her."

"That's not the way she tells it," Claudia argued. "She's always told me you were the bravest man she'd ever known."

"There was nothing brave about getting drafted."

"She isn't talking about your service in Vietnam," she clarified. "She's talking about when you came back. Mom said you were in a million pieces and fought your way back to health—and all the while, you were taking care of me. That took a lot of courage." She smiled nostalgically. "She showed me this old music box you used to play for me. Do you remember? It played 'Edelweiss.'"

"Yeah, I remember that." He shared her smile, then grew solemn. Would Joelle really have gone out with him in high school? They'd been such close friends, dating her would have seemed incestuous. "The bottom line was, your mother hoped to marry Drew Foster," he said quietly. "She had to settle for me."

"I think she loves you more than you realize," Claudia said, reaching across the table to squeeze his hand.

"And I think you're a daughter trying to keep her parents together." Noticing a darkness on the inside of her elbow, he frowned. He'd glimpsed it earlier and assumed it was just a shadow, but when she extended her arm he saw more clearly that it was a bruise. "What happened to your arm?"

"Oh, this?" She glanced at the discolored skin just below the crease of her joint. Then she met his gaze. "I went for a blood test yesterday."

"A blood test." His heart pinged, like a car engine with a malfunction.

She squeezed his hand again. "Whatever happened in the past wasn't that boy's fault. I don't know how I feel about everything else, but I can't just turn away and let that boy die. He's my brother."

That boy might die anyway. Claudia might not be a match. And all the pain, all the brutal truths that had rampaged through that door when Drew Foster had forced it open might have been exposed for nothing. If Foster hadn't barged back into Bobby and Joelle's lives just one week ago, they might have gone on happily, forever.

But now Claudia believed she had a brother. Not just Mike and Danny, but another brother. Drew Foster's son.

She broke into his ruminations, as if trying to tear him away from the idea she'd just presented to him. "Seeing a marriage counselor might be a good idea."

"I hate that stuff," he said, not ready to be torn. *He's my brother,* Claudia had said. Foster's kid was her brother.

"Sometimes it's easier to talk your problems out with an objective outsider. You could get it all out in the open. You could say things to the counselor that you can't say to each other."

"Like that's such a great idea," he muttered, then sipped his coffee. "I don't think there's all that much inside me, anyhow. And if there is, maybe that's where it belongs. Inside me. Left alone."

Claudia finished her coffee and stood. Her hair was the color Joelle's used to be before a few streaks of gray had sneaked in, but straighter. It fluttered around her face as she carried her mug to the sink and washed it. After propping it in the drying rack, she faced Bobby. "Either you and Mom can talk to each other and get things out into the open, or you can go back to pretending everything's fine when it isn't."

"We can't go back," he said.

"Right. You can't. Because even if you wanted to pretend everything was fine, you can't pretend that I'm…" She drew in a breath and let it out. "You can't pretend I'm your daughter anymore. I mean, I *am,* but…"

"Yeah. I know." From the living room drifted the sound of Jim Morrison singing, "You're lost, little girl." Bobby considered storming into the living room and shutting off the damn music—or maybe dragging the CD player off its shelf and stomping on it. What more did he need in his life? His wife gone, his daughter telling him she wasn't his daughter and the Doors providing the sound track. And violent urges rising in him. Maybe they'd been behind that door, too, just one more nasty bit of truth, his father's legacy. The door was open and now he was going to become the beast his father had been.

He'd denied Claudia her genes. Maybe he'd denied his own, as well.

"I'd better get back home," she said. "Gary's probably tearing his hair out by now. The kids can be pretty demanding first thing in the morning."

Bobby nodded. He pushed away from the table, stood and wondered whether he should kiss Claudia goodbye.

She answered that question by crossing to him and kissing his cheek. "Things will work out, Dad."

"You're sure of that?"

She shrugged, then patted his arm. "Promise me you'll remember to eat. I'll call you this evening to see how you're doing."

"I'll be fine," he swore, hoping his words weren't just another lie. "Will you tell me the results of the blood test when you get them?"

"I'm not sure," she said, then turned and left the kitchen.

He should have accompanied her to the door, but he couldn't bear to watch her walk out of his house and away. She was right; he could no longer pretend she was his daughter. *You're lost,* the song reminded him.

As if he didn't already know.

TEN

May 1987

THE SPRING SUNLIGHT WAS LIKE a warm, white bath soaking Joelle as she sat on the stiff folding chair. To her left was her mother, who'd traveled all the way from Ohio for this day. To her right were the boys, Mike flipping through the program and Danny squirming incessantly, kneeling, sitting, climbing down from his chair to get a closer view of an ant plodding through the grass. On their other side sat Claudia, just a couple of weeks short of sweet sixteen and acting as if she had no idea who the two rambunctious little boys beside her were.

Joelle didn't care if the boys were restless. She didn't care if Claudia wished she were seated in another row, a member of another family. She didn't care that Wanda was there—her mother could be a pain, but she'd insisted on coming and then requested that Bobby and Joelle pay her airfare, since she couldn't afford it herself. None of that mattered.

This was truly one of the greatest days of her life.

Twenty rows in front of them, under a white canopy, a man in a long, black robe spoke ponderously into a microphone, his voice distorted by echoes and amplification as it drifted across the field.

"I'm bored," Danny whined.

Joelle dug in her tote bag and pulled out an Etch-a-Sketch. "Here," she whispered. "Play with this—but don't talk. People are trying to listen to the speech."

"It's boring," Danny muttered, although he subsided in his chair, crossed his legs and twisted the Etch-a-Sketch's dials.

Amazing that they'd gotten here, Joelle thought. Amazing that they'd reached this day, this place, this sun-blessed corner of western Connecticut. Amazing that Bobby was graduating from college.

How did people get from point A to point B? she wondered as the orator droned on. How did sixteen years fly by so quickly? It felt like mere days ago that Bobby returned his cane to the V.A. hospital. "I hate New Jersey," he'd said as he'd left the rehab clinic for the last time, walking with only a slight limp. "Let's get the hell out of here."

One of the physical therapists he'd worked with had a cousin who ran a masonry business in Bridgeport, Connecticut. Bobby and Joelle knew nothing about Bridgeport, Connecticut, except that it wasn't New Jersey—and it wasn't Ohio. Bobby phoned the cousin and got himself hired.

Joelle and Bobby decamped for Connecticut and moved into a two-bedroom apartment they could barely afford. Bobby learned how to do brickwork and stonework for the new subdivisions and office parks sprouting across the region. People hated talking about the Vietnam War, but they seemed happy to hire a veteran. When Joelle suggested to Bobby that she'd like to return to college, he told her to go ahead.

Claudia, fortunately, was an easy child. She loved her preschool and didn't cling to her mother—probably because she'd spent so much time with Bobby during her first few years. Joelle was able to schedule her classes at Fairfield University in the mornings, so Claudia attended preschool for only a half day, which saved on the tuition. In the afternoons, Joelle played with Claudia and taught her the finer aspects of shopping: "Always use a coupon if you've got one," she'd explain as she pushed Claudia up and down the grocery-store aisles in a shopping cart. "Always look for a Sale sign," she'd instruct in a clothing store. After a while, Claudia began to recognize the letters. *Sale* was the first word she ever read.

Bobby's job healed him as effectively as the surgeries and physical therapy had. Bending, lifting, laying stone and lugging thirty-pound sacks of concrete powder honed his body. He came home every evening filthy and exhausted, but smiling. In the evenings, after dinner, he would play with Claudia while Joelle studied. Seated in the kitchen with her textbooks and notes spread across the table, she would hear Bobby and Claudia chatting and laughing and watching *The Muppet Show* together in the living room. Before bed, Bobby would always read to Claudia. "Make Eeyore's voice," she'd order him as he worked his way through *Winnie the Pooh* with her. "Make it funny, like you did last time."

He would summon Joelle when Claudia was ready for her good-night kiss. Joelle and Bobby would tuck her in, turn on her seashell-shaped night-light and close her door. And then they'd retreat to their bed.

As expensive as it was, a two-bedroom apartment was worth every dollar it cost them. Back in New Jersey, Joelle had finally moved Claudia's crib and changing table out of the bedroom and into the living room. She'd hated having her baby so far away—

and stuck in a room that clearly wasn't a bedroom—but she and Bobby couldn't have sex while Claudia was in the room with them.

And sex with Bobby was a revelation. In the months after his return from Vietnam, Joelle had learned so much about physical pleasure, partly because she'd had so much to learn and partly because Bobby's body was broken. He had no strength in one leg. His balance was off. He was thin and fragile and, despite her reassurances, embarrassed about his scars. The nightmares would strike without warning and he'd shout his friend's name while his body jerked and flinched. Joelle pleaded with him to talk to a therapist, but he hated the idea of opening up to a stranger.

He opened up a bit to Joelle, at least. They would lie beside each other in the dark, and he'd tell her about his platoon's routine patrols, how frightening they were, how pointless they'd seemed. He'd tell her about the bone-deep envy he'd felt whenever one of his platoon mates finished his hitch and got to leave. He'd tell her about the heat and the humidity and the insects as big as a woman's fist. He'd tell her how he would keep his fear of dying at bay by reminding himself that if he died, she and the baby would get widow's benefits, so something worthwhile would come from his death. He'd tell her about the mud and the eerie green cast of the morning light and the sense he sometimes had that he was standing in quicksand and would never escape—until he pulled out the photo she'd given him, taken the evening of the senior prom. And he would gaze at her, looking so pretty, so clean and healthy and lovely, and he'd be reminded that a life was waiting for him back home, if he could only keep himself from getting killed.

These bedtime conversations were as intimate as making love. And when they weren't talking, they did make love. Bobby would ask her to try different positions. When his leg and back were hurting him, he'd move her around on the bed and use his hands and his mouth on her. Their bed was their own magical world, a place of adventure and safety, a place where Joelle believed that everything would work out, that her marriage would last her lifetime.

The clouds that had followed him back to America from Vietnam gradually dissipated. Months would go by without his shouting Schenk's name in his sleep, and then years. A Vietnam veterans' group in southern Connecticut sent him invitations to events, but he never attended. "That's over," he'd say. "It's history. I don't have time for that stuff."

Wanda didn't come to Connecticut for Joelle's college graduation. She was still working full-time at the Bank Street Diner then, and Joelle and Bobby and Claudia had driven out to Ohio during Joelle's spring break less than two months earlier, where they'd spent four hideous days shuttling back and forth between Joelle's mother and Bobby's father. Louie DiFranco had been surly and vicious, reeling from the news that Bobby's brother, Eddie, was gay. "I never shoulda let him go to college," Louie had railed. "Shoulda made him join the military, like Bobby. That woulda made a man out of him." Eddie had wisely moved to San Francisco, leaving Bobby to receive the brunt of his father's bitterness. One morning, as he fumed about his pathetic younger son, Claudia beamed a smile up at him and said, "I like fairies, Papa Louie. They can do magic." That had shut him up.

At least Wanda didn't have a temper. But she did little to conceal her disappointment that Joelle had married Bobby when, had she only played things right, she could have wound up with Drew Foster. "You say you're happy, so okay," Wanda would mutter. "But honestly, Joelle. For years you had to work to support him, and now that he's finally able to work, he's a laborer. He comes home every night with dirt under his nails. And he limps."

"Hardly," Joelle had defended Bobby. "And he knows how to wash his hands."

Joelle graduated from college with only Bobby and Claudia to cheer for her as she accepted her diploma, and she landed a kindergarten teaching job in Arlington. "That takes some pressure off you," she told Bobby. "I'll be working, we'll have two incomes—things'll get easier."

"Easy is boring," he argued. "I don't mind pressure. I've been thinking, Jo. Now that you'll be earning a steady income and we can get insurance through your job... I want to start my own landscaping business."

Bobby knew bricks and stones. He knew grass and shrubs. But running a business? What did he know about that?

She kept her doubts to herself. "Go ahead and do it," she said.

His boss in Bridgeport mentored him. He went out in search of customers far from the city and discovered communities in the northwest hills where New Yorkers were buying up old properties and hiring contractors to fix them up. He enrolled in an evening class in marketing at the local campus of the state college system. Just to get a little business knowledge, he'd insisted. Just one class.

Eight years later, he'd built DiFranco Landscaping into a thriving enterprise. He'd done extensive renovations on the fixer-upper he and Joelle had bought in Gray Hill. He'd fathered two sons. And he'd completed a degree at Western Connecticut State, majoring in business and minoring in botany.

"This I've got to see," Wanda had said when Joelle told her about Bobby's graduation. He himself hadn't wanted to participate in the commencement ceremony, but damn it, he'd worked so hard to get through college—when he hadn't even had to, given that his business was thriving. No one hired a landscape designer for his educational pedigree. They hired DiFranco Landscaping because the company had an excellent reputation for getting a job done on time and on budget.

But he'd wanted the degree. Something beyond his business had motivated him. Two courses a semester, an occasional summer class... He'd fought for every credit, every B-plus. And Joelle resolved that he would wear a cap and gown and march with his fellow graduates and have the dean of the college place in his hand his very own diploma, rolled into a tube and tied with a ribbon.

The orator in the black robe finally ran out of steam. Joelle glanced to her right and saw that Mike had taken over the Etch-a-Sketch and Danny had curled up like a snail on the seat of his chair and was fast asleep. Claudia sat with her head back and her legs slightly angled, trying to maximize the sun's rays so she could improve her tan.

Joelle felt a slight breeze against her left arm. Glancing in that direction, she found her mother using the commencement program as a fan. She considered suggesting that her mother might be cooler if she removed the jacket of her suit, but Wanda had boasted about buying the outfit new at Beldon's just for this trip. The jacket's shoulders had padding bigger than a linebacker's. "Krystal Carrington on *Dynasty* has a suit just like this," Wanda had insisted.

Joelle opened her own program and smiled to see they'd reached the "conferring of diplomas" portion of the ceremony. She pulled her camera out of her tote and removed the lens cap. She was seated much too far away to get a good shot of Bobby— she didn't have a zoom lens—but she didn't care. Even if all she got was a blur of cap and gown, she would know that blur was Bobby, doing something no one had ever expected of him.

The dean intoned each graduate's name. In alphabetical order, the graduates marched across the platform, accepted their diplomas, shook the dean's hand and then walked back to their seats. They all looked so young. At thirty-five, Bobby was surely one of the oldest graduates.

"They're starting the *D*s," Wanda whispered to her.

"I know." Joelle stood and edged past the kids' chairs to reach the grassy aisle. She lifted her camera and waited.

"Robert L. DiFranco," the dean announced.

Joelle snapped three photos. Three blurs of Bobby striding across the platform, his hair straggling out from under his mortarboard and brushing the neckline of his robe. Unlike some of the young graduates, who appeared to be wearing shorts under their robes, and sneakers or sandals, he wore black trousers and dress loafers. He held his head high, and Joelle could see his lips move as the dean handed him his diploma.

She sidled back to her chair and sank happily onto it. "He needs a haircut," Wanda muttered.

"I like his hair that way," Joelle defended him. "So does he."

"Can we go now?" Mike asked in a stage whisper.

"Soon," Joelle promised.

Once the graduation ceremony finally ended, Joelle had to shoot more photos. A photo of Bobby holding his diploma. One of him and Claudia and the boys standing in front of the student union. One of him with a groggy Danny in his arms and the plant studies laboratory in the background. One Wanda clicked of all five of them.

Joelle refused to quit taking pictures until she'd used up the roll of film. Only then, reluctantly, was she willing to leave the campus.

After Bobby returned his rented cap and gown to the student union, they piled into the minivan he'd bought last fall and drove to the Arlington Inn, where Joelle had reserved a table for six. She issued stern instructions to the boys through tight lips as the maître d' led them to a circular table covered in a heavy white linen cloth. "I want your best behavior," she warned. "No wild stuff. This is a fancy restaurant."

"Can I get a hamburger?" Mike asked.

"Yes."

"Can I get choco milk?" Danny wanted to know.

"If they have it, yes."

They had chocolate milk—and also crayons and paper place mats with pictures on them that Danny and Mike could color. Claudia ordered a 7 Up and Wanda insisted on wine for the adults. Bobby reluctantly allowed the waiter to fill a glass for him.

"A toast," Wanda announced, raising her glass. The boys spiritedly raised their glasses, too, and Joelle, seated between them, steadied their hands before they could spill their drinks. "A toast to Bobby, who now has two remarkable accomplishments to his name. You got my daughter to marry you, and you got yourself a college degree."

Bobby grinned. "Not bad for a Tubtown boy, huh?"

"The degree I can understand," Wanda said. "You always were a smart kid, even if your prospects weren't so hot. How you managed to snag Joelle, though—that's a mystery." She was smiling, teasing him, but Joelle sensed a serious undercurrent in her tone.

"He snagged me just by being Bobby," she said, shooting him an affectionate look. "He didn't have to do anything more than that."

He smiled back, but she could tell from the chill in his eyes that he'd felt the barbs in Wanda's words. He consumed a tiny sip of his wine, then put down the glass and settled back in his chair. "So now that I have a bachelor's degree, does that mean I'm a bachelor?"

"Ha-ha," Claudia muttered, rolling her eyes.

The rest of the meal went smoothly. No more digs from Wanda, no major misbehavior from the boys. Claudia thought one of the busboys was cute and repeatedly visited the ladies' room so she could walk past his station. He clearly thought she was cute, too, since he followed her with his gaze every time she entered his field of vision path. When he came to the table to refill her water glass, he blushed.

Joelle glanced Bobby's way and noticed him observing the flirtation. He turned in time to catch her eye. His eyebrows arched. So did hers.

They were too young to have a daughter old enough to be interested in boys. But then, they'd done everything too young—left home, gotten married, had Claudia. And they'd gotten their college educations too late, Bobby even later than Joelle. Their timing was abysmal, yet somehow everything had worked out.

After dinner, they drove back to Gray Hill. The evening was mild and dry, and sitting out on the back patio would have been pleasant—except that Bobby hadn't finished building the patio yet. A pile of flagstones stood near the door, awaiting his attention. Now that his schooling was done, he might be able to complete that job.

Joelle sent the boys into the backyard to run around for a little while and tire themselves out. She asked Claudia to keep an eye on them, then went upstairs to make sure Danny's bedroom was ready for her mother. Whenever Wanda visited, Danny's room became the guest room and he moved into Mike's bedroom for the duration. Mike had a bunk bed and he loved the excuse to sleep on the upper bunk.

Danny's bed was made with fresh linens. Joelle left a bath towel and washcloth on the dresser for her mother, then opened the window to allow in some cool evening air. In the twilight, the boys chased each other, shaping their hands into guns and making bullet noises.

She heard footsteps behind her, two sets. Turning, she saw her mother enter the room, followed by Bobby, who was carrying her suitcase. "I'm going to change my clothes," he said as he set the bag down. He nodded at Wanda and then left the room.

"Those boys," Wanda said, joining Joelle at the window. "Where on earth do they get their energy?"

"They're boys," Joelle answered, as if that explained everything.

"I guess." Wanda pushed a shock of hair back from her face. Her hair had naturally been a dark blond shade, but now that she was coloring it it seemed a bit brassy. Her suit had wilted in the heat, but beneath it she still had a decent figure. In her late fifties, she was tenaciously holding on to her looks. "I never had to deal with little boys," she conceded. "I don't know if I'd have the energy."

"They're wonderful," Joelle said. Tiring, yes. Challenging, always. But God, how she loved them.

"They resemble Bobby strongly," Wanda noted. "Both of them. I tell you, you look at them standing next to him, and you don't have to guess who their daddy is. Now, Claudia... there's nothing of Bobby in her at all. Absolutely no resemblance whatsoever."

Joelle stiffened and peered behind her. To her dismay, she saw Bobby lurking in the hall just outside the door. He'd heard Wanda. A shadow flickered across his face.

She spun back to her mother. "Claudia has Bobby's eyes," she said, then looked over her shoulder again, in time to watch him entering their bedroom and shutting the door behind him.

"You think so? I don't see it at all."

"Well, it's there." Joelle hoped her mother didn't hear the belligerence in her tone. More quietly, she said, "I'm going to give Bobby a hand. He can't hang up a suit without getting it all wrinkled. You should have everything you need. Toothpaste's in the bathroom, shampoo in the shower. If you want a hair dryer, I can lend you mine. Claudia is kind of possessive about hers."

"My hair's fine," Wanda said, although Joelle barely heard her. Her attention was on the door Bobby had closed, on the man behind that door.

Entering the master bedroom, she found him standing in front of the open closet door. His jacket was off, his dress shirt unbuttoned and untucked and his tie slung unknotted around his neck as he wrestled his jacket onto a hanger. Hanging the trousers first would be easier, but she didn't give a damn if his suit wound up as wrinkled as a raisin. She crossed the room to him and hugged him from behind, her hands meeting on the warm skin of his chest. She turned her head and pressed her cheek to the smooth cotton of his shirt. "Bobby," she murmured.

"She knows."

"She just made a stupid comment. People say that kind of thing without thinking."

He drew in a breath, then let it out. She felt the surge and contraction of his diaphragm against her palms. "She knows," he said. "Did you tell her?"

"Of course not." Joelle was insulted that he'd accuse her of such a thing. "Nobody knows."

"*We* know," he said. He hung up his jacket, then eased her hands from him and faced her. "If she saw it, other people see it."

"Stop it, Bobby. Nobody knows. Nobody talks about it."

"*We* know," he repeated. "We don't talk about it, but we know."

"It doesn't matter," Joelle said, understanding the truth in the words as she spoke them. They were a family. Bobby was a father, Claudia a daughter.

"It's like..." He gazed past her, as if searching the air behind her for the right words. "It's like a piece of shrapnel that never came out. It's just floating around inside me. I don't feel it. I don't even know it's there. But yeah, it's there, and it could migrate to my heart and kill me."

Joelle shook her head. "Claudia is your daughter." Eager to steer his thoughts in a better direction, she reached around him and pulled a bag down from the closet shelf. "I forgot to show you what I bought," she said with artificial cheer. She slid a picture frame from the bag. "For your diploma."

"You want to frame it?" he asked, eyeing the frame warily.

"It'll look great." She carried the frame to the bed, then grabbed his diploma from the top of his dresser and untied the ribbon.

"You never framed your diploma."

"Where would I put mine? In the classroom?" She twisted the clamps at the back of the frame and removed the backing. "You can hang yours in your office."

"Why would I want to do that?"

She glanced up at him and smiled. "Pride?"

"People come to my office to talk about the price of pine mulch or the delivery date of gravel. They don't come to review my credentials."

She smoothed the diploma against the batting and glass. The parchment was curled, but the frame flattened it. "Well, you can hang it wherever you want, then," she said, displaying the framed document for him. "In the den. In the bathroom. It's beautiful, isn't it?"

Two strides carried him to her side. His chin was harsh, his eyes unfathomable. His hair was definitely not too long. It was just the right length for Joelle to ravel her fingers through it, to stroke it back from his face.

He lifted the framed diploma out of her hands and tossed it onto the bed. "I didn't go to college so I could hang a piece of paper on a wall," he said.

"Why did you go?"

"To learn something. To run the business better." She raised her hand to his face again, but he caught her wrist before she could touch him. "To prove something to myself."

"That you could do it?"

"Yeah."

"Of course you could do it. Anything you put your mind to, you can do," she said, meaning it as much as she'd meant everything else she'd told him in the past few minutes. He could do anything. His diploma was beautiful. He was Claudia's father. No one knew different.

She wished she could make sense of the emotion in his eyes. He seemed uneasy, dissatisfied, not at all proud. Could her mother's idiotic words have deflated him so completely? Did he not know what a fantastic father he was, what a magnificent man?

He lifted her hand to his lips and kissed her knuckles. Then he lowered it to her side and took a step back. "You deserved a husband with a college education," he said, returning to the closet to put away his tie.

She stared after him, unsure she'd heard him correctly. "You mean, because I had a degree?"

"Because you always wanted to be the wife of a college man," he reminded her without looking at her.

Drew, she realized. She'd told Bobby, years ago, when they were just friends, that she'd hoped to marry Drew, who was heading off to Dartmouth. But that was so far in the past. Bobby would never have even thought about Drew if her mother hadn't opened her stupid mouth.

She followed him back to the closet, planted her hands on his shoulders and forced him to face her. "I'm the wife of the best man in the world," she said.

He managed a smile, and when she pulled him down to her, he gave her the kiss she wanted. Then he straightened and turned away, moving to the bureau and taking a pair of jeans from a drawer.

Allowing him his privacy as he undressed, she left the bedroom and went downstairs, through the kitchen to the back door, where she could call for the boys to come inside and start getting ready for bed.

Claudia followed the boys through the door. Her hair color lightened every spring, the sun painting streaks of platinum through the blond. The older she got, the prettier she grew. Teenage boys phoned the house constantly.

Joelle was determined not to pressure Claudia the way she herself had been pressured. Claudia would never feel she had to reel in a good catch, as if boys were fish. She would be successful on her own terms, by her own actions. She wasn't a Tubtown kid. She'd grown up secure, close to both her parents, loved by both. No rambling man had passed through her life a few times, left her with a doll and a coloring book and then died in a highway accident.

Claudia knew who she was: the daughter of a woman who would never imply that her worth was based on whom she dated, and the blessed, beloved daughter of Bobby DiFranco.

ELEVEN

THE WEST SIDE MOTOR LODGE on Rockwell Turnpike had not aged well. It was clean and the staff was friendly, but Joelle seriously doubted the motel had undergone any significant renovations since she'd left town thirty-seven years earlier. The pattern in the lobby's carpet had faded so badly that the black circles resembled oil stains marring the green background. The trite still-life paintings on the walls were faded. The leaves on the fake potted plants had been bleached by time to nearly white.

The room rate was cheap, though, and the night clerk hadn't balked when Joelle had checked in at nearly midnight last night. She probably should have stopped for the night somewhere in Pennsylvania, rather than driving all the way to Holmdell in one day. But she didn't want to be in Pennsylvania.

She wasn't sure she wanted to be in Ohio, either. All she had was a vague idea that returning to the place she and Bobby had agreed to get married might help her understand how their marriage had reached this crisis.

She'd considered driving straight to her mother's house last night, but she hadn't even warned her mother that she was coming to Holmdell. If Joelle had rung her mother's bell in the middle of the night, Wanda would probably have had a heart attack. Joelle didn't need that calamity on top of everything else she was dealing with.

So the West Side Motor Lodge had been her home for the night. She'd staggered into the room, taken a quick shower and found herself too agitated to sleep, even though she was exhausted and aching. She'd unpacked her cell-phone recharger, plugged it in, then lifted her phone and listened, for at least the dozenth time, to Bobby's message: *Come home. Please.*

The "come home" she could handle. The "please" filled her eyes with tears.

She couldn't bring herself to call him. She'd tried to talk to him all week and he'd shut down on her. Well, now it was her turn to shut down. She'd phone him when she was ready—and she wasn't ready yet.

She'd crawled into the hard motel bed and willed herself to rest. The sheets had smelled of starch and bleach. The air conditioner had rattled like a tin can rolling down the sidewalk. The curtains at her window didn't meet, and through the narrow slit she'd seen the occasional flash of headlights as a car barreled down Rockwell Turnpike, heading toward Indiana.

Eventually she'd drifted off. But the first gray light of dawn to slice through that crevice in the curtains roused her, and by seven-thirty she was seated in the motel's sleepy restaurant, sipping coffee that tasted burned and waiting for a platter of scrambled eggs.

Was Bobby awake yet? Was he eating a decent breakfast? Had he ever grilled the shrimp?

Her phone rang, and she checked the caller ID. Bobby again. Why did he want to talk to her now? Why couldn't he have talked to her before she'd left, when she'd been begging him to open up?

The phone stopped ringing, and she checked to see if he'd left another message. He hadn't. If she'd answered, he probably would have only asked her to come home. Maybe he would have said "please" again.

She didn't want to go home, not until she knew what she was going home to.

She was on her third cup of coffee when Claudia called. As soon as she answered, she realized Claudia was phoning from Joelle and Bobby's house. She heard Doors music in the background—not a listening choice Claudia would make in her own home. Claudia assured her that Bobby was all right and Joelle told her to tell Bobby about the Prius's outstanding highway mileage.

She signed her breakfast bill to her room, then left the motel. More than ten years had passed since she'd last been back in her hometown. It was so much easier to fly her mother to Hartford than to try to haul everyone to Holmdell for a visit, especially now, with Jeremy and Kristin in the family. Since her mother had more or less retired from her job at the Bank Street Diner, she had no real constraints on her schedule and could visit Connecticut without having to negotiate for vacation time.

She still went to the diner a few days a week to run the cash register, because sitting around her apartment was boring. She had no family in town; she'd told Joelle that her coworkers at the diner were her substitute family and she'd go there when she felt like seeing them. She'd station herself behind the cashier's desk and schmooze with the customers, and most people seemed to think Wanda Webber's presence at the Bank Street Diner meant all was as it should be.

Joelle drove up the turnpike into town and turned onto Bank Street, stopping at the corner where the diner sat, only because a red light forced her. The eatery's windows were cloudy, the interior dimly lit, but the awning shading the windows appeared new, its green-and-white stripes vivid in the pale morning light.

The traffic signal changed and she continued down the street. The sidewalks had been inlaid with bricks in a herringbone pattern, she noted, and a few concrete planters had been installed along the curb, holding clutches of impatiens. Evidently Holmdell had hired the local version of DiFranco Landscaping to spruce up the downtown area. Although limp in the late-June heat, the flowers were pretty.

She noticed that Fontaine's Beauty Salon was gone, replaced by something called Kwik-Kuts, and Clement's Hardware had been taken over by one of the national retail-hardware franchises. Beldon's Department Store had looked like something out of the thirties when Joelle had been a child; it still looked like something out of the thirties, its limestone facade boasting an art deco flavor and its outer walls stained from decades of auto exhaust. A Starbucks stood next to Harley's convenience store, where Joelle used to work. Even Holmdell had its own Starbucks now, Joelle thought with a smile. The Bank Street Diner had better improve the quality of the coffee it was serving if it hoped to compete.

She passed the bank building, a massive structure with a clock embedded in its front wall. When Joelle was a child, the clock had been round, with ornate hands and gothic numerals. That clock had been replaced by a digital panel that flashed not just the time but the temperature in Fahrenheit and centigrade. The clock was off by eight minutes, and the thermometer claimed it was only sixty-five degrees. It felt warmer than that to Joelle.

She turned off Bank Street and headed toward Tubtown. The gentrification that had improved Holmdell's business district hadn't reached this part of town. The neighborhood was still dreary, houses and duplexes crowded together, sidewalks crumbling or nonexistent, buildings crying out for paint or a new roof. At least every fourth house had a bathtub shrine adorning its front yard.

She steered down one familiar street and then another until she reached the DiFranco house. The last time she'd been here, her goal had been to empty the house and shut it down after Bobby's father died.

Mike and Danny had driven out to Ohio with Bobby and Joelle when they'd received word that a neighbor had found Louie lying dead on his kitchen floor. The coroner wasn't sure how long he'd been there—a couple of days, at least. Fortunately a funeral home had already carted his body away by the time Joelle and the family arrived. All medical evidence had indicated that Louie DiFranco had died of a massive stroke, although according to the autopsy, he'd had a great deal of alcohol in his blood.

Claudia and her new husband had flown in for the funeral. Eddie had traveled east from San Francisco, leaving his partner behind. Louie hadn't left a will—that would have made things too easy—but his estate hadn't been large or complicated, and Bobby and Eddie had agreed to split whatever was left after expenses. The funeral service at St. Mary's had been sparsely attended. Wanda had offered to pay her respects, but Joelle told her not to bother.

Joelle had felt sadder viewing Bobby's mother's grave than watching Louie's casket as it was lowered into the ground beside her. Bobby had remained expressionless throughout the entire ritual, one hand holding Joelle's and his other arm looped around Eddie's shoulders, as if he still felt he had to protect his baby brother from Louie's fists. There would be no more fists, no more violence.

Joelle and Bobby had sent the boys home on a plane with Claudia and Gary, and then they and Eddie tackled the daunting task of emptying Louie's house. Running fans in the windows, they managed to chase most of the foul, musty smell from the rooms. They threw out empty pizza boxes, bags of stale bread, a plastic container of rice pudding edged in blue mold and all the liquor Louie had left behind, scattered in bottles throughout the house. While Joelle scrubbed the kitchen, Bobby and his brother sorted through Louie's belongings in the rest of the house, stuffing his old clothing into boxes, gathering up the unpaid bills piled on his dresser, filling trash bag after trash bag with the contents of his drawers and cabinets.

Bobby tuned his father's radio to an oldies rock station so they'd have music to distract them while they worked. Above the din of Bruce Springsteen and the Eagles and Pink Floyd, she'd hear Eddie shout, "Hey, look at this!" or Bobby holler, "Damn—remember this?" When their words were followed by laughter, she'd smile and scrub the stained counters and sing along with whatever was playing on the radio.

After three days of sweaty labor, the house was as empty and clean as it would ever be. Bobby gathered the few items he intended to bring back to Connecticut with him—an old, weathered baseball glove, a ratchet set and a crucifix that had belonged to his mother—and hired a Realtor to sell the place for him and Eddie. Then they'd driven away.

"Are you sad?" she'd asked him.

He'd thought awhile before answering. "I'm sad that I don't feel sadder."

Someone had painted the house yellow since that August day so many years ago, but the place still seemed shabby and mournful. The roof was missing a few shingles, the shrubs were overgrown and the Madonna statue in Bobby's mother's bathtub shrine listed as if she'd been guzzling some of Louie's leftover booze. Joelle knew someone else had bought the house the spring after Louie's death, and maybe more families had moved in and out since then, but the place seemed abandoned. No cars in the driveway, no tricycles or basketballs on the lawn, no plants visible along the windowsills. Joelle parked, strolled up the front walk and knocked on the door. No one answered.

She wandered around to the back of the house. The back porch still sagged and the back door's screen still sat crookedly on its hinges. She recalled a night when light had spilled through that screen door and she'd heard voices coming from inside. Bobby had stood behind her in the shadows, fearing for his life, while she'd peeked through the door into the kitchen and seen Louie with his busted nose.

Oh, Bobby... Maybe one of the things she'd loved about Drew Foster back then was that he'd been so simple. No deaths in his family, no drunks, no father swinging his fists. No ghosts in his soul, no torment in his eyes. Whatever he'd wanted, he'd gotten. He had never had to fight for anything.

Bobby had always had to fight. He'd fought here, in this house. He'd fought in Vietnam. He'd fought his own body after a land mine had shattered it. He'd fought to create a viable business, to become an educated man.

And now he was fighting Joelle. He was fighting Drew. He was fighting to hold on to the lie on which they'd built their lives—but he'd already lost that fight.

How could she get him to stop fighting?

Sighing, she trudged back around the house, across the scraggly front yard to her car. Her heart was so heavy it seemed to pull her off balance. When she gazed through her windshield at the bathtub shrine, she wondered whether perhaps the Madonna's heart was heavy, too, and that was why she couldn't stand straight.

JOELLE STEERED AWAY FROM the DiFranco house, away from the leaning Madonna and the memories and drove back through downtown, past the rivet factory on Bailey Street where Bobby's father had worked; past the cemetery; past the high school, to where the altitude and the economic status were elevated. The houses on the Hill were spacious and solid. No vinyl siding here, no rusty rain gutters, no driveways with weeds growing through cracks in the concrete. No half-buried bathtubs.

The curving roads in this part of town bore names like Cedar Lane and Glenville Terrace and Harvard Street. The air smelled of newly cut grass and sun-warmed roses. The houses featured elaborate stonework, leaded windows and heavy oak front doors with polished brass knockers. The two-car driveways that weren't vacant held Audi coupes and Lexus SUVs.

She cruised down Harvard Street, then veered onto Birchwood Drive. The road arched around the golf course, the rear yards of the houses separated from the fairway by rows of Scotch pine and aspen. When she reached the house where Drew Foster used to live, she coasted to the curb and turned off the engine.

Drew's house, a symmetrical mansion of brick and stone with a peaked slate roof flanked by chimneys on either side, had once seemed like a palace to her. The few times she'd been a guest there she'd felt like a village peasant paying homage to nobility.

It seemed a bit less grand to her today. She'd grown used to the rambling houses of northwest Connecticut—and she'd grown, period. She was no longer a poor girl in awe of her hometown's wealthiest residents. As she gazed at the Foster house, she acknowledged that the Fosters had a grandson who might die too young from a terrible disease. How could anyone envy them?

The front door opened and a slim woman with short red hair emerged. She had on a tank top and cargo shorts, white anklets and sneakers. She might have been dressed to go for a jog, or to clean house. If Joelle were home right now, she'd be dressed much the same way, and she'd be dusting and polishing furniture, pushing the vacuum around, making the bathroom sinks sparkle.

Instead she was in Holmdell, spying on a stranger as she strolled down the slate front walk to the mailbox at the curb. The woman opened it and emptied it of its contents, then marched back up the walk to the house.

Watching as the woman vanished behind the ornately carved wooden door, Joelle acknowledged that the Fosters no longer lived there. They'd probably decamped to Florida or Arizona or wherever rich retirees who no longer wanted to deal with snow lived.

She stared at the house for a minute longer, trying to envision herself living in it, ambling down that front walk past rows of flowering spirea, past a lawn as smooth and green as the surface of a billiards table, to pick up her mail. She couldn't picture it. Even if Bobby hadn't married her, she could not imagine herself living the life of a Foster.

She started her car's engine, U-turned and drove back to Harvard Street, to Glenville Terrace, down the hill, toward town. On Jackson Street, she slowed as the black wrought-iron fence bordering the cemetery loomed into view. Alongside the cemetery's border, she eased to the curb and yanked on her parking brake. Through the fence she saw the rows of head-stones, all different sizes, different sentiments. Somewhere up the rise, near an umbrella-shaped oak tree, was a marble bench beneath a tree where she'd found Bobby one September afternoon and asked him for a favor.

Why had he proposed marriage that day? Friendship and fear, she realized. Friendship for her and fear for himself, for what lay ahead of him in Vietnam. "I'd have something to come back to," he'd said.

He'd been coming back to her ever since—from Vietnam, from his injuries, from his nightmares. From work at the end of each day. She'd been there waiting for him, never expecting him to stagger home drunk, to arrive late after spending time in a tavern with another woman.

The day he'd asked her to marry him, she had trusted him more than anyone else in her life, anyone else in the entire world. She wanted to trust him like that today, but she longed for something more: she longed for him to love her.

He'd never spoken the words. He had never handed her his heart, never offered her his soul. He'd lived with her, made babies with her, created a family with her—but never once, in all the years she'd known him, had he said, "I love you."

FIVE YEARS AGO, WHEN Mrs. Proski had died and her son had put the duplex on Third Street up for sale, Wanda had bought it, with help from Joelle and Bobby. They'd provided the down payment, and she'd paid the mortgage using the rent she collected from the Tranhs, a family of Vietnamese immigrants who'd moved into the upstairs apartment. Unlike the old DiFranco house, the duplex was spiffed up: recently painted, new roof, air-conditioning units in several windows and the old washtub flowerpot gone, replaced by azalea bushes blossoming pink and magenta. Since Joelle and Bobby considered the house an investment, they made sure Wanda was diligent about maintaining the property.

Joelle walked up the neatly edged path to her mother's front door and rang the bell. She half expected her mother not to be home, but Wanda opened the door. She was wearing an old housedress, a loose-fitting thing of thin cotton with snaps down the front, and her hair was unbrushed, the gray roots in need of a touch-up. Seeing Joelle on the front step, she appeared at first thrilled and then stricken. "What happened?" she asked.

"I just...needed a road trip," Joelle said. "Nobody's dying, I swear. Everyone's fine. Can I come in?"

"Of course." Wanda swung open the door and beckoned Joelle inside. From the living room drifted the babble of a television show, people conversing energetically in saccharine-sweet voices. "I slept in this morning—up late last night. Me and Stan Sherko, you remember him? We went down to the Dog House Tavern to watch the Reds game on the wide-screen TV and have a few beers. And that's all we did," she added emphatically. "We're just friends."

"I didn't say a thing." Joelle stifled a smile.

"I fixed a pot of coffee. Would you like some? It's fresh. You hungry? When did you get to town? Where are you staying? Here, of course," she answered herself. "You're staying here. Where's your suitcase?"

"I got in late last night," Joelle said, following her mother into the kitchen and settling onto a chair at the table. Her mother's high-voltage chatter tired her as much as driving eight hundred miles had tired her yesterday. "I took a room at the West Side Motor Lodge for the night."

"No sense paying them when you've got a comfortable bed here."

Joelle wasn't so sure her narrow childhood bed was all that comfortable. But her mother's coffee couldn't possibly be worse than what she'd been served in the motel's restaurant. "I'll check out and stay here," she agreed.

The kitchen hadn't changed since the day Joelle had propped a note to her mother against the salt and pepper shakers and left town with Bobby. Same Formica-topped table, same vinyl-padded gray chairs, same clock in the shape of a rooster fastened to the wall above the window. Same graduated canisters filled with flour, sugar and tea bags, same two-slot toaster plugged into the wall, same stained porcelain sink.

She thought of her own kitchen, and of the note she'd left propped up for Bobby yesterday morning. And the note he'd left propped up for her a week ago. He'd said he had gone fishing. Maybe she'd done the same thing. Maybe she was fishing for something here in Holmdell.

Her mother hustled into the living room and switched the television. She moved fast for a woman on the far side of seventy-five. All those years waitressing had kept her reasonably fit. Age had left is marks all over her—skin hung loose from her bony arms and her upper lip was pleated like a fan. But she remained light on her feet as she glided to the counter, filled two cups with coffee and carried the cups and saucers to the table without splashing a drop.

"So," she said, sitting across the table from Joelle and glowering suspiciously at her. "Suddenly here you are in Holmdell."

If Joelle hadn't intended to tell her mother why she'd traveled to Holmdell, she wouldn't have rung her mother's doorbell. Yet she wasn't sure what exactly to say. Wanda had never been the sort of warm and cuddly mother a woman would want to confide in.

"Bobby and I needed a break," Joelle said. "And I—" she shrugged "—I had this urge to visit my old haunts."

"What kind of break?" Wanda leaned forward. "You tell me that boy is cheating on you, Joelle, and I swear I'll fly to Connecticut and tear his eyes out."

"He's not cheating on me," Joelle hastened to assure her mother. Her mother's loyalty would have been more welcome if Joelle had actually believed Bobby had done something wrong. He hadn't, though. He'd just been himself—closed in, shut down, sucked into a black hole.

"Then what kind of break? You hungry? I've got some Danish, left over from the diner. It's a little stale, but still good. Cheese and apple," she said, rising and moving to the refrigerator. She removed a platter covered in aluminum foil and deposited it on the table. Then she sat back down and peeled the foil back. "Here, take one. This one's apple," she said, pointing. "You always liked apple Danish."

"No, thanks." Joelle's stomach felt leaden from the eggs she'd eaten at the West Side Motor Lodge.

"You look thin. You're not on one of those crazy diets, are you? South Beach or whatever. Why do they always name diets after fancy towns? Why isn't there a Holmdell Diet?"

"Or a Tubtown Diet," Joelle joked.

"That would be a liquid diet," Wanda muttered with a grin. "Lots of beer and whiskey." She grew abruptly solemn. "He's not drinking, is he?"

"Bobby? No," Joelle said, praying that it was the truth.

Wanda lifted a cheese Danish from the platter, pulled a napkin from the plastic holder on the table and used it as a plate, tearing the pastry in half and arranging the halves on the napkin. "It took me twenty-five years to decide that marrying Bobby DiFranco wasn't the dumbest thing you ever did in your life. I'll admit it, Joelle—he turned out a hell of a lot better than I would have predicted. A businessman, a college education—who would have guessed that long-haired boy in torn jeans and boots would wind up like that? I always thought he was wild, with that good-for-nothing father of his and no mother to take him in hand, and that god-awful truck he rattled around in. He had no prospects, no money, nothing but an induction notice when you ran off with him."

"He was a good man. I always knew that."

Wanda nodded. "He's a good man. He's proved it a whole bunch of times. So why are you here and he's in Connecticut?"

Joelle sighed. Crumbs fell from her mother's hands as she broke her Danish into bite-size pieces and popped them, one at a time, into her mouth. Even as she ate, her eyes remained on Joelle, sharp and assessing. "He won't talk to me," Joelle finally said, the power of her mother's stare forcing the words out. "It's always been a struggle to get him to open up, but now he won't talk to me at all. How can you have a marriage when your husband won't open up?" As if her mother were in any position to offer marital advice.

Wanda devoured another chunk of pastry, then dusted the crumbs from her hands onto her napkin. "It's Claudia, right?"

Joelle flinched. "What?"

"How many years now, Joelle? Thirty-seven? Tell me the truth."

"What truth?"

"Bobby isn't Claudia's father."

Joelle fell back in her chair. How had her mother guessed? What should Joelle do, now that she *had* guessed? She and Bobby had vowed to keep the truth hidden, and they'd maintained the lie successfully for all these years. No one in Holmdell knew. Maybe her mother had suspected, but why should Joelle confirm her suspicions?

"I may not be the sharpest knife in the drawer, but I'm not blind," Wanda said, her voice low and firm. "My daughter spends her whole senior year of high school dating a rich boy from the Hill. He's her ticket out of here, her gateway to a better life. They're going steady. They go to the prom together. And then all of a sudden she runs off with another guy—a guy who's her ticket to nowhere and her gateway to nothing. Why does she do that?"

"You know why I married Bobby," Joelle said, her voice scarcely above a whisper.

"Because you *loved* him." Her mother sneered. "Seven months later you have a baby. You think I can't count?"

"I've never denied that I was pregnant when Bobby and I got married."

Her mother glared at her. "You're dating Drew Foster, Mr. Wonderful—Mr. *Rich*-and-Wonderful—and on the side you let Bobby DiFranco knock you up? You weren't stupid, Joelle, and you weren't careless. You wouldn't have risked your chances with Drew Foster by getting involved that way with Bobby. Besides, you weren't the type of girl who slept around. If you were going steady with a boy, that was who you would have given yourself to."

Joelle drank some coffee while she tried to figure out what to say. No, she hadn't slept around. If she had, she'd bet Bobby would have known how to use a condom better than Drew had. Bobby would have protected her. He was that kind of boy, that kind of man.

"How I got pregnant is irrelevant," she said.

"I'm aware of *how* you got pregnant, honey. There's really only one way for that to happen." Her mother shook her head. "Claudia is Drew Foster's daughter, right?"

Once the truth was out, it was out, Joelle supposed. Sustaining the lie about Claudia's parentage was pointless. Claudia might as easily have told her grandmother who her father was, now that she'd been informed of the fact. It was no longer Joelle's secret to keep. "Claudia is Bobby's daughter," she said quietly. "Drew Foster provided the sperm."

Her mother made a face. "God, I wish I still smoked," she muttered. "I could use a cigarette." She reached for another Danish, instead. "I guess you *were* stupid. You're pregnant with Drew's baby—why didn't you make him do the right thing?"

"I didn't want to *make* him do anything," Joelle retorted. "I sure as hell didn't want to marry him, not after he told me to get an abortion. He even sent me money and the name of a doctor."

Wanda, not the most religious woman, clicked her tongue and crossed herself. "That would have been a sin. And it wasn't even legal then."

"Legal or not, it wasn't what I chose to do. I wanted my baby."

Her mother's piety departed as quickly as it had arrived. "So you had the baby. That baby was Drew's. You could have milked him for child support, or gone after his snooty parents. You could have made Drew pay through the nose. If he wouldn't marry you, the least he could have done was give his daughter a good life."

"Bobby provided her with the best life in the world," Joelle countered, irritated by her mother's crass calculations. "I didn't want money, Mom. I wanted my daughter to have a father. I wanted her to have a real family. I didn't want her to grow up the way I did, never really knowing the man who provided the sperm for me."

Her mother bristled. "Dale Webber—"

"Dale Webber was a trucker passing through. You invented that nice story about how you and he got married, but I knew better. I had no father."

"He visited you," her mother argued. "He gave you a doll."

"And then he conveniently died in a highway accident." Sarcasm stretched Joelle's voice thin. "The way I figure it, that insurance check you got from his sister was insurance against your going after him. And his sister was probably his wife. Or maybe him. 'Here's some money, Wanda. Now, stay out of my life.'"

Wanda's eyes narrowed and her mouth tightened. The lines grooving her brow dipped into a frown.

"That's not what I wanted for my child," Joelle said. "I wanted a husband. I wanted my daughter to grow up knowing who her daddy was." And she did, Joelle tried to reassure herself. Bobby was Claudia's daddy. Always. Still.

"Fine. So you had yourself a little Father-Knows-Best family," her mother snorted. "And now your husband isn't talking to you. I guess things didn't work out so well for you after all."

The vindictiveness in her mother's tone stung. Joelle had come here for comfort, for support, maybe even for advice. She'd come because she had desperately needed someone to talk to, and Bobby was no longer listening. She hadn't come so her mother could break her into pieces like a day-old piece of breakfast pastry.

"You're right," she said, pushing away from the table. "Things didn't work out well. Thanks for pointing that out."

Before she could stand, her mother had clamped a hand over hers. Wanda's hand was hard, her joints knobbed with arthritis, her skin freckled with age spots. But her palm was warm and she held Joelle tightly. "Don't go running off, honey," she murmured. "You're hurting. I'm hurting for you. Seems to me there are worse things in this life than having a man who lives with you, gives you a nice home and good children, pays the bills, doesn't drink and doesn't like to open up. Men can be that way.

I've known a whole lot more of them than you have, Joelle. They're like clams. They could have a pearl inside—a whole damn pearl necklace—but God help 'em, they won't open up and let you see the good stuff."

Just the touch of Wanda's hand was enough to thaw the knot of anger inside Joelle. Her words turned that thawed knot into a warm rush of tears and gratitude. "He doesn't love me, Mom," she said in a wavering voice. "That's the bottom line."

"He doesn't love you? What are you, nuts? He's crazy about you."

She shook her head. A few tears slithered down her cheeks, and she pulled a napkin from the plastic dispenser and wiped her face dry. She didn't want to weep. She didn't want to believe her situation was bad enough for tears. Yet here she was at her mother's house, hundreds of miles from home, hundreds of miles from Bobby.

"I've seen him with you," Wanda said. "He looks at you like a teenager checking out a centerfold. It's all he can do not to drool."

"That's lust, Mom. Not love."

"Don't knock it." She loosened her grip on Joelle's hand, then patted it gently. "Lust'll get you a lot closer to love than you realize."

Not close enough, Joelle thought. The last time she and Bobby had made love was the night after they'd told Claudia the truth about her conception. Bobby hadn't reached for Joelle that night. She'd initiated their lovemaking. And afterward, Bobby had warned her that the wall they were perched on was about to collapse and hurl them down.

Lust couldn't get her to love. If anything, it demonstrated just how far from love she and Bobby were.

TWELVE

June 1998

BOBBY GAZED AROUND THE interior of Our Lady of Lourdes and decided he could survive an hour in church. He'd gotten through both his sons' christenings without melting down— he'd missed Claudia's christening, thanks to 'Nam—and he could get through today. The church was just a place, after all. Just a building.

Before Mike's christening, the last time Bobby had been in a church he'd been twelve. St. Mary's in Holmdell had been a dreary church in the best of times, with dark stone walls and stained-glass windows depicting the most gruesome scenes in the life of Jesus. That day when Bobby was twelve, all those fractured images of Christ with is head wrapped in thorns, and Christ dead on the cross and Christ bleeding in his mother's arms, had served only to magnify Bobby's misery.

A coffin had stood in front of the altar, smooth and polished, shining like a freshly waxed car. His father had said, "That's your mother in there," and Bobby had wanted to kick things. Instead he'd held Eddie's hand and let their father lead them down a hall to the priest's office.

"Let me talk to the boys alone for a minute," Father Paul had said, ushering them inside.

The room had smelled of cedar and cigar smoke. Eddie had been too small for the chair next to Bobby's; he'd had to shift forward so his legs wouldn't stick straight out in front of him. His face had been blotchy red and damp. By Bobby's calculation, Eddie had been crying pretty much nonstop for four days.

Father Paul had sat behind a huge desk, facing them. He'd been old and balding, his face as round as a volleyball. He'd seemed to have no neck, just his clerical collar. It kept his head from rolling away, Bobby had thought.

"Do you boys know why your mother died?" he'd asked. Eddie had given his head a vigorous shake, but Bobby had remained still, staring at Father Paul, daring him to come up with any possible justification for such a tragedy. "She died because God loved her so much. He wanted her in heaven with him. He knew that was where she belonged."

Eddie had sniffled. Bobby had pulled a Kleenex from the box on Father Paul's desk and handed it to him. Doing that had kept him from saying what he was thinking: that God must not have loved Bobby and Eddie very much if he would take their mother away from them.

"Your mother is an angel," Father Paul had told them. "She's an angel among angels, in God's kingdom, where God wants her to be because He loves her so much."

Bullshit, Bobby had thought.

"Now your father is all alone, and he's suffering," Father Paul had gone on. "It's very important that you boys mind him. You don't want to increase his suffering. So whatever he tells you to do, you do it. Don't disobey him. Don't talk back. Don't give him a hard time. He's lost his wife, and your job from here on in is to be obedient, well-behaved boys and do as your father says. Whatever he asks of you, you do it. Do you understand?"

Eddie had been blubbering openly by then. Bobby had nodded, because he'd figured agreeing with Father Paul was the fastest route to escaping from the stuffy office.

"Very well." Father Paul had stood, which had given Bobby and Eddie the freedom to stand, as well. "Be good boys, now. Don't make your father's life harder than it is. Do as he says. I don't want to hear about you giving him a hard time."

"Okay," Eddie had mumbled, and Bobby had echoed him.

Out in the hall, Eddie had collapsed against Bobby. "Do we have to do whatever Daddy says?" he'd asked plaintively.

"Nah. That was a crock. You steer clear of Dad as much as you can. I'll take care of things."

He wasn't sure he'd done a particularly good job taking care of things, but somehow, thirty-plus years later, he was standing at the back of a church, sunlight streaming in colored shafts through the much cheerier stained-glass windows of the Catholic church in Gray Hill. The pale oak pews were filled with people, among them Eddie and his partner, Stuart, and Louie, the man Father Paul had ordered Eddie and Bobby to obey. Joelle had arranged the seating so that Louie was positioned at the end of a pew, Joelle's mother next to him and Eddie and Stuart on Wanda's other side. After all these years, Louie DiFranco hadn't yet come to terms with the fact that his younger son was gay.

Coming to terms with things wasn't one of Louie DiFranco's strengths. He was much more adept at mouthing off like a fool and drinking like a fish.

He was sober this morning, at least. Eddie had assured Bobby of it. Eddie and Stuart and Louie were all staying at a hotel in Arlington, and Eddie, who had rented a car, had volunteered to chauffeur Louie wherever he had to be. "You're the father of the bride," Eddie explained. "You've got enough on your plate. I'll babysit Dad."

Father of the bride. God, how had that happened? Bobby shook his head and grinned.

Mike and Danny looked spiffy in navy-blue blazers, khaki trousers, white shirts and burgundy ties, each with a red rose boutonniere pinned to his lapel. Claudia had decided they didn't need to wear tuxedos just to be ushers. Lucky boys, Bobby thought. Wearing a tux made him feel as if he ought to be trick-or-treating. He, Gary, Gary's father and the best man had all gone to a tuxedo-rental place in Arlington, where they'd agreed on the least frilly, fancy style available—plain black with black satin lapels, straight black trousers, pleated white shirts and black bow ties. Bobby had struggled a bit with the shirt's studs, but Joelle had gotten them all fastened and tied his bow tie so it lay smooth under the weird stand-up collar and didn't resemble a fat butterfly too much.

She was beautiful, almost as beautiful as the bride. She'd sewn her own dress, a simple thing of flowing blue silk that fell to midcalf, with a blousy jacket over it. It was the same color as her eyes, the same color as the prom dress she'd sewn for herself so many years ago. Bobby still remembered that day. He remembered the pang he'd felt when Drew Foster had shown up—looking ridiculous in a matching blue tux, as Bobby recalled—and Joelle had looped her hand through the bend in his elbow and gazed at him with adoration.

Bad memory. Bobby shook his head again, then stepped aside

as Claudia's bridesmaids began their procession down the church's center aisle, leaving clouds of perfume in their wake. Claudia inched closer to him, her dress rustling. Joelle had sewn Claudia's dress, too. It had taken her two months, and it was a work of art, panels of ivory silk with a gently curving neckline and a sweeping skirt that trailed behind Claudia. Rather than a traditional veil, she'd pinned a scarf of lace into her hair. In her hands was a bouquet of red, pink and white roses.

"Are you sure you want to go through with this?" he teased as they watched her bridesmaids march down the aisle. "It's not too late to change your mind."

"Gee, I don't know," Claudia whispered back. "If I marry him, will you still be my dad?"

"Forever and ever." He wasn't joking anymore.

Her smile was so real he knew she wasn't joking, either. "Good," she said, then tucked her hand around his arm and led him through the doors, into the church.

THE RECEPTION WAS HELD at a country club in northern Fairfield County. Gary's parents were members, and they'd made the arrangements, even though Bobby had insisted on paying. The venue was damn expensive, although Gary's father had informed Bobby that because he was a member of long standing, the place had offered them a generous discount.

Discount? Bobby would hate to think what the undiscounted price was.

But he could afford it. If this was what Claudia wanted, she would have it.

The club was pretty, at least. The room they were in was bright, afternoon sunlight flooding through the French doors that lined one wall and opened out onto a fieldstone patio. The tables were draped in linen, the bartender was filling orders nonstop in one corner of the room and a three-piece combo played mellow music. Claudia and Gary had considered hiring a deejay, but they'd gone with a band instead, for which Bobby was thankful. Not that they showed any flair for playing Doors and Jimi Hendrix songs, but at least they weren't playing hip-hop, or that deafening heavy-metal junk the boys were listening to these days.

Claudia was in her element, circulating among the guests, dancing with Gary, laughing, hugging, kissing and showing off her ring set. The wedding band had diamonds in it, and the engagement ring contained a rock so big Bobby needed sunglasses to stare directly at it.

Joelle glided over to him, holding a glass of white wine for herself and a club soda for him. The sense of dislocation he felt in this ritzy room, hosting this ritzy reception, was replaced by an even greater amazement that a woman so elegant and confident could be his wife.

"How are you holding up?" she asked as she handed him his drink.

"Fine. You?"

"I don't know." Her smile was bittersweet. "I'm not old enough to be someone's mother-in-law."

He chuckled and glanced toward his own mother-in-law. Wanda was seated at a table with some of Gary's relatives, blathering about something. As mothers-in-law went, he supposed there were worse. Over the past few years, she'd started acting as if she liked him, or at least respected him. He supposed she had to be nice to him, as long as he and Joelle were helping her out financially. And since she lived in Ohio, he didn't have to see her too often.

"You'll be a great mother-in-law," Bobby assured Joelle.

"And you're a wonderful liar." She reached up to adjust his collar. He'd untied the bow and unfastened the shirt's top stud a while ago, which had undoubtedly destroyed the odd shape of the collar.

He eased her hand away from his neck and gave it a gentle squeeze. Then he studied her ring. So plain, so thin. It had been all he could afford twenty-seven years ago. At least it was fourteen-carat gold.

"I should buy you a diamond," he said.

She was in the middle of a sip of wine, and she coughed a couple of times. "A diamond? Why?"

"Your daughter's walking around with the Rock of Gibraltar on her hand. That stone could cover the boys' tuition costs when they go to college."

She stretched out her arm and inspected her wedding band. "I like this ring just fine."

"It's cheap."

"It's priceless," she said, then rose on tiptoe and kissed his lips.

He closed his eyes and sank into the kiss, astonished that he—Bobby D—could be lucky enough to have this woman as his wife. When someone seated at a table near them whistled softly, he chuckled and pulled back. And immediately frowned when he spotted his father at the bar again.

How many drinks had the guy consumed? At least four, and the formal dinner hadn't begun yet. There weren't enough appetizers in the entire country club to absorb all the booze he'd been swilling.

If his father got drunk… Hell, he was already drunk. At this point, the only question was whether he'd get drunk enough to start breaking things.

Bobby cursed softly and handed his club soda to Joelle. "I've got to head Dad off at the pass," he said, squaring his shoulders and working his way across the room. It wasn't easy. Too many people had to stop and congratulate him. Who were all these folks, anyway? He and Joelle had very small families, but they'd invited neighbors, friends, a few of Joelle's fellow teachers, a few of Bobby's colleagues and associates from work. Bobby's first boss in Connecticut, the cousin of his physical therapist. Suzanne, the woman Joelle had lived with while Bobby was in 'Nam. A goodly portion of Claudia's classmates from high school and college. It seemed as if every single one of them had to stop him and offer congratulations, or share some anecdote about Claudia, or reminisce about some silly thing Gary had done years ago.

By the time he reached the bar, his father had already been served a highball glass full of Scotch. Glenlivet, expensive stuff—wasted on Louie. At this point he'd probably think motor oil tasted great, as long as it had a high enough alcohol content.

Louie turned from the bar and wove toward a table. Bobby swooped down on him, slung his arm around the old man's shoulders and said, "Let's take a walk." Before Louie could muster any resistance, Bobby had him through the room's door and out into a chilly, air-conditioned hallway.

"What's going on?" Louie asked.

"You and I could use some fresh air," Bobby said, steering him down the hall, past the pro shop and the restrooms, through the airy lobby and out the front door. The patio that bordered their reception room ran the length of the building, but in front of the main entry it extended outward into a broad stone stairway that descended to a plush lawn and a circular driveway. Meticulously pruned arborvitae lined the driveway. Blossoming rhododendron flanked the patio. Not bad, Bobby thought. DiFranco Landscaping could do better, but the view was attractive and the lawn was extremely green.

"I don't need fresh air," Louie groused, wrinkling his nose as the summery evening wrapped around him. Like Bobby, he'd loosened his tie. His shirt and the jacket of his suit were wrinkled. Bobby wondered when he'd bought the suit, and where. It looked old, but his father never gained weight. He might have bought it when Bobby was a kid. Lapel widths came and went, and Bobby had no idea which width was considered fashionable when.

"I think you do need fresh air," Bobby said quietly. A blue-bird alighted on the stone ledge bordering the patio and then flew off. A couple of pink-faced men in casual apparel, with golf bags slung over their shoulders, emerged from the building, nodded a greeting at Bobby and Louie and then headed down the steps to the driveway.

"A flipping golf club," Louie muttered. "Since when did you get so fancy?"

Bobby chose to laugh off his father's implicit criticism. "It was what Claudia wanted," he said, his gaze settling on the glass in his father's hand. Was there a tactful way to get it out of Louie's grip? A way that wouldn't cause Louie to snap?

"You spoil that girl rotten, Bobby."

Anger bubbled up inside Bobby, but he swallowed it back down. He wasn't going to let his father goad him, not today. "It's her wedding. The only wedding she's ever going to have."

"People get divorced all the time," Louie pointed out.

"There's a happy thought." Keeping his voice mild required greater and greater effort. "If she gets a divorce, she's still doing this——" he gestured toward the building "——only once. One big wedding, and after that she's on her own. But I don't see a divorce happening here. Gary's a good guy, and Claudia's crazy about him."

"Lucky to marry a woman who's crazy about you, huh," Louie said, his tone tinged with sarcasm.

What the hell was that supposed to mean? Was he implying that Joelle wasn't crazy about Bobby? She'd said her simple little wedding band was priceless. That sounded pretty crazy to Bobby.

His father slugged down some Scotch. His eyes had a milky appearance, but he wasn't staggering or reeling. "So, how much did this shindig set you back? You got that much money to spare?"

"We budgeted for it," Bobby said cryptically. He wasn't sure what direction the conversation was taking, but he didn't like it. "How about a cup of coffee, Dad?"

"I don't want coffee. I've got a drink." He took another sip from his glass. Damn the bartender for having filled it so full. "I hear you send money to Wanda."

"We don't send her money." They only helped her out when she needed it. They'd paid her airfare to visit Connecticut—and they'd paid Louie's airfare for this wedding, too, and his hotel room. But he'd been union at the rivet factory, and he received a decent pension in retirement. That he spent most of it on booze wasn't a justification for Bobby to give him financial support. "Dad, you're getting in a mood. I think you should have some coffee."

"What mood? I'm not in a mood." Louie shot him a defiant glare. "I'm here, okay? I came to the flipping wedding. Put on a suit, got on a plane, saw the girl get married. This part's called the reception, right? This is when we get our reward for sitting through the boring parts."

"Reward yourself with a cup of coffee. There's going to be a nice dinner soon, and—"

"Oh, a *nice* dinner. Everything's very nice here. Who are you trying to kid, Bobby?"

Bobby sighed. His gaze was still on his father's glass. He felt his eyes swiveling in their sockets, following the movement of Louie's hand as he moved it, the glass shifting right and then left.

"You're a piece of crap like me, Bobby. You can dress up in a fancy tuxedo, but it doesn't change what you are. A kid from Tubtown. Cannon fodder, all shot up in Vietnam. Now you lug stones and plant shrubs. You wear boots to work and breathe dirt. You married that snotty blond girl—I don't know why. Why didn't you marry the dark-haired one? She was like us. This one—" he gestured toward the doors "—this Joelle, she always put on airs. Thought she was better than us. I never liked her."

"I'll be sure to tell her," Bobby said dryly. "Give me the glass, Dad."

"Like hell." He took another sip. "I never liked her. She had a superior way about her. I don't know why the hell you married her—"

"Dad."

"But I can guess. I can guess, Bobby. You think I'm an idiot? She was pregnant. You got her in trouble. You were stupid, sleeping around with too many girls. Thought you were the stud of Holmdell, but Mr. Stud got caught."

"Give me the glass," Bobby said, extending his hand.

His father stepped back, out of reach. "At least you had the balls to get a girl pregnant, which is more than I can say for your pansy brother. But I'll tell you this, Bobby, since you're too stupid to figure it out yourself. Joelle tricked you. She conned you. That pretty little girl you walked down the aisle today? You claim she's my granddaughter, but she sure as hell doesn't look like a DiFranco."

Rage exploded, flaring red in Bobby's brain. He made a dive for the glass and wound up catching his father's wrist. The glass tipped, splashing Scotch onto the fieldstone beneath their feet. With his free hand, he wrenched the glass from his father's grip and hurled it over the ledge, onto the grass below.

"You little punk," his father snarled.

"You've had too much to drink, Dad. You're saying things you don't mean to say—"

"I mean every word of it." He yanked his arm away from Bobby and started toward the door. "I'm getting another drink."

"No. You're done drinking for today."

"You think I'm a drunk?"

"I know you're a drunk."

The punch came so quickly, so unexpectedly, Bobby didn't have a chance to duck. He felt the sting in the corner of his mouth, the grinding ache in his cheek as his feet danced under him, struggling to hold him upright. Behind him he heard someone shout, and then a pair of hands pressed against his shoulders, steadying him. "Christ," Eddie muttered. He pressed a frosty glass and a cocktail napkin into Bobby's hands. "Put some ice on your lip. I'll take care of Dad."

Bobby's vision slowly cleared. He watched his brother storm across the patio to Louie, who was trying to climb over the ledge to retrieve his glass from the lawn below. Sucking air into his lungs, he lowered his gaze to the glass in his hand. Some sort of liquid in there, a stirrer and ice. He pulled out a cube and pressed it to the corner of his mouth. The cold felt good, but the alcohol made his lip sting even more.

The ice melted fast, dripping between his fingers. He used the cocktail napkin to dry his hand and then his mouth. When he drew the napkin away, he saw blood on it.

Eddie seemed to have calmed his father down. He held him tightly and led him back toward Bobby. "How 'bout that?" Louie said, studying Bobby's face and smiling with dazed pride. "Didn't know your old man had it in him, huh."

"I always knew you had it in you," Bobby retorted, wondering if the hatred burning in his gut was visible in his eyes.

"It's not that bad, Bobby," Eddie assured him. "Use more ice."

"You can just tell folks you walked into a door," Louie said, then laughed. Maybe he wasn't so drunk after all. Or maybe being drunk didn't dull his memory. This punch, Bobby understood, was payback. It was settling a very old score. It was letting Bobby know that the hatred was mutual.

"I'm going to drive him back to the hotel," Eddie said.

"I can call a cab for him."

"Here? In the middle of golf country?" Eddie snorted.

"I don't want you to leave. They'll be serving dinner soon."

"That's all right. I'll get him into his room and come back. You can tell Stuart where I've gone. Anyone else, just tell them Dad wasn't feeling well."

"I'm feeling fine," Louie protested. "I'd feel even better if I had a drink."

"I'll talk to the bartender at the hotel lounge," Eddie added.

Bobby shook his head. "If the bar cuts him off, he'll just go through whatever's in the minibar in his room."

"At least he won't be drinking in public. Let me leave so I can come back."

Bobby glanced at his father, who appeared to be deflating, adrenaline no longer pumping through his veins. Just blood and booze. "Eddie, I—"

"Hey." Eddie silenced him. "How many times did you shield me from him over the years? This is the least I can do for you.

Now, your princess just got married. Go back inside and be a proud papa."

Bobby felt his energy drain away. "Thanks."

He watched as Eddie led their father toward the stairs and down. Louie's legs seemed rubbery beneath him, even though Bobby was the one who'd gotten walloped. If he and Eddie were lucky, the son of a bitch would collapse as soon as he got to his room and sleep until morning. If they weren't lucky, he'd work his way through the minibar, make himself sick and stick Bobby with a whopping bill at checkout time.

Screw it. Eddie was right. He had to go inside and be a proud papa. With a split lip and a bruised cheek.

He made his way back to the building, shivering as the air-conditioning blasted him. Refusing to show his face in the reception room until he'd cleaned up, he ducked into the men's room.

The bathroom was brightly lit and as he studied his reflection in the mirror that stretched the length of a wall above a row of sinks, the striped green wallpaper made him look even paler than he was. His hair was mussed, the skin above his jaw slightly puffy. Blood leaked from the corner of his mouth. At least it hadn't dripped onto his tux. How would he have explained the bloodstains when he returned the suit to the rental place?

I walked into a door, and the door won.

Frickin' bastard, he thought as he tossed the cocktail napkin into the trash can and twisted the faucet.

The door swung open. He hoped it wasn't one of the wedding guests. His peripheral vision caught a flutter of pale blue and he spun around. "Jo? What the hell are you doing here?"

"Someone in the lobby said you were in here."

"It's a men's room."

"Big deal." She swept across the room, pinched his chin between her thumb and index finger and inspected his face. "Did you hit your father?"

"No." He eased out of her grasp and turned back to the sink. "I wish I had," he added before bowing and splashing water onto his face.

"Where is he now?"

"Eddie's driving him back to the hotel." He lifted a paper towel from the stack beside the sink. It was as soft as cloth. He dabbed his lip, then stretched it to see where the blood was flowing from. Just inside, where his teeth had jammed into the flesh.

"Let me," Joelle said, taking a fresh towel, soaking it and pressing it lightly to his mouth and cheek. "I think you'll live." She smiled, obviously trying to cool his anger as much as his face.

"I look like shit."

"You look like the most handsome man at the wedding," she argued. "With a slightly puffy lip. If you smile, no one will notice."

He attempted a smile. It hurt not just his face but his soul.

Behind Joelle, the door cracked open and a man started to enter. "Oh—excuse me," he said, hastily retreating.

"Come on in," Joelle called to him. "Don't pay any attention to me."

"No, that's all right—I'll find another restroom." The man vanished, letting the door whisper shut behind him.

Joelle grinned up at Bobby. "I scared him away, huh."

She was the scariest woman he'd ever known. So calm, so sure of herself, so determined to whip him back into shape. He could force a smile so the wedding guests wouldn't notice his swollen lip, but he was a long way from back into shape. The anger inside him had mutated into something else, something that felt like panic, or helplessness. Something weak and frightening, something Bobby didn't want to be.

Joelle must have sensed it. "Talk to me, Bobby."

"I'm fine," he insisted.

"You're upset, but your father's gone. Eddie's taking care of it. Put it out of your mind, okay?"

"It's not——" He swallowed. When she gazed at him that way, her eyes so blue, so beseeching, he wished he could tell her everything. He wished he could sob on her shoulder. But he couldn't. He was a man, her husband, the person who had promised to make everything right for her. "I'm not upset," he said.

"You are, Bobby. Why do I always have to fight with you to get you to open up? For God's sake, talk to me."

What could he say? How could he admit what he was feeling? "I hate my father," he admitted at last.

"I don't blame you."

"Not because of him, or this." He brushed his hand against his throbbing mouth. "Because...because what kind of father can I possibly be if he's who I learned from? He's all I know about how to be a father." Eddie was wise not to have kids—even gay couples became parents these days, but Eddie and Stuart had no interest in that. Bobby should have been that wise, too. He carried his father's genes in him, his father's imprint. He'd spent every day of his life struggling to be a better man, but what if he'd failed? What if he was his father's son?

He should never have married Joelle. He'd done it only because she'd been desperate and he would have done anything for her—even if it meant turning into his father.

She cupped her hands on either side of his face and forced him to meet her gaze. Her fingers were cool, firm but unbearably gentle. "You are the finest father I've ever seen," she told him. "You're nothing like him."

"I'm his son."

"He's not a father." Her voice dipped to a near whisper. "Contributing sperm isn't what makes a man a father, Bobby. You know that. I know that."

Bobby's father probably knew that, too. The words he'd said outside, the insinuations—had he guessed the truth? Did it matter?

"*You,* Bobby DiFranco—*you* are what it means to be a father." She guided his face down to her and kissed him, a sweet, warm touch of her mouth to his, light enough not to hurt his injured lip. Then she released him. "Come," she said, slipping her hand into his and leading him out of the bathroom. "You have to make a toast to the bride and groom. Try to smile, okay?"

Smiling would hurt. But for Joelle he would do it.

THIRTEEN

DANNY SHOWED UP AT FIVE-THIRTY, lugging a shopping bag full of take-out Chinese food. The aroma of soy and ginger emanating from the bag tore through whatever had been wrapped around Bobby's appetite all day. One whiff and he realized he was starving.

He wasn't sure what to make of his kids' fussing over him, though. That morning Claudia had barged in and ordered him to eat something. Now Danny was standing on the front porch, armed with food.

At least he hadn't taken inspiration from his brother and shown up with booze. Of all the mistakes Bobby had made in the past week—and he still wasn't sure what all those mistakes were; he just knew he'd made plenty—downing drink after drink with Mike at the Hay Street Pub had been the biggest.

Or maybe not. Joelle hadn't left him after that debacle. Maybe meeting with Helen Crawford behind Joelle's back had been a worse mistake.

Or maybe his biggest mistake was that he was who he was— a man who couldn't give Joelle what she wanted. A man who could provide her with a home and a car, all the security in the world, but couldn't go all touchy-feely about his emotions.

She wanted him to open up and let everything out? Well, damn it, he'd been as open as he could be. She wanted to know what was inside him? Rage. He'd sure as hell let that out.

"How about it, Dad?" Danny said with forced cheer. "Can I tempt you with some General Gao's chicken?"

"Come on in." Bobby waved Danny inside, then shut the door. The house didn't have its usual Saturday fresh-scrubbed smell. He supposed he could have cleaned the place in Joelle's absence, but instead he'd spent much of the day working on her garden. She labored over it, and she liked to believe it was hers, but gardening wasn't her forte. She didn't understand that you had to thin out the carrots and radishes if you hoped to harvest edible vegetables and not scrawny little roots. You had to check the undersides of the tomato leaves for aphids, and you had to weed ruthlessly. Joelle insisted that her garden be organic and she'd forbidden Bobby from spraying weed killer and insecticide on the plants. But you couldn't get a crop of organic produce if insects ate whatever the weeds hadn't choked to death.

He'd finished gardening a couple of hours ago, taken a long shower and thought about how, if he were a drinker, a cold beer would have hit the spot. Instead, he'd poured himself a glass of iced tea, left another message, less pleading and more demanding, on Joelle's cell phone and then called Wanda. "Have you seen Joelle?" he'd asked.

"I don't want to get in the middle of this," she'd replied, which indicated that she *had* seen Joelle and knew something about what was going on.

"She won't return my calls," he'd said.

"I suppose she will when she's good and ready."

"Will you ask her to get ready soon?" He'd been unable to sift the impatience from his voice. "We can't work anything out if she won't talk to me."

"Or if you won't talk to her," Wanda had said.

He'd almost retorted that he'd been attempting since yesterday to talk to Joelle, but she kept refusing to accept his calls. But why argue with Wanda? She didn't want to get in the middle of this, and he didn't blame her. "Tell her I called," Bobby had said. "Tell her I'll keep trying."

"You better try *something*," Wanda had said cryptically before hanging up.

Discouraged, he'd turned the CD player back on. The carousel was still full of Doors disks, and the first song to play was "The End." He'd sat listening to the dirgelike number, absorbing Jim Morrison's howls of pain. "The end of laughter and soft lies," Morrison sang, leaving Bobby so depressed he almost hadn't heard Danny ringing the doorbell.

All right. Food had arrived, food and his youngest son. He was still depressed, but not quite as much as he'd been a few minutes ago.

"Lauren says Asian cuisine tastes better with chopsticks," Danny said as he removed plastic tubs and waxed cardboard containers from the bag and spread them out on the kitchen table.

Bobby reminded himself that Lauren was Danny's girlfriend, the woman who'd dragged Danny off to Tanglewood to listen to symphonies. Bobby had met her a couple of times, most recently at a barbecue at Claudia and Gary's house to celebrate Memorial Day and Claudia's birthday. Lauren seemed nice enough—but she also seemed like the sort of person who'd use words like *cuisine* and insist on using chopsticks.

"This is America," Bobby said. "I'm using a fork."

Danny grinned and accepted a fork, too. He helped himself to one of the microbrewery beers in the refrigerator door while Bobby poured himself a fresh glass of iced tea. Then they settled at the table and dug in. While Bobby inhaled a third of the General Gao's chicken and a small mountain of steamed rice, Danny described the client he and Mike had visited earlier that day. "He asked for terracing, but his property doesn't slope. If we did terracing, we'd have to recontour the land first. It seems like an awful lot of effort just so the guy can have terraces."

"It's a profitable job," Bobby explained. "If that's what he wants, we'll rent some earth movers and recontour his property. And we'll make a lot of money doing it."

"Yeah, well, Mike and I wrote down the guy's specs and figured you'd have to calculate the cost. We weren't sure whether the company can do that kind of job."

"We can."

Danny nodded. He was eating even faster than Bobby. Twenty-four years old and he still went through food like a ravenous teenager. He piled some spring rolls onto his plate, then picked one up with his fingers and chomped on it, managing to consume half of it in one bite.

"So, what's the deal?" Bobby asked once Danny had made it through all his spring rolls. "You kids are on some kind of rotation?"

Danny gave him an innocent look. "Rotation?"

"Yeah—taking turns feeding me. Is Mike scheduled for tomorrow morning?"

"Mike." Danny snorted. "He's pissed. I told him to stay away from you."

That brought Bobby up short. He lowered his fork. "Why?"

"Because of the whole Claudia thing. He doesn't want to forgive you for not telling us the truth."

"You *do* want to forgive me?"

Danny shrugged. Along with his adolescent appetite, he still had a lanky adolescent build. Working for DiFranco had added some heft to his torso, however. His chest and shoulders filled his T-shirt well. The front of the shirt featured a picture of a rock band Bobby had never heard of. "I figure, what the heck," he said. "Claudia's my sister. End of story."

"You don't mind that your mother and I lied to you?"

"People lie. They have their reasons." He rummaged through the food containers, apparently contemplating what to eat next.

Danny had apparently made his peace with Bobby and Joelle's decision not to tell anyone about Claudia's origins. Why couldn't Mike? Was it simply that Danny was a mellower guy, or happier because he was in love? And where did Claudia fit on the scale? She'd agreed to have her blood tested, but she seemed agitated about the whole thing.

Beyond the kids, what about him? What about Joelle? What would they do if Claudia wound up being a genetic match for Foster's son?

Would they even still be married by then?

"So, when do you think Mom'll be coming home?" Danny asked after washing a dim-sum dumpling down with a swig of beer.

"I don't know. She won't talk to me."

"Man, what did you do to her?"

"Nothing," Bobby said, then pressed his lips together and stared at the thick brown sauce spread like an oil slick across the surface of his plate. He'd done *something*. Saying he'd done nothing was just another lie.

He and Joelle had survived worse, hadn't they? They'd survived his return home from Vietnam, his nightmares, his long, arduous months of rehab. They'd survived years of scrimping, years when the only vacation they could afford was a day at an amusement park with the kids, when their idea of a new car was anything less than ten years old.

"Maybe you ought to go out to Ohio," Danny said as he scooped a pile of beef and broccoli onto his plate. "Sit down with her and talk things out."

"I just told you—she won't talk to me," Bobby said.

"Maybe you ought to get in her face. Then she'd have no choice but to talk to you."

Bobby regarded Danny. Danny tended to be more impulsive than Mike or Claudia. He thought a thing and then he did it. *Get in her face,* he'd said. *Go out to Ohio.*

Bobby wasn't one for dramatic gestures, and he'd never chased after a woman who didn't want him. But this wasn't just a woman. This was JoJo. His wife.

The woman who'd betrayed him. The woman who'd taken his daughter away from him.

The woman he'd adored since he was ten years old.

He couldn't fix this mess alone. He wasn't sure he and Joelle could fix it together. But apart, they would never make things right.

"I wonder how soon I could get to Ohio," he said.

JOELLE'S CHILDHOOD BED WAS A lot less comfortable than her bed at home in Gray Hill. It was even less comfortable than the hard king-size bed in the room at the West Side Motor Lodge, where she'd stayed her first night in Holmdell. Yet after checking out of the motel and moving into her old bedroom at the rear of the first-floor flat on Third Street, Joelle slept as if someone had clubbed her over the head, a thick, black sleep without dreams.

The small room overlooking the backyard was warm and

stuffy. Her mother had never installed an air conditioner in that room, and she left the door shut most of the time so the air-conditioning gusting through the rest of the apartment wouldn't be wasted in a room she rarely used. She'd set up her sewing machine on Joelle's desk, and an ironing board along the far wall. A pile of fabric squares in a basket next to the sewing machine indicated that she was working on a quilt. Joelle could sew it while she was in town, but it was her mother's project, so she left the fabric and the machine alone.

She used to sew a lot when the kids were younger. They were always outgrowing things, always in need of a new shirt or dress. Ratty old furniture had to be spruced up with new slip-covers and pillows. But lately she'd been neglecting her sewing. When she went home, she'd start a new project.

When she went home. Once she decided it was time to return to the house in Gray Hill. Once she knew whether the mistakes she'd made were reparable, whether her children would forgive her, whether her husband would ever, ever open his heart fully to her.

Until she was ready to face everything that awaited her in Connecticut, the cramped back bedroom on Third Street would do, even without air-conditioning. The scuffed chest of drawers that used to hold all her clothing now contained stationery supplies, old magazines and odds and ends, but the bottom drawer was empty, enabling her to unpack her suitcase. The closet was empty, too—except for her high-school prom dress, still hanging from the rod, draped in clear, protective plastic. As if she'd ever wear the thing again. Just touching the synthetic fabric made her skin itch.

The pillow on her bed smelled musty, but the sheets were cool. She'd opened the window to let in the night air and asked her mother to let her sleep late. She hadn't slept well for so many nights. Maybe a night alone, without Bobby lying right beside her yet light-years away from her, would allow her to get some rest.

It did. In her thin T-shirt, with the blanket kicked to the foot of the bed, she lay unmoving in the heat. She might have slept straight through Sunday if she hadn't heard a tapping at the window.

She opened one eye and found the room hazy with a gray light seeping through the voile curtains. Then she heard the tapping again, and a whisper: "JoJo?"

She bolted upright, blinking furiously. Once her eyes were in focus, she saw the familiar silhouette against the floating curtains. Inhaling deeply to steady her nerves, she swung out of bed, crossed to the window and spread the curtains apart.

There stood Bobby, just as he had when they'd been children, when he'd sneaked over to visit her late at night and hadn't dared to ring the front doorbell. She stared at him through the screen, his face shadowed, his shoulders broad and strong. "What are you doing here?" she asked.

"Danny said I should get in your face," he told her.

Her brain moved sluggishly, still woozy with drowsiness. She blinked again, took more deep breaths, shook her head to clear it. "I mean *here,* at the window."

"No one answered the front door."

"What time is it?"

He lifted his wrist. "Almost eleven."

Her mother must have gone out. Maybe she'd met Stan Sherko at the Bank Street Diner for brunch. Just friends, indeed.

Unsure what to do, Joelle decided to concentrate on facts and chronologies. "How did you get here? You were still in Connecticut last night. You phoned."

"And you had your mother run interference." He sounded annoyed when he said that, but his tone grew more conversational when he explained, "I hitched a ride to Cincinnati on a FedEx plane."

"What?"

"Danny's girlfriend, Lauren—her father is an attorney for some big shot at FedEx. Danny talked to Lauren, and she made a few calls and got me a seat on one of their overnight flights. Me and a bunch of fruit crates and sandals from L.L. Bean. I like that girl." She saw the outline of his cheeks move and realized he must have smiled. "I rented a car at the airport."

"You must be exhausted."

Although she couldn't see his eyes, she felt his gaze. "You look a lot more tired than I feel."

"Bobby..." She sighed. "I'm not sure I'm ready to talk to you yet."

"Too bad. I'm in your face."

She smiled, imagining Danny giving him in-your-face coaching.

"So, are you coming out or am I coming in?"

"I'm not climbing over the windowsill," she said. "I'm too old. Go around to the front door. I'll let you in."

She turned from the window, wondering whether she should get dressed before she let Bobby inside the apartment. Why bother? He hadn't touched her in days. The last time he had, it had felt more like fear than love. No way would he interpret her sleep apparel as seductive.

She ran her fingers through her tangled hair and yanked the knob on the bedroom door. The heat had made the wood swell, and the door stuck for a moment before opening. Willing herself to full alertness, she strode barefoot down the hall to the front door.

Bobby stepped inside, closed the door behind him and stared at her. He had on a pair of old jeans worn to flannel softness and a plain navy-blue T-shirt that hinted at the lean strength of his body. She ached to bury her face against his chest, to feel his arms tight around her. But he didn't reach for her, and she kept her distance.

"Are you okay?" he asked.

"Yes."

"It was a long drive for you, all alone."

She shrugged. "Would you like some coffee? Something to eat?"

"Why is everyone trying to feed me? You all think I don't know how to feed myself?"

Irked by his response—by his presence—she pivoted on her heel and stalked into the kitchen. Bobby might not want coffee, but she did.

He followed her into the kitchen and opened the blinds while she prepared a pot of coffee. "What have you been doing here?" he asked.

By here, she knew he meant Holmdell. She wasn't sure she should say anything when she was still not completely awake, but having Bobby talk to her, pepper her with questions, attempt a conversation, was a treat after the past week. She ought to encourage him. "I've been retracing my steps," she told him.

"What do you mean?"

"Figuring out how I wound up where I did."

"Have you figured it out?"

"I don't know." The coffeemaker churned. She pulled two cups and saucers from the drying rack and set them on the table. Typical Bobby: he wanted her to give him a simple answer. He wanted her to say yes, she'd figured it out, so he wouldn't have to offer anything of himself. In fact, she *had* figured it out, at least some of it. She'd figured out that for the past thirty-seven years she'd been married to a loyal, reliable, generous man who couldn't face the demons inside himself, who couldn't face the even greater goodness there, who couldn't love her the way she'd always dreamed of being loved. But how could she tell him that?

The coffee finished brewing, and she lifted the decanter from the machine. "I'll go to a marriage counselor with you," he said, startling her so much she nearly dropped the pot.

She steadied herself before carrying the pot to the table and filling the cups. "You will?"

"I can't stand the idea, Jo, but if it'll make you happy, I'll do it."

"I don't know how successful counseling would be if you went into it saying, 'I can't stand the idea.'"

He snorted. "Sitting in an office and baring my soul to a stranger? I don't do that kind of thing."

You don't bare your soul to anyone, she thought, returning the pot to the counter.

"I don't even know what we'd talk about," he added.

"We'd talk about why…" Her voice started to crack, and she took a sip of coffee to cover the sound. "We'd talk about why you can't talk about anything. About why when you're angry or afraid, you won't talk to me. You lock everything up inside yourself and pretend it doesn't exist."

He ignored his coffee, his attention fully on her, his eyes as intense as lasers. "Sometimes that's a pretty smart strategy."

"But the truth doesn't always stay locked up. It escapes."

"Yeah." He looked past her and drank some coffee. "Why don't you get dressed and go downtown with me. I can drop off the rental car at the bus station. No sense having two cars here."

He was shutting down again. Despair whispered in her heart, but she refused to listen to it. He was here. He'd traveled all the way to Cincinnati on a FedEx cargo plane. Maybe that was as close as he'd ever get to telling her he loved her.

Abandoning him to the steaming coffeepot and whatever edibles he might scrounge—there were probably some more stale Danish stashed somewhere—she detoured to her bedroom to grab a robe, then headed for the bathroom to shower. She didn't need to wear a robe around him. He was her husband; he'd seen her naked plenty of times. But she still felt a barrier between them, like the spring-pressured gates he'd bought to block off the stairways when the boys were toddlers. The gates wedged between the walls at the top or bottom of a flight of stairs, or in a doorway and tension held them in place.

Tension was holding a barricade in place between her and Bobby, too.

She showered, brushed her teeth and returned to the bedroom to dress. Her mouth tingled with mint. She wondered whether Bobby would kiss her. He'd traveled all this way—in a cargo plane—but he hadn't even touched her.

Dressed in shorts and a polo shirt, her hair brushed and sandals buckled onto her feet, she emerged from the bedroom. She found Bobby where she'd left him—in the kitchen, staring out the window above the sink. All he could see from there was the duplex next door. The buildings along Third Street were separated from one another only by alleys no wider than a car. When Joelle was about ten, a fat woman with poodle-curly hair lived in the neighboring building, and she liked to stack Andy Williams and Dean Martin albums on her hi-fi and waltz around her flat. Joelle used to spy on her, half amused and half transfixed by the way the woman danced, as graceful as a ballerina despite her size. She'd moved away a couple of years later and a family with a bunch of bratty children who were always screeching moved in. In the summer, when people kept their windows open because no one in those days had air-conditioning, the children's constant whining and bickering became an excruciating sound track to Joelle's dinners.

Now everyone had air-conditioning units and all the windows were closed.

Bobby gave her a tenuous smile and led her out of the building into the overcast morning. His car was a nondescript dark green sedan. Before folding himself behind the wheel, he reminded her that the car-rental drop-off was at the bus station. She nodded, climbed into her Prius and followed him down the street.

Once he dropped off his car, she'd have to drive him places, or else he'd appropriate her car to drive himself around. Maybe it would have been better for him to keep the rental.

Except that he'd journeyed to Holmdell to get in her face, and she had to admit she wanted him there. Maybe he was ready to start talking, *really* talking. In any case, that he'd go to such an effort to be with her had to mean he wasn't ready to give up on their marriage.

The bus station's parking lot was full, every space occupied and a huge Greyhound bus occupying most of the curb. Bobby double-parked and approached her car. She pushed the button to open her window. "I'll park in the lot behind the bank," she said. It was less than a block away.

Nodding, Bobby slapped the roof of her car and then strode into the terminal.

Since it was Sunday, the bank was closed, but several cars were parked in the lot. Parking on the downtown streets was metered, so people often left their cars in the lots behind the stores and office buildings. Joelle eased into a space between a Dodge Ram and a glossy Mercedes sedan. Swanky car, she thought as she climbed out of the Prius, careful not to let her door bump the Mercedes. No doubt it belonged to someone from the Hill.

By the time she'd walked back to the bus station, Bobby had completed his task. She observed him as he swung out of the terminal. Although their marriage was in shambles, he walked with a confidence that dazzled her. He'd had that long-legged, sure-footed stride for as long as she'd known him. Even during the year he'd been on crutches, undergoing rehab on his left leg, he'd hobbled with a certainty and determination that announced to the world that he knew where he was going.

"Hi," he said, meeting up with her at the parking lot's entrance. The gray sky washed his face with wan light.

"Is there anything you need to do downtown?" she asked.

"No." He gazed down at her, his expression inscrutable.

"Well, what should we do? We're not going to find a marriage counselor on a Sunday morning."

He laughed, a welcome sound above the rumble of the bus's idling engine and the whisk of cars cruising down the street. "Downtown didn't use to be so busy on a Sunday," he said, observing the traffic. "Everyone used to be in church."

"Or sleeping late. And all the stores used to be closed. I guess they did away with the blue laws. Lots of stores are open today."

"Holmdell meets the twenty-first century." He shrugged and started toward the bank. "Let's get some lunch. It's too late for breakfast."

She wasn't particularly hungry, but she supposed he was, after his overnight flight on the cargo plane. They couldn't go to the Bank Street Diner, though. Her mother might be there, and if she was, she'd meddle.

As Joelle and Bobby entered the parking lot behind the bank, she spotted a woman ahead of them, approaching the Mercedes. The woman had silver hair as smooth and shiny as a mirror, and she wore white slacks and a sleeveless cotton blouse. Her hair placed her well past middle age, but her tan and freckled arms were firm and muscular, as if she swam or played a lot of tennis.

She reached her car just before Joelle and Bobby reached the Prius, and when she pressed the button on her key to unlock the sedan, she turned to offer a friendly smile. It froze on her face, and her eyes widened in astonishment. "Joelle Webber?"

The woman's shock arced like lightning, striking Joelle and causing her to flinch. She recognized that nut-brown face, the elegant cheekbones, the prim lips glossed with pink lipstick. Drew Foster's mother was the sort of woman who never left the house without first donning a full layer of makeup.

"Mrs. Foster," she said politely, trying to hide her surprise. Hadn't she seen a strange young woman picking up the mail at the Foster house yesterday? Hadn't she concluded that the Fosters no longer lived there? Stupid assumption. The young woman could have been a guest, or hired help.

Joelle scrambled for something innocuous to say to Drew's mother. But before she could come up with a friendly observation, Mrs. Foster had stepped out from between their cars, marched over to Joelle and slapped her cheek.

The slap didn't hurt—for all the muscle tone in her arms, Mrs. Foster was a petite, elderly woman. But it hurt Joelle's composure. She sprang back and Bobby sprang forward. Joelle gripped his arm, afraid he'd take a swing at Drew's mother and send her clear across the lot.

"How dare you!" Mrs. Foster railed. "How dare you keep my granddaughter from me!"

"Don't touch my wife," Bobby growled.

"Bobby, no." Joelle tried to calm him.

"You're her husband?" Mrs. Foster glowered at Bobby, her

expression as lethal as his. "You're the man who stole my granddaughter?"

Before Bobby could retort, Joelle yanked on his arm, moving him back a step. "No one stole your granddaughter, Mrs. Foster," she said.

"Then tell me why my son had to hire a detective to find out he even *had* a daughter."

Joelle could feel Bobby bristling next to her; energy pulsing through him. He wanted to defend her, he wanted to lash out. Yet he restrained himself. She knew how much that restraint cost him.

"Drew ran away from his daughter," Joelle said, her voice muted. Something cold and wet struck her cheek and she glanced up to see a dark cloud passing over the parking lot. "When I told him I was pregnant, he asked me to get an abortion."

"He didn't know any better," Mrs. Foster said, defending him. "He was just a child. He was scared."

"I was young and scared, too."

"You should have come to Marshall and me. We would have supported you, paid your medical expenses."

And then stolen my baby from me, Joelle completed the thought. She wasn't sure why she believed this, but she did. The Fosters had never cared for her. She'd been a poor girl from the wrong side of town, and while they'd tolerated her and maintained a pleasant civility around her, they'd never embraced her.

If she'd shown up on their doorstep with the news that their son had gotten her pregnant, they would have hated her. They would have done the right thing—they were the kind of people who recognized their obligations—but they wouldn't have done it for her. Only for her child.

"I made the choice I believed was best," Joelle said firmly, ignoring another raindrop that struck the tip of her nose. "And I'd make the same choice today."

"Keeping our granddaughter from us? Does she even know she has grandparents?"

Joelle felt another wave of energy surge through Bobby. She slid her hand down past his wrist to twine her fingers through his. The tension in his grip could have broken her bones if he'd let it. "She knows her grandparents," Joelle said, not bothering to add that Claudia's allotment of grandparents was pretty skimpy.

"Marshall and I need to meet her. She's our grandchild, too."

"She's an adult. If she wants to meet you, I'm sure she'll arrange it."

Mrs. Foster closed in on her. "You have no idea," she said, her teeth clenched and the tendons in her neck standing out beneath her skin. "You can't begin to comprehend what it's like to have only one grandchild and he's dying. In your worst nightmares, you can't begin to imagine it."

Joelle suffered a pang of sympathy for the woman, but it was fleeting. If Mrs. Foster had raised her own son to be more responsible, she might have spent the past thirty-seven years doting on a granddaughter. But things happened. One decision led to another, and to another, until people wound up so far down one path that they could never retrace their steps and try another route.

"I've had my own nightmares, Mrs. Foster," Joelle said quietly.

Bobby broke in, apparently unable to hold back any longer. "We're done here." He dug into the pocket of Joelle's purse where she stashed her keys and pressed the button on her car key to unlock the doors. Swinging the passenger door open, he nudged Joelle onto the seat, then loped around the car and crammed himself behind the wheel, not bothering to adjust the seat for his larger frame before he ignited the engine and backed out of the parking space. In the side mirror, Joelle saw Mrs. Foster calling to them, her face stretched into a grimace, her hand hacking the air.

Bobby didn't speak as he drove out into the street, his knees banging against the steering wheel. Stopped at a red light, he slid the seat back and tilted the rearview mirror to accommodate his height.

She considered asking him where they were going, then thought better of it. He was seething with anger, most of it aimed at Drew Foster's mother but some of it reserved for Joelle, too. She knew Bobby well enough to understand he was furious with her for having spoken gently to a woman who had slapped her. Joelle should have been furious, too. But...God help her, maybe she deserved that slap. And maybe she deserved Bobby's wrath. She'd made a choice so long ago, the only sensible choice she could grasp at the time, the only one that would enable her to keep her baby and her dignity. It might have been the wrong choice, but she wouldn't have done anything differently if she'd had it to do all over again.

Next to her, Bobby said nothing. Random raindrops had accelerated into a drizzle and he flicked on the wipers. She could tell he was gnashing his teeth by the twitching muscle in his jaw.

He drove through downtown Holmdell, past Harley's and the new Starbucks. He drove past where the A&W stand used to be. It was gone, replaced by a car wash. Farther down the road, a Home Depot had sprung up, a large concrete structure surrounded by an even larger parking lot. Bobby kept driving.

She realized where he was driving her when he veered off the main road and onto a two-lane strip of asphalt that snaked into the woods outside of town. Over one hill, a jag in the road, up another hill and the trees thinned out, opening onto a stretch of dirt and gravel and beyond it the lake.

No other cars were there. Sunday at noon wasn't exactly a popular time for teenagers to make out in cars—if they still did that sort of thing these days—and the damp day kept swimmers from gathering along the edge of the lake on the narrow strip of sand that Holmdell residents extravagantly called a beach. Bobby had his choice of places to park, and he angled the car to provide a clear view of the lake and the pine forest surrounding it. The water was slate-colored, pockmarked by the rain striking its surface. When he turned off the engine, Joelle heard the tap of raindrops against the roof.

"You never brought me here before," she said.

"Yeah, I did." He pushed his seat back as far as it could go and attempted to stretch his legs. "We'd bike up here to swim."

"When we were kids. I meant..." She remembered the summer nights Drew drove her to the lake in his Corvette and she'd struggled to figure out how far she ought to let him go.

"I know what you meant."

More silence. More raindrops pattering on the car's roof.

Joelle stared at the lake and ran her fingers lightly over her cheek where Mrs. Foster had slapped her. "You wanted to kill Mrs. Foster back there, didn't you," she finally said.

"And you wanted to shoot the breeze with her."

"I did not!"

"You treat the Fosters like they're decent people. They're not. They're spoiled, demanding, manipulative users. And that woman hit you. I can't believe she did that."

"I can."

"It's her son's fault she never knew about Claudia. She shouldn't be blaming you."

"Maybe she should." Joelle felt as bleak as the grim, gray clouds lying low above them. A sob filled her throat and she gulped it down. "I did everything wrong, Bobby. I shouldn't have had sex with Drew. And when I got pregnant…"

"Don't say you should have gotten rid of the baby." His voice was taut with indignation.

No, she shouldn't have gotten rid of Claudia, either through abortion or adoption. She couldn't imagine her life without Claudia in it, her precious daughter, her blessed firstborn. She couldn't imagine her life without Claudia—or without Bobby. If it hadn't been for Claudia, he would never have married her.

He reached across the gear stick and captured her hand in his. It was the first time he'd touched her voluntarily, with affection, since Drew Foster had entered their house a week ago. He pulled her hand toward him, sandwiched it in both of his, traced his thumb aimlessly over her palm. "You weren't acting alone, Jo. If you did everything wrong, so did I."

The caress of his thumb felt so good she wanted to moan. She wanted to vault herself over the gearstick and into his lap, and hold him and kiss him and believe he loved her the way she loved him. But there was no room, and her seat belt was still fastened and she was afraid to risk having him push her away. So much remained wrong between them, so much unsaid. "Maybe marrying you was just another thing I did wrong. But I can't help feeling it was the right thing to do."

He twisted in his seat to face her. She kept her eyes on the lake, but she sensed his movement. She felt his scrutiny, his gaze solid and warm. "We were nuts to think we could keep the truth about Claudia a secret forever," he conceded.

"We kept it a secret for a long time." At last she looked at him, but now he'd turned away and was staring at the lake, at the rain streaking the windshield. "Unfortunately we never figured out what we'd do if the secret got out."

"What should we do?" he asked.

"If I knew, we wouldn't be here now."

His lips moved, as if he wanted to taste his words before he actually spoke them. "You walked out on me, Jo."

"We walked out on each other," she corrected him. "I just traveled more miles."

His thumb moved back and forth against her palm, exploring the lines, the skin worn dry by so many years of cleaning, digging weeds, sewing, demonstrating craft projects to her students, writing, hugging, clinging to her children and then prodding them out into the world. "All my life, I've tried to give you what you want," he said, his voice low but steady. "I did the best I could. But I don't think it's enough."

No, she acknowledged. It wasn't enough. He'd given her so much, but not the one thing she truly wanted. "I need to know what's in your heart," she said. "That would be enough."

He exhaled. "I—I don't do that stuff. Baring my soul and all that. Talking to shrinks, punching pillows to get out the rage, meditating, chanting, whatever. That's not the way I am."

She agreed with a nod.

"But I've tried."

She eyed him skeptically. "Have you?"

"I told you what happened in 'Nam. I didn't want to, but you pushed me, so I told you. And when I was starting the business, I talked to you about the finances, the loans, everything I was worried about. Everything I dreamed the business would be." He hesitated, and his voice emerged hoarse when he said, "I told you I hated my father. And I told you how I felt when Foster walked into our house last week. What more do you want?"

"I want..." God, she hated to beg. She hated to ask him for what he couldn't give. But they were actually talking, and he was holding her hand and she couldn't back out now. If the truth hurt... Well, it often did. She would simply have to endure the pain. "I want you to love me, Bobby."

"What?" He half shouted the word, half laughed it.

"You've never said it. Not once in all the years I've known you, all the years we've been married. You've never told me you love me."

"I tell you all the time. Maybe not in words, but—come on, Jo. You ask for a Prius—I buy you a Prius. You decide to try gardening—I give you a garden. Anything you want, anything I can give you—"

"Those are things, Bobby." He might be laughing, but she heard anger in his words, as well. She herself was far from laughter. It was all she could do to keep from erupting in tears. "When you were in Vietnam, every time I got a letter from you, I'd say a little prayer that you'd signed it 'Love, Bobby.' Then I opened it, and it never said *love*. I was sure you were planning to divorce me as soon as you got home. That was the deal, after all—we'd get married and then we could get a divorce. You never said you loved me, so I figured you didn't. But then you came back broken and wounded, and you couldn't divorce me while you were in rehab, and then you kind of got in the habit of being married to me and—"

"Are you insane?" He tugged her hand, urging her to meet his gaze. "I've been in love with you since the first day of Mrs. Schmidt's fourth-grade class."

"You were ten years old. How could you have been in love with me?"

"Damned if I know. But I was."

"You never told me, Bobby. You never even hinted——"

"Because you were Joelle Webber." He sighed, his gaze pinned to the horizon. "You were going places. I realized even then that you were going to wind up someplace better. You were going to escape Tubtown. You weren't going to tie yourself to a boy whose father drank a lot and knocked him around, who went off to Vietnam because even that hellhole was better than his own home. I loved you enough to stay out of your way."

"I did wind up someplace better," she said, wishing he didn't look so distraught. "You were right about that."

"Everything I did, Jo—buying a house, building a business, getting the damn college degree—I did it so you would never have to think you'd gotten ripped off. You had dreams, you had expectations, and I did everything I could not to disappoint you. You married me only because you were in a bad situation, but——"

"The day you asked me to marry you was the best day of my life," she said. "I'd walked up that hill in the cemetery certain it was the absolute worst day of my life, and you turned it into the best day."

"You didn't know that at the time," he argued.

"No. It took me a while to figure out, but I know it now." She unclasped her seat belt and leaned across the console to kiss Bobby. "Tell me. I need to hear the words."

"I love you, Jo," he said. "I always have."

They kissed, a deep, lush, loving kiss. His hand remained around hers and his mouth took hers, possessive, hungry... loving. She believed that. He'd said the words, and this time the truth didn't hurt at all.

By the time they stopped kissing, she was half in his lap, one knee propped on her seat, the steering wheel digging into her shoulder and the car's windows steamed. Bobby cupped her face with his free hand, brushed her hair back from her cheek and peered into her eyes. "So here we are at the lake, and this car is too small."

"It's not too small."

"It's too small and I'm too old." He smiled and caressed her mouth with his fingertips. "I'm sorry I never took you here to do anything besides swimming."

"You were busy with half the girls in Tubtown. I don't think you're all that sorry."

"I am," he insisted. He grazed her lips with his, and then her cheek and then the sensitive spot just below her ear. Desire throbbed deep inside her. "I would have made it good for you if I'd brought you here," he murmured, and she knew he would have. He'd made it good for her on their wedding night, when all she understood about sex was that it was unpleasant and painful and embarrassing. He always made it good for her, even when they were tired or angry or distracted. If only Bobby had told her he loved her back then, when she'd been young and hadn't made any terrible mistakes yet, who knew where they'd be today?

As if he could read her mind, he let his hand fall still and his eyes grew darker. "I could say I love you nonstop for the rest of our lives, Jo. But that wouldn't make things any better."

"Why?"

He closed his eyes for a moment, then opened them. "I'm still going to lose Claudia."

If Bobby had loved Joelle as a teenager, Claudia would never have existed. They would never have had their wonderful daughter. "You won't lose her, Bobby. She adores you."

"She went for a blood test."

Once again silence filled the car. The rain was falling harder now, drumming against the car's surfaces, blurring the world beyond the windows.

"If she isn't a match, it's all over," Joelle said, wishing she could convince them both of that.

"It's not over." His gaze slid past her and fixed on the silver shimmer of the rain. "She said he was her brother. Foster's son—her brother." He stared into her eyes, the sorrow and accusation in his gaze piercing her. "You told her about Foster, and now I'm losing her. You want me to bare my soul? Here's what's in my soul, then. I love you, Jo. I always have and I always will. But when you told Claudia that Foster was her father, you took her away from me." He turned from her, once again staring out at the rain spilling down into the lake.

"She loves you."

"She calls him her father." He swallowed, his eyes distant, seeing not the scenery outside the car but something invisible, something inside himself. "I love you, Jo, but I wish to hell you'd never let Foster into our lives."

"He was in our lives all along," she pointed out sadly.

She felt Bobby's withdrawal, a subtle motion, a slackening of his hold on her. He seemed to slip away from her like the rain slipping into the lake, water vanishing into water. "Yeah," he muttered, nudging her back into her seat and reaching for the car keys. "He was, wasn't he."

Joelle watched him, struggling to read his expression. For one fleeting moment he'd opened to her and spoken his heart. Now he was locking himself up again, sealing himself away. What she'd said was only the truth, but like the truth that he feared had cost him his daughter, this truth might cost Joelle her husband.

Don't close down, she wanted to plead. *Don't leave me.* But he was easing away, drawing back, in full retreat. She'd had him for that one precious moment, and now he was gone.

FOURTEEN

Two weeks later

"Here you go," Mona said, entering Bobby's office with a stack of application forms. "I put the three best prospects on top. One's a college kid just back from a school program in London. He plans to make some money before he has to go back to college in September. The other two are cousins of Hector Cabral's wife. Here legally. I checked their papers. They don't speak English too well, but Hector vouches for them. They said he told them you're a good boss." She grinned. "You want to fire him for lying?"

Hector had been working for DiFranco Landscaping for several years. Bit by bit, he was transporting his entire extended family from Brazil to New England, and Bobby had already hired several Cabral relatives. Over the years, he'd learned a lot about immigration law.

"You ought to move on these soon," Mona continued, placing the stack on his blotter. "You really need some more employees. The price of success, Bob. You've got more contracts than you can staff."

"I'm not complaining." DiFranco Landscaping had landed a lot of jobs this summer. His staff size waxed and waned with the seasons, but this year the firm was in serious demand. He was desperate to add some more personnel, and he would.

He eyed the top application, from the college student. The words made no sense to him; the letters were just squiggly ink shapes. "Something on your mind?" Mona asked.

He shoved back the pile. "I can't concentrate. My daughter's undergoing a medical procedure tomorrow morning."

Mona's eyes widened. "Nothing serious, I hope."

"She'll be fine." Bobby was reasonably convinced of that, even though marrow extraction was a lot more complicated than getting a tooth filled or suturing a cut. Claudia would be given general anesthesia, and then a doctor would insert a needle into her pelvic bone and suck the marrow out. Bobby consoled himself with the understanding that Drew Foster would hire only the best doctors in New York City to treat his son. The doctors would know what they were doing with Claudia.

"If her procedure is tomorrow morning, those applications can wait until tomorrow afternoon," Mona said, tapping the pile with her fingernail and giving Bobby a sympathetic smile before she turned and left his office.

He dug his thumbs into his temples and rubbed, trying to stave off the headache that had been circling his skull all morning. Claudia would be fine, he assured himself. She wanted to do this. It was her choice.

And he ought to review the applications and find some new hires.

He slid open the top drawer of his desk to get a pencil so he could jot down notes. His gaze snagged on the photo of Joelle he kept there, and he paused.

Despite the washed-out colors of the photo, Joelle glowed in her pretty prom dress, with her loose, loopy curls and her bright smile. She'd been so happy that evening, so excited about attending the prom.

With Drew Foster.

It wasn't just the medical procedure that was eating at Bobby. It was the knowledge that Claudia was about to meet her real father.

Foster had arranged for a car to pick up Claudia that morning and drive her to the city so the extraction could be done in the same hospital where his son was a patient. They were all going to meet with the doctor later that afternoon, ostensibly to discuss the procedure. She would spend the night as the guest of Foster and his wife and then get to the hospital by seven the following morning.

Bobby couldn't obliterate the pictures in his mind of Claudia meeting Foster, acknowledging their kinship and believing that she'd finally found her real father. No matter that Bobby had been the only dad she'd ever known. There was a bond between her and Foster, and once they were in the same room, it would blossom.

Thinking about their meeting opened the doors to his headache, which rushed into his brain with booms and flashes of red. Damn. Claudia and Foster. Claudia and her father. Claudia and the guy who'd escorted Joelle to the prom the night that photo was taken, the night she'd worn that beautiful blue gown and worried about whether she had enough class to hang off the arm of a boy from the Hill.

Bobby shoved the drawer shut, locked his desk and stormed out of his office. "I can't work," he told Mona, who peered up at him from her desk in the outer office. "I'll review the applications tomorrow. I just can't do it today." Before she could question him, he swept out of the building.

He was halfway home before he paused to figure out what the hell he was doing. His mind swam with images of Claudia and Joelle's old boyfriend, Claudia searching the man's face and seeing in it a reflection of herself. Bobby had tried so hard, since the day she'd phoned to tell him and Joelle that she was a match for Foster's son, to be calm and reasonable about the whole thing. He'd tried to focus on his work, to make conversation with Joelle over dinner, to slip into the comfortable routines that had marked his days before Foster had barged in and screwed everything up.

He'd tried to be the husband Joelle wanted him to be.

But just as Foster dreaded the possibility of losing his son, Bobby dreaded the possibility of losing his daughter. And in his case it was his own fault. His and Joelle's. They'd lied, and now they were paying the price. He hated himself—and he hated Joelle, too.

He sped up the driveway to their house, slowing only for the automatic garage door to open. Slamming out of the truck, he took a deep breath to calm himself. It didn't help.

By the time he reached the door to the mudroom, Joelle had opened it and was staring into the garage, frowning. "Bobby? What's wrong?"

He strode past her, his boots thumping against the floor, and halted in the kitchen. Several shopping bags stood on the counter. Apparently she'd just arrived home from the supermarket.

"What happened, Bobby?" she asked, concern planting a flutter in her voice as she joined him in the kitchen.

He must have looked half-mad, because she shrank back when he turned to her. "She's going down there today," he said.

"Of course. I know."

"She's going to meet him."

Joelle watched him. "Yes."

"I can't stand it." He roamed around the kitchen, too edgy to stand still. "I've been trying to be a good sport about this, but I…" Emotions tore at him like thorns. "We shouldn't have told her."

"Who? Claudia?"

"We shouldn't have told her about Foster. We should have kept the secret."

"We couldn't, Bobby."

He bore down on her and she shrank back again, pressing against the counter, her eyes wide with alarm. Did she think he would hurt her?

His anger frightened him, too, and he wrestled with it, forcing it down into his gut. He would not become his father. He would not throw things, break things, hit the people in his life.

He spun away from her and moved to the window, hoping the sight of their perfectly landscaped backyard would soothe him. Joelle's garden lay lush and fresh in the late-morning sunlight. He'd done a fine job of weeding and pruning it after she'd run off to Ohio, and she'd done a decent job of keeping it tidy since they'd returned home.

If only raising children were as simple as raising tomatoes and zucchini. If only maintaining a marriage was as simple as digging out a few weeds and adding a little fertilizer.

"We should have kicked Foster out of our house that day."

"If we had sent him away…" Her voice sounded tight, breathy with anxiety. "He would have gone behind our backs to find her. He'd hired a detective, Bobby. He knew about Claudia. He would have found her, with or without our help."

He refused to look at her. "You're sure he'd do that? You know him that well?"

"I'm a mother," she answered, her voice drifting across the room to him. "I know what a parent will do for a child."

"You're a mother. He's a father." What was Bobby? When it came to Claudia, what the hell was he?

He closed his eyes, unable to bear the sight of Joelle's thriving garden anymore. But closing his eyes left his mind free to see what he didn't want to see: Claudia and Foster together, shaking hands. Hugging. Claudia calling that son of a bitch Dad.

"I've tried," he said slowly, his voice breaking. "Ever since we got back from Ohio, I've tried to accept this. I've tried to forgive you and me both." He sighed. "I just can't do it."

For a minute neither of them spoke. The hum of the refrigerator's motor spread around them, and the hiss of one of the upstairs air conditioners cooling down the bedrooms. Then Joelle said, "All right. Let's go."

"Go?"

He heard the bell-like rattle of her keys and the clapping of her sandals hitting the soles of her bare feet as she headed for the mudroom. "Let's go," she repeated.

He had no idea where they were going. Away from the garden, away from the patio he'd built, away from the house in which he'd raised his sons—and his daughter. Away from this house Claudia had once called home.

Going couldn't possibly be worse than staying. He followed Joelle out.

EVEN WITH THE PASSENGER SEAT shoved all the way back, Bobby seemed cramped in the Prius. He also looked forbidding, his eyes dark and brooding, his brow low as he stared at the road in front of them. Waves of tension, hot and pulsing, rolled off him.

She should have changed her clothes. She had on a pair of

khaki shorts and a cotton shirt with a pastel striped pattern. Her hair was arranged in a ponytail, but as she drove she tugged off the elastic and ran her fingers through the locks to loosen them.

Ponytail or no, she looked like a dowdy middle-aged suburban lady, someone who'd abandoned a pile of groceries on the counter and bolted on an insane mission. To save her husband, to save her daughter, to save her marriage—for all she knew, everything she cared about was beyond saving by now. At least she'd gotten most of the perishables into the refrigerator. She'd saved their groceries.

"Where are we going?" Bobby asked.

"I'm not sure. Do you have your cell phone with you?" At his nod, she said, "Call Gary."

He eyed her dubiously but punched in his son-in-law's number. After listening for a couple of seconds, he said, "Gary? It's Bob. I…uh…" He flashed a quizzical glance at Joelle.

"Ask him Drew Foster's address."

Bobby's frown intensified. He said nothing.

"Go ahead. Ask him. Somewhere in Manhattan. I need the address."

Bobby continued to glare at her. Into the phone, he said, "No, I'm still here. I just…"

"Ask him," Joelle ordered.

Twisting away, he spoke into the phone. "Do you know Drew Foster's address?" He listened for a moment, then said, "Thanks. No, nothing's wrong. I'll talk to you later." He folded the phone shut and grunted, "Nothing's wrong? Add that to the mile-high heap of lies."

"What's the address?" she asked. "Write it down so we don't forget it."

"We're not going to New York."

"Yes, we are."

Skepticism mingling with the tension that radiated from him, he opened the glove compartment, pulled out a pen and a wrinkled napkin with a fast-food logo on it and jotted the address. "I wrote it down. Now, turn the car around and take me home."

"You don't want Claudia to do this. You won't admit it, Bobby, but it's obvious you don't want her to do it. So we're going to New York to get her."

From the corner of her eye she could see his disbelief. "We are *not* going to New York to get her," he retorted. "This was her decision. She wants to do it. She's a grown-up. If this is what she wants to do——"

"But *you* don't want her to do it. You don't want her to save that boy's life."

"That boy's life has nothing to do with it," Bobby snapped. "Of course I want the boy to live. Damn it, Jo…"

He seemed as furious as he'd been in the kitchen. But at least he was strapped in by a seat belt, trapped in a moving car. He couldn't act on his anger as long as she kept her foot on the gas pedal.

She had tried to reach him through talk. She'd tried to reach him through food, preparing his favorite meals. She'd tried to reach him physically. Since their return from Ohio, their bed had seen its share of activity——but something had been wrong. There was no hostility when they made love, but there was no rapture, either. There was no life at all. The bed was like a garden without water. Nothing could bloom there.

She'd tried leaving him, and he'd chased after her and brought her home. He'd told her he loved her. But still the demons danced inside him. He was in agony, and in the pauses of their lives, in the quiet moments when conversation died, when sex was over and they retreated to their own sides of the bed, she felt blame flowing from Bobby and spilling all over her.

If the only way she could save her marriage was by snatching Claudia away from Drew Foster, she would do it. She'd tried everything else.

Perhaps she should have thought through this mission a little better. She wasn't sure she was ready to meet Drew's wife—the woman who'd insisted she and Bobby were two corners of a trapezoid when they'd gone out for drinks. Drew's wife would be sleek and chic, and Joelle would be frazzled and ragged. She'd be forced to tell the woman her son would have to find another donor, because until Bobby got his daughter back, he would never forgive Joelle for allowing Drew to cross their threshold. How could Joelle do that? How could she deny a woman the chance to keep her son alive?

"This is nuts," Bobby muttered.

"I don't care if it's nuts. You want Claudia? We'll get her."

"This isn't about Claudia," he said.

Joelle was so startled she almost veered off the road. She straightened the wheel, glanced at him and refocused on her driving. "Of course it's about Claudia."

"It's about you," he argued, spite edging his voice. "It's about you and Foster."

Joelle took a minute to collect herself. All along, Bobby had been anguished about Claudia, about losing her, about losing his place in her heart. He'd never acknowledged that anything else was troubling him. Of course, that was Bobby. He never said anything at all, anything that mattered.

"There is no 'me and Foster,'" she said quietly.

"There was."

"Years ago."

"All right." He sank back in his seat, his hands curled into fists on his knees, and shut his eyes. "Never mind."

He was finally opening up. *Never mind* wouldn't do. "Talk to me, Bobby. For once in your goddamn life, talk to me."

She heard him inhale, then let his breath out on a broken sigh. "I always loved you, Jo. Maybe I didn't say it in words, maybe I didn't express it the way you wanted, but I always loved you. And you loved Drew."

"In high school," she emphasized. "I was young, I didn't even know what love was. It was a schoolgirl crush."

"You wanted to marry him. You planned your future around him." Now that he was talking, *really* talking, the words sprayed from him like water from a garden hose, soaking and chilling her. "I asked you to marry me because I loved you. You were the only good thing in my life back then, and I saw a way to keep you in my life, and I grabbed it and held on tight. That's why I married you. And you married me because you couldn't have Drew."

"That's not—" she stumbled over the next word "—true." But it *was* true. If, when she'd phoned Drew to tell him she was pregnant, he had sent her bus fare to travel not to an abortion doctor in Cincinnati but to New Hampshire, to his college campus, so he could marry her, she would have gone. She would have been his wife and had his baby.

And she would never have had the life she'd lived with Bobby. She would never have struggled with him and celebrated each triumph with him, whether that triumph was his tossing away his cane or starting his own business or earning a college degree. She would never have had her two glorious sons. She would never have built her own world with Bobby. She would never have had all those loving nights in their bed, trusting, touching, connecting in the most elemental way.

"Back in Holmdell, you accused me of never saying I love you," he reminded her, sounding oddly drained. "And I've spent this whole damn marriage knowing I wasn't your choice, I wasn't the one you loved. You settled for me in desperation. The son of the town drunk. The kid who mowed the grass at the cemetery. You didn't marry me for love." He sighed again, almost a moan. "You want me to open up, Jo? There. I've done it."

She didn't realize she was crying until the double yellow line striping the road turned into a blur. Somehow she managed to steer onto the shoulder and stop the car. How could he have thought she'd *settled* for him? Hadn't she loved him enough? Hadn't she given him everything she had—her joy, her sorrow, her patience, her passion?

He had lived the past thirty-seven years doubting her love, just as she'd lived the past thirty-seven years doubting his. If only he'd opened up, if only he'd shared his feelings with her. If only she'd known he felt that way.

The last time she and Bobby had kissed in this car, he'd been in the driver's seat and she'd had the wheel jammed into her back. This time, she climbed over the console to the passenger seat and settled onto his lap. She clung to his shoulders and wept into his shirt until he closed his arms around her. Only then did her sobs subside. "I love you so much, Bobby," she murmured, brushing her mouth against the hollow of his throat with each word she spoke. "The only thing I love about Drew was that his stupid selfishness sent me to you."

"You came to me because you were panicked," Bobby insisted.

"No." She lifted her head and gazed at him. "When I found out I was pregnant, the first person I thought of was you."

His eyebrows arched in surprise. "We'd never done the deed," he reminded her. "You couldn't have pinned it on me."

She managed a feeble smile. "I wouldn't have pinned anything on you. It was just...you were the one I wanted to share my pregnancy with. My first thought was, 'I've got to tell Bobby.'"

"Why?"

She struggled to remember that day, when the nurse at the community college clinic had given her the news and she'd immediately thought of Bobby. "Because you were my friend?" she said, testing the idea as she spoke it. "Because you were my soul mate? Because——" she let out a damp, bleary sigh "——because I trusted you in a way I never trusted anyone else. If that's not love, Bobby, I don't know what love is."

He twined his fingers into her hair, pushing it back from her tear-soaked cheeks. Then he kissed her forehead, tucked his thumbs under her chin and angled her face so he could kiss her lips. A soft kiss, not steamy, not erotic, yet it was the most loving kiss he'd ever given her. "For all these years," he said, barely above a whisper, "you kept me going. You rescued me from that graveyard, from Holmdell, from 'Nam, from a million kinds of hell. And I always told myself that was enough. I loved you, you saved my life, and that was enough. If Foster hadn't come through our door that day, I probably could have kept on going, believing it was enough. But he came through our door...and I realized it wasn't."

"Is it enough now?" she asked. "Knowing I love you with all my heart—is that enough?"

He kissed her again. "It'll have to be, because I can't go through this opening-up shit every day. It hurts, Jo."

"Not every day. Just now and then," she assured him. "When it's absolutely necessary." They kissed again, and she felt the dampness on his cheeks, too. Her tears or his? She didn't know and didn't care.

"We don't have to go to New York," he said. "Claudia'll be 'fine. Let her save some poor boy's life. Just like her mother." He kissed her again, one last, deep, lingering kiss. "Can we go home?"

She wanted to go home, too—home with Bobby, her husband, the man she loved. But she didn't want to leave the warmth and safety of his arms. She wanted to remain this way with him forever. Their lips touching, grazing. Their bodies pressed together. "Will you take me to bed?"

"Yeah," he said, then smiled gently. "I'll do that."

She returned his smile and blinked back a few fresh tears. Reluctantly she eased off his lap and back into the driver's seat. She turned on the engine, merged back onto the road and risked an illegal U-turn. Then she cruised north, away from New York City, away from the Fosters and her daughter and the boy whose life she would save.

Joelle and Bobby drove away from their past, away from the lies, away from the doubts, heading home. The sooner they got there, the sooner they would be in each other's arms, in their bed, expressing their love in the most honest way they knew.